# A PLACE NEAR KOLOB

## JOHN McRAE

© 1999 John R. McRae
All rights reserved. No part of this book may be reproduced in any form or by any electronic or mechanical means without the written consent of the publisher. Contact the publisher at Ross House Publishing, 12658 South Bridgewood Lane, Draper, UT 84020.

Ross House, Draper, Utah 84020 Telephone 801-523-2425

Printed in the United States of America.

ISBN 0-9673990-0-9

Cover design by Tom Child

• • •

*To all those who have pondered "the last days"
and wondered how and why.
Not even the angels know when.*

*This novel is not about prophesy.
It is about people and events in this world
... and those beyond.*

*The time is—well, you decide.*

• • •

# A PLACE NEAR KOLOB

## PART ONE

# 1

## NEW WASHINGTON, MISSOURI

The military jumbo jet landed at Stark Air Force Base in Missouri, about twenty miles south of the city of New Washington, at 2232 hours—10:32 p.m. in civilian time. The giant plane carried only two passengers, Quinn Adams and his wife Joanna. They had slept through much of the flight from Israel, but both showed signs of fatigue. There had not been much sleep these past weeks, and stepping down onto the tarmac brought a feeling of relief that they were finally back on American soil.

Two limousines pulled up alongside the plane. The chauffeur of the first limo opened the rear door and a woman and man got out, crossing to greet Quinn and Joanna.

Anne Ashford had a trim figure, wore an expensive black tailored suit, and was very attractive. No one disputed that she was the most attractive Vice President ever elected in the United States. She was now serving her second term in that office.

Right behind Anne was her husband, Fernando Francisco de Branca, chairman of the governing council of the Coalition of Allied States of the Americas, headquartered in Brazilia. As the official representative of CASA, Fernando divided his time between Brazilia and New Washington these days. His marriage two years ago to Anne Ashford had helped heal deep wounds between North and South America. The birth of the new United Sovereign States of the Americas, or USSA, had followed, binding both hemispheres closely together by treaty. There was still a lot of distrust and jealousies to overcome, however. In the last few years, the acronyms USA, CASA and USSA had become familiar symbols throughout the world. As for Anne and Fernando, they were almost idolized in the Latin countries.

A half dozen unsmiling, dark-suited security agents piled swiftly out of the second limo, alertly taking perimeter positions about their charges.

Quinn and Joanna were delighted to see Anne and Fernando. The two women embraced, the two men shook hands warmly.

"This is an unexpected surprise," Quinn grinned. His glance turned questioningly toward Anne Ashford. "Are you two just being friendly, or is this official business?"

"A little of both," Anne smiled back. "After what you both just went through in Israel, we thought you'd appreciate some friendly faces on the ride home—"

"Most certainly," Joanna murmured. "I am worn out, physically and emotionally."

"And the business part—?" Quinn asked.

"President Baldwin wanted to be sure you were up to the meeting tomorrow morning. He tried to say he'd be willing to postpone it, but he couldn't get it out. He really wants to meet with both of you as soon as possible."

"How does ten o'clock sound?"

"Not as good as eight o'clock, which the President mentioned," Anne smiled, "but I'll tell him how absolutely terrible you both look, and he'll understand."

"If I look the way I feel," Joanna sighed, "terrible is a good word."

Now in her late forties, Joanna Adams still was a beautiful woman. She was olive complexioned, her dark hair showing some signs of gray but not much. Her figure was as trim as it had been twenty years ago when Quinn first accompanied her and a squad of Israeli commandos on a raid to eliminate a nest of terrorists in the Libyan desert. She had always possessed a magnetism that drew the attention of both men and women, and this had matured over the years into a poise and confidence that made her equally at home in a shopping mall or a gathering of heads of state. She did look exhausted tonight, however.

Joanna gave her husband a quick look. Normally, Quinn didn't show fatigue. He'd had his fiftieth birthday a few months ago, but always looked more like a perennial thirty-nine. Quinn was showing strain now, his face tired and gray. There were deep, dark circles under his eyes. The last two months in Israel had been extremely difficult for both of them, particularly Joanna. An Israeli by birth, she felt the agony of her people very deeply.

Anne Ashford was also studying Quinn. This man had become a legend over the past decade. She had no idea what had happened, because all records were sealed, but she knew the fate of the nation had hung in this man's hands at least twice. He never said anything about those times, but she knew that without him, the United States would have fallen. Joanna knew a small part of the story, but she never talked about it either.

Anne shifted her stare to her friend, seeming to know what was going through her mind. "The worst is over, Joanna," she said softly. "Better days lie ahead."

"At least the dead are buried," Joanna muttered. "I'll never forget all those valleys piled with bodies. They were enemies, but it was still horrifying."

"How is Dovid holding up?" Fernando asked.

Dovid Shazebak was the prime minister of Israel, and the brother of Joanna.

"As well as can be expected," Quinn answered. "You can't even imagine the devastation in that part of the world, Fernando. Millions of bodies still rotting in the sun in dozens of countries hit by our nuclear raids. The dead within Israel's borders are mostly cleaned up now, but it will take years to get those other countries into livable condition."

"That's what the President wants to talk about, of course. He's anxious to provide all the assistance we can."

"When the United States agreed to unleash Operation Armageddon," Joanna muttered, "we saved Israel, but we destroyed the rest of that whole region. The destruction is indescribable."

"Well," Fernando said briskly, "let's get you two home. I'd suggest stopping off for a late snack, but I don't think you'd be good company. You both need some serious rest."

Quinn nodded wearily.

Moments later, the two couples were being whisked away from the airport. As tired as he was, Quinn couldn't resist powering the window down and staring out at the blazing lights as they headed north through the city. Although it was over nine years since New Washington had been officially dedicated as the new capitol of the United States, it was still an awesome sight at night.

They were traveling the new Interstate 1, the major freeway that cut through the heart of the city. On each side of the freeway rose a forest of government high-rise administration buildings, all severely plain in architectural style, with none of the gothic columns and impressive granite grandeur of the old government buildings that had adorned Washington, D.C., before it had been destroyed in a nuclear holocaust twelve years ago.

There was a much more startling difference between the old and the new cities than architecture, however. Every building in New Washington was a tower of light. Walls blazed in a brilliant glow, bathing the entire city in light, reflecting into the sky so brightly that the night sky overhead appeared almost as bright as daylight. Quinn and Joanna had spotted that reflection when the jet was still four hundred miles out from the city. Even the surface of the freeway stretching ahead of the limousine was lighted. Though he was familiar with the development of the solar-illuminated laser plastics a decade ago at a secret research site in a Utah desert, Quinn still was overwhelmed by what had come from an accidental discovery. People came from all over the world to see this astounding city of light, rising from the ruins of what once had been Kansas City.

The limousine sped through the capitol and on toward the adjoining city of New Jerusalem, similarly blazing with light from the solar panel construction. There really was no demarcation between the two cities, with just as many high-rise towers in both, although those in New Jerusalem were mostly residential complexes. The city was the bedroom community for many of the government workers and the hundreds of thousands of civilians who had left the protection of the old western Federal Zone to start rebuilding the devastated central and eastern states. It was mind-numbing to even think about all the shattering things that had happened in these last few years, not only in the United States but throughout the whole world.

Quinn raised the window, the light outside now dimmed by the heavily tinted glass. Anne and Fernando sat across from them, saying nothing. Quinn reached over and squeezed the hand of his wife, who was leaning her head back against the soft leather, her eyes closed. She didn't move her head but he felt the pressure of her fingers as she returned the squeeze. Quinn closed his eyes too, trying to shut out thoughts of the past—and the last two months in Israel. He was too tired to relive any of those horrors. Besides, it was the present that needed attention.

Quinn Adams, the man known as Pharaoh One, who headed the National Emergency Coordinated Command Organization, known in intelligence circles as NECCO, had no idea how many things would need his attention, nor how quickly they would spin utterly out of control.

Quinn and Joanna were dropped off at the prestigious Ashford Tower, overlooking New Jerusalem's huge central park area, promising to spend an evening soon with Anne and Fernando. The Ashford was named in honor of Anne Ashford, who as Vice President had made significant contributions to the political and social well being of the country. It was an impressive building, constructed of the new solar panels, and designated as a high security residence complex.

Their condominium occupied the fifty-ninth floor of this sixty-floor tower, security maintained round-the-clock by a company of elite NECCO Rangers. That security net had been penetrated only once, several years ago in a similar tower back in Virginia, and it had almost cost Quinn Adams his life. It was a lot more difficult, if not impossible, to breach the precautions now in place at the Ashford. The top floor was reserved for conference facilities and off-hours communication between Quinn and the far-flung network of NECCO stations. Every occupant of this building held high-level clearance.

Quinn took a long shower and Joanna relaxed in the jetted tub, ridding themselves of some of the wear and tear of travel. They were snuggled on the large sofa in the living room, discussing some of the things facing them in the next few hours, when they heard the doorbell ring. Quinn went into the entrance lobby, peered through the viewfinder, surprised to see who was standing outside. He quickly opened the door.

Dr. Jules Henshaw gave him a worried, apologetic look. "Sorry, One," he muttered. "Please forgive the intrusion. I know you and your wife just got back from Israel, but this simply can't wait."

Henshaw never referred to Quinn Adams as anything but 'One'. He had been one of the fifteen Pharaohs who directed the NECCO force since the beginning. In fact, Quinn had been responsible for bringing Henshaw into the highly secret organization. As Pharaoh Thirteen, directing scientific activities, Henshaw had made many outstanding contributions to the work of NECCO.

He hadn't changed much over the past fourteen years. He was still thin, academic looking, peering over small glasses with thick lenses. His hair was reduced to a few thin lines straggling across an almost bald pate, but Quinn couldn't remember it ever being much thicker. Henshaw had a large adam's apple that bobbled in his throat every time he spoke. He looked genuinely sorry to be there, and profoundly concerned. Quinn invited him inside.

"If you say it's important, Jules," he told him, "I'm sure it is. Joanna's in the living room. Can we talk there, or shall we meet privately in my study—?"

"Mrs. Adams should probably hear this, too," Henshaw said. "I'm really terribly sorry—"

"Nonsense, Jules," Quinn smiled. "You've certainly got my attention."

After a brief exchange of greetings, Henshaw accepted the invitation to sit down but declined any refreshments. Joanna was secretly relieved, because she had glanced in the refrigerator earlier and found nothing that looked edible. Henshaw sat on the very edge of a large leather armchair, clutching his briefcase to his chest with both hands, seeming to be searching for a place to start. There was no doubt he was highly agitated.

"I understand you'll be meeting with the President in the morning," he said.

Quinn nodded. "Joanna and I will be making a report on our findings in Israel. You were there a month ago—you know the conditions."

"Not good," Henshaw muttered. "But trust me, One, what I have in this briefcase is far more urgent."

He reached into the briefcase and pulled out a large manila envelope. The contents were bulky and the envelope had a wax seal, with the bold notation:

TOP SECRET. PHARAOH ONE EYES ONLY.

That was surprising, Quinn thought. Henshaw wasn't usually so secretive with his reports. No wonder Pharaoh Thirteen looked agitated. Henshaw withdrew a second envelope, similarly sealed, but marked

PRESIDENTIAL EYES ONLY.

"This is a copy for President Baldwin," Henshaw said, handing both envelopes to Quinn. "I leave it up to you whether or not you give it to him."

Quinn stared at Henshaw in surprise. "Why wouldn't I give it to him, Jules? What's is in this report, anyway?"

"Only a projection, One—but it scares me like nothing has in my entire scientific life."

Quinn looked at the envelopes. "Do you want me to read this, or are you going to brief me?"

"I'll give you the highlights, but I hardly know where to begin. My mind doesn't want to accept the logic of these conclusions, but I've checked and double-checked, and the information is incontrovertible."

Joanna was tired and getting a little impatient. If this was so important, it was time to get it out. "Information about what, Jules?"

Henshaw was staring thoughtfully at the carpet, his mind obviously far away. Quinn's voice echoed the sharpness of his wife.

"Your report, Jules—what's happened?"

"It's what might happen, One," Henshaw said, looking up and blinking his eyes. Quinn got the impression he had rejoined them. "If my calculations are correct, it's what is going to happen. I hope I'm wrong, but I don't think so."

They waited, for it appeared Henshaw was about ready to give his briefing.

He put his briefcase on the floor, knitted his fingers tightly together, and leaned toward them.

"As you know, one of my main duties lately is to track potential earthquake hazards, here in the United States and around the world." He stared at Quinn, fell back into thought for a moment, then cleared his throat and continued. "Ever since the last world-wide shifting of crustal plates, my group has been maintaining intensive surveillance on all known faults. Pressure readings. Ocean floor monitoring. The rate of creep. Anything and everything that will provide meaningful statistics—even statistics that don't seem meaningful."

"The results are impressive," Quinn nodded. "I'm aware of the huge scope of the monitoring network and what you and your people have been doing. Has a problem surfaced?"

Henshaw drew in a deep breath. He frowned, staring thoughtfully at a corner of the ceiling. Well, Joanna thought, at least it wasn't the carpet.

"The recent nuclear bombings by our people brought some concerns," Henshaw murmured. "It was so saturated and so wide-spread, it threw a lot of our monitoring stations around the world completely out of service. That's why I went to Israel, of course, to put as many stations as possible back on line."

"I thought you were pleased with those results—"

"Oh yes, most definitely. Too bad we don't have access like that to the rest of the monitoring probes in the Far East and Middle East."

"I didn't think those were areas of major concern. Not like here in the states, and in South America."

"Ordinarily, that would be true. But apparently we are dealing with a massive international event."

"Event?" Joanna queried. "Is that another word for earthquake—?"

Henshaw's shoulders drooped. "Yes, Mrs. Adams. A series of earthquakes, to be more precise."

"Is that what this is all about, Jules—you've picked up on another possible worldwide round of earthquakes?"

"More than just possible, I'm afraid." The adam's apple bobbed several times. "Our information indicates highly unusual crustal activity around the world. If it continues, especially at the rates of creep that are being registered, we are almost certain to see a major disaster—worldwide. Possibly—probably," he corrected himself, "greater than the last time."

Joanna was frowning. "Rates of creep—? Refresh me on that, Jules."

"The earth's surface—its crust, if you will—is broken into a jigsaw puzzle of separate pieces. All floating on a molten core, but all fitting together, of course."

"Those are referred to as plates—" she said.

"Tectonic plates," Henshaw nodded. "They are all constantly shifting—unfortunately, in different directions. Some are moving eastward, some westward. Very slowly, of course—at least, they have been until just very recently. That's what we scientists call 'creep'—that slow movement of the crustal plates in one direction or another. On top of that, each plate has its own cracks, or faults. The movement of the large plates creates pressure along the smaller fault lines."

"You're saying this crustal creep is speeding up," Joanna said, trying to speed up the report. "That is what's causing this alarm—?"

"Our American plate, which covers most of the United States, has suddenly doubled its rate of creep," Henshaw said, frowning again. "That means we're moving westward at about six inches or more a year. In geological terms, that's almost supersonic speed."

"Is that likely to produce earthquakes here in the states?" Quinn asked. "Last time you were worried about our rate of creep, we lost California."

"We shouldn't experience undue building of pressure along the San Andreas fault this time. That's already ruptured and broken free—with terrible loss of life, as you know. It would be possible, of course, but very unlikely. Where we're highly vulnerable is in the Aleutians and the Bering Sea, as well as the entire eastern Pacific seaboard from Russia to New Zealand—the Ring of Fire, as it's called."

"And South America—?"

"Our projections are very grim. A southeast section of the Pacific Plate that subducts under South America's western coastline has also picked up speed. If it can't subduct fast enough—"

"I'm sorry, Jules," Joanna interrupted again. "Subduct—I think I know what you mean but I need to be sure."

"Each plate, after it has moved and created pressure against the next plate, usually slides under the edge of the restricting plate. We call that subduction."

"Slides under—?

"Slips down beneath the opposing plate and apparently simply melts back into the core. But if the northwest section of the Pacific plate, for example, which is moving north and west, doesn't subduct under the Aleutian plate fast enough, it will cause a terrible pressure build-up. It appears that is happening now at many widely scattered points, especially in

South America. Earthquakes along the entire coastline of the continent seem imminent, on a scale we've never experienced before. That's not the real concern, however—"

Quinn Adams stared at him. "Not the real concern? What is, Jules?"

"The mid-Atlantic rift. That will probably cause the most trouble worldwide," Henshaw replied soberly. He could see the question forming on Joanna's face, and answered it before she spoke. "There's a rift—a break, or a weak spot—in the earth's crust that runs some forty thousand miles down the middle of the Atlantic ocean floor. Magma, or molten lava, has been welling up along that fault for millions of years. It's pushing the Atlantic ocean wider every year, and shrinking the Pacific—"

"The oceans are changing size—?" Joanna said incredulously.

"Only a matter of inches, of course, but there will be a change in your lifetime, Mrs. Adams, of approximately your height. That's how much wider and narrower the oceans would normally change. The rate of expansion, however, has doubled in the past few months."

"You can measure that—?"

"Very precisely. The Atlantic is closely monitored because it creates enormous pressure along fault lines, or plates, all around the world. It pushes westward against the American plate, and eastward against Europe. All the data now being received from the Atlantic rift is alarming—very alarming. There is a great deal of strange activity being recorded along the whole length of the rift—that's over forty thousand miles, remember."

Quinn's thoughts were racing. There had been worldwide upheaval of these crustal plates only a few years ago, with devastating results. He understood why Jules Henshaw was so nervous about it happening all over again.

"Do we know what's causing this new activity?" he asked.

"No idea," Henshaw replied. "I'm assuming it's some new imbalance deep within the core. No way of gathering absolute information."

"Is there anything we can do?"

Henshaw shook his head grimly. "Just be prepared to handle a whole series of major disasters—"

"—that could happen anywhere in the world," Quinn finished wryly. "Is there a probable timeline?"

"There's absolutely no way to predict the pressure build-up along all those plate lines. The only certain fact is there will be crustal upheavals, probably very soon. All the data inescapably supports that conclusion."

"Can you even speculate when this might happen—?"

"Could be a matter of days. Perhaps months. The data suggests it won't be long in coming."

Quinn looked soberly at the scientist. "This is frightening news—"

"But that isn't what's worrying me the most. I wish it was."

Quinn's eyes widened. "There's more—?"

The turmoil inside Henshaw was a visible thing, which was even more disturbing, because Jules was a scientist, not given to emotional trauma. Without knowing what was troubling him, Quinn felt his whole nervous system tighten. He glanced over at Joanna, saw she was leaning forward with the same intensity on her face that he was feeling.

"What could be more troubling than what you've just told us, Jules?" he asked quietly.

"What I'm going to say sounds crazy. It even sounds crazy to me, but it's true. It's absolutely, scientifically plausible. I've worked the equations a score of times just since yesterday, and it keeps coming out the same."

"Go on—"

"It's not just the earthquakes. It's what might happen if all the crustal plates shifted suddenly, as the readings indicate could theoretically happen. If something like that actually occurred—"

Henshaw stopped, staring off into his thoughts again. Quinn spoke sharply to him.

"What would happen, Jules? What if all the crustal plates shifted at the same time—?"

"Well, the plates would probably fragment to some degree—break into smaller sections. If the mid-Atlantic rift cracked open—and the data indicates that is a frightening possibility—we would have a massive pouring of cold seawater down into the crack. When it meets that molten core, it could produce an explosive force of titanic proportions."

"What would that do—?"

"It could cause the whole planet to be thrown off balance."

"And what would that do—?"

"At best, profoundly affect the world climactic structure. Even a few degrees change in the tilt would result in dramatic change. Upper air flows disrupted. The temperature of the oceans fluctuating. A melting of the polar caps. Change in the seasons. Ocean levels would increase. It all adds up to chaos."

Quinn exchanged glances with his wife. She was having difficulty absorbing what Henshaw was saying. So was Quinn.

"That's the best scenario—?"

Henshaw gave an almost imperceptible nod.

"I hate to ask this," Quinn muttered, "but what could be worse?"

Jules Henshaw looked from one to the other, hesitating before answering that question. He started shaking his head, as if not wanting to see the pictures now in his head.

"If the Atlantic rift were to split open, the sudden meeting of molten magma with cold seawater could result in the entire ocean turning to steam. If that happened, it would occur with explosive force—a jet force of incredible magnitude. It is possible—and this exceeds the limits of all known physics—that our planet could become a projectile. If you include the consequences of the same things happening at the same time in the Pacific, and along other undersea faults, there is a clear mathematical probability that the earth could be thrown out of orbit and head out into space."

Quinn could say nothing. He could only stare at Henshaw, his mind refusing to accept what the scientist had just said. His voice fell to a whisper.

"What is the probability of that happening—?"

"It is a definite mathematical possibility."

"I'm asking about the probability—"

"There is no way to calculate that."

"What would happen to the earth if we did get blown out of orbit?"

Henshaw shrugged. "I can only speculate—"

"Then speculate."

"It's impossible to project the trajectory. Gravity would tend to draw it toward the sun. But it could escape into deep space."

"In either of those possibilities, what would happen to us—to any form of life on earth?"

"If gravity pulled us too close to the sun—beyond the planetary life zone—we would be looking at millions of degrees Fahrenheit and this planet would be turned into a red-hot sphere of magma. All life as we know it would cease to exist—human, animal, plant, even micro-organic. Nothing could survive."

"That could happen—we could be drawn into the sun?"

"It certainly could happen. It is just as likely the planet would be thrown out into deep space, hurled like a gravitational sling-shot."

"And if that happened—?"

"There is no friction in space, so we wouldn't burn up. However, the impact on all life on the planet would be the same. No form of life would survive, not without atmosphere and in such super-cold."

"So regardless," Quinn said, his voice a whisper, "everyone on earth dies."

"I'm afraid so, One. That is my projection, at least."

"How many people know about this?" Quinn muttered.

"I'm the only one who's taken the theoretical possibilities this far, as far as I know."

"Don't repeat any of it, Jules," Quinn warned, "not to anyone. Not even to anyone in the agency."

Henshaw nodded. "I hope you understand why I had to see you as soon as possible. I felt that—"

"It was absolutely the right thing to do. Be at Pharaoh headquarters early tomorrow—no later than nine. The President has to be told. And in case you figure out an exact time all this is going to happen—I don't want to know."

It was about two o'clock in the morning when Quinn and Joanna finally went to bed. Strangely, they hadn't talked much about Henshaw's report. Quinn had started to read it aloud but both found it too disturbing. Neither of them could deal with the mental images that came. Their minds would not allow Henshaw's projections to become real. It put a depressing stamp of futility on everything.

Instead, they went over the events of the past weeks that had occupied them in Israel. They tried to put details into order, sort out the positive aspects of their report to President Baldwin. That didn't work, and neither could fight a numbing sense of frustration. Rest was urgently needed, they realized. Perhaps it would all look different in the morning.

There was no way to tell how long they slept before being suddenly awakened by a violent shaking sensation. Quinn and Joanna reached over and clung to each other. A great rushing sound engulfed them, as if a tornado was ripping directly through the room. The first thing that jumped into their minds was Jules Henshaw and his projections of disaster.

Was it happening?

More frightening than the shaking and the noise, however, was the bright light filling the room. The drapes were heavy material, double lined, to keep out the glow of the city outside. Quinn glanced quickly to see if they had fallen, but they were still in place. The light in the room was so intense it was painful to even open their eyes.

Suddenly the sense of motion increased. At the same time, the air seemed to be sucked out of the room. Quinn and Joanna started gasping, trying to draw in breaths that would not come. Each felt a dizziness overtaking them. All they could do was cling desperately to each other.

Quinn's last conscious thought was the realization that Ashford Tower was collapsing. There could be no other explanation. In seconds, all sixty floors would be a pile of rubble and everyone in the building, including Joanna and himself, would be dead.

Both of them long ago had come to terms with the probability of violent death. It was a price too often paid for walking the dark and dangerous paths of their secretive world.

But dying in an earthquake—

# 2

## A Place Near Kolob

Quinn opened his eyes and stared up at the ceiling. It took a second or two before the importance of that registered in his thoughts. There was a ceiling. He could see it even in the darkness.

And he was lying in bed beside his wife.

He suddenly raised up, peering at Joanna. The motion roused her, and her eyes blinked open. They fastened on her husband, a bewildered expression on her face.

"You're alive. We're both alive—"

"That's my first impression."

"Open the drapes, Quinn—"

He jumped out of bed and crossed to the windows. He pulled the drapes open and light flooded into the room and they both winced at the sudden change from darkness. They both looked around the bedroom.

Not one thing seemed out of place. Nothing had fallen over. Even the photographs on the dresser on the far wall still were upright. There was absolutely no sign of the tremendous shaking and upheaval and whipping wind that had awakened them earlier, other than the small clock on the dresser. That read three-fifteen. The daylight outside said it was much later than that.

"What's going on, Quinn?" Joanna whispered, still looking about the room.

Quinn opened the door to the balcony outside the bedroom. He forced himself to look down, not knowing what to expect but knowing something terrible had happened during the night. They hadn't dreamed that terrifying experience.

Nothing.

Everything in the city below looked exactly as it had the day they left for Israel. No collapsed buildings, no screaming emergency vehicles or fire engines. No crowds. No visible damage anywhere. If anything was unusual, it was seeing just a small number of people walking around. It must still be very early, Quinn thought. The only other thing he noticed was there were no cars in the streets. That was unusual at any time, day or night.

Joanna's voice, fearful, came from behind him in the bedroom.

"What is it, Quinn? What's happened?"

He came back into the room and once again stared around it. Nothing had changed in the last few minutes. Nothing was broken or out of place.

"It's weird."

"What—?"

"Nothing happened. Apparently there was no earthquake. There's no damage anywhere."

"There has to be," Joanna exclaimed.

She jumped out of bed and came out onto the balcony, staring at the city below. Like Quinn said, everything looked completely normal.

"We didn't dream that, Quinn—"

"If we didn't, where's the damage? I felt this whole building coming down. We were about to be blown out of bed. And all that blinding light. Yet those photographs are still standing."

"Are you saying we did dream it—?"

Quinn shrugged. "We were both exhausted. The pictures Jules put into our minds with that report would scare anybody."

"I don't believe it." Joanna shook her head firmly. "Last night was real—we both felt it."

Quinn pulled on a pair of pants and a sweatshirt.

"Let's check the rest of the place. If it looks the same as the bedroom—well, no matter how we feel, that whole thing had to be a dream."

There was no sign of disturbance anywhere. They sank down on the long sofa in the living room and stared at each other. Then Quinn looked at the ornate clock on the wall. It read three-fifteen. He glanced down at his wristwatch.

It also had stopped at three-fifteen.

"I'll tell you one thing," he muttered, looking up at his wife. "Something happened at three-fifteen this morning. Every clock in the place stopped at that precise moment."

Joanna looked around again. "Something did happen, Quinn—"

"You're right," he said grimly. He crossed and picked up a phone.

"Security will know."

He dialed a number and waited. There was no answer—there was no ring, he realized. He frowned at the phone.

"It's not working. That's impossible—it has a fail-safe back-up."

"Try the regular phone," Joanna said.

He changed phones and dialed a number. There was no hum, no answer. He dialed another number. Still no answer.

"Okay, the phones are out," he muttered, putting it back in the cradle. "I'm going down to the lobby. Somebody must know what's going on."

He left. Two minutes later, the front door opened again and Quinn came back. He stared at his wife, frustration on his face.

"The elevators are out."

"That's odd—"

"It's more than odd. This building has three back-up power systems—"

"Don't take it out on me. I'm not responsible."

He stared at her, anger showing. Then a grin slipped onto his face.

"Did I mention this whole thing is weird—?"

"Let's give it a few minutes," Joanna said. "If the power doesn't come back, I'll walk down the stairs with you."

"Fifty-nine flights—?"

"Well, maybe we give it a lot of minutes."

Joanna went in to take a shower. Seconds later, Quinn heard her scream.

He rushed into the bathroom and found his wife staring into a mirror.

"What's wrong?" he cried, looking about the room.

"Look at me, Quinn—"

He did—and for the first time, noticed what had brought the scream from her. He moved closer, staring.

"You're beautiful, Joanna—"

"I know I am. But last night I had wrinkles—forty-seven years worth of wrinkles."

"You haven't got them now. I don't know why I didn't notice that—yes, I do. You face isn't the only weird thing that's happened this morning—"

"Thanks a lot," Joanna said, slapping at his chest. She stared into the mirror again, running fingers across her cheeks.

"So where did they go—"

He grinned. "You want them back?"

"Of course not. Look at me—I'm thirty again. How did that happen?"

"I don't know," Quinn muttered, "but I'll bet you one thing. It happened at three-fifteen this morning."

Joanna turned from the mirror and looked at her husband. She started shaking her head.

"Look at yourself, Quinn—"

He peered into the mirror, and shock swept through him.

"Is that me—?"

"Pretty handsome, I'd say," she murmured. "I remember that face—it was the one you were wearing when we first became lovers during that mission in Greece. That was about twenty years ago, wasn't it—?"

He was staring at himself in disbelief.

"I'm young again, Joanna—you're young again. What's going on—?"

"Whatever it is," she murmured, "this part I like."

They both showered, quickly checking the mirror afterward. They hadn't changed—or rather, they still were changed. This was beyond weird. This had to be part of the same dream as the earthquake.

There was no way of knowing the exact time, but it was now full daylight outside. Quinn went out onto the balcony again, looking for the sun.

It wasn't there.

It obviously was up, so that meant it had to have already arced out of sight over the building. Which meant it wasn't morning at all, but afternoon. Quinn found his body-clock unwilling to accept that.

He came back inside, saying nothing. After all, how did you tell someone the sun wasn't where it was supposed to be? Especially someone who was running her hand over her face, still unable to believe how smooth the skin was to the touch.

The front doorbell rang.

"Let's hope it isn't Jules," Quinn grimaced, "with a positive timeline."

He went to the door and peered out through the viewer. Shock swept through him, and his knees actually sagged. He opened the door and stared at the man facing him.

"Race—is this really you? You were reported killed in that California terrorist raid—that was two years ago. It can't be you—" Another thought struck him. "How did you get up here? The elevators aren't working—"

"That's it?" the man in the hall said. "After two years all I get is a cold stare and a question about the elevators?"

"You are dead, Race—"

Race Courtney was wearing a broad grin, and he stretched his arms wide.

"Do I look dead, buddy?"

Joanna appeared behind Quinn. She stared at their visitor, shock paling her face.

"This can't be—"

"I'm beginning to feel a little unwelcome—"

Quinn stepped out and threw his arms about him. The two men gave each a long hug. Finally Joanna pushed between them and put her arms around Race's neck.

"Race—it's wonderful to see you! You must have an incredible story to tell—"

Race grinned again. "You could say that."

Quinn pulled him into the house. Once they were all inside, they went into the living room. Neither of them could take their eyes from Race Courtney.

Quinn had grown up with Race, back when both their families lived in Seattle. They had gone to college together, graduated, and both went into intelligence work. Race began to work for the FBI and made quite a name for himself. No one ever knew what intelligence agency Quinn was in, although Race was always convinced it was the CIA. Then in the violence that shook the country almost twenty years ago, both men found themselves working together in the Pharaoh Force intelligence unit. Quinn went on to head the entire NECCO organization, and Race became head of its intelligence unit.

The lives of the two friends became even more interlocked when Race married Quinn's sister, Stacy, and Quinn married Race's sister, Jill. Quinn's marriage to Jill ended tragically and he later married Joanna. Race and Stacy stayed happily together over the years. Quinn realized with a shock that was nineteen years ago. He stared curiously at his friend.

"It's happened to you, too—"

"What's happened?"

"The way you look, buddy. You're fifty, same as me, but you look thirty."

"So do you."

"I know it. So does Joanna. Why do we all suddenly look twenty years younger, Race—?"

"You expect me to know the answer to that—?"

"If you can come back from the dead after two years, you can answer a simple little question like that."

"Sorry, buddy. Just enjoy it." He looked at Joanna, nodding approval. "He's right—you've never looked lovelier."

"Where have you been these past two years?" Quinn asked, still staring at his friend with an incredulous expression. Another thought struck him. "Does Stacy know you're back—?"

Race shook his head. "First priority was to make contact with you and Joanna—"

"Before you let your wife know you're back from the dead—?" Joanna exclaimed. "Better not tell her that."

"She'll understand. At least, she will after I explain."

"We're headed for a meeting with Baldwin," Quinn said. "Is your priority higher—?"

"As a matter of fact, it is," Race answered, "but President Baldwin will be there too."

Quinn frowned at him. "You're over my head, buddy. You show up after two years being AWOL, and you're dragging Joanna and me to a meeting with someone higher than the President of the United States?"

"Strange, isn't it," Race grinned.

"Who's calling this meeting?"

"Can't tell you. You know how it goes—you've pulled the same stuff on me scores of times."

Joanna was staring hard at him. "What's happening here, Race? Some mighty strange things occurred last night, and now I'm looking like Miss Israel again. I'm all for it, you understand, but what's going on—?"

"She's right," Quinn frowned. "We didn't imagine last night, although there's no evidence that anything unusual happened. Other than all the clocks stopping at three-fifteen. It feels like we're in some kind of time warp."

"In a way," Race nodded, "that's right."

"A time warp?" Joanna repeated, disbelief in her voice. "I thought that only happened in the movies—"

"We shouldn't get into this," Race said quietly, "not before the meeting."

"Race," Quinn exclaimed, "if you know anything, you really need to tell us."

"You're not going to believe a word I say—"

"You do know something," Joanna said quickly. "Tell us—please."

"We know there was some kind of earthquake last night," Quinn said. "It felt like this whole building was falling down."

"It was being lifted up."

Quinn stared at him. "You got to know how much sense that makes—"

"This building—the whole city—was transferred last night."

"Transferred—?"

Race nodded.

"What does that mean? Transferred where—?"

"That's going to be hard to explain," Race said hesitantly.

"I'll accept any explanation you come up with—"

"We'll both accept your explanation, Race," Joanna added, "even if we don't understand it."

"And I have a strong feeling we won't," Quinn muttered. "We were lifted up last night, you say. That's a little mind boggling. Can you be more specific—?"

"You're not on earth anymore, buddy."

Quinn wheeled away, putting both hands to his head. "Come on, Race. I looked out the window this morning. It was all there—"

"I told you the whole city was transferred—New Jerusalem and New Washington together. Everything looks the same outside because it is. It just isn't where it was yesterday."

"You sure you didn't spend the last two years in an asylum?"

"I told you we should wait until the meeting. There'll be people present who are a lot better at this than I am. I barely understand it myself."

"Understand what, Race?" Joanna asked. "You're not making any sense."

"Last night," Race said patiently, "you and the whole city were transferred off the earth to here."

"Just us—Joanna and me?"

"Of course not. Everyone who was Justified was Quickened."

"Justified—? Quickened—? Transferred—?" Quinn was shaking his head. "What kind of language is that, Race? Are we supposed to understand it?"

"Not really."

"All right," Joanna interrupted, "if we're not where we were, where are we now?"

"A place near Kolob."

"Kolob—?" Quinn repeated. "Do you mind telling us where that is?"

Race shook his head. "We should definitely wait on that."

Quinn went over and sat down. "Not one thing you've told us makes the slightest sense."

"I said you wouldn't understand."

"You said we wouldn't believe you. You didn't say that was because we couldn't possibly understand you."

Race sat down in a leather armchair and stretched out his legs. "It's not that difficult, buddy, once you get over the first hurdle."

"Which is—?"

"Accepting the fact that you're not on earth anymore."

Quinn scrubbed his hands through his hair. He looked up at Race with an apologetic smile. His voice was lower, none of the previous exasperation showing.

"Let's go over this again. We had a rough night, but we don't seem able to prove it. You show up after two years and lay some incredible—no, some absolutely unbelievable—stuff on us. I have to tell you buddy—I'm having a tough time with this."

Joanna interrupted again. "Race, I don't really want to ask this question, but I feel I need to hear the answer." She hesitated, looked across at her husband, then blurted it out. "Are you dead—?"

Race took a moment before answering, then smiled at her. "I'm not dead, Joanna. You can see that. I'm not a ghost, either—those hugs we gave each other felt pretty real, didn't they?"

Joanna was frowning at him. "But something is different about you, right?"

"Okay. I did die—what you call death—two years ago in California, but now I'm Unified."

Quinn let his head flop back on the sofa, showing his exasperation. "First you're not dead, now you are. If you died two years ago, how can we be holding this conversation—?" He stopped, looking at Joanna. "Are you sure there's three of us in this room. I think there's a high probability we're crazy—having some giant hallucination."

Race grinned and answered before Joanna could. "You're not hallucinating. Let me give you the simple version. It'll still blow your mind but I promise things will all fall into place once we get to the meeting. So just listen, and no questions, okay?"

"Deal," Quinn nodded. "Only talk slow. You've already fried my brain."

Race settled back in the armchair.

"The planet earth has been going through several stages since the beginning of time—all part of a plan, which we won't go into. Last night, it started changing to prepare it for its next-to-last stage. This will be easier to understand at the meeting because you'll actually see it happening."

Quinn looked like he was going to ask a question, but Race waved it off. "All you need to know for now is the simple truth that all life on the planet temporarily ended last night."

Quinn and Joanna exchanged quick glances.

"I'd say that happened about three-fifteen, right?"

Race nodded.

"I know we aren't supposed to ask questions," Joanna said, "but did this have anything to do with the earth going out of orbit—becoming a ball of molten magma?"

Race smiled and nodded. "Jules nailed it. Even to the timeline. Nobody up here had it pinpointed that close. We knew it was going to happen, of course, but nobody knew exactly when. The word came down from Kolob just minutes before it happened."

Quinn leaned forward, his face now serious. "I hate to admit it, but this just might start making sense—"

"Just before earth shot in close to the sun, then was sling-shotted out into space," Race continued, "New Jerusalem and New Washington were transferred here. Don't try to figure out why, or how—it's all perfectly within the laws of celestial physics, I assure you. It's been done before."

Quinn was listening intently, trying to grasp as much as he could. Joanna was doing the same.

"Everyone alive who was found to be a basically good person was transferred here," Race continued. "They—and that includes the both of you—are now in a state we call Quickened. That means you didn't die, you were just temporarily changed. When the time comes, you'll go back to earth, live out your life, then return here again."

"If I'm understanding even a small part of this," Quinn murmured, "we're not dead, but you are. We're Quickened, but you're Unified—isn't that what you called it? But looking at the three of us, we all seem to be the same, buddy."

"We are all basically the same. We're individual spirits, which are all the same stuff, but we have different kinds of—well, outer shells. That depends on what stage of existence we're in—I'm sure this all sounds very strange and confusing."

"You got that right."

"Go on, Race," Joanna urged.

"Just a little more, perhaps," Race smiled, "then you'll both be on overload."

"More like being scared to death," Quinn muttered. He flashed a wry grin at his friend. "Death. Is that a bad word up here in—where did you say we were?"

"A place near Kolob."

"I hope someone explains where Kolob is. That will help pinpoint 'a place near it'."

"All in good time. That undoubtedly will come up at the meeting."

"I'm beginning to look forward to this meeting."

"Good, because we're headed there in just a few more minutes."

Race studied them, wondering what more he should say. Finally he pointed at the clock on the wall. It still showed three-fifteen.

"Any idea why all the clocks stopped?" he asked them.

They looked at each other, got no inspiration. Quinn shrugged.

"All that light we saw—or didn't see. I figure it must have been some kind of electrical storm. Strong enough to blow all the circuits and somehow drain or short out all the batteries. I don't believe one word of that, of course. Truth is, we don't know. Tell us, why did the time stop at three-fifteen?"

Race started smiling. "You just answered your own question. Time stopped."

They both stared at him, trying to understand.

"If that's your answer, Race," Joanna murmured, "it seems kind of obvious."

"I don't mean the clocks stopped. I mean time stopped."

Joanna felt a shiver of apprehension. "You're telling us that all time stopped when we were transferred here—"

"Exactly," Race nodded. "Well, all earthly time stopped—not down there, just up here. It's confusing, I know. Time is measured differently on this sphere."

"How different?" Quinn frowned.

"Trust me, buddy—that really will blow your mind."

All three of them rose, and Race reached out and touched both their foreheads with a finger.

"We have to get to the meeting. Don't ask me how this works, but it's called thought transport. It's the way people get around up here."

Race pressed down with both fingers.

All they felt was a tingling sensation.

# 3

## OLIBLISH ADMINISTRATION CENTER

Quinn and Joanna, accompanied by Race, stood in the center of a lobby of what appeared to be a huge, magnificent office building. One moment they were in the apartment, the next they were here in the lobby. There was no awareness of any motion or travel.

Joanna looked down at herself. Everything seemed to be intact. She glanced at Race.

"I'd say this is a great way to get to the office. What did I miss?"

"Nothing. Except traffic, of course."

Quinn was also examining himself. Nothing missing, as far as he could tell.

"Thought transport. You just thought us here—?"

Race grinned. "You're gonna love celestial physics. Right now, we need to get to that meeting."

Quinn glanced around him. The lobby was circular, at least twenty stories high, and capped with a glass dome. Actually, it appeared to be more than glass. The light streaming through it sparkled with an iridescent rainbow of hues, as if it were a giant diamond, or at the very least, high quality crystal. The colors it showered down were breathtaking.

Quinn noticed that large, round pillars were spaced around the perimeter of the lobby. They continued up through each succeeding floor, all the way to the dome, one on top of the other as if they were single columns. Quinn became aware that the columns were lit from an interior power source. All the columns, and surrounding office walls, were made of some kind of marble. The stone seemed translucent, not solid. Neither Quinn nor Joanna had ever seen anything like it.

Quinn saw his wife staring down at the floor of the lobby. At first glance, the floor was made of thick glass, clear but with a deep blue base. There was a pattern showing amid the blue, and he suddenly recognized it was a panorama of a night sky. There were millions of little stars stretching across the entire lobby floor. Then he noticed something else, the thing that obviously had already drawn the fascinated attention of Joanna. The stars, and the occasional sweep of milky, crowded galaxies, were twinkling, as they did when viewed on a clear night. The scene looked real, and there was something familiar about it. It was Joanna who recognized what it was.

"That's our heaven, Quinn. Look—there's Aries—the Dippers—the North Star. And Mars—"

"You're right," Quinn nodded. "It's like looking up from earth. That's an amazing reproduction."

"We call it the telestial sky," Race told them, "and it's more amazing than you think."

A pleasant looking man in a white suit approached them. He shook hands with Race.

"They're waiting for you in Monitoring Room Ten. That's down C Hall, off to your left."

Moments later, the three of them entered a large circular room. A conference table ran around the room, leaving an open space in the center. The table was made out of the same translucent marble they had seen everywhere. Quinn and Joanna noticed the floor in the center space appeared similar to that in the lobby, thick clear glass with a dark blue base. There were no twinkling stars in this one, however.

That was all they had time to notice, because their attention became riveted on the nine people already seated around one side of the conference table. Quinn and Joanna had experienced more than their share of jolting surprises in their years of intelligence work, but nothing even came close to the hammering shock of seeing these nine.

The first to wave in greeting to Quinn and Joanna were Dovid and Sophia Shazebak. These four had shared many forays into dark intelligence operations in the Mediterranean, an unusual but highly effective alliance between Israel's Mossad and the United States overseas arm of intelligence, the CIA. All four were friends and lovers long before joining in marriage. It was still difficult for Quinn to think of Dovid as Israel's top politician. It was shocking to see them, because Quinn and Joanna had just bade them farewell yesterday at Tel Nof, the Israeli air force base just south of Tel Aviv.

But shock was piled on shock.

Seated next to Dovid Shazebak was Anne Ashford. Beside her was her husband, Fernando Francisco de Branca.

Quinn's attention fastened on the man seated next to Fernando. He stared closely, not immediately recognizing him. Then he realized why the man looked so familiar. It was Sam Baldwin, President of the United States, the man he had been scheduled to meet with this morning. Quinn realized the same thing had happened to the President that he and his wife had experienced. Baldwin was sixty-seven, he knew, but now he looked no more than thirty-five. He hadn't known Sam thirty years ago, so the President looked really different.

But the shock of seeing a younger Sam Baldwin was nothing compared to the sudden realization of who was sitting next to him. The man was younger, like the rest of them, but there was no doubt it was Warren Hughes. It brought a greater shock than seeing Race Courtney.

A beloved American president, Warren Hughes had been murdered in an abortive plot to overthrow the government some twenty years earlier. Warren was more than president to Quinn. He was a close friend, and his death left a sadness that never really went away—not even after Quinn personally brought retribution to the man who killed him. Now here he was, looking fresh and dapper in a white suit, a broad grin on his young face. Hughes got up and came over to greet Quinn with a bear hug.

"Been looking forward to this moment, Quinn," he told him. "I know what you did for me back then, and I appreciate it."

"I don't believe this, Warren. You, of all people—"

"You don't think I'm smart enough for this group?"

"I think you're the smartest man I ever met. I just didn't expect to see you. But," Quinn added wryly, "I can't say I expected any of the things that have happened these last few hours."

"Know what you mean," Warren said, slapping him on the back. He looked back at the table. "Me and Sam been swapping a few stories. Neither one of us picked a good time to be president, did we. Have to admit, though, Sam sure has better taste in vice presidents."

Race went to greet the man and woman who were waving to him from the table. Austin and Vanessa Wells were his aunt and uncle, and had been an important part of drawing up the Phoenix Plan that had ended a war and brought the two American hemispheres together in a peaceful coalition. Race gave each of them a quick embrace. He reached over to shake the outstretched hand of the man sitting next to them—Jules Henshaw. Race had worked closely with Jules over the years they had served together on the Pharaoh Force.

"Congratulations, Jules," he smiled. "From what I hear, you were smarter than any of the folks up here. You hit it right on the button."

Henshaw was staring at him blankly. "I thought you were dead, Race. We heard you were killed in that raid on the terrorist camp in California—"

"Don't believe everything you hear," Race grinned. Explanations could come later.

"Then again," Henshaw muttered, glancing covertly over his shoulder, "I know President Hughes was killed. I saw his body in the coffin, and I attended his funeral in Arlington. Look at him, Race—he's a young man. I didn't recognize him before he introduced himself."

"Seen yourself this morning?" Race grinned. "You've got hair."

"I know," Henshaw frowned, stroking the top of his head. "A lot of crazy stuff is going on, Race. I don't know where I am or how I got here. Most of all, I don't know why I'm here." He glanced furtively about, and lowered his voice even more. "I don't recognize this place, Race. I know it sounds crazy, but I'm to the point of thinking we may not be on earth."

"You'll get answers soon, Jules. That's the purpose of this meeting."

The door opened and a man entered. He was dressed in a white suit, just like Warren, wearing a white shirt and white tie. He looked young but had snow-white hair that was neatly combed. There was an aura of authority about him that Quinn easily recognized. Whoever this man was, he was a leader.

Everyone automatically stopped talking and took a seat at the table. The man in the white suit sat down across from them. He studied them for a moment, his hands folded in front of him.

"I'm very pleased you all could come," he said finally. The voice was soft, well educated, and friendly. "You all know each other, so we'll use first names, if that's all right with everyone. You can call me Adam. Though I haven't met all of you personally, I am very familiar with what you've accomplished."

He paused, but no one said anything. Adam smiled.

"I know each of you has a thousand questions. All of them will be answered, but I'll begin with a brief statement that I hope will clear up some of your confusion. It probably won't, however."

There were smiles around the circular conference table.

"First of all, you are no longer on earth. You are on a place near Kolob. Kolob is the primary governing planet for all terrestrial and telestial solar systems. Without going into details, I assure you that is a lot of systems.

"This planet you are on is next in administrative order to Kolob—in other words, this is where the work gets done."

That brought some chuckles.

"I know you've all wondered if this place has a name. For now, we'll use the name the ancient Egyptians gave it—Oliblish. It's a terrestrial order, and I'll explain that in greater detail later. You are now in one of the administrative complexes on Oliblish."

He pointed down at the center circle of glass floor. "That is a space monitoring screen. I'll now show you why we call it that."

They all stared at the blue circle of glass. There was a fuzzy milkiness, then it cleared and everyone gasped as a clear, sharp picture of a planet filled the whole screen. It reminded everyone of the view astronauts had while circling the earth.

The planet was strange to everyone. They could see rotation, and glimpses of a land mass beneath a cover of thin clouds. The clouds obscured most of the planet.

"Does anyone recognize this planet?" Adam asked.

Everyone studied the monitoring screen. Jules Henshaw, his voice hesitant, spoke up.

"It's not a planet I recognize," he said, "although it seems vaguely familiar. It appears to have one land mass, circled east to west by a vast ocean. There are no separate continents. I'm guessing those clouds are steam, caused by intense heat probably emanating from the planet itself. The steam indicates there is an atmosphere similar to that of earth. I think the planet is hot, but cooling. Otherwise, that ocean would simply evaporate and disappear."

"Very good, Jules," Adam nodded. "I'm impressed. May I personally congratulate you on the very accurate conclusions you reached about what was going to happen to earth. Especially your conclusions on timing. You show a remarkable grasp of geological sequences. You took the knowledge available to you as far as you could. I might add that celestial laws of physics were involved in your transfer here, and in moving earth to a new order of planets. You could not possibly have known about that, but your conclusions were excellent."

"Thank you, sir," Jules said. "However, I have to admit to being completely bewildered now."

"Let me give a few reference points," Adam said quietly. He looked down at the planet again. "That is the planet earth, in its new form—"

"Pangaea," Jules blurted out, interrupting Adam. "That's earth as it was originally, in one land mass, millions of years ago before continents began splitting off and drifting apart. Pangaea—that's why it looked familiar. A re-creation of the world of Pangaea used to be on display in the old Smithsonian." He looked across at the man in the white suit. "That's what happened, isn't it. It all melted back together into one land mass and one ocean again."

"Once again, Jules, you're absolutely right." He flashed the scientist a quick smile. "And this time it has a solid surface crust—no broken or shifting plates."

Henshaw was suddenly frowning. "But if that's earth—" He looked up at Adam, the truth finally registering. "We're really not on earth, are we—"

"I wouldn't want to be there right now," Adam said. "Your conclusions were very plausible, Jules, about the possibility of the earth becoming a fiery ball. As I said, some celestial laws also were invoked. The earth did burn up, however, and it's still very hot. It will have to cool before it becomes habitable again."

Jule's head was nodding, a thin smile on his face. "So it did go out of orbit—" He gave Adam an apologetic shrug of his shoulders. "Please forgive my excitement, sir. This is all terribly fascinating."

"The earth was destined to leave its old solar system," Adam explained, "and has now been reorganized into a terrestrial order. It was in a telestial environment before, so it needed to be moved to a terrestrial order of heavenly systems."

Adam looked around at the faces of the others. It was very evident that while his explanations to Jules might have helped the scientist, they had only served to confuse the others.

"I can see I'm confusing you. Let me just say, there are three major orders of systems. Telestial—the lowest. Terrestrial—a middle order, but awesome in splendor. And celestial—the highest order of existence. The glory of that is beyond any words I can put together to describe. However, we will be dealing only with the terrestrial order during your stay on Oliblish. You have all been assigned to what we shall call Alpha Team. Each of you will be given assignments vital to the success of the earth's terrestrial phase."

Quinn was frowning. "May I ask, Adam, what will happen to the earth after that?"

"It all starts again—in just over a thousand earth years," Adam said. "The earth will be consumed once again, but this time it will emerge as a celestial planet. Many changes will occur, including removal to yet another solar system, but those are not our concern."

Sam Baldwin raised a hand, and Adam nodded at him. Baldwin cleared his throat, scratched at his cheek.

"One thing has me real puzzled, Adam," he began. "Seems like the people in this room aren't all in the same—well, the same condition, if you follow me. I know Warren here is dead—or he was. More than one of us here saw him put into the ground. He tells me he's Unified now, or something, and no longer dead. Never was dead, according to him. I guess I'm in some other category. I'm not sure what that is, where I am, or where I'm headed. Is that something you can clear up—?"

"I can try," Adam responded, "but with all this being so new to most of you, it will be difficult to understand."

"As it is," Baldwin muttered, "I'm totally confused."

"All right, let's give it a try." Adam stared around the group. "Sam is right—not all of you are in the same category. We are dealing with a fairly simple situation. Only two basic categories concern us at the moment—Quickened and Unified. Everyone here is one or the other. Understanding that becomes a little more difficult, however, when you factor in the several shadings of each category.

"Most of you here are in the Quickened state. That means you were transferred to Oliblish before you underwent a physical death on earth. You will all have to return to earth and eventually die a mortal death. I might add that a mass re-transfer back to earth is scheduled for tomorrow."

That brought an exchange of puzzled looks between the others in the room.

Quinn voiced what was in all of their minds.

"We're only going to be here in Oliblish for two days—?"

"That's two days Kolob time," Adam replied. "I'll get back to that, but first let me continue to explain the individual status of each of you. All of you who are Quickened have been found to be honest, truthful, and basically good people." He flashed another smile. "I'm sure all of you will agree with that assessment."

Everyone smiled and quickly nodded.

"A few of us here," Adam continued, "are what we call Unified. That simply means we have undergone death on earth, left our mortal bodies behind us, and returned to our original state. Now we have been Unified into one, inseparable body—or put in earthly terms, we have been resurrected. On earth, we actually had two bodies—a spirit body within a mortal body. In our separated state, we continue to have the same body we had before going to earth. For most people, there is little difference in appearance, because the spirit body was the model for the mortal one. Unfortunately, that isn't true for everyone, for some entered their mortal life with special challenges. Have I lost any of you yet—?"

"I'm a bit behind you," Sam Baldwin grimaced, "but you're leaving a reasonably clear trail to follow."

Adam nodded understandingly. "It takes a radical adjustment in thinking. Anyway, when the earth went through its recent change, the righteous dead—well, the most righteous of all the dead—were once again united with their mortal bodies. Being Unified simply means those two bodies are now inseparably locked together in one, immortal body. Achieving that state is one of the most important reasons for the whole experience of going down to earth."

Warren Hughes raised a hand.

"Adam, perhaps you could explain the difference between being Unified and Sanctified. That term will undoubtedly come up, and it can be very confusing."

"Good point, Warren." He again looked around the room. "I've explained what Unified means. Being Sanctified, simply put, means an individual has undergone a preliminary review of his life by those in authority, and been judged to meet the criteria of eventually living in the highest celestial order. There's a lot more to it, of course, but that gives an overview. That judgment is usually made at the time of Unification."

He looked around the table, saw that most were absorbing the essentials of what he had told them. Dovid Shazebak had a couple of questions.

"How long has this unification process been going on?" he asked. "And why isn't it referred to as a resurrection? That's the only way we've ever heard it described."

"The Unification process—or resurrection—began today with the events on earth. Unification occurred in a large group once before, and there have been a few individual unitings since then. However, this is the first time such large numbers of people have been involved. When earth is inhabited again, there will be more such events. In fact, another is scheduled in a few hours.

"As for not using the term resurrection, Unification is preferred because it more accurately portrays the event. Resurrection is a word used to communicate in simple terms to humans, but it conjures images of dead bodies arising from graves. It adds to a sense of life ending with mortal death, when nothing could be further from the truth. However," Adam smiled, looking around the group, "if it helps to look upon Warren, and Race, and myself as resurrected beings, please do so. Either way, we're Unified and now immortal."

Warren Hughes looked down the table at Dovid. "Can't tell you how happy folks are up here about being Unified. It means a lot to be in the first resurrection."

Dovid looked at Adam again. "So everyone wasn't involved—?"

"Not everyone who lived in the past two thousand years—since the Savior was Unified—participated in this first phase," Adam replied. "Only those authorized to receive sanctification status were Unified at this time. Two more Unification events are scheduled, however."

"And everyone came here to Oliblish—?"

"No," Adam said. "Actually, they were all transferred to a planet that has served as a temporary waiting place ever since earth was put into the Plan. You people, along with many others in New Jerusalem, and old Jerusalem, were brought to Oliblish to receive specific assignments and training for the next phase of the Plan."

"Why us?" Sam Baldwin asked. "I know most of us worked together at one time or another, but we seem an odd lot to put together as a team. I mean, we're all patriots, and all basically good people I suppose, but not many of us are what you'd call religious. Seems like that would be an important requirement for you folks—"

Adam gave a quick shake of his head. "Not in the least. You all represent an important diversification of skills and talents. You will be working closely together after returning to earth. Many groups with special skills and ethnic backgrounds have been brought to Oliblish for training, just as you people have. Their religious background is important only to them, as individuals. Religious salvation is something entirely different from what we are dealing with now."

"Well, I hope you're good at giving instructions," Sam muttered. "I'm staring at a blank page."

"All of you are," Adam smiled. "Your assignments will be made very clear before you go back. Much needs to be accomplished on the new terrestrial earth once it becomes habitable again, and it must be done in a relatively short period of time."

"I'm wondering, Adam," Warren said, "if you could outline our central purpose—give us some recognizable goals."

"That's a good place to start," Adam nodded. "Each of you is important to getting the new terrestrial order organized. Your assignments will reflect your individual expertise and begin immediately after the transfer occurs tomorrow."

He looked around, pleased at what he saw on their faces. These people had been chosen well, and would make sure their assignments were completed. He felt very confident about that.

"Don't forget that everything on earth relating to organized society was just destroyed. Although far more beautiful, and much friendlier to cultivation and development, it is now a planet empty of humans. Restarting society for all the millions who will be returning is your major task." He gave a knowing smile. "That may sound like an awesome challenge, but I promise you it will be much easier to accomplish than when I faced a similar situation. You will enjoy open communication with Oliblish, and receive all the scientific and educational assistance needed."

An almost eager anticipation could already be seen on some faces. The assignments were beginning to take shape in their minds, even before they were given.

"This new period of earth's existence is primarily to connect the entire human race—everyone who has lived on earth, or will live on it during the terrestrial phase—into genealogical chains. There's no time today to explain why that is so important, but it is. And almost every one of those people will have some kind of personal problem, an unresolved personal relationship connected to mortality that needs solving while mortal time still exists. We need organizations and systems to accomplish what will undoubtedly be a monumental task. It all must be finished before earth's mortal phase ends."

Quinn spoke up again.

"Obviously, time stopped this morning at the moment of this—transference. I'm wondering, when will it start again?"

"What you say is not quite true, Quinn. Time did not stop on earth, but it has little relevance here in the Kolob system. We operate on a completely different time order."

"Could you explain that, please—?"

"Hate to clutter your minds with it," Adam smiled, "but it is important to your understanding of what's going on, I suppose. Here on Oliblish, we operate on Kolob time. That means one day here is the same as one thousand years on earth."

He could see that stunned everyone in the room.

It was Warren Hughes who first picked up on the significance of what Adam had just told them.

"You're saying that the two days we'll be spending here in Oliblish will actually see two thousand years pass in earth time—?"

Adam nodded. "Now you see why two days gives the planet plenty of time to cool off."

Sam looked at himself, poking a finger into his chest. "I'm going to be two thousand years older when I go back to earth—?"

Adam smiled and shook his head. "Technically that's true, but not physically. You will experience no physical deterioration, and just pick up where you left off when Quickened. After that, each of you will live until you are one hundred earth-years old. At that time, you will be instantly Unified. No funerals, no burials."

"That's an established date—one hundred years. What if you get sick—?"

"You won't," Adam said. "Things will be a lot different on the terrestrialized earth. You'll live to be exactly one hundred years old—and the good news is, that entire time you'll feel like you're in your thirties."

"I'm going to like this new world," Baldwin grinned, "although I have a friend in the funeral business who's going to hate it. Come to think of it," he added, "Charlie probably didn't make the first cut."

"One thing more, before we get into the details of your assignments and separate for individual training sessions this afternoon," Adam said. "When you leave here today, each of you will be given your Life Key. A modification is at this moment being made in your homes. A large wall screen is being installed. It's television like you've never seen before. Three-dimensional, crystal clear, absolutely life-like. In fact, the pictures are life-size.

"There is a control box near the screen. Insert your Life Key and you will be able to view every second of your life on earth. Or, if you wish, you can program the viewing to a specific date or time."

"Sounds like the mother of all home movies," Sam grunted. "Not sure I want to see every second of my life—too many things I'd rather forget."

"Everyone shares that feeling, Sam, but I should tell you it's already been reviewed in minute detail. That's part of the reason you were Quickened in this terrestrial phase."

"Are you recommending we view our whole life?" Joanna asked. "We don't have time for that, do we—?"

Adam gave another little smile. "You're forgetting one thing, Joanna—watching your whole life in Kolob time will take about an hour. Just relax and enjoy the movie—"

# 4

## THE LIFE KEYS

"None of this is real, Joanna. It can't possibly be happening."

"How can you say that—?"

"Nothing makes sense."

"Why not—?"

"We're talking to dead people, Joanna. Think about it—we just came from a five hour meeting sitting around a table with people who died years ago. And if we believe Adam, the meeting didn't last five hours—we sat in that room for over two hundred years. Is that unreal, or what—"

"You don't accept what Race or Adam told us—?"

"Forget what they said—I don't accept them as real. Race was killed two years ago—there was positive identification. I didn't want to accept it then, and obviously I still don't. And Adam. If he's who I think he is, he certainly wasn't walking around in a white suit when he was on earth."

"When was that—?"

"About six thousand years ago, using the Biblical calendar."

**"That** Adam—?" she breathed incredulously.

"We're imagining all this, Joanna. We've both been under a lot of stress—we must have cracked."

"Cracked at the same time, and sharing the same crazy dream? How long do dreams last, Quinn? We've been having this one since last night—in stereo. Now that's unreal—"

"Anything can happen in a dream. Maybe it just seems that long."

"You're fighting this—why?"

"Because if this whole crazy situation is real, I don't know how to cope with it."

Quinn and Joanna returned directly to their condominium after the meeting. Race obliged by returning them via thought transfer—which was something else Quinn couldn't accept. Thought transfer. It didn't even happen in the movies—a person needed to get zapped by some power source before being beamed anywhere. It was just one more thing that defied all logic.

Joanna stared around the apartment. It looked the same. Even down to the clocks still stopped at three-fifteen.

"Are we dreaming now?" she asked her husband.

Quinn crossed to the balcony door and stepped outside. As before, there was nothing unusual about the scene below. Same buildings along the street, none of them damaged. Same central park. There were still no automobiles in sight, he noticed. There was no doubt, however, this was the same view of New Jerusalem they had always enjoyed from their condo. He came back inside, plopping wearily down on the sofa.

"You tell me," he muttered. "If this is a dream, I want out."

The doorbell chimed. Joanna went to answer it, and moments later, she came back into the living room followed by her brother Dovid and his wife Sophia.

"Why don't you ask them?" she told Quinn.

"Ask us what?" Dovid queried, frowning at them. "Is there a problem—?"

"Now that's a strange question, Dovid," Quinn said, unable to keep the sarcasm out of his voice. "We're walking around on some strange planet, talking to dead people, and attending meetings that last for two hundred years. Yesterday, you and Sophie were in Tel Aviv, up to your ears in at least a year's worth of problems, yet here you are in Missouri—or Oliblish—or wherever we are. Do you see a problem in any of that, Dovid?"

A grin broke over Dovid Shazebak's face. "I know where you're coming from—Sophie and me had the same conversation awhile ago. Here you are in New Jerusalem—and we're just a thought away in old Jerusalem. Unlike you guys, however, our surroundings don't even look the same. We're in Jerusalem, but not in Israel—unless someone leveled the mountains. So Sophie and me are asking the same questions. Is any of this real? Are we all wandering around in the same dream? Are we all crazy? Where exactly are we? I can answer one of those questions—the one about where we are. I'm not touching any of the others."

Joanna motioned for them to sit down, and she joined Quinn on the sofa.

"So where are we, Dovid? Knowing that will at least be a start—"

"He doesn't really know," Sophia told her. "He asked a question and he got an answer, but we still can't say where we are."

"Sophie's right," Dovid said. "I don't have a name. It's more like I know where we aren't—"

"If this is going to be another riddle, Dovid," Quinn grimaced, "we have enough of those already."

"So where aren't we—?" Joanna asked.

"We're not on Oliblish. We were this morning, but not now."

"Would it be too much to hope we're back in Missouri—?" Quinn grunted.

"Not Missouri—we're on a third planet. The temporary waiting place Adam mentioned this morning. Everyone was transferred there just before earth went flying out into space."

Quinn gave him a look of frustration. "Listen to yourself, Dovid. You're telling us that in addition to just spending two hundred years in a meeting on Oliblish—which we all know by now is a place near Kolob—we also threw in a little inter-planetary space travel?"

"Tough to swallow, isn't it."

Quinn stared hard at his friend. "You're buying this, aren't you—"

"About it all being real? It's the only logical conclusion, isn't it."

"I've been trying hard to make it illogical—"

"Give up, my friend. As hard as it is to accept, this is all really happening—I'm convinced of it. Don't ask me to explain any of it, but I believe what Adam told us this morning."

"He didn't tell us who he is—"

"He didn't need to, did he."

"Well, I had no idea," Joanna said quickly. "Quinn just laid that one on me a few minutes ago."

"Me neither," Sophia added. "I'm still not sure I believe it."

"And you know who is prominently not mentioned by anyone?" Quinn added. "No one has mentioned God. I thought he was central to everything in life after death."

Sophia was nodding. "You'd think the name of Jehovah would have come up—"

"It's all being kept on a business-like basis," Dovid said. "Almost as if God—or Jehovah—has nothing to do with it."

"I'm sure he does," Joanna said quickly. "I feel a deliberate separation is being maintained. Like Adam said, religious salvation is not a part of the mechanics we're involved in."

The front doorbell chimed again. Joanna went to answer it and this time came back with Race and Stacy. Seeing his sister, Quinn jumped up and threw his arms around her, giving her a long, tight squeeze. He finally stepped back, giving her a quizzical inspection. She looked great—younger, of course, like the rest of them. Still perky, and looking radiantly happy. He hadn't seen her look like that in the last two years, since Race had been killed—maybe killed, he added to himself.

"You seem real enough," he said. His glance went to Race. "I'm not sure about you—"

Stacy turned and put her arms around her husband's waist, holding herself tightly against him.

"He's real," she said, looking up at Race. "He's alive—I've got him back. Isn't that wonderful!"

Quinn flashed a wry smile. "If hanging around with a dead husband makes you happy—"

"You still can't accept it, can you, buddy," Race said, shaking his head. "What's it going to take to convince you—?"

"Maybe walking through a few walls, like the other ghosts do—"

"You're not a ghost, buddy. I keep telling you—you're not dead."

"But you are—"

"If you want to call it that. But nobody really dies—not in the way you think of it. You don't stop living—you just change locations."

"I can deal with that," Joanna said, "but here we are, all mixed together. You're dead, and we're not. That seems too strange—"

"Ordinarily, it wouldn't be happening," Race agreed, "but this is a whole new phase of the Plan—"

"That's another thing," Quinn interrupted. "I keep hearing references to this Plan—what's that all about?"

"It's a plan of existence that's been operating forever," Race said. "Earth is leaving its telestial phase, and going back to a terrestrial order. That means a whole lot of changes. All of us are involved in getting society and industry functioning again on earth. Don't forget there's no longer a North America, or a South America, or an Australia. It's all one piece of land now. Enough time will have passed to allow the restoration of natural things—forests, grasses, rivers, things like that. There will be no more mountains—did anyone mention that? Anyway, it's all going to be strange, and a tremendous challenge."

Quinn sighed and sat down again on the sofa. "It's all very weird. Still, I'm beginning to feel I might be the one out of step here—"

Joanna motioned for everyone to sit down. She suddenly had a strange thought.

"I just realized the only food Quinn and I have had since yesterday is a rather poor excuse of a meal on the jet coming back from Israel. I'm not hungry though—is anyone else?"

"You don't really get hungry here," Race said hesitantly. He and Stacy were snuggled against each other on the love seat. "I almost brought over a basket of fruit—you can't believe how indescribably delicious the fruits and vegetables taste here—but finding Stacy made me forget everything else."

Dovid shot a questioning stare at him.

"Did you know the new temple we just finished building in Jerusalem was not destroyed. It's here—wherever we are."

"All temples of worship were transferred to this planet. They'll be transferred back tomorrow. They'll all be needed for the ordinance work that needs to be done."

Joanna was nodding. "You can see the Mormon temple from our terrace. Apparently nothing is damaged."

Their condominium was located on the east side of Ashford Tower—at least, it had been in Missouri—and afforded a spectacular view of the Mormon temple grounds. Although neither Quinn nor Joanna belonged to the Mormon faith, they had many friends who did and all of them were openly envious of that temple view.

The majestic temple built in New Jerusalem occupied over a square mile in the center of the city. It included a complex of temple buildings surrounded by a huge park. This new temple square, more than eight times larger than the familiar square in Salt Lake City, was a breathtaking triumph of architecture. There were twenty-four main temple buildings, all connected by graceful arches spanning a huge central court. It was seeing these arches still in place that first convinced Quinn no earthquake had occurred. It there had been one, those arches almost certainly would have fallen.

Race studied the faces of his friends. They were all showing the strain of trying to understand what was going on.

"I think maybe it's time for some serious talk," he said quietly.

Everyone started nodding at the same time. They were indeed ready.

"A great deal of effort has been expended to make this transition as understandable as possible," Race began. "It may not seem like it, but it's been a major concern for people here. Any part of what's just happened on earth is enough to blow the average mind."

"So far," Quinn said dryly, "I agree with you completely."

"You may have noticed that some references have been avoided. We haven't talked about the celestial kingdom, or God, or the Messiah—I know you've been curious about that. It was done to lessen the confusion, make things sound more natural and easier to accept. We know the reality of what is happening is very difficult to cope with."

"I'm not sure it wouldn't have been easier to understand all this stuff if you'd used more familiar terms from the very beginning," Quinn muttered.

"Trust me, buddy, you'd all be in shock," Race said. "There's too much fear associated with words like death, resurrection, paradise, hell—too much mystery. Adam explained why the term Unification is used, rather than resurrection. Then there's the Millennium—another word surrounded in mystery. That's what we're talking about, of course, now that earth has entered its terrestrial order. And the Savior, or Messiah, as the Jews have long referred to him. He's directing everything that's happening but that must not overshadow the fact that each one of us has an important role to play."

"It helps to put it on the table," Quinn agreed. "I know I'd feel caught up in some religious web that was far bigger than me."

Dovid was exchanging looks with his wife. It was obvious something was troubling them. Race knew what it was.

"You don't have to be secretive about it any longer," he told them. "The man who's been visiting Israel ever since the Jihad—go ahead and tell them about him."

"What man?" Joanna frowned.

"The Messiah," Sophia said, the words so quiet the others could hardly hear her. Tears jumped into her eyes. "He's the man they called Jesus of Nazareth. Every Jew in Israel accepts that as truth now. And we are all feeling tremendous guilt."

"It was part of the Plan," Race said softly. "No need to feel blame or remorse. What happened was decreed before He came to earth."

"But we crucified him—"

"It was the Plan—it had to happen. He knew that. He places no blame."

Sophia put her head in her hands and her shoulders began to shake. Dovid reached over to comfort her.

"There can be no doubt," Dovid said, looking at the others. "We have all seen the marks on his hands and feet—"

Stacy was staring at him, obviously puzzled.

"Are you saying the Savior has been seen in Jerusalem?"

"Many times. Ever since the war ended."

"And you didn't tell anyone?"

"It was His wish—"

"Do you know what a shock this is?" Tears gathered in Stacy's eyes. "The Savior has been on earth, in Israel—"

"It's been a difficult secret to live with, Stacy. Of course, it was also a supremely joyful one."

Stacy looked at her husband. "You knew about this—?"

"It was on all the monitoring systems up here," Race said. "Everyone knew it meant the timeline was getting very short."

There was silence for a long time.

The Savior walking the streets of Jerusalem once more. The Jewish people accepting Him as their long-awaited Messiah. It was overpowering to deal with.

Race reached into a coat pocket, taking out a strange-looking square rod covered with rows of markings. He held it up.

"Does everyone have their Life Key?"

The rod didn't look like a key, not the usual kind used on earth, at least. It was light, seemingly made of some translucent plastic material. It was an inch wide on all four sides, and about eight inches long. Each of the group had received one similar to it, but there hadn't been an opportunity to use them yet. The huge wall screen and control panel were installed, however, just like Adam promised. Everyone indicated they had their Life Key with them.

"May I suggest we take a look back, refresh our memories about all that's happened in the last few years."

"Whose life are we going to start with?" Stacy asked. "Not mine—"

Race grinned. "I agree. We should see that when we're alone, Stacy. The lives of all six of us were pretty tight the last few years. Let's all put in our keys and pick a time to start reviewing. Any suggestions when that would be—?"

Joanna looked at Quinn. "Perhaps my phone call to you the night they tried to kill you. Seems like that's when things started moving pretty fast."

Quinn nodded. "We were certainly all involved after that."

Each put their Life Key into spaces in the control panel. Dovid stared uncertainly at it.

"Race, do you know how to operate this thing?"

"It's mainly thought controlled—"

Quinn's eyebrows raised in mock surprise. "Now why didn't I think of that—"

They made themselves comfortable. Stacy snuggled closer to her husband as they all stared at the screen.

"Anyone else have a sudden urge for popcorn?" Stacy murmured

The huge screen came to life. It was startling. So real, so dimensional, it seemed they actually were inside the bedroom that now showed on it. And so huge—like being engulfed in the front row of a movie theater.

"That's you and Jill in bed," Joanna said. She gave her husband a curious stare. "Where is Jill, anyway?" The stare swiveled to Race and Stacy. "Either of you two seen her?"

"She hasn't been Unified yet," Race answered. "She's in the Place of Contemplation. She'll be called in the next event, I'm sure."

Joanna shook her head. It was all too much to figure out. The picture on the screen was moving in on the bed with the two sleeping figures.

"I'll bet the next sound you hear," Joanna said, "will be me calling Quinn from Tel Aviv—"

It was.

# THE MANDRIN SPIDER

## PART TWO

# 5

## Assault On Pharaoh One

On the second ring, Quinn Adams squeezed open an eye and peered at the clock on the bedtable. Five minutes to two. He groaned softly. There was no flashing red light or muted bleep to signal a message coming in on the black phone connected to NECCO headquarters. This strident intrusion came from the white, personal phone beside it. On the fourth ring, Quinn grabbed the receiver.

"Yes—?" he growled.

"That you, Quinn—?"

The woman's voice was stressed but warmly familiar, triggering an instant flood of memories. No, not memories. More like fragmented glimpses of his life exploding in his mind, blurred moments shared with a dark-haired young woman. Moments of killing. Moments of passion. Quinn Adams sat up, swung his feet onto the floor, while on the other side of the bed, his wife stirred restlessly. Jill was trying to ignore the disturbance and stay asleep.

"Joanna—where are you calling from? This call isn't routed—"

"Tel Aviv. No time for channels. Is your wife with you—?"

"Yes. It's two o'clock in the morning—"

"Both of you get out of there—"

Nerve ends started crawling. Quinn knew this woman too well not to recognize the urgency in her voice.

"What's happening?"

"Just get out. Immediately."

"Give me something, Joanna—"

"You're targeted. I don't know why, but you are. The report came in from Morocco not ten minutes ago. It's reliable. Pharaoh One. Air assault. Tonight. Get out, Quinn. Call me back when you can—I'm at the office."

The line clicked as Joanna Shazebak ended the call.

Quinn reached over and used the dimmer switch on the small lamp beside the phone to bring up just enough light to weaken the solid darkness. His wife rolled over, propping herself up on one elbow to stare at him.

"Who was that?"

Quinn was already pulling on cotton pants and stepping into loafers.

"Joanna Shazebak. Grab some clothes, we have to get out of here."

Jill sat unmoving. "Why is Joanna calling? Is she here in Washington?"

"She's in Tel Aviv." He pulled a sweatshirt over his head. "She thinks someone is coming to kill us."

"Why would she think that?" Jill peered at her husband, trying to determine if the shadows hid something on his face. Quinn's warning of danger was alarming, but for the moment she was more concerned with reaction to the telephone call from a former lover. "How did she get our number? Have you been in contact with her again—?"

"There's no time for this, Jill."

Quinn opened the drawer on the bed table, took out a .45 caliber pistol. He reached under the drawer, pulled off the loaded ammo clip taped there and banged it into the pistol grip.

"I suggest you get dressed."

Jill was concerned about the call, but Joanna wouldn't have called if the danger wasn't real. Jill started to say something but he held up a hand to silence her. Outside, he heard the sound of approaching helicopter rotors. He crossed swiftly to the bedroom window and opened the curtains a slit. Their condominium was on the twenty-fifth floor and nothing but black sky could be seen in the darkness outside.

The beating of the rotors grew rapidly louder. Quinn assumed the helicopter was heading for the landing pad on the roof of the building, just five floors above. Joanna's information out of Mossad's secret station in Morocco was deadly accurate. Quinn realized armed terrorists would soon be starting down from the roof with the mission of eliminating the man who headed the National Emergency Coordinated Command Organization. Pharaoh One. Quinn Adams. He wheeled from the window.

"Out, Jill—now."

Jill jumped out of bed, quickly pulling on the slacks and sweater left on the bench at the foot of the bed. There was no time for anything else. Quinn grabbed her arm as they raced from the bedroom. At the front door, Quinn stopped to listen, snapping a bullet into the chamber of the automatic. When he jerked the door open, the hallway outside was empty.

As they ran to the elevator, Quinn paused long enough to smash the butt of the pistol through the glass of the fire alarm box, setting off clanging bells.

They reached the elevator and Quinn punched the button. Glancing up at the indicator lights, alarms went off in his head.

The elevator was arriving from the floors above, but at this time of the morning, it should have been coming up from the lobby.

He looked down the hall to the "Exit Stairs" sign—too far to reach in time. Quinn shoved his wife back against the wall.

"Get on the floor," he hissed. Jill was slow to react, and he pulled her down as he dropped to the carpet. The loud clanging of the fire alarm blocked out the faint bell announcing the arrival of the elevator, but he saw the door begin to open. He rolled away from the wall just enough to give him an angle of vision inside the elevator.

Lying flat on the floor, elbows propped in front of him with the pistol gripped in both hands, he saw the two hooded men dressed in black a half-second before they looked down and saw him. It cost them their lives. Quinn pumped two bullets into the foreheads of each of them. At that range, one of the hollow-nosed .45 slugs would have sufficed, but two left no nerve signals intact even for reflex action.

Both assassins were hurled backwards by the force of the bullets. One slid down into a sitting position, the other bounced off the rear wall of the elevator and fell forward. His head, or what was left of it, protruded out of the elevator into the hallway.

Jill still cowered against the wall, covering her ears against the blasts of the .45 that echoed loudly in the confines of the hallway. Quinn grabbed her and pulled her to her feet. Her eyes were wide with shock as she stared down at the blood pooling around the hooded head sticking out of the elevator. She quickly averted her eyes from whatever was bubbling out from the back of the dead man's skull.

Quinn signaled Jill toward the door to the stairwell.

"Keep going down. You won't meet any more bad guys."

She looked at him in alarm.

"You're not leaving me—?"

He gave her arm a reassuring squeeze.

"It's all right. There are NECCO special forces on duty here twenty-four hours a day. This is a secure building—"

"Sure it is," Jill grimaced, glancing back at the elevator door bumping insistently against the shattered head obstructing it.

"Just do it, Jill!" Quinn said sharply. "You'll meet Rangers on the stairs. Tell them I've gone to the roof."

Quinn turned and ran back to the elevator. He pushed the dead man's head back into the elevator with his foot, stepped inside and punched the button marked "Heliport". As the elevator moved up, he took the automatic weapons from the assassins and slung them over his shoulders. He ripped off the hoods but didn't see what he expected. There wasn't a whole lot left of their heads but he could tell both dead men were Latinos. With Joanna's warning coming out of Morocco, he had expected to see Arabs. He frowned, wondering how an Israeli intelligence unit operating out of Casablanca picked up on an assassination attempt in the U.S. that did not involve Arabs. Maybe Joanna would have some answers when he was able to question her about the alert.

Before he shoved the automatic pistol into the belt of his pants, he smashed out the overhead light and plunged the elevator into darkness. If the two men at his feet had done that, the outcome in the hallway might have ended differently.

The elevator stopped on the thirtieth floor. Quinn tensed and crouched low as the door opened but there was no one waiting. A short flight of steps led up to the glassed enclosure providing access to the heliport. There was no sign of any NECCO Rangers, who were normally on duty round-the-clock in the reception area, checking arrivals and departures in the Level Five security residential tower. He slung one of the automatic rifles into position, checked to make sure the safety was off, then lunged out of the elevator toward the stairs.

At the glassed-in entrance, he saw the bodies of two Rangers sprawled outside on the roof. The position of the bodies left no doubt the men were dead. A helicopter stood on the pad outside, blades rotating in a blurred circle, ready for a fast lift-off. The helicopter was clearly marked with Army insignia but Quinn didn't let that disrupt his concentration. Army or not, this copter had brought men to kill him, terrorists who already had committed murder.

One man dressed in black stood beside the copter with what looked like another man inside at the controls. It was too dark to be sure. With that quick picture set in his mind, Quinn shot out the overhead lights and lowering the muzzle, fired through the glass at the helicopter.

The terrorist on the roof saw someone burst up the stairs and shoot out the lights. The man started firing but by then Quinn was through the shattered glass, out onto the roof, and rolling into the deeper shadows of the brick elevator control wall. Quinn fired in the direction of the helicopter and heard a man cry hoarsely in pain.

The helicopter started to take off. As it lifted from the roof, a man clung to the landing strut. Quinn fired again and the copter veered upwards and turned sharply. The man on the strut fell into space. If he wasn't already dead, he would be after a thirty-story fall.

Quinn Adams stood up and took deliberate aim, emptying the magazine at the helicopter. He quickly changed weapons and emptied the second magazine. He felt a surge of anger as the copter veered and rose until it was nearly out of range. Suddenly the craft rolled over and started tumbling. Quinn ran to the edge of the roof and watched the helicopter hit the ground and explode. Quinn felt a grim satisfaction as he watched the flames.

Four to one. And you lose.

It took several hours for the bodies to be removed from the building and Quinn to repeat all he knew about the attack to the various levels of investigating Ranger officers. He said nothing, of course, about the call from Tel Aviv, nor his own involvement with NECCO. As far as anyone knew, Quinn was a high-level official in some branch of Intelligence, and that was all they were supposed to know.

A sky-blue helicopter bearing the red triangular NECCO insignia arrived at the heliport. Quinn boarded and the copter flew off into the Virginia countryside.

Dawn was breaking as the craft approached a five-sided, completely enclosed concrete building hidden in the wooded terrain some twenty miles southwest of the Capitol.

The building resembled a small Pentagon, except no windows were on the exterior. The lone entrance to the building was to the east, reached by a narrow, twisting two-mile-long private road with four barricaded checkpoints along it. A sign at the turn- off from the state highway indicated the private road led to the National Archives Repository Annex.

It didn't.

The road led to the headquarters of the National Emergency Coordinated Command Organization—known as NECCO. Only a handful of people in administration and a small number of politicians and citizens remembered the organization from its brief surfacing into the public spotlight seven years ago, during the debacle of Operation Eagle Red. NECCO was no longer super-secret, as it was before Eagle Red, but it had quickly, and deliberately, sunk as far back into anonymity as possible. Almost no one remembered what the acronym stood for, or the fifteen section heads—Pharoahs—who ran the organization.

The helicopter landed in the inner quadrangle of the building. Armed NECCO Rangers, dressed in blue military uniforms with white neck scarves and leggings, immediately emerged from the building. One of them greeted Quinn with a warm handshake.

"Sorry that happened, sir."

General Frank Kantros was a major seven years ago when he proved his loyalty and ability to command while stamping out the revolutionaries of the so-called American Liberation Army. Since then, Kantros rose to commanding officer of the special forces of NECCO, with its elite groups of commandos strategically located in every section of the country.

Quinn fell into step beside Kantros as the Rangers escorted them toward the building.

"Any word on who they were or where they came from—and why they came after me?"

Kantros shook his head. "Latinos. No positive identification yet. The one in the chopper was burned to a crisp. The man who fell was pretty well splattered, but the ones you killed in the elevator should give us a fast track. Not much left of their faces but the bodies should tell us something."

"Let me know as soon as you get anything," Quinn muttered. "They must have thought I was an easy target. There were only four in the strike unit—and they acted pretty amateurish. I doubt they were hard-core terrorists. I don't know whether to be insulted or grateful."

"You can be assured it won't happen again," Kantros said grimly. "With your permission, sir, we'll be keeping a tighter net around you and the other Pharaohs from now on."

Half an hour later, after a short meeting with Kantros and other concerned Ranger officers, Quinn rode the elevator to the depths of the headquarters building where a special electric tube train whisked him to Pharaoh Operations, the nerve center of NECCO hidden entirely underground several miles from the main building.

It was almost seven in the morning when he finally settled behind the desk in his office. The first thing he did was put in a call to Mossad headquarters in Tel Aviv. It took only a few minutes, routed through a patch between U.S. and Israeli COMINT satellites. When the phone rang, Joanna Shazebak was on the line.

"I owe you, Joanna—again."

"So it did go down—"

"Just like you called it."

"I was worried when I didn't hear back. You sound like you're still in one piece—"

"Thanks to you. It was close."

"What kind of unit was involved?"

"Latin."

There was a pause. "That's surprising."

"I agree, especially after the source you mentioned."

"Don't repeat that, not even over COMINT."

"That station is deep, I take it."

"Very deep. There are other reports we've been cleared to share—but not over open lines. No courier channels, either."

"Is this important?"

"Very important."

"We're talking about a face-to-face meeting?"

"Yes. It will have to be over here, with you and no one else. My people are very jumpy about dealing with unknowns right now."

"Agreed. Just like old times."

"Well, not quite. You do have a wife now. How did she handle being a target?"

"She was a little shook. About the guns—and you."

"Give her my regards."

"I don't think so—"

He could hear the smile in Joanna's voice.

"In and out in a couple of days. She won't even know you've been here, if you don't want to tell her. The meet is important to both our companies, though. I'll set it up and call you back." Her voice fell a notch lower and he thought he detected the merest quaver in it as she added, "Glad you made it, Quinn."

The line went dead.

He hung up the receiver and with Joanna's words fresh on his mind, wondered if he should tell Jill he would be spending a couple of days in Israel. He told her about Joanna before they married, and many of the missions they had shared together. He'd even told her that he and Joanna were lovers at one time. That news was difficult for Jill to handle, but he thought it was all put behind them a long time ago. Now he wasn't so sure.

Judging from his wife's reaction this morning when Joanna called, there was still jealousy there, some womanly-type fear that her husband's commitment was not full and complete.

It was natural enough, he supposed. Jill realized she could never share the intense life-and-death moments that would forever link Quinn to the beautiful Israeli woman. Still, he and Jill would share the rest of their lives together and Quinn had hoped that was enough. Jill could not doubt his love for her. He shook his head, wondering how in the world a man understood a woman.

There was a knock on the door. Race Courtney, the head of NECCO intelligence—and Quinn's brother-in-law—stuck his head into the office.

"Just talked to Stacy. Jill's okay."

"Glad to hear it. It isn't every day she's a target for assassination."

"Heard Joanna called in the alarm." He stared at Quinn with mock seriousness. "Not a good idea, buddy, to have your lover call while you're in bed with your wife. From what Stacy said, Jill's not too happy about that."

Race knew Quinn spent most of his years in the CIA working the Mediterranean theater. That was where he met Joanna Shazebak and her brother Dovid, both highly placed in Israel's Mossad intelligence organization. Quinn and Joanna became lovers, but the relationship ended abruptly when Quinn was recalled to Washington and detached from the CIA.

In the months that followed, Quinn helped put together NECCO, an organization dealing with a wide range of high-security information. This included people, materials, industries, and national and military resources, information vital to planning responses to any kind of catastrophic disaster that might strike a state, a region, or the entire country. NECCO operated independently of any Congressional supervision or oversight. As Pharoah One, Quinn answered directly, and only, to the President of the United States. Race Courtney joined the NECCO intelligence force during the days of Eagle Red. No one doubted he earned his promotion to become head of the very elite, very secret, intelligence arm of the NECCO organization.

Quinn motioned for Race to sit, giving a weary shake of his head.

"Joanna saved our lives. We'd be on those slabs in the morgue if she hadn't called."

Race grinned at him. "Seems Jill isn't totally convinced that's not where you belong."

Quinn was exasperated.

"She knows Joanna is not my lover—"

Race raised both hands.

"I'm on your side, buddy—"

A telephone rang. There were three phones on Quinn's desk, red, white, and black. This was the red one, which connected to only one place.

Quinn picked it up.

"Yes, Mr. President."

Sam Baldwin, President of the United States, sounded relieved to hear Quinn's voice.

"Congratulations. I heard you were one mean dude this morning."

Race stood up to leave but Quinn waved him to stay.

"Any information on that assault team, Mr. President?"

"Just got through meeting with Akker and Dean." Stuart Akker was the director of Central Intelligence, Norman Dean the head of the FBI. "The chopper apparently came from a small base near Baltimore. No one knows how those Latinos got hold of it. In fact, no one seems to know anything about this whole incident. Do you—?"

"Not yet, Mr. President," Quinn said grimly, "but I will."

"Can you whip over here? I want to go over some items with you. Right away."

"Anything I should bring with me?"

"Bring Courtney. Some of this stuff involves his area."

"We'll be in your office in thirty minutes."

"Good. You want me to send a helicopter—?"

"Not necessary, Mr. President. We'll use one of ours."

"I'll alert security you're coming."

Quinn hung up the phone and looked across at Race. "That's you and me, bud. In the Oval office. Pronto. You ready to go?"

"Any clue what this is about—?"

"He sounded testy. Not a good sign."

\* \* \*

Sam Baldwin walked across the Oval office to greet Quinn and Race, hand outstretched. Baldwin was short, balding, and overweight. He hadn't been elected because he looked like a politician but he was a scrapper for what he believed in and as honest in his beliefs and actions as a politician can ever be. He was a people's man. People liked the earthiness and lack of polish displayed by this former senator from Wyoming. He shook hands first with Quinn, giving him one of those penetrating stares the President was famous for. Baldwin seemed to have an uncanny ability to peer through a person's eyeballs and read what was going on in the mind behind.

"I don't blame you," Baldwin said.

Quinn looked surprised. "Sir—?"

"Being ticked off at Akker and Dean. They should have picked up on the assassination attempt and stopped it before it happened."

Quinn shook his head in amazement. "You continually amaze me, Mr. President."

"Any fool can see you're angry. There's no reason to be mad at me so I'm assuming you're ticked at Akker and Dean. Don't blame you. There's no doubt they weren't on top of things. A brazen assault like that wasn't decided over lunch yesterday. Someone's been planning this for months."

"My thoughts exactly, Mr. President."

The President quickly studied the two men in front of him.

Quinn Adams was in his late thirties, a little taller than average, with a lot of sandy hair that Baldwin envied. Adams looked tanned and fit, with an athletic build and virtually no body fat. His features were rugged and craggy but somehow gave an impression of refinement.

Adams looked like one of those all-around nice guys, but the president knew this man was skilled in killing. He knew Adams played a vital role in holding the government together during the crisis seven years ago when two presidents died in three days. Baldwin had no idea what that role was, but no one else did either. All he really knew about Quinn Adams was he ran one of the finest, most tightly organized intelligence gathering agencies he'd ever come across, and the man was completely loyal to the United States of America.

Race Courtney was about the same age as Quinn, Baldwin guessed, but somehow kept more of the boyish, All-American college look, which was deceptive. Baldwin had gone over what little information about Courtney was available outside the sealed files of NECCO, and knew this man too was a deadly killer when occasion demanded. It was his natural ability for covert operations that pushed Courtney to the post of director of NECCO intelligence. Courtney was respected by all his co-workers, and even Akker and Dean voiced admiration for his talents.

Baldwin turned to Courtney now, shaking his outstretched hand. "Dean raised the question maybe you should have known about this attack on Quinn—"

Race flushed in embarrassment.

"I accept that criticism, Mr. President. We should have picked up on it."

Baldwin gave him a friendly pat on the shoulder.

"No one's blaming you, Courtney. I can't really blame Dean, either. Who would have thought some crazies would launch an air attack like that."

The President returned behind his desk and sat in his leather chair. He motioned for the other men to sit in the easy chairs in front of him.

"What's bothering me, is why would they want Quinn out of the way? We have to assume this has something to do with NECCO—or have you been humping some Latin diplomat's wife?" he grinned at Quinn.

"Not even a daughter, sir," Quinn replied, a flicker of a smile crossing his face. "I'm puzzled too. I don't understand why I suddenly need taking out. Nothing unusual is happening at NECCO. Everything's at full readiness, so there's not much activity going on that would catch anyone's interest. It doesn't make sense."

Baldwin frowned at Race, "I want you to come up with some answers, Courtney. You have my permission to make Dean look like an incompetent jerk, and Akker too, if it reaches overseas like it probably does."

"You understand, sir," Race cautioned, "that we'll be stepping pretty hard on FBI and CIA toes."

"I don't care," Baldwin grunted. "Something's going on and I want to know what it is."

The President turned his attention back to Quinn Adams.

"Quinn, my desk is piled with a bunch of reports I can't put together."

"Like what, sir?" Quinn asked.

"Well, you know the entire world is crawling with intelligence agents—spiders, I call them, because they're all spinning some kind of web. Trouble is, no one knows who's spinning what, or why. We can't ignore all that activity, however."

"Any specific concerns, Mr. President?"

"Plenty. Got a call late yesterday from London. The Prime Minister is concerned about rumors going around in the EC that something is going on in Russia. Nobody knows what exactly, but there's talk about dissident generals and missing arms supplies. The PM wanted to know if we'd heard anything. The CIA hadn't, of course—I think Akker needs a hearing aid."

Quinn was surprised. "Military action in Russia—?"

"To be specific, Russia, Ukraine, and Belarus."

"Those three have something in common—"

"Nuclear arsenals," Baldwin nodded, "and control of virtually all the military forces left adrift after the Soviet breakup. That includes some very significant naval fleets in the Baltic and the Black Sea."

"What do the Europeans think is happening?"

"They have no idea. That's not all. Akker tells me strange reports are coming out of South America—"

Race Courtney straightened in the chair. "We can vouch for that, Mr. President. We've been keeping pretty close tabs on the Latins." He glanced uneasily over at Quinn. "Which makes me all the more tender about the attack this morning."

"What's happening down there—?" Baldwin asked.

"A lot of contact between top diplomats. Covert meetings. That kind of stuff."

"Military activity—?"

"Not much—nothing to be alarmed about. Just about all governments in Central and South America seem to be involved."

The President frowned. "It's not happening officially. This country hasn't been invited to any meetings like that. You say your people are on top of this—?"

"Some of our best, sir."

"Keep me posted on anything that surfaces. You don't mind if I pass this along to Akker, do you?"

"We're all working for you, sir."

"Some a whole lot more efficiently than others." Baldwin cast a curious glance at Quinn. "You don't seem too surprised by any of this—"

Quinn shrugged. "Our responsibility at NECCO is clearly defined, sir—be ready to respond to any major disaster or threat to the United States. We've been interpreting that pretty loosely of late, sir. These last few months, in view of all the activity in other intelligence communities, NECCO—particularly Race's intelligence unit—is on global status. Stu Akker might interpret that as intruding into the CIA's arena, but I don't really care, not when the security of this country is at risk."

"That's what I want to hear, Quinn," Baldwin said quickly. "I'm not interested in territorial squabbles. Do anything you have to do, and don't worry about not consulting with Akker or Dean—which you obviously don't," he added. "Anything else your people picked up?"

"I may have something in a few days, sir. The Mossad called this morning to warn me about the attack. One of their units picked up on it and passed an alert on to Tel Aviv. I talked to Tel Aviv about an hour ago. They said they have important information they're willing to share. I have to go there, however. Just me, face-to-face, no electronics."

"You go back a long way with the Mossad, as I recall—"

"Yes, sir. I've shared quite a few parties with them over the years. They feel they can trust me."

"Then get over there."

"This is Wednesday. I should be back by Friday, maybe Saturday."

"Keep me posted. Maybe the Israelis can help sort out this mess."

"That's what I'm hoping, sir."

Once again the President fastened him with one of those penetrating stares.

"Bottom line, Quinn—take off the gloves. You say NECCO is at full readiness. Keep it there—we might need it. More than anything else, though, I need to know what's going on. Too many spiders—agents, spooks, whatever you want to call them—spinning too many nasty little webs. I want to know why." He hunkered down in his chair. "I hate spiders."

# 6

## SPIDERS IN RIO

Spiders began converging on Rio de Janeiro on Wednesday morning. The first to arrive were Otto Konsdorff, a German businessman, and his striking young wife. Birgit Konsdorff, who appeared to be ten to fifteen years younger than her husband, was a natural blonde in her late twenties who could have posed for a poster of the perfect Aryan beauty. They arrived after a long and tiring flight begun three days earlier in Hong Kong. They flew United Airlines non-stop to Los Angeles, stayed overnight at a hotel adjacent to the bustling LAX airport, then boarded a flight to Brazil early the next afternoon. For some reason, the stopover in Miami was longer than scheduled and the plane did not leave until after midnight. As a result, the flight arrived at Rio's international Galeao airport thirty minutes late, shortly after 9:30 a.m. Wednesday.

The couple carried German passports and papers that identified Otto Konsdorff as an import-export dealer in heavy machinery for a company in Stuttgart. Needless to say, Konsdorff did not bother customs with the detail that he and his wife were agents of the BND, the German Federal Intelligence Service, nor that Birgit was once an agent for Stasi, the infamous East German Secret Police.

Birgit specialized in getting information out of a parade of visiting politicians and high-ranking military officers invited to her bed. Otto arrested her shortly after the Berlin Wall came down. After three days of alternating interrogation and passionate intercourse, Otto offered to destroy her file if she would become Mrs. Konsdorff.

Shortly after their marriage, Konsdorff introduced her to his superiors. Unaware of her former connection to Stasi, they eagerly recruited Birgit into the BND. Otto knew he faced dismissal and possibly imprisonment for concealing Birgit's past but every night he spent with her made the risk worthwhile. He had long ago shut out of his mind why his beautiful young wife was so skilled in the art of making love.

Another spider who slipped almost unnoticed into Rio that same Wednesday was Hamdi al Hadi Moussak. He carried credentials identifying him as a second secretary in the Egyptian foreign service, en route to a meeting in Brazilia.

Hamdi boarded a British Airways flight in Athens, bound for London. Anyone watching Hamdi carefully would have noticed the short, perspiring, over-weight Egyptian seldom took his eyes off another passenger on the plane, an Oriental who connected with the Athens to London flight after a circuitous route eastward from Hong Kong through Bombay.

Again, if someone was watching carefully, they would have noticed Hamdi and the Oriental from Hong Kong, a quiet, unassuming man in a black business suit who wore thick spectacles and did not speak to any of his fellow passengers, were once again on the same BA flight scheduled from London to Lisbon and Rio de Janeiro.

Hamdi al Hadi Moussak, of course, was not just a low- level attache in the Egyptian foreign service. He was an agent for Mukhabarat, the Egyptian intelligence service. In fact, Hamdi also served the foreign branch of Israeli intelligence, the Mossad, as a double agent.

On this assignment, however, Hamdi did not have an opportunity to serve either one of his masters. Upon entering the terminal at Galeao, Hamdi headed for the nearest telephone. He was observed making the call, which was short and apparently upsetting, but when authorities tried to trace it later, the call was lost forever in the maze of the Brazilian telephone system.

Fifteen minutes after placing the call, Hamdi al Hadi Moussak was found sitting on a toilet in one of the airport restrooms. He was stabbed in the heart, his throat was slit, and his tongue cut out of his mouth.

Hamdi, in those last seconds, undoubtedly knew if his double existence became fatally flawed on one side or the other, or if death was the price for making a mistake somewhere between Athens and Rio. No one else knew, or cared. The police listed his death as the result of a robbery. When found, Hamdi was still wearing a diamond ring, an expensive watch, and his wallet was bulging with money. None of these items were listed on the police report and none went back to Egypt with Hamdi's body.

By Thursday noon, Wallace Harrington, owner of the Superior Pan-American Travel Agency, with offices in Sao Paulo, Rio de Janeiro and Brazilia, identified six arriving agents from five intelligence services. Three of them he knew well.

Sir Geoffrey Helms-Waterford, the distinguished-looking owner of a security systems company in London who actually worked as a South American specialist for Britain's MI6.

Wilfreid Blokstadt, a Belgian executive in the maritime insurance business who really was not a Belgian but an Israeli operative of the Mossad.

And an attractive young woman from San Francisco, Joyce Williams.

Joyce worked for the real owners of Superior Pan-American Travel—the Central Intelligence Agency, headquartered in Langley, Virginia. Anyone checking on Joyce would find she was an associate law professor at Berkeley enjoying a three-week vacation in South America. It would not be true, but that's what they would find.

The other intelligence operatives Harrington knew were in Rio were the Konsdorfs, from Germany's BND, and an Egyptian agent of the Mukhabarat. He heard of Hamdi al Hadi Moussak's arrival and departure at the same time.

Harrington, a lean, tanned man with sharp blue eyes and a clean-shaven, intelligent face, served as CIA station head in Rio for the past five years. In that time, he proved himself capable at his job and a dismal failure as a husband. His wife hated Brazil, and Rio in particular. After two years, she divorced him and returned to Portland, Oregon, with their two young children. Harrington consoled himself with the realization the divorce was inevitable. His wife simply didn't like living in a world of shadows and lies.

The CIA station head found the beautiful, restless city of Rio fascinating. Teeming with intrigue and violence, it was a favorite rendezvous for people with secret deals and larcenous schemes. Planners and plotters could relax in Rio, reasonably isolated from the busy European centers of prying eyes and ears.

For the most part, Rio was warm and friendly to its visitors, except those who strayed into the dark and lawless favelas, the shanty towns sprawled behind the glitter. The miles of beaches stretching along the densely populated South Zone welcomed an endless parade of tanned, semi-nude young women and young men, allowing for all inclinations. Rio offered its guests a colorful cornucopia of almost every vice and entertainment known to mankind.

Harrington was alert to the fact that this sudden influx of shadowy spiders undoubtedly meant trouble was descending on his part of the world. He didn't know what form the trouble would take, and unfortunately, didn't foresee how many spiders would suffer violent death in the next few hours.

The Rio offices of Superior Pan-American were located on the mezzanine floor of one of the older, but still resplendent hotels overlooking the beaches at Copacabana. This district in the South Zone was where those who could afford the good life came to live, in the splendid residential communities of Botafogo, Copacabana, Ipanema, or Leblon. All clung to the beaches or Lagoa Rodrigo de Freitas, the most prestigious of Rio's lagoons.

For the visitors and the tourists, there were the endless miles of towering luxury hotels. For the special customers of Superior Pan-American, there was an inner, sound-proofed, electronically swept suite of offices behind the reception area of the travel agency.

Joyce Williams was admitted to these inner offices shortly after noon Thursday by the beautiful, vivacious woman who greeted her at the reception desk. The Latin woman introduced herself as Lolita. If ever a woman deserved such a glamorous name, Joyce decided, this one did.

Following behind her down a short hallway toward the rear offices, she couldn't help but notice the sensuality rippling with every step, catch the expensive fragrance of imported French perfume. Lolita was wearing a brightly colored, off-the-shoulder silk blouse that did an excellent job of showing off full breasts, and a tight, very short, black skirt that more than adequately displayed her long, shapely legs.

Joyce was glad when the door at the end of the hall opened and she saw Wally Harrington coming around his desk to greet her. Walking very far behind Lolita could destroy a woman's self-image, Joyce decided ruefully.

"Not bad, Wally," she murmured, after the door to the office closed, leaving only Lolita's scent. "Do you ever get any work done?"

Harrington grinned as he shook Joyce's hand warmly.

"She has an effect, doesn't she. She's a good employee, believe it or not."

"She looks like she'd be good," Joyce said dryly.

Harrington motioned for Joyce to sit down in a comfortable chair. He went around and sat in the leather recliner behind his desk, giving the woman across from him a quick scrutiny.

Joyce was about five-seven, in her early thirties. She was not in Lolita's sensual mold but she was reasonably stunning in her own right. The white suit she was wearing looked expensive and did good things for the trim body in it. So did the lavender silk blouse, stylish with a loose cowl neck. It snugged and clung in all the right places. Joyce possessed the outdoor beauty that went with a California image; blonde, leggy, a tanned look that spoke of sun and sand, overlaid with a smoky sophistication and worldliness.

Harrington knew by reputation that the woman in front of him could put lights into those brown eyes that made a man throw caution to the winds—and not live long enough to regret it.

"So what brings you to Rio?" Harrington asked. "What's bringing the whole world to Rio, for that matter? I've never seen so many agents in one place, at the same time, in my entire life."

"Everybody wants out of the cold, Wally," Joyce smiled, "and into a warm Lolita."

"I've received no briefing," Harrington pressed, "but something is sure going on. Can you tell me anything about all this activity?"

Joyce Williams sat back and crossed her legs. Harrington couldn't help but let his eyes drop and Joyce shook her head gently.

"Lolita wouldn't like what you're thinking, Wally."

"You've got great legs," Harrington shrugged. "It's sort of expected down here to appreciate things like that. So what's the word from Langley? They're ignoring my cables."

Joyce shook her head, a little frown gathering the corners of her mouth. "It's a puzzlement, Wally, even to the thinkers. You're not being ignored—nobody has an explanation to give you. They just know people are on the move and they don't like it."

"I take it the policy is everybody follows somebody because they must be following someone else—"

"Pretty close. That's why they sent me here. They know you're short-handed at the moment with people on vacations and they don't want to strip the station."

"They already have," Harrington complained. "Cut four from my staff here in Rio. I'm down to two people in Sao Paulo and three in Brazilia. I keep telling Langley I can't cover everything that's going on down here. They tell me to call the White House. One of these days I'm going to get drunk enough to do it." He looked questioningly at the California operative. "Who are you following—?"

"No one, specifically."

"I'm the station chief, Joyce—"

Joyce Williams gave a lift of her shoulders. "It's true, Wally. Langley got a report from MI6 that they were sending one of their men to Rio—"

"Helms-Waterford. He got in this morning."

"MI6 was hoping we could tell them something. We couldn't. Their man is supposed to be on the trail of a Chinese banker who left Hong Kong several days ago headed east. He made it to London the hard way, through Bombay and Athens, then disappeared. He surfaced again Wednesday, spotted leaving on a flight to Rio. BA has the man listed as Wu Zhenkang. The British think he's a high-level official in Chinese military intelligence, stationed in Beijing. Both companies want to know what the Chinese military is doing in Rio."

"Apparently so do a lot of other people," Harrington muttered. "Six agents in town in the last twenty-four hours that I know about, representing five different companies. One of them was murdered yesterday at the airport."

Joyce looked up in surprise. "Who was it?"

"An Egyptian named Mouzak, or something like that. Somebody slit his throat while he was on the throne." Harrington's forehead suddenly pulled into creases. "Come to think of it, he must have come in on the same flight as your man from Beijing."

"Can you put me in touch with the agent from MI6—what was it you called him—Helms-Waterford? Sounds terribly British."

"No problem," Harrington said quickly. "Sir Geoffrey always stays at the same hotel, just down the road in Impanema. We usually have lunch or a drink whenever he's in town."

"Sir Geoffrey. That's what I call a high class cover. I'm impressed. Are you friends with all the competition?"

"I communicate with some of them and sometimes we help each other, when it's mutually beneficial. There are no friends on the other side of the fence—any fence. You know that, Joyce. Friendly acquaintances. That's as far as it goes in this business. So your target is this Wu Zhenkang—"

Joyce shrugged. "Until someone more interesting shows up. If I stay with Zhenkang, I'm to find him, follow him, and if necessary, kill him."

"Watch yourself in the bathroom," Harrington muttered. "The back of my neck tells me there's a connection between Zhenkang and the Egyptian."

"You watch yourself in the bedroom. A woman like Lolita can cause a man your age to dangerously overheat."

Harrington grinned. "I know how to handle Lollie. She's been my mistress for almost four years."

"Let's see," Joyce mused, "that would be almost a year before your wife left you, wouldn't it—?"

"Right out of the field operator's manual," Harrington tossed back. "Piece together all the little scraps and come up with the wrong picture. Lollie became my mistress after my wife decided to move into her own bedroom."

"Wally, I'm only kidding. You look like a happy man and there aren't many of those in our business. How do I meet your friend from MI6?"

Harrington reached for the phone. "Let's do lunch—that is, unless I'm not invited."

Joyce smiled at him. "You're the station chief, Wally. Of course you're invited."

Harrington dialed the number of the hotel. The telephone operator confirmed that a Sir Geoffrey Helms-Waterford had checked in but as she started to tell Harrington she was putting him through, she suddenly stopped in mid-sentence. There was a silence, some clicking, then a man's voice came on the line.

"Yes, sir. This is the assistant manager. May I help you—?"

"I'm trying to call Sir Geoffrey Helms-Waterford. He arrived this morning and I understand he's already registered. Is there a problem?"

"Are you a relative of Sir Geoffrey?"

"No, I'm not a relative. This is Wallace Harrington. I'm a friend and business associate. Has something happened?"

"I'm afraid it has, Mr. Harrington. Sir Geoffrey just passed away."

Harrington looked across the desk at Joyce Williams, his face telling her something was very wrong. "What happened?" he asked the man on the phone.

"Sir Geoffrey was having a drink at the bar, sir. He was alone. He suddenly just collapsed. We believe it must have been a heart attack—a doctor is examining the body now. Such a terrible thing to happen. Sir Geoffrey was a regular, as you probably know."

"There's no doubt he's dead—?"

"None whatsoever. It all happened in a matter of seconds, according to the bartender."

"I'd like to speak to that bartender."

"That's not possible at the moment, I'm afraid. He was very upset and asked to be relieved."

"He's gone—?"

"He's still somewhere in the hotel, I'm sure. The police want to talk to him, too. Do you know how to get in touch with Sir Geoffrey's family, Mr. Harrington?"

"Yes. At least, I know people in his company. Would you like me to contact them?"

"That would be very nice of you. This is such a terrible thing—"

"I'll get in touch with them right away."

Harrington hung up the phone. "Damn it. Sir Geoffrey was a good man."

"How did he die?"

"Supposedly a heart attack. I'm not ready to buy that. MI6 doesn't send out field operatives with bad hearts."

The telephone rang. It was a red phone on a credenza behind Harrington's desk. He looked at it, then glanced at Joyce.

"That's the Langley phone." He picked up the receiver. "Superior Pan-American Travel. This is Harrington. How may I help you?"

"There's a young lady arriving from San Francisco who might need help with travel arrangements—"

"Yes. She's already contacted us. I'm sure we can give her any assistance she may require."

"Good. There's another friend traveling in your area who might need some help—"

"Could you be referring to Sir Geoffrey Helms-Waterford, the businessman from London?"

There was a momentary silence. "As a matter of fact, that was the friend we had in mind."

"I'm afraid I have bad news. Sir Geoffrey just passed away—sudden heart attack, I understand."

There was a longer silence this time. "That's very sad," the voice said finally. "Heart attack, you say—?"

"So I heard. Sir Geoffrey was so healthy though, wasn't he."

"Yes. Has his family been notified?"

"I wonder if you might do that. It just happened a few minutes ago. Miss Williams and I were going to have lunch with Sir Geoffrey. We'll stay here until we find out if there's anything his family would like us to do."

"We'll get right back to you."

It was less than fifteen minutes later when the red telephone rang again. Harrington answered it.

"Superior Pan-American Travel. Harrington here—"

"Mr. Harrington, we've contacted the family of Sir Geoffrey. They were surprised, of course, and upset. They wondered if you would do a favor for them. They would like a doctor that you recommend to examine Sir Geoffrey—just to be completely sure of the cause of death."

"I'll take care of it immediately."

"We do hope this will not affect any plans Miss Williams may have—"

"I'm sure it won't. We'll give her as much help as we can in taking in all the sights."

"Good. Get back to us with the results of the autopsy, won't you."

"Without delay."

"Thank you, Mr. Harrington. Hope you have no more unpleasantness."

"I wouldn't bet on it."

Harrington hung up the phone again and swiveled his chair back toward Joyce. "MI6 wants an autopsy. And our employers want you to stay on the job."

"There can't be more than one Wu Zhenkang who arrived yesterday from London."

"I'll get Frank Kopeinig on it. Frank's not only good—he's the only one left who isn't on vacation. Passport registrations should point a finger in the right direction."

Joyce stood up. "I'm going to nose around on my own. I'm staying at this hotel, of course. Let me know if your man pinpoints Zhenkang. I'm a tourist—what should I see?"

"The Statua do Cristo-Redentor. It's close and you may never get a better chance to see it. It's also a good place to orient yourself to Rio. Take a taxi to Morro do Corcovado—Mount Corcovado. Look up outside the hotel and you can't miss it."

"Always wanted to see that. Anything else—"

"Probably won't be time. You could take the railway up Sugar Loaf, but you won't see anything you don't see from Corcovado. If you have to kill time, go to the Jardim Botanico. It's close and it has a lot of interesting stuff."

"I take it you're not particularly thrilled by botanical gardens."

"See one, see 'em all," Harrington grunted. "Keep checking in with me. And take one of those guarda-chuvas by the door. Don't be fooled by the sun—it always rains in Rio."

"Find Zhenkang," Joyce said, going to the umbrella stand. "He's beginning to sound like a bad dude."

"Maybe he's just an innocent Chinese businessman starting up a new chain of laundries."

"And maybe Lollie will join a convent."

# 7

## DEAD SPIDERS

Otto and Birgit Konsdorff checked into a second-class hotel in the central district of Rio. Birgit hated the shabbiness, especially since she could look out of the window and see the tops of the luxury hotels marking the beaches in the South Zone. She knew however that her husband was doing the best he could with what the BND allowed, and still provide her with little luxuries that could be hidden in the expense account.

Otto came out of the bathroom in his underwear, a grin on his face. Birgit sighed inwardly. Men were such animals, always with one thing on their mind. If they only knew how easy it was to read them, to manipulate them.

She already knew the bed was going to be hard and the springs would squeak very noisily. Ten minutes later, Birgit got up and went into the bathroom. The tub was permanently grimed, the water was barely warm, and the shower curtain, if it could be called that, was stiff with scum and slime. Well, since being with Otto, she'd seen places a lot worse. However, she never lost sight of the reality that all of them were better than a prison cell.

It was now late Thursday afternoon and so far they had done nothing about their assignment. Otto was still lying on the bed.

"I'm surprised there were no messages again today," Otto yawned. "I'm still not sure what they want us to do."

"We should have followed Zhenkang."

"How could we do it—? He got in a car and was gone. I told them in Berlin we would need a car waiting for us. Get one when you get there, they said. Now we've lost him. Do you have any idea how many millions of people there are in Rio?"

"Why are we following this man, anyway? What do we expect to learn?"

"I have no idea. Neither does anyone in Berlin. They think some Russian generals may be involved in some kind of a plot. They think some former East Germans officials may also be involved. Only they don't know what kind of a plot or how these people may be involved. The whole thing is stupid. The only reason they could give me for following this Zhenkang is that his name showed up in a report that may or may not be linked to whatever may or may not be happening. And it may or may not be happening in Rio. They've all panicked. I've seen it before. Do anything so you can't be accused of doing nothing. So, we go through the motions of finding Zhenkang and enjoy this little holiday. I suspect they will recall us soon enough."

Birgit finished brushing her hair and turned to her husband. "Get up, Otto. I'm starving."

Otto grinned at her. "I was thinking perhaps we might have another helping of dessert before dinner—"

Birgit shook her head firmly. "Not until after we eat. I want to see more of Rio than the ceiling of this grubby little room. Get dressed. I'll check on the car."

"Call the concierge," Otto said, disappointment clearly in his voice. "It should be here by now."

The concierge wasn't there, but someone at the reception desk answered after a dozen rings. The man's voice sounded tired.

"Please—?"

"This is Birgit Konsdorff. My husband and I ordered a rental car. It was to be delivered by noon—"

"It's here," the tired voice interrupted. "Green Volkswagon. Parked out in front. Keys are in it."

"Thank you." She turned excitedly to Otto as he came out of the bathroom, this time dressed. "It's downstairs. Let's see Rio then have a magnificent dinner overlooking the ocean."

Otto kissed her. He loved it when she was excited over anything. "A good dinner," he promised, " even if it costs three days allowance. A drive along the beaches, maybe even a ride up Sugar Loaf. Then we come back for dessert, right?"

She smiled and kissed him. "Lots of dessert, Otto. I promise you. You are right—we should pretend we are on holiday."

They held each other tightly as they rode down in the jerky little elevator. They hurried arm in arm across the lobby and went outside. The green Volkswagon was one of the old Beetles and the paint was faded and daubed with primer in places but the rental price was more than reasonable and would allow them to squeeze more important luxuries into the expense account.

Birgit smiled happily as she climbed in. She was still smiling as Otto got in on the driver side, slammed the door shut, and turned on the ignition.

The explosion blew Otto and Birgit into a thousand pieces.

\* \* \*

Wilfreid Blokstadt was short, with a thick-set build that gave the impression of being overweight. This was not true, for Blokstadt kept in excellent physical condition and most of his bulk was pure muscular power. He had black, close-cropped hair, making his face appear sallow in contrast, emphasized by the fact that Blokstadt preferred shadows over sunlight.

He was scowling angrily now as he stopped the rented Mercedes in front of a small synagogue in a poor neighborhood far out in the North Zone of Rio. The synagogue looked as poorly kept as the dilapidated clusters of high-rise apartments surrounding it.

That wasn't what was bothering Blokstadt, however. It was the fact he was summoned to a building that would directly link him to a Jewish background. For some people, those with trained, intelligent minds, it would need only a small step beyond that to link him to the Mossad.

On top of that, the location was frustratingly hard to find. Several times Blokstadt had found himself lost in sections that made even him nervous.

Closing the front door of the synagogue behind him, Blokstadt stood unmoving for a few moments, adjusting his eyes to the deeper gloom of the interior. He saw a figure approaching and his grip tightened about the pistol concealed in the pocket of his jacket. As the man neared, Blockstadt saw he was dressed in the dark attire of a rabbi. More importantly, he recognized the face. His finger eased from the trigger.

"You got even shorter, goat turd," the approaching man grunted. "Uglier, too—although I didn't think that was possible."

"You tempt the vengeance of God, Menachem," Blokstadt growled, "putting on those clothes."

Menachem Rotan gave a flicker of a smile. These two went back a long ways, working together in dark schemes spawned in the bowels of Aman. In those days, the military arm of Jewish intelligence was all powerful, the newly born Mossad struggling for purpose and identity. Over the years, bitter power struggles resulted in Aman reluctantly relinquishing most of its overseas intelligence work to the Mossad, where it properly belonged.

Wilfreid transferred to Mossad operations; Menachem remained with

Aman. Blockstadt felt himself getting angry again; old friend or not, Menachem was not part of this assignment.

"What are you doing in Rio?" Blokstadt asked gruffly. "If I'd known it was you who sent the message, I never would have come. You shouldn't be using Mossad codes. What do you want? Why are sticking your nose into Mossad business?"

"Were you followed?" Menachem asked, paying no attention to the questions.

"I'm not a fool," Wilfreid hissed.

"Then why leave real intelligence work to go play with the children in Mossad."

"There are more than Arabs in this world," Wilfreid retorted, "who would destroy our country. You people in Aman never could see beyond the desert."

"It is Arabs who bring me to Rio," his friend said, his voice low and serious. "What do you know about this man from Chinese military intelligence—Wu Zhenkang?"

"Our station has him under constant surveillance. I know where he is staying. I know who has visited him since he arrived yesterday. This morning I learned he is here to attend a meeting with high government officials from several Latin countries. I know he does not leave the apartment, so when he does, it probably will be to attend that meeting. Then I will know more."

"I am impressed," Menachem murmured. "Mossad apparently has not completely dulled your wits. But then, your Rio station is quite heavily staffed, isn't it."

"Enough to handle this without any help from the military. What is Aman's interest in Zhenkang?"

"We believe he has come to meet with Arab envoys—not Latins. It has something to do with pulling all of the Arabs into a single alliance against Israel."

"The Arabs have tried to do that for years," Wilfreid shrugged. "They don't trust each other enough to crowd into the same tent."

"Our people are picking up very disturbing rumors. Something is happening. A lot is going on beneath the surface, especially in Iran—"

"Nothing is ever out in the open with the Arabs, Menachem. Everything is hidden, everything is a plot. It is their way."

"This is different," Menachem insisted. "I would like to join you in the surveillance of Zhenkang—together, like in old times."

"These are not old times," Wilfreid replied, giving a quick shake of his head. "He has made no contact with Arabs. No Arabs have arrived in the last forty-eight hours at either the international or the domestic airports. My people would know. I have not seen an Arab since I arrived in Rio. I don't know what is going on, my friend, but I'm sure it has nothing to do with our enemies in the desert."

"An alliance is being put together, Wilfreid. It is the only conclusion that can be made. We in Aman are sure of it."

"You are afraid of making another Omission," Wilfreid snorted. "You see war under every rumor."

Blokstadt referred to a painful lapse in Aman intelligence two decades earlier when it failed to detect the Yom Kippur attack on Israel by Arab foes. No one in Aman ever forgot October of 1973, not even the newcomers. Certainly not Menachem Rotan, who felt an unreasoning flush of guilt and anger toward his former associate.

"You were a part of that, Wilfreid. It pains me that you bring back such a memory—"

"Not a memory, Menachem—it has become the mote in Aman's eyes. We must see clearly today, watch everyone, suspect everyone, trust no one—not even our friends. We have more than Arabs to fear in this new world, Menachem."

The two men were so intent on memories and the differences in their beliefs that neither heard the van pull up across the road from the synagogue. They were unaware of the rear doors opening silently, the four hooded men clambering out, each lifting a Stinger missile to their shoulder.

Both Israelis were trained enough in the arts of war, however, to look up at the first instant of firing, recognizing the swoosh of sound for what it was. It was too late. The small wooden building disintegrated in a quick series of explosions. There was not enough left of the two Israeli intelligence operatives to let mystified investigators know anyone was in the building when it was destroyed.

\* \* \*

Standing at the foot of the towering statue of Christ the Redeemer atop Mount Corcovado was as emotionally stirring for Joyce Williams as she had imagined it would be. An experience of a lifetime. It brought tears and a sense of relief that she could still feel a spirit of good in a world so filled with evil.

The view of the city of Rio spread below Corcovado was almost as breath-taking as the statue. She studied the landmarks carefully, making mental notes of their relationship to each other. Sometimes it helped to at least know if you were headed in the right direction.

The visit to Mount Corcovado had taken longer than expected so Joyce decided to return to the hotel and check with Harrington. She was anxious to see if Frank Kopeinig had been able to ferret out Zhenkang.

As she got out of the taxi in front of the hotel, she was approached by a young man dressed in clean white cotton pants and a colorful, neatly pressed shirt. He was obviously Latin, well mannered. He nodded his head politely.

"Senorita Williams, is it not?"

The young man's voice was soft, respectful, the words spoken in English with only a trace of accent.

"Strangers who know my name make me very nervous," Joyce replied coldly.

She studied him carefully, looking for any sign that would give a warning. The pistol in her purse could be reached and fired with deadly accuracy in under three seconds. She could feel the adrenaline already starting to pump. He merely smiled and offered her a piece of folded paper.

"I know you only from your picture, Senorita. If you would read the message on the paper, please."

Joyce unfolded it, glanced down. It was a computer print-out on what appeared to be an ordinary sheet of bond paper. The message was printed in capitals:

IF YOU WOULD LIKE TO SPEAK TO WU ZHENKANG,PLEASE ACCOMPANY THE BEARER OF THIS MESSAGE.

There was no signature.

Joyce looked up at the man, eyes narrowing. "Accompany you where?"

"There is a car waiting a short distance from here. I am to take you to the car and then I leave. That is all I know, Senorita. I was told it must be your choice, to go or not."

Joyce looked up at the hotel entrance. The young man spoke up quickly. "You must go alone. You must go now. If that is not agreeable, I will leave."

She was torn. Every instinct told her this was the wrong thing to do. Her training and her experience were sounding loud warning bells in her head. On the other hand, this could put her into direct contact with the man who had drawn the attention of practically every intelligence agency in the western world.

She felt the weight of the weapon in her purse, and the fire of the adrenaline. She had handled tighter situations than this, she reminded herself. The decision was made. Sometimes the reward was worth the risk.

She folded the piece of paper and slipped it into her purse. If nothing else came of this, perhaps there would be fingerprints or other information to be gleaned from the message itself.

"Which way—?" she asked.

The young man smiled and started walking south down the sidewalk a few steps ahead of her.

About a hundred yards down the street, the rear door of a waiting black Mercedes limousine opened. She hesitated for a brief moment, then got in. The door closed and the car pulled away.

The young man kept walking. So many beautiful women in Rio, he thought. He had a feeling there would soon be one less. Darting across the wide, busy boulevard, he continued walking along the beachside. It offered a better view.

\* \* \*

Dr. Raoul Ramirez looked uncomfortable as he sat across the desk from Wally Harrington. There was no reason for it; he had done enough favors for this man in the past few years to know Harrington trusted him. Still, it was always a little unnerving to sit in an office with a view of the dark side of the world.

He never asked about the assignments he received from Harrington. He accepted the travel agent's advice that the less he knew, the better. He would not even admit consciously that he knew what Harrington really did for a living. Travel agent was just fine.

Harrington saw Ramirez was uncomfortable and smiled reassuringly at him. "You're certain it was poison—?"

Ramirez nodded emphatically. "Don't know exactly which one. I need to run more tests."

"And you're sure it was in the drink—?"

"Had to be. Whatever it was, it shut his heart down almost instantly."

Harrington frowned. "Wish that bartender hadn't got away."

"The police still have not found him?"

"He's probably in Paraguay by now," Harrington muttered. "The regular bartender got sick, or so he says, and this man substituted for him. That was an hour before Helms-Waterford checked in. Obviously, they knew when he was arriving."

"Do you want me to do a complete autopsy?"

Harrington gave a quick shake of his head. "Doesn't seem necessary. Would we learn anything—?"

"Only what he had for breakfast. I have enough blood and tissue samples to complete tests on the poison."

Harrington stood up and shook hands with the doctor. "My thanks again. As usual, this never happened."

"What shall I do with the body?"

"I'm sure his family will want it shipped back to England. I'll confirm arrangements as soon as I hear from them."

A few minutes after the doctor left, Lolita entered the office. She came close and leaned over him. She put both hands on his cheeks and crushed her open mouth against his.

"You working late tonight?" she asked softly.

"Not after that, I'm not."

The telephone rang, the black phone on his desk. He answered it as Lolita sat on his lap.

"Superior Pan-American Travel. Harrington—"

"Mr. Harrington, this is Colonel Jorge Fariocha. I'm with security—"

Harrington sat up, pushing Lolita off his lap. Fariocha was not just with security—a catch-word that encompassed a number of city and state law enforcement agencies that few people questioned. He was head of military intelligence of the First Military District, the most elite regional army unit in all of Brazil. The colonel probably didn't know Harrington knew that, so the station chief kept his voice calm, almost disinterested.

"Yes, Colonel. Is there something I can do for you?"

"I'm not sure, Mr. Harrington. I am at the scene of a rather brutal murder. The only identification we can find on the body is one of your business cards."

Instinctively, Harrington felt a sick churning in his stomach. However, he avoided asking any question that might lead Fariocha to suspect he knew something about the murder or the victim. With this man, it was better to wait until facts were offered.

"That's strange. I do hope it isn't one of the clients of Pan-American. Where was the body found?"

"The Parque Julio Furtado."

"That's the park close to the war ministry building, isn't it?"

The colonel brushed aside the question. "I wonder if you would oblige us by seeing if you can identify the body, Mr. Harrington."

The colonel was playing it close, offering no help. Harrington felt a little uneasy about that.

"Of course, Colonel."

"I've taken the liberty of sending a car. It should arrive at your establishment any minute now. I knew you would be anxious to see if the victim was someone doing business with you."

"I'll be waiting."

Harrington hung up the phone and gave Lolita a troubled look. "They found a body in the park. I have a bad feeling it might be Joyce Williams. That was Fariocha—from military intelligence. He's already sent a car for me."

"Did he say it was Joyce?" Lolita asked.

Harrington shook his head. "He didn't even say it was a woman. He was playing me, seeing how I'd react. I wonder if he knows as much about me as I know about him—?"

Fifteen minutes later, Harrington climbed out of the unmarked police car that sped with sirens wailing to the group of uniformed men and flashing emergency lights clustered near the center of Furtado Park. He recognized Colonel Fariocha as he approached. Fariocha was thin, tall for a Latin, although considerably shorter than Harrington. He had a pencil-line moustache that served to accent a downward curve at the corners of his mouth. Fariocha tried to look friendly as he approached Harrington but could not hide the coldness in his eyes. He made no offer to shake hands, merely pointed toward a nearby clump of trees.

"I hope you are not a squeamish man, Mr. Harrington. The body is over here."

Joyce Williams was propped in a sitting position against the trunk of a tree. She wore only the coat of her white suit and it was soaked in the reddish brown of blood from the long gash across her throat, difficult to see because of the four-foot snake coiled about her neck. The snake was not moving and apparently it too was dead. Joyce's blouse was missing, as was the skirt and all underwear. Her legs were spread out to keep her balanced in the sitting position.

Harrington was sickened by the sight. Judging from the amount of blood, someone had tortured Joyce with savage ferocity. Harrington felt hot anger surge through him. And pain, that any woman could be subjected to such horrible suffering and indignity.

Harrington forced himself to take in the rest of the murder scene. Painted in vivid colors on Joyce William's forehead and stomach were a series of symbols. They had no meaning for the station chief, although there was a vague tugging at his memory. Joyce's body was encircled by a scattering of aromatic leaves, evidently some type of pungent herb

Harrington did not recognize.

Fariocha saw Harrington's anger, saw the man's fists clench, the eyes narrow. There was no doubt Harrington was shocked and horrified by what he saw. The security chief expected such a reaction but he wanted to be sure.

"I warned you it was brutal," Fariocha said. "Do you know this woman, Mr. Harrington?"

Harrington nodded. "Joyce Williams. She arrived this morning from the States. She dropped into our offices about noon, I think it was. Said she was traveling alone, going to be here for two or three weeks. She wanted information on things to see in Rio."

"That would explain your business card in her suitcoat pocket, I suppose." Harrington detected something in the colonel's voice that bordered on disappointment.

Fariocha leaned forward and pulled the coat apart. The symbols on her torso stood out plainly but Harrington's eyes narrowed as he saw more signs of torture.

"Macumba," the colonel grunted. "Your Miss Williams must have strayed into places where tourists are not welcome—if she was a tourist."

"With all due respect, colonel," Harrington said quietly, "what makes you think macumba is involved?"

The military intelligence chief looked at him sharply. "Look again, Mr. Harrington. The painted markings. The dead snake. The circle of herbs around the body. These clearly point to a ceremonial killing."

"This woman has been mutilated. From my limited knowledge of the magic rituals, such things are not part of macumba."

Fariocha was staring at him suspiciously. "If you know so much about our native customs, Mr. Harrington, what do you believe happened here?"

"I'm not a professional in such things, of course," Harrington replied slowly, "but I doubt if this is where she was killed."

"Why do you say that? the colonel asked.

"There is very little blood on the ground—there would be more if she bled to death here. Also, I cannot help but notice the burn marks all over her body—small burns, possibly inflicted by a cigarette or a burning rod. This woman was savagely tortured before she was killed—that is not part of macumba magic. Besides, what was done to her almost certainly would not be done in a public park."

He wanted to add that a building where acts of such cruel torture could and did take place regularly was located just across from the park entrance—the edifice of the war ministry, with its infamous rooms of interrogation and death. However, nothing would be gained by openly antagonizing Fariocha, and it couldn't help Joyce Williams.

"For a non-professional," Fariocha murmured, "you are very observant, Mr. Harrington."

Harrington shrugged. "I spent several years in the military before going into the international travel business. They teach you to notice the unusual. I think some very vicious killers made a poor attempt to make this look like macumba."

"If you are right, we must conclude that Miss Williams was more than an ordinary tourist. Is there anything else you can tell me about this woman, Mr. Harrington?"

Harrington pursed his lips, thought for several moments. "I'm afraid not, colonel. She purchased her ticket through one of our affiliates in the United States. I can check that out, if it will help—"

Colonel Fariocha flashed a frown of annoyance. "We will do our own checking, Mr. Harrington. If you have no more observations," he said, placing a deliberate emphasis on the word, "the car will return you to Cocacabana."

The travel agency offices were closed and locked when Harrington arrived back at the hotel. He glanced at his watch: barely a quarter after eight. Someone usually was in the office at least until nine in the evening. That was dinnertime for most Latins.

He found a note from Lolita on his desk. There was one word:

Hurry!

He would have smiled but the picture of a mutilated Joyce Williams propped against a tree was too fresh in his mind. He checked to see if there were any messages needing attention but there weren't. He locked up again and took the elevator up to the twelfth floor suite he shared with Lollie. Their love nest, she called it. In the budget Langley approved, it was referred to as a safe house.

Harrington turned to close the door after entering the apartment, calling out to Lollie. It was the last sound Wally Harrington uttered. He felt the prick of a needle in his neck but blackness engulfed him before he could turn around.

It would be late the next morning before a maid found Lolita and Wally wrapped in each other's arms, both dead. Wally was holding a small-caliber revolver in his hand. The weapon had put a hole in Lolita's heart, and one in Harrington's head. Police called it a murder-suicide.

There was one other death that afternoon. Frank Kopeinig, the only other agent not on vacation at the Rio station, found what he was looking for in the police records. An address where a Chinese banker by the name of Wu Zhenkang was staying. Unfortunately, as he left the building and headed for his car, he was run down and killed by a hit-and-run driver.

\* \* \*

That same afternoon, Colonel Jorge Fariocha escorted General Wu Zhenkang, political liaison officer, Latin Hemisphere, Central Military Commission, Chinese People's Liberation Army, into a long, luxuriously appointed hall. The hall had no windows but was ablaze with light from a row of ornate chandeliers hanging over a polished conference table. The table ran down the center of the hall for at least fifty feet.

There were only six men seated near one end of the table, three on each side, and all stood up respectfully as Zhenkang entered. A high-backed chair was sitting empty at the head and Fariocha led the Chinese general toward it. Zhenkang sat down and motioned for the others to do the same.

For several moments, Zhenkang looked at the men in the hall, studying each of them. It was impossible to tell what he was thinking. The other men were seasoned enough to say nothing, to wait until the newcomer was ready to break the silence.

Five of these men, Zhenkang knew, represented the executive council of the newly-formed Coalition of Allied States of the Americas—CASA. One house, in all of Central and South America. A difficult task, pulling all those volatile personalities and national policies together. Zhenkang spent five long, frustrating years of secret negotiations and billions of U.S. dollars to bring CASA into existence. Now it was time to move on to the next objective. The sixth man at the table was the general who would have the responsibility of making sure that objective was achieved.

Zhenkang leaned back in the chair, glanced over at Fariocha. The security chief did not join the other men at the table, standing back a respectful distance.

"Colonel Fariocha," Zhenkang said quietly, "I am impressed by your efficiency. Not only are those following me now dead, but their deaths were accomplished in a manner certain to confuse those who sent them. My congratulations, Colonel, and my thanks."

Fariocha gave a quick bow. "It is an honor to be of service to the People's Republic, sir."

"Did you learn anything from the American woman?"

Fariocha shook his head. "She knew nothing of importance."

"Are you certain of that?" Zhenkang pressed. "Did you learn why the CIA sent her to Rio?"

"A report from London—nothing of consequence. Neither the Americans nor the British have any idea why you are here—not even a theory. We used heavy chemicals on the woman to interrogate her. She spoke the truth—she couldn't help it. Actually, the chemicals killed her. The torture and macumba was only to confuse the Americans."

Zhenkang gave the intelligence chief a hard, direct look. "It is essential that utmost secrecy be maintained—"

"I understand," Fariocha murmured. "You may be assured it will be, Colonel."

Zhenkang turned his attention to the six men at the table.

"It is time, gentlemen, to discuss your readiness to launch Operation Scourge—"

# 8

## RED STAR IN YALTA

In a cramped, cluttered office on the third floor of the military headquarters building in St. Petersburg, the important Baltic Sea port of the new Russian Federation, General Viktor Kuchakov stood up and turned to look out of the small window. The panes were grimy from years of unwashed winter soot. There was not much to see anyway.

Drab buildings lined a drab street that led to a small, drab park. Although it was mid-April, spring was slow in coming and the limbs of the few trees he could see from the windows were still winter-gaunt, with no leaves. It was a sign, Kuchakov thought grimly.

Kuchakov was short and heavy-set. His gray, pocked features gathered into an angry frown, thick eyebrows pulling down, dark eyes sunken into deep sockets. A kindly person could perhaps excuse the red blotches staining the general's sallow cheeks as the residue of exposure to more than sixty raw Russian winters, but not the puffiness, nor the watery eyes, nor the jowls that hung flabby and loose. These unquestionably were the legacy of too many years of self-indulgence, too little activity, and far too much vodka.

If things had not changed, Kuchakov told himself bitterly as he stared out of the window, if he were still the commander of Soviet ground forces, the mightiest, proudest military power in the history of the world, those trees would be waving new coats of leaves, the sun would be shining, and all would be well in the Union of Soviet Socialist Republics.

But everything had changed. Nothing was right any more. There was no Soviet Union. No unity in anything. Fifteen squabbling republics, or was it twelve? No one could be sure—alliances and allegiances changed with the weather. Even the proud city of Leningrad was no more, forced to step backward in time to become St. Petersburg once again, to become once again a symbol of all that was decadent and distasteful. Kuchakov felt the anger and the hatred welling up inside him, swelling a purplish color up through his neck.

The proud Soviet military machine was splintered and torn apart, with no central direction, rendered virtually useless. Kuchakov himself was banished from the new inner circle of military power, reduced to a second-line command position of a demoralized, disorganized regional military unit that had no loyalty or purpose. Every morning when he awakened and faced the new reality that there was no limousine waiting to speed him to his richly paneled office in the Kremlin—an office that would make ten of his present quarters—Kuchakov tasted a bitter frustration. There was no way around it; the terrible changes had to be undone. And they would be. Very soon.

Looking down at the leafless trees, Kuchakov was convinced he was doing the right thing. He glanced around the tiny, spartan office—totally unbefitting even the lower station he now held—and took satisfaction in knowing he never would come back to it.

The meeting he planned to attend in a few hours in a secluded dacha in Yalta would almost certainly assure that a new page was turned in history, just as it had decades ago when the great Stalin wined and dined and out-negotiated the pompous Roosevelt and his faithful British bulldog, Churchill. Events would soon roll inexorably toward the beginning of a new era of Soviet power, even greater than before.

He shrugged into his overcoat and buttoned it slowly, allowing himself a quick thought of the palm trees and pebbled beaches of Yalta, on the southern shores of the Crimea. Even if the Black Sea resort did not meet the ridiculous standards of the bourgeois west, it was pleasant enough for a true Russian. He wondered if it was too early for all those topless sunbathers. Regardless, he was sure his host would make suitable arrangements on the agenda for a few hours of pleasurable female companionship.

General Viktor Kuchakov left St. Petersburg aboard a military jet half an hour later. He was now in civilian clothing, a poorly fitting dark blue suit, and was the plane's only passenger. It didn't seem to be an important event but it was duly watched and reported by intelligent eyes, along with the general's flight plan to Minsk, the capital city of the neighboring independent republic of Belarus. It was difficult for Kuchakov to think of Minsk that way. In his mind, it was just part of the Soviet Union.

The plane stopped at the airport in Minsk long enough to pick up a single passenger. General Sergei Yazenko, wearing a brown pinstripe suit that did not fit any better than Kuchakov's, sank down in a seat beside him and moments later the plane was airborne again. The new destination was reported as Odessa, on the Ukranian coast of the Black Sea.

Yazenko appeared to be almost a twin of Kuchakov. The same short, overweight build. Approximately the same age, in their early sixties. The same flabby jowls and unhealthy flush in their cheeks. The same fondness for vodka and women. And both had endured humiliating demotions under the political breakup of the Soviet Union.

Yazenko had lost his prestige as commander of the European defense forces of the Soviet army. He was still in a position of power and importance, however, commanding the army of Belarus. Although that force was small compared to the armies maintained by Russia and Ukraine, there was a great equalizer also under Yazenko's control—a sizable arsenal of nuclear weapons placed there as part of the former Soviet Union's strategic defense plan.

Kuchakov filled a paper cup from the bottle of vodka he had brought from Leningrad—he could give it its proper name now that events were in motion to reverse the damnable changes—and handed it to Yazenko. He filled another cup for himself and lifted it in toast to his companion.

"To Operation Red Star—"

Both men drank, emptying the cups.

The conversation, beyond that one toast, was guarded. The two generals talked of days now past, of suicides of former officers not able to stand the humiliations and frustrations of the new order, of rumors that reached insidiously in every direction, in every republic. One common thread of all the fears was the inevitability of more change, more splintering, more shattering of what, such a short time ago, seemed so invincible. After several more refills from the bottle of vodka, both men became weary of the past and fell asleep.

They did not awaken until the plane made a bumpy landing at the airport in Odessa. That wasn't the pilot's fault, it was the condition of the runway, sadly dilapidated since the maintenance budget long ago was drained and left dry.

The two generals were met by a black limousine as they stepped off the plane. They were taken to a private twin-prop plane waiting at the farthest runway. The pilot, a colonel in the Ukranian air force, was standing at the open entrance to the plane. He gave the two generals a snappy salute.

"Colonel Spiekov, at your service."

Kuchakov glanced inside the plane, saw that it was empty. "Is Admiral

Chekonovich joining us?"

"Admiral Chekonovich left two hours ago, sir. He said to tell you the guest arrived early. We are to proceed at once to Simferopol."

Yazenko stared at the colonel sharply. "Not Sevastopol—?"

Sevastopol, on the southwestern tip of the Crimea, was a secure military headquarters, home port to the former Soviet Black Sea fleet. Russia and Ukraine had been locked in a bitter struggle since the Soviet breakup about who was now rightful owner of the two hundred ships listed on the official fleet roster—the actual number of ships berthed in the Black Sea port was considerably higher. Both generals assumed they were heading to Sevastopol.

"No, sir. Admiral Chekonovich said it would be better to go directly to his dacha at Yalta. He said you would understand."

Kuchakov nodded. "Proceed, Colonel."

At the airport in Simferopol, the capital of Crimea located some forty miles north of Sevastopol, the generals transferred to a waiting helicopter. They lifted off and flew over the mountains and dense forests of central Crimea toward the resort town of Yalta, near the southeast tip of the peninsula. Twenty minutes later, the helicopter settled down in a clearing beside the imposing dacha of Admiral Chekonovich.

The building, located in the forested hills above Yalta, was built solidly of stone and was larger than most of these resort hideaways of the Russian elite. The dacha had two stories, with a steeply sloping slate roof from which extended several high antennas. The forest was cleared away on the east to provide an unobstructed view of the Black Sea, glittering several hundred feet below them.

Two black limousines were parked in front of the dacha, and a rough dirt road could be seen leading back into the forest to the west. No other building was in sight, for the nearest neighbors were over a mile away to the north and south, those further separated by dense forest. Anyone accidentally, or deliberately, wandering through those forests would find them riddled with high-tech security systems connected to a squat building beside the dacha. Security personnel were always stationed in this building, whether or not the admiral was in residence.

Generals Kuchakov and Yazenko were shown into the long living room fronting the dacha. Admiral Chekonovich rose to greet them, as did a Chinese man sitting in one of the comfortable leather chairs in front of the expanse of windows.

Chekonovich was taller than his counterparts, thin to the point of appearing gaunt. His hair was white and bushy. He too was dressed in civilian clothes, dark baggy slacks and a grey knitted sweater that hung loosely. He was obviously a little younger than the other two military officers, somewhere in his fifties.

The Chinese man was slender, dressed in a dark silk business suit fitting with the perfection that spoke of the finest tailors in Hong Kong. He did not smile as he stared at the newcomers, studying each man in turn. Both Kuchakov and Yazenko felt uncomfortable at being so intensely scrutinized. The Chinese man must have sensed it, for a thin smile flitted across his face. There was no warmth in it, however.

"Please forgive me, General Kuchakov—General Yazenko. It is a habit I have a difficult time with. I do not intend to be rude."

Chekonovich spoke up. "Generals, I would like you to meet General Wang Jingwei, chairman of the Central Military Commission of the Chinese People's Liberation Army."

They shook hands and Chekonovich motioned for them all to sit in the chairs, arranged in a semi-circle. The sweeping sea view was temporarily interrupted as a uniformed, armed guard marched across the far edge of the lawn.

"General Wang has indicated a need to complete our discussions and return as soon as possible to Beijing. So we should get right to the purpose of this meeting." He looked over at the figure of the Chinese general, sitting straight and unsmiling at one end of the circle. "I am sure you have some questions, General—"

Wang fastened his stare on Kuchakov. "General Kuchakov, what is the current status of Operation Red Star in the Russian Federation?"

"All the major steps are accomplished. We are ready to assume control of all army and air force bases in the territory. Our command structures at both major naval installations are already in place. We will be an organized, unified fighting force the moment Red Star is launched."

"You are sure of the loyalty of your commanders—?"

"Each man is completely dedicated to the restoration of the Soviet Union."

"That will not happen, General Kuchakov," the other said thinly.

Yazenko spoke up quickly. "What General Kuchakov means is the restoration of power and unity within military ranks, General Wang—the restoring of a unified military command throughout all the republics. We realize that future political structures must be decided in cooperation with Beijing."

"You should not be wary of that liason," Wang said softly. "The government of China has absolutely no wish to assume control of any republic of the former Soviet Union. We simply do not wish to see the former political union restored as it was before. A military unification is called for and the People's Republic supports that. We look forward to a new era of mutual cooperation."

Kuchakov was looking directly at Wang. "I have assured my commanders that China does not intend to occupy any Russian territory or the territory of any other republic—"

"That is correct," Wang said firmly. "My government only wants the assurance that people we can trust are in control of your military forces. We do not want to risk any interference with—" there was a slight pause, "—any other activity that the People's Republic might wish to engage in. You may be assured that such activity, if it occurs, will not threaten any of your borders or affect your own military operations."

It was Yazenko's turn to question the general from Beijing. "It is our understanding that these other activities, as you have referred to them, do not involve the use of nuclear weapons. Is that still the position of the People's Republic—?"

"There is no change. My government expects the non- nuclear policy to be enforced by your forces, also. Beijing is absolutely insistent on that."

"None of us wants nuclear war," Kuchakov said stiffly.

"One assurance of that is to adhere to the operational plan," Wang snapped, his tone hardening. "Operation Red Star is to be confined strictly within the borders of your own republics. No military action is to be launched against any country of the European Community. Not even an overt threat of action. The People's Republic will react strongly if this policy is violated in any way."

"What does that mean?" Kuchakov growled.

"It means you are to follow the agreed plan, General Kuchakov. No deviation will be tolerated. It means military force will be used against you by the People's Republic of China if you do not stay within the bounds outlined for Operation Red Star. Does that make it perfectly clear, General?"

Once again Sergei Yazenko interceded, casting a warning frown at Kuchakov. "No one has any intention of expanding the operation, General Wang. We will have enough on our hands maintaining control in the republics. We do not want to involve the EC any more than you do."

"It is not just the EC that is of concern," Wang said, still showing anger. "Attack Europe and you bring in the United States. We do not want that to happen. We do not want escalation. We do not want any risk of nuclear response."

"We are all in complete agreement with that," Yazenko nodded.

General Wang frowned at Kuchakov then turned his attention to Chekonovich. "Admiral, many ships are still not delivered as promised."

"The last of the vessels from the Black Sea fleet left three days ago," Chekonovich replied. "Another aircraft carrier, a cruiser, five destroyers, and four more submarines. They should be in your hands within three weeks."

"The time is running short—"

Chekonovich shrugged. "There have been inspection teams at Sevastopol for three months, arguing over disposition of the fleet. It was necessary to detach the ships without drawing undue attention. The vessels have all cleared the Dardenelles but for security reasons, they are being routed in several directions. Some will take the long way, around the Cape and through the Indian Ocean. Some will go through the Suez. They are widely scattered, to avoid causing alarm. False orders have been issued that give various reasons for the ships putting out to sea, none remotely of any military significance. The destinations listed are also false, and also widely scattered. They will undoubtedly be tracked, but people will lose interest once it is determined no battle groups are involved. However, it all takes time—"

"And the shipments of enriched uranium?"

"Five hundred tons are aboard the carrier, another two hundred tons are en route overland. With the eight hundred tons already in your possession, that will complete the agreed upon fifteen hundred tons."

"You are sure there are no records of this uranium—?"

"It was produced in utmost secrecy. The only records were in the plants that produced it, and those records are destroyed. Officially, these supplies do not exist."

Wang looked at Kuchakov. "And the ships from the Baltic fleet—?"

"All en route, as promised. We had to space departures and provide misleading information about ports of call, for the reasons Admiral Chekonovich just gave. It is not easy to detach that many naval vessels without sounding alarms in other countries. It has been accomplished, however. The ships should all reach the People's Republic on schedule."

"That is good," General Wang said, nodding in satisfaction. "It is better that this build-up of Chinese naval power be accomplished without unduly alarming other countries. Your cooperation in this matter is warmly appreciated in Beijing."

Kuchakov was frowning. "There is something I do not understand,

General Wang. Why have so many Soviet planes been delivered covertly to South America? It was part of our agreement, and it has been accomplished as scheduled, but I cannot help being curious about the purpose of such deliveries."

"Do not be curious, General Kuchakov," the man from Beijing said coldly. "Do not think about it, and most certainly do not speak of it. Your only concern is Operation Red Star."

## 9

## RED TIGER IN TEL AVIV

Quinn Adams arrived at Tel Nof, Israel's military air base south of Tel Aviv, feeling surprisingly fresh and alert. That was partially due to the supersonic speeds the U.S. military jet maintained after leaving Andrews Air Base, slowing only for mid-air refueling over the Atlantic. Another reason Quinn felt so good was the anticipation of once again seeing Joanna Shazebak.

As he stepped from the plane, a small, white sports car raced across the runway. It braked to a stop and Joanna climbed from the driver's seat with a decorous flash of dark-stockinged legs.

Despite the fact that he was happily married now, Quinn could not help but feel the impact of old emotions. Joanna was as radiantly beautiful as he remembered, perhaps even more so. She was petite, the classic beauty of high cheekbones and delicate chin framed in a perfect, oval face. Her dark eyes, under the long lashes, were as large, and flashing, and exciting as any of the pictures in his mind.

She had done something different to her hair—it was shorter, blowing free, with a casualness that can only come from meticulous grooming. She was wearing a pale pink silk dress molded perfectly to a figure that had not lost any of its slim sensuousness. Color-matched, high-heeled pumps provided a perfect accent to those long, eye-stopping legs.

All of this registered in the few seconds it took Joanna to cross the tarmac and throw her arms tightly around his neck in greeting. The familiar scent of expensive perfume reached into his memory, recalling similar times they held each other close. Joanna was the one to greet him almost every time he flew into Israel in those intense years of working with the Mossad in scores of covert operations.

She gave him a light kiss on the cheek and stepped back. "I won't ask if you've missed me," she said, a light glinting in those dark eyes, "but I hope you have."

"I'll always miss you, Joanna," he told her. "We shared too much together to ever forget any of it."

"Enough said," she replied, grasping his hand. "Now we must get you to Dovid. He's waiting anxiously to talk to you."

Seated beside Joanna as the sleek car left the air base and threaded up toward the fashionable hillside estates overlooking Tel Aviv, Quinn half-turned and openly studied the woman beside him. Memories again churned inside him, some of death and violence, but mostly of warmth and passion. They had never really talked of marriage and growing old together; life unfolded one day at a time, to be lived and appreciated to the fullest. The future always was too filled with uncertainties.

Joanna felt his stare and looked over at him. "I suppose you're looking for lines and gray hairs," she smiled.

"Your beauty is ageless, Joanna. You'll be just as stunning thirty years from now. You haven't aged a day in these past seven years."

She flashed another quick smile. "And you lie just as genuinely as ever. To be truthful, you look a little beat. They must be over-working you."

"I like to think of it as maturing gracefully."

"Well, never doubt that I think you're the most handsome, sexiest man I've ever met," she said, her hand reaching over to clasp his, "and I'll still think that even when you're fat and bald."

Their hands gently squeezed. It said more than any amount of words, especially words that no longer could be said.

The car climbed higher into the hillside residential areas, toward the more isolated estates where the Shazebaks lived. They said nothing for awhile, then Quinn had a question.

"Did you uncover anything more about my visitors?"

"Not much. That was really strange."

"How did your people pick up on it?"

"They were interrogating a Chinese agent who said he wanted to defect."

"To Israel? Certainly not to Morocco—"

"Actually, he wanted to defect to the United States. The man didn't trust the usual channels. He claimed there are too many paths being criss-crossed these days, too many countries involved."

"Involved in what?"

"He didn't know—like the rest of us."

"He knew about the attempt on my life—"

"A message was passed through him confirming the timetable. He knew it originated in Colombia, and was to be forwarded to Beijing."

"If the report went to Beijing, the Chinese are involved—"

"Not necessarily. The timetable was passed along by their agent in Colombia, but that doesn't mean the Chinese planned the raid. Frankly, I think they would have used their own people."

"Unless they didn't want to be identified with the hit."

Joanna nodded. "Always a possibility. Our station in Washington is of the opinion it was too loose an operation to be run by the Chinese."

"It was certainly loose," Quinn agreed, "but why would the Colombians want to take me out?"

"Are you sure your wife hasn't taken a Latin lover—?"

"Jill—?" Quinn broke into a smile, suddenly realizing Joanna was teasing. "Why would she want one? She has me."

"Well," Joanna said, her expression serious, "I understand muscle tone starts to break down with age—"

Dovid Shazebak and his wife Sophia were waiting in the driveway as they pulled up before the family home. Dovid had put on a little weight, Quinn saw, but still looked trim and athletic. Sophia was as beautiful and voluptuous as the last time he saw her. Quinn received warm hugs from both of them.

"Good to see you, my friend," Dovid grinned. "With you here again, it must be party time."

Dovid was referring to the fact that whenever Quinn showed up in the past, there was usually some kind of covert operation about to get underway.

"I'm not sure I could still handle one of your Mossad parties," Quinn grinned. He cast an appreciative glance at the woman standing beside Dovid. "You look beautiful, Sophia. Marriage agrees with you."

Sophia laughed. "You haven't looked closely. Either that, or you're too polite to mention the pounds it's put on me."

"If there are more," Quinn murmured, "they all went to the right places."

Sophia was a sabra, a native born Israeli, and her looks were as deceptive as Joanna's. Both women could kill efficiently, with any weapon or with their bare hands. Sophia became an Israeli agent at the age of fourteen. Both she and Joanna fought in the Israeli army, with deadly distinction. Sophia and Dovid were lovers the last time Quinn had "partied" here in the Mediterranean.

"Sophia and I bought the house next to this one," Dovid said. "I keep telling Joanna that with our parents gone, this place is too big for her, but she refuses to sell."

"Like the song says," Joanna smiled, "I love it for sentimental reasons."

The house had the same exterior of drab, brownish stone as most of the buildings in Israel—a matter of law, not choice. Inside, however, it showed the taste and refinement that was Joanna, splashed with just the right amount of color in walls and accessories to also reflect her joy of life. Nothing much had changed, Quinn noted, since the times they shared together in this fine old house.

Joanna served cool drinks and they all sat down in the comfortable living room. They chatted for a while about old times and old friends, then Dovid put down the drink and his expression became grim.

"Have you heard about the slaughter in Rio?" he asked Quinn. The blank expression on Quinn's face was answer enough. "It happened yesterday. We lost an operative, and we think an Aman agent was killed too. Your station was wiped out."

"Our CIA station?"

Dovid nodded. "Four of them, including a special agent sent down to help out. Did you know any of them?"

Quinn shook his head. "What happened?"

"A different story for all of them. The Germans lost two, the Mukhabarat lost one. No one knows the total count."

"Any common thread?"

"Apparently they were all interested in a member of the Chinese military intelligence—Wu Zhenkang. Strike any chords?"

Again Quinn gave a shake of his head. "But there's that Chinese connection again. They're up to something."

"We received proof of that two days ago," Dovid said, his voice automatically falling lower, though Joanna's house, and his own, were both screened from electronic eavesdropping. "That's why you're here. One of our people in Shanghai came into possession of a copy of the battle plan for an Operation Red Tiger. I'm assuming you haven't heard of it."

Quinn gave a quick shake of his head. "This is definitely beginning to feel like old times."

"I'll take you to headquarters later and go over everything in detail, so you can put the full picture in front of your people. But Operation Red Tiger is a plan for China to take over all of mainland Asia."

"What—?"

"The Chinese already cast a large shadow over most of those Asian countries. The plan deals mostly with occupation strategies—apparently very little military resistance is anticipated."

"What about Japan. They'll certainly resist—"

"The Chinese strategy involves only the mainland. Japan and Taiwan won't be bothered. They don't want to test the defense treaties those countries have with the United States."

"Viet Nam. Korea. We have treaties there, too."

"China is gambling your country will not go to war to defend them again. Not when it will result in direct confrontation with Chinese forces, and not when China is in control of all Asia. They project the U.S. would consider it too costly, without hope of success. I tend to agree with them."

"What about India and Pakistan—?"

"Resistance is expected in most of the southern countries. But by then, China expects to be so dominent and powerful, opposition would be quickly crushed."

"Are we talking about another hundred year war—?"

"A hundred days might be closer," Dovid said grimly. "None of those Asian countries are going to mount any serious resistance. The Chinese just might sweep through without firing a shot."

"When is all this supposed to happen?" Quinn asked, his brow furrowed in thought. This Chinese gambit would present tremendous complications for the United States.

"There's no date that we know of, but reading the battle plan indicates it will be soon."

"You believe this Operation Red Tiger is the real thing, not just an exercise?"

"We're checking, but it looks real. There's no doubt a massive mobilization is underway. They're being clever and secretive, but it's happening."

"Any indication they plan to attack the United States?"

"None. Apparently they want to make it difficult for your country to become involved. Can you see your president, or the Congress, voting to go to war with China without a direct threat?"

"Sounds like the Chinese will be pretty busy in Asia," Quinn frowned. "What are they up to in South America?"

"Maybe that's just a diversion," Dovid said. "I suggest we move this meeting to headquarters and start providing you with the scary details."

Two days later, early in the morning, Quinn Adams was seated in the Oval Office. The office was unusually crowded. There was President Baldwin, Vice President Anne Ashford, Duff Jenkins, the White House chief of staff, Secy. of State James Van Durlin, and Admiral Harry Brunswick, head of the Joint Chiefs. They had all been hastily summoned to this meeting with no indication of what it was about.

At the invitation of Sam Baldwin, Quinn Adams filled them in on his visit to Tel Aviv. When he finished, there was stunned silence.

"Somebody say something intelligent," Baldwin muttered, looking at the faces circled around him.

"Crap."

It was Admiral Brunswick, known to everyone in the room as "Boots". He was respected for his ability to probe to the core of a situation and apparently he had done it again, for no one even smiled.

"I think that describes the essence of the situation, Admiral," Baldwin nodded, "unless someone wants to go for 'deep doo-doo'."

"There's no doubt about the accuracy of this report?" Anne Ashford asked. Anne was single, an attractive brunette, and brought one of the sharpest minds to the vice presidency in many years. She was respected not only for her dedication to domestic affairs, but for her keen grasp of the international scene.

"The evidence is incontrovertible," Quinn replied. "I have slides and maps broken down from the battle plan—this is all very real."

"The Chinese seem to have gone to great lengths to keep us out of it," Van Durlin said. "No direct confrontation, incredibly high risks in our voluntary intervention. Extremely difficult for diplomatic approaches, and the U.N. would be helpless to oppose such a large-scale venture."

"Can we use this advance knowledge to our advantage?" Baldwin asked.

"Not diplomatically, Mr. President. Any move on our part will probably cause them to move up their timetable. The Chinese do not bend to foreign political pressures."

Admiral Brunswick was frowning into his thoughts. He looked up at Quinn. "You sure there is no tie-in with the Russian republics?"

"Not sure of anything," Quinn said. "We have a lot of bits and pieces that don't fit together. Those Russian ships that put to sea awhile ago—they seem to be sliding as unobtrusively as possible into Asian waters. No clear reason why. We do know that the Chinese battle plan specifically orders no infringement on any territory of the former Soviet Union. There is no indication that any of the republics will be involved in Tiger Red operations."

"I can't believe they'll let China gobble up all that territory around them," the admiral muttered. "Something's not right. The Ruskies have something up their sleeve."

"What do we do?" Baldwin barked, looking around the circle again. "Anyone care to lead us in prayer—?"

"We have several military priorities, Mr. President," Boots Brunswick said briskly.

"Like what—?"

"We need to bolster European defenses as quickly as possible, under the auspices of NATO. This Operation Red Tiger may not spell out an attack on Europe, but it's a logical sequence of events after they seize Asia. We need to beef up defenses here in the States, too. Both the Atlantic and Pacific seaboards."

"There is another consideration, Mr. President," Anne Ashford said quietly. "It sounds ridiculous, but after the attempted revolutionary coup seven years ago, we all know anything is possible. We must face the possibility of an attack on the United States, either from a foreign power or forces inside the country. Are we prepared for that?"

Baldwin pursed his lips thoughtfully. "Absolutely right, Madam Vice President—we can't rule anything out." He looked up at Quinn. "Mr. Adams, everyone in this room knows you're the head of the National Emergency Coordinated Command Organization, but probably no one fully understands what NECCO does. Anne raises some good questions. Under the circumstances, I think an overview of NECCO's plans for emergency contingencies is in order."

"Very well, Mr. President," Quinn said. He looked around, almost smiling at the eagerness on the faces around him. An open insight into the workings of NECCO was a rarity appreciated by all of them.

"As most of you are aware, NECCO's purpose is to prepare to respond to any major national emergency. There is no duplication of other emergency response organizations. We deal in catastrophic disasters, either natural or military, that might threaten the existence of the United States."

Quinn glanced over at the President, who gave a nod to continue.

"We've divided the country into ten regions, with a member of NECCO directly responsible for all emergency actions within it. Highly trained forces of NECCO Rangers are stationed in each area, along with complete air and ground support facilities. These operate independently of the regular armed forces, although there is close cooperation between them."

"Each of these regions has a designated command center capable of handling relocation of the entire governmental structure, should that become necessary. So, to answer Madam Vice President's question directly, we do have emergency capabilities to keep the government running should the nation be attacked, from within or abroad."

Quinn glanced questioningly at the President. Baldwin looked around at the expectant faces, saw their deep concern.

"You might add a few more details concerning the possibility of an attack on the Capitol, Mr. Adams."

"Contingency plans for that scenario have been underway for several years," Quinn told them. "Relocation of many of our national treasures has already been effected. The Constitution, the Bill of Rights, nearly all of our irreplaceable documents are already out of the area."

Van Durlin looked up, surprised. "I saw the Constitution just a few days ago—"

"You saw a copy, Mr. Secretary," Quinn told him.

"A copy—?"

"In that light, who can tell the difference," Baldwin grunted.

"Gold reserves are also relocated, both ours and those deposited by foreign nations in our keeping—"

"You've moved the gold from Fort Knox?" Brunswick asked, obviously startled.

"There's not much left," Quinn replied. He looked around the room. "I think you all get the picture. Our Rangers are ready to evacuate key people in all areas of government, business, and industry to a safe region. There are plans to extradite materials and key industrial components—everything possible to keep the country running under the impact of a major catastrophe." Once again Quinn looked over at the President. "Is that sufficient detail, Mr. President—?"

Baldwin nodded. "It's all they're going to get. Mr. Adams, we appreciate the briefing. Of course," he added, glowering around at the others in the room, "what you just heard is absolutely top secret. It must not be discussed even with your closest staff members—and that includes the Joint Chiefs, Boots."

Brunswick gave a nod of understanding. "I suppose it would be going too far to ask where—"

"Absolutely," Baldwin said, cutting off the question. "Even I don't know where NECCO has put the stuff. And I've given orders for Quinn not to tell me even if I ask. What we don't know, we can't tell."

"I presume there are safeguards," Van Durlin murmured. He glanced at Quinn. "I'm thinking of the attempt on your life a few days ago—"

"Adequate safeguards, Mr. Secretary," Quinn smiled. "Nothing is going to get lost."

Duff Jenkins, the White House chief of staff, raised a hand for attention. "With all the news about this Operation Tiger Red, we shouldn't overlook the incident in Rio a couple of days ago—"

"Incident—it was a slaughter," Baldwin growled.

"We reviewed that matter with Stu Akker this morning. It caught everyone by surprise. As you know, the whole CIA station in Rio was eliminated."

"I understand a Chinese military general was involved in some way," Anne Ashford said. "Is that correct?"

"Yes, but we can't determine that the man was actually involved in the killings," Jenkins replied. "He was tracked to Rio by the British, and perhaps others. There's no indication the Chinese had anything to do with the massacre. Akker is investigating, but all we have so far are dead agents. All of the intelligence communities affected are keeping a tight lid on things."

"If the CIA follows through in their usual efficient manner," Baldwin said sourly, "in a year or so, they should come up with a tentative theory about what might have happened."

"It won't take the Mossad that long, Mr. President," Quinn said quietly. "They'll have a detailed report in a matter of days."

"That makes me feel better," Baldwin growled, standing up, "but it also makes me more disgusted with the CIA. As for this Chinese attempt to take over Asia, we can't just stand by and watch it happen. Admiral, draw up plans for beefing up NATO defenses, and our own. Mr. Secretary, get back to me on how much of this we should share with our friends. Madam Vice President, I'd like you to work closely with Quinn, become familiar with what NECCO is all about. Run interference for him if it's needed. He needs to stay in the background as much as possible." He again glowered around the room. "That means everybody keeps their mouth shut about everything discussed at this meeting. Thank you all. Now get out of here and start working the problems."

# 10

## WRONG DECISIONS

Quinn went back to his office at NECCO Operations and was just beginning to review a stack of files on his desk when Race Courtney entered. He closed the door and dropped into one of the comfortable chairs in front of the desk.

"I suppose you destroyed the peace and tranquility of everyone at the meeting," Race murmured.

"And I'm about to do the same for you," Quinn replied. He leaned back in his chair. "You comfortable about the arrangements at Granite Mountain—?"

Race nodded firmly. "Secure as anything can be. We've completed all the modifications and expansions and Frank Kantros' Rangers don't even let fresh air in without checking it. Everything is tight—a mosquito gets within half a mile and it's gone."

"The Utah authorities cooperating—?"

Race nodded again. "Turned it over completely. With all the miles of new tunnels we've put in, they won't recognize the place when—and if—we turn it back to them."

"Everything on the list has been relocated?"

"All safely tucked away."

"I want you to get out there."

"I was just there two weeks ago—"

"This time I want you to stay. I want you to take personal charge of all operations at Granite Mountain."

"Won't that upset Frank?"

"Kantros is a soldier. He knows the chain of command."

"We expecting trouble—?"

Quinn frowned. "I don't know what we're expecting, Race. That's the problem. We have to be prepared for anything."

"If it comes to Condition One," Race asked quietly, "would we evacuate everything to Pyramid Seven?"

"That makes sense to me. What do you think?"

"I think we should initiate alert status. Something is going to blow up. If anything spills over onto us, we have to consider Washington will be a primary target."

"I agree. I'll give the orders to go immediately to Condition Three, with Pyramid Seven as first option. That will get things rolling. You alert the Utah authorities their tourist business is going to pick up dramatically in the next few hours."

"Hill Air Force Base is ready."

"It just thinks it's ready," Quinn said grimly. "Get out there fast and keep me posted. Utah is about to become the center of the universe."

An hour later, one of Quinn's three phones started ringing. It was the black security phone. He picked it up.

"Yes—?"

It was a familiar voice at the other end. "We need to talk, Quinn." It was Joanna, obviously calling on a secure COMINT satellite line.

"We just talked yesterday."

"And we just got an interesting call from Aunt Freida today."

"How is dear Aunt Freida?"

"Very nervous, and very upset."

"You can't tell me about it over the phone—?"

"It's much too personal. You came here last time, so it's my turn to log some jet lag."

"How soon will you be leaving?"

"Today."

"I'll make arrangements at Andrews."

"See you tomorrow."

Quinn called his sister's house, where Jill was staying while he was gone. Stacy answered and he asked for his wife.

"Say sweet things, brother," she murmured into the phone. "You're in big trouble."

When Jill came on the line, Quinn tried to ignore the tightness in her voice. "Thought we might do lunch—"

"You're back. I suppose it never occurred to you to come home before you went to the office—"

"Sorry. I went directly to the White House. Can you meet me?"

"I suppose so."

"Usual place, usual time."

He hung up, staring at the phone for a moment. There was no doubt Jill was upset. He wondered briefly if he should tell her about Joanna.

Quinn made a wrong decision. In fact, he made two wrong decisions. He told Jill about Joanna coming to Washington, and he told her where he was the last three days—not just out of the country, but in Tel Aviv meeting with Joanna and her brother. That was just before the waiter put a cup of onion soup in front of Jill.

An angry reaction by Jill overturned the cup. There was a deadly silence as the waiter sopped up the spilled soup and put a couple of fresh cloth napkins on the table in front of Jill. When they were finally alone, Jill gave her husband a chilling, accusing stare.

"You're having an affair with her, aren't you."

"Of course not. You know that's not true."

"She called you in the middle of the night on our personal, unlisted telephone—"

"To warn us we were about to be killed."

"You just spent three days with her in Tel Aviv and didn't tell me about it."

"I wasn't 'with her'—not like you're inferring."

"I can't trust you, Quinn—"

"This is crazy. I love you, Jill. Where is all this coming from—?"

"I know I'm not the sexy spy-type she is—"

"Joanna isn't like that at all." Well, that wasn't exactly true, but this was no time to go into details. "When she arrives, we'll all go to dinner. You can get to know her—"

"I don't want to go to dinner with her," Jill said icily. "I don't want to know anything about her. And I sure don't want you 'knowing' her, either."

"It's just business—"

"I'm certain it is—old business."

Quinn was exasperated. "You're being totally unreasonable. Are you PMS or something—?"

Jill slammed down her napkin and stood up. "Sleep with her if you want—I don't care."

She stalked out of the restaurant. Quinn stared out of the window, mostly to avoid the curious glances and knowing smirks of people in the proximity of his table, fervently grateful he was not well known. All in all, he concluded, lunch had not been a good idea.

Jill returned to Stacy's house, intending to pack the few things she had brought with her and return to her own home. She almost knocked down Stacy's daughter as she came in the front door. She quickly gathered the seven-year-old into her arms, hugging her. Leah was a doll, with large brown eyes, long curls, her lips a perfectly shaped cupid's bow. Her little arms went around Jill's neck and gave her a tight squeeze.

"You almost squished me, Aunt Jill—"

"I would have felt so bad, darling," Jill told her, returning the hug.

Stacy poked her head out of a bedroom down the hall. "That was a short lunch—"

"It was terrible," Jill said, shaking her head. "I'm sure Quinn hates me."

Stacy tossed the sweater she was holding back into the bedroom. "Here, Race—I need to talk to your sister."

"Race home already?" Jill said, surprised.

"He's catching a plane to Utah in an hour." She broke into a smile. "He came home to catch me first. What's this about Quinn hating you—?"

"I was a total witch."

"Aunt Jill," Leah said, her eyes wide, "you said a bad word."

Stacy came forward and took her daughter. "Go play in your room, Leah. Aunt Jill and I need to talk—real grown-up talk."

Race came out of the bedroom with a travel bag. "This'll do for now." He leaned over and gave Stacy a kiss.

"If I need more, I'll get it there."

"If you need more," Stacy said impishly, "you wait for me."

"I'm talking about clothes," Race grinned.

"How long are you going to be gone?" Jill asked.

Race shrugged. "Several weeks. Could be longer."

Stacy glanced at Jill, then back to her husband. "I've got a great idea—"

Race winced. "Those usually cost me money."

"How about us women taking the van and driving out to Utah?" She looked excitedly at Jill. "How long has it been since you and Race saw your aunt and uncle—what's their name?"

"Austin and Vanessa Wells," Race answered. He glanced at his sister. "Stacy's right. Quinn is going to be tied up for a few days, and after that, he'll probably be flying to Utah himself. You up to a three-day drive, sis—?"

Jill nodded eagerly. "Sounds fabulous. Maybe Stacy can help me sort out my head—it's really in a mess."

"Why?" her brother asked.

"I can't shake pictures of Quinn and his Israeli playmate. That's stupid, I know, but I can't help it."

"She's not his playmate, Jill," Race said, shaking his head. "She's an Israeli intelligence agent. Quinn wouldn't cheat on you."

"I know that," she muttered. "I just can't believe it."

Race shook his head, giving his sister a wry grin. "On that note of womanly reasoning, I'm leaving." He gave Stacy another kiss. "I'll call Aunt Vanessa and let them know you're coming. I'll be staying at Hill Field, but it's only a few miles away."

"If we're not there in a week," Stacy smiled, "don't call out the Rangers. It'll just mean we've found a couple of better guys."

# 11

## CASA ALERT

It was a little after 3 a.m. when Joanna Shazebak, escorted by two NECCO Rangers, was admitted to Quinn's office. Quinn, dozing on the sofa, roused himself and gave Joanna a hug. He excused the Rangers and both Quinn and Joanna collapsed on the sofa.

"It's been a long day," Joanna sighed wearily.

"The last full night's sleep I can remember is the night before you called. Let's see—that was about five days ago, I think."

Joanna patted his cheek sympathetically. "Poor baby. Think how much fun you're having."

Quinn caught both her hands in his. "How can you look so good at three o'clock in the morning—?"

"—and with my clothes on, too," she smiled. "Oh well, you probably never think of the good old days when we were lovers."

"Was that the reason for this hurried flight—to fall into my arms?"

Joanna closed her eyes for a moment. They looked beautiful even closed, Quinn noticed. She opened them and caught him staring at her.

"Do you have room service in this dungeon?" she murmured. "I haven't eaten all day."

Quinn ordered a light meal brought in. Joanna ate heartily then leaned back on the sofa, giving a contented sigh. She glanced at Quinn.

"I'm ready to go to work."

"You said Aunt Freida was upset. Is she still in Berlin—?"

"Her spirit lives on. She has a full beard now. Sounds like a man, too."

"Must be the water," Quinn said solemnly.

Aunt Freida was the name they gave the fierce head of the Mossad station in Berlin when Quinn and Joanna worked together and spent a couple of months in Germany several years back on assignment. Freida was a spinster who never smiled, never joked about anything, never spent one moment of her life not being an agent. She disliked Joanna, thought a woman so soft and feminine could not possibly be a good field agent, ready to kill when it was called for. She was very wrong. Apparently Aunt Freida was dead now, replaced by a bearded man as fun-loving as Freida.

"Why is the Berlin station upset?" he asked. "Nazi ghosts again?"

"Germany didn't bring me here," Joanna said. It's what our Berlin station uncovered about the Russians."

"What Russians? They come in all flavors now."

"Red Guard. Dyed-in-the-wool Soviets, complete with hatred of all things democratic."

"We're talking military, I suppose."

"Have you ever heard of an Operation Red Star?"

"You're doing it again, aren't you," Quinn muttered. "Showing us up. No, I've never heard of Operation Red Star. I'll wager the CIA hasn't either."

"Don't feel bad," Joanna smiled. "We just picked up on it yesterday."

"So what is it—?"

"We're not really sure. Our people in Berlin stumbled across a reference. They did some checking. What they found is scary."

"Is it connected to Operation Red Tiger?"

"Yes—and no."

"That's perfectly clear."

"Red Star appears to be a strictly Soviet operation, not tied to the Chinese Red Tiger gambit in Asia. At least, not directly."

"But you think there is a connection somewhere—"

"It's the timing. Both operations launched at the same time—the Soviet and Chinese operations must be linked. No way it can be coincidence."

"I take it Red Star involves more than the Republic of Russia."

"All of the republics are involved, according to Berlin. They believe the former Soviet military hierarchy is attempting to put humpty-dumpty back together again."

"Restore the Soviet Union—?"

"There's no evidence the politicians are part of it. It seems to be exclusively military."

"Bring back a unified military structure that controls all of the republics. If they managed that, the generals could put in their own slate of politicians—starting with themselves."

"Is that possible—?" Joanna asked.

Quinn thought, then nodded. "The right people could pull it off. They would have to keep it internal, not involve anybody outside the republics."

"They must know NATO isn't going to ignore something like that—nor the United States."

"They must also be very confident China isn't going to object to the Russian bear rising from the dead." Quinn frowned, following his own train of thought. "The generals must know we're beefing up NATO."

"They do. Our people in Berlin say the Russians are anticipating a huge U.S. defense build-up in Europe."

"That doesn't bother them?"

"Apparently not."

Quinn locked his hands behind his head and stared up at the ceiling. "What's wrong with this picture—?"

"I really hate to ask this," Joanna said quietly, "but have you heard of CASA?"

"Casa. That's Spanish for house."

"It's an acronym for Coalition of Allied States of the Americas."

Quinn stared blankly at her. "Never heard of it."

"Well, I don't want to trash your American intelligence system any more than necessary, but you should have."

"From where—?"

"Pick a country. Anywhere in Central or South America."

"We have our own NECCO people down there—"

Joanna said nothing, just gave a shrug of her shoulders and arched her eyebrows.

"You just did it again," Quinn growled.

"Sorry," Joanna smiled. "Would it help if we sent you copies of our reports—?"

Quinn broke into a grin. "As a matter of fact, I'd appreciate that. Can you arrange it?"

"If the Knesset approves."

"Actually," Quinn said, his tone becoming serious, "Race's intelligence unit did pick up on a lot of recent political activity down there. Nothing military, and nothing about this CASA. A coalition of Latin countries, you say. Who's in it?"

"Just about every country in the hemisphere."

"Is there an agenda?"

"I'm sure there is, but we don't know what it is. Besides, we thought we should leave something for you Americans to do."

Quinn tried to ignore the barb. "Strange, isn't it. China. Russia. South America. All in motion. What's going on, Joanna?"

"I think we'd better find out, don't you."

\* \* \*

At noon, Joanna began the long return journey to Tel Aviv. Quinn summoned Lincoln Banes, second-in-command of NECCO, and Frank Kantros to his office.

Linc Banes was an imposing figure. Black, standing six-four and a solid two-forty, Linc carried himself with a jutting chin and an aggressive forward lean, a stance developed in the days of rising through the ranks of labor unions and federal labor bureaus. He was recruited into NECCO as one of the original Pharoahs, and Quinn knew Linc was completely loyal and dedicated. Banes had served as Pharoah Two for the past six years.

Quinn briefed the two men on what the Israelis uncovered in Berlin. They both pondered the news and finally Kantros frowned at Quinn.

"I'm having trouble seeing a clear and present danger to the United States. There probably is one—but where's it coming from?"

"It's puzzling," Quinn agreed. "It doesn't seem possible the Chinese would tangle with us at the same time they're marching over Asia."

"Same with the Russians," Kantros grunted. "Pulling off a coup like Red Star won't be easy. Those republics like their independence from Moscow, bitter-sweet as it might be. There was trouble in the smaller republics even before the Soviet break-up. Now there's full-scale revolution in some states."

"And this CASA stuff," Banes muttered. "It's almost impossible to get those countries into lock-step over anything. Now they're in a kissy-huggy coalition? It just doesn't sound right."

"Still, I can't see a threat to national security coming from that quarter," Quinn frowned. "Put them in the ring with us, and they're not going to last the first round."

Kantros looked dubious. "They're pretty rag-tag as independents, all right, but if they were organized into a united force—"

"—they still wouldn't have enough manpower or firepower to pose a threat," Banes finished.

"You're right," Quinn agreed. "South America can't be considered a major threat."

"Which means we're looking at the possibility of assault from two directions—as crazy as it sounds," Kantros said. "China and Europe."

"I'm thinking we're near a Condition Two situation," Banes said grimly. "Even if we don't come under direct attack, we're going to be involved in whatever happens in Europe and Asia. That puts us a blink away from war with either of our friends and neighbors—or both."

Quinn nodded again. "I agree. It's time to shift NECCO into high gear. Condition Two will get the extraction procedures rolling, without causing a national panic by initiating full-scale evacuation. Most of the national treasures and gold reserves are already relocated to Pyramid Seven. Race is out there now. The Intermountain region offers the best protection if we do get attacked. Do either of you have second thoughts about that—?"

Both men shook their heads.

"Linc, get the Pharoahs back to Ops. I'll let the President know we're recommending activation to Condition Two."

Kantros raised a hand. "I have a request—"

Quinn flashed a thin smile. "Vacation denied."

"Let's also activate Aaron."

Quinn and Linc Banes both stared hard at him. General Aaron Stark had headed the military action against the terrorists attempting to seize the government seven years ago. Stark was undeniably one of the best military tacticians the country had produced in several generations. After the military phase of crushing the coup was completed, Stark chose to quietly retire.

"How do you see using him?" Banes asked.

"Central command in Pyramid Seven," Kantros replied. "With Condition Two activated, I'm going to have my hands full coordinating evacuation and relocation of people and materials. The Joint Chiefs are going to have their own priorities with Europe and our coastal defenses. I'd feel better if Aaron was in Utah, making sure the NECCO operations, civilian and military, were all coming together properly."

Linc frowned at the general. "Would you intend General Stark assuming top command—?"

"I wouldn't be comfortable giving Aaron orders," Kantros said. "I'd be honored to serve under him again."

"It's a good idea, Frank," Quinn said. "There's no doubt Aaron would be an asset. Are you sure about this? No one has any doubts about your ability to command."

"This isn't competition between quarterbacks," Kantros said firmly. "Aaron is the best, and we need him. Besides," he added with a smile, "if I know Aaron, he'd re-enlist as a private just to get into action again."

An hour later, the men designated as Pharaohs, heading the various pyramids of NECCO operations, were seated at the long table running down the center of the cavernous underground Operations Room. It really wasn't a table; it was a series of communication stations linking the Pharoahs to each other and to NECCO operational centers across the United States. There were fifteen stations, a line of six on each side of the table facing each other, and three across the top, near the entrance. Each station had two small television monitors, several phones, a shielded computer terminal that provided access to the nation's deepest and most protected secrets and statistics, and a surrounding console of sophisticated electronic communication equipment.

The far wall at the end of Operations was covered with three banks of television screens, sizing down from the three huge screens on the top level to six in the middle and a dozen smaller screens along the bottom. Linked by satellites, these screens could provide the Pharoahs with simultaneous live coverage from NECCO centers strategically located across the United States.

All of the Pharoahs, with the exception of Race Courtney, were in their places when Quinn Adams entered. These were the men who had done all the planning, and now would have all the responsibility for removing key people from harm's way. People in government, industry, research, education, every type of activity necessary to maintain a working governmental and social structure in the event of any kind of catastrophic national disaster. In addition, the Pharoahs knew exactly where all strategic resources and materials were stockpiled across the nation, with plans in place to extract them out of danger zones.

Linc Banes was seated to the left at the head of the table, Frank Kantros on the right. Quinn sat down between them.

Quinn flipped a switch and put himself on one of the monitors. With all the surrounding equipment, it was difficult to see faces around the table and the monitors made it easy to follow conversations.

"Gentlemen, we are activating Condition Two emergency status," Quinn told them. "That means immediate evacuation of priority personnel and key strategic materials and resources. Pyramid Seven is the relocation site."

One of the Pharoahs punched himself onto a monitor. "This must mean we're expecting imminent trouble—"

Quinn's face was grim as he briefed the group on the reports of Operations Red Tiger and Red Star. A map of the world was brought up on one of the large screens at the end of the room.

"As you see, gentlemen, anything is possible once the Russians and

Chinese launch their offensives. We are at risk everywhere. The military is pouring men and materials into Europe, into Hawaii, into Japan—everywhere we can show deterrent force."

"Do we know their timetable, sir—?"

"No. But it could be only a matter of hours."

"Will we escalate to Condition One when the trouble starts in Europe and Asia—?"

"Not unless there's a direct assault on the United States."

"Are we going public with this, sir?"

Everyone could see Quinn shake his head. "We need to be as discreet as possible. I'd say we have maybe twelve hours before the media picks up on it. The White House will run interference for us as long as it can, but you know how that goes. No one will reach us here in NECCO but be sure your people in the field say absolutely nothing."

One of the phones rang in front of Quinn. It was the white one. Quinn answered it.

"Yes, Mr. President."

"I know this is bad timing," Baldwin said, "but I need you to meet Anne Ashford at Andrews right away. She's in Air Force Two, waiting for you."

"Something happened—?"

"I'll let her brief you. Can you get away—?"

"I'll leave immediately."

"Good. Check with me later."

Twenty minutes later, Quinn entered the lounge of Air Force Two, waiting on a side taxi runway at Andrews Air Force Base, the huge jet engines already churning at a low whine in preparation for take-off. Anne Ashford motioned for him to sit down.

"Glad you could make it, Quinn."

"The President seemed disturbed—"

"We all are. I got a call earlier today from Margaret Groethe, our ambassador to the U.N. You know her, I suppose."

Quinn smiled. "I've known Maggie since she first went over to State. Smart, and tough. I take it she picked up on something—"

"Maggie discovered the Latin U.N. delegations have all left New York."

"All of them—?"

"All the top people. We did some checking and found the same thing here in Washington—skeleton staffs at the embassies. Everyone who counts is gone."

"Do we know where they went—?"

"They're supposed to be in Las Vegas, attending some hush-hush strategic planning conference, or something."

"Doesn't sound very sinister."

"Except none of them are in Las Vegas."

Quinn frowned. "Where are they—?"

"We don't know for sure. The President had me contact Race Courtney. He went to Vegas to look around. The Latins had reservations, and were checked in by travel reps. However, no one has actually seen any of them—and all the rooms are empty."

"Now we're getting sinister—"

"Exactly."

"What's Race's read on it—?"

"He's as confused as the rest of us. He asked me to brief you, tell you he would keep checking."

"Sounds like you're ready for take-off," Quinn said. "How do I get in touch with you—?"

"I'm headed for Utah. Some of the officials out there are very uneasy about being designated the nation's safety net. Race asked if I could hold a few hands."

"Where's Race now?"

Anne shook her head. "I don't know."

"You should know we're activating to Condition Two, so there's going to be a lot dumped into that safety net in the next few days. Utah, Idaho, Oregon, Wyoming, Nevada, Arizona—everything between the Rockies and Sierra Nevadas. You might prepare all those governors for the possibility— the probability—of martial law being declared. Keep in close touch, Madam Vice President."

"Race suggested I stay at NECCO headquarters at Hill Field—"

"Excellent idea. I'll have them clean out a closet for you."

"You keep in touch too, Quinn. The President—Maggie and me— we're all a little up tight."

Four hours later, Race Courtney reached Quinn at his office in NECCO headquarters.

"You still playing the slots in Vegas?" Quinn asked.

"Not hardly. I'm in Mexico City. Maggie's friends moved the party down here."

"That's interesting. They still partying—?"

"Nobody in town. They all caught connecting flights home within an hour of arriving."

"Very strange."

"Flight reservations were made weeks ago. Charter flights out of New York, direct to Mexico City."

"So Las Vegas was never in the plan—"

"A dust storm to confuse people like us."

"What now?"

"I'm nosing around. Something's going on, buddy. I'll try to contact Vicente—he should have some answers. By the way, have you called Jill?"

Quinn felt a flush of guilt. "Not yet—"

"Don't bother. She's gone."

"Gone where—?"

"She and Stacy took off for Utah yesterday in the van—Leah's with them. I encouraged it. A good way to get them out of Washington for awhile."

"Good. We're moving to Condition Two. And Anne Ashford is on her way to Salt Lake as we speak."

"I'll be in Utah no later than tomorrow. Do me a favor. Call our embassy in Mexico City and have a Marine helicopter standing by. I may need a fast exit. The airport is crawling with uniforms and I'm attracting a lot of attention. I don't think it's my personality."

"Watch yourself, Race. Whatever's going down, it smells."

"That could be me. I just had a taco and beans—"

# 12

## CONDITION TWO

Race was unable to make contact with Vicente Cabrillo, the NECCO agent stationed in Mexico City. Vicente was not in his apartment, the tourist gift shop he operated was closed, and Race did not spot him at any of the regular rendezvous points. Race left messages at two dead drops then took a room at a cheap hotel out of the tourist zone.

The next morning, Race sat at a window table in a small cafe. He had toast and fresh-squeezed orange juice, then drank several cups of strong coffee. He pretended to read the newspaper but maintained a constant surveillance of the busy stream of people outside. Perhaps that was why he was surprised when a waiter put another cup of coffee in front of him and leaned over to brush at the crumbs of toast on the stained tablecloth.

"After all that coffee, you must need to pee," the waiter murmured. Race's eyes lifted to see Vicente, studiously avoiding eye contact. Vicente straightened, and pointed toward the back of the cafe. "El inodoro, senor."

Vicente left and after a couple more swallows of coffee, Race got up and made his way back to the toilet. It was small and dirty, and smelled very bad. It was also empty—at least, it appeared that way until Vicente appeared from one of the stalls. Race started to speak, but Vicente put a finger to his lips and pressed his ear against the door leading back to the cafe. He suddenly backed away, and both men moved back into the stalls. Vicente's hand reached over the partition between them, holding a pistol.

"You may need this, amigo," he hissed.

Race took the pistol, automatically checking to make sure it was loaded and ready. He looked down and grimaced as he saw the toilet was clogged and had not been flushed after apparently being used more than once.

Filthy water, toilet paper and other things had slopped over the bowl onto the floor. Fortunately, it was only a few seconds before the outer door opened.

"You here, Vicente?" a voice hissed softly.

Vicente stepped out of the booth. "Were you followed?" he asked the small, nervous man who entered and quickly closed the door.

The man shook his head. "I don't think so."

"You need to be sure of such things."

"How can you be sure? Fariocha's men are everywhere."

Vicente called softly to Race, who stepped out into the open. The small man went from nervous to frightened and looked as if he might bolt. Vicente quickly raised both hands to reassure him.

"This is my friend from the United States—so he is also your friend," Vicente said swiftly. "He is here to help us."

Race thought it would be bad timing to tell the little man the situation actually was reversed—he was counting on Vicente to help him. The man appeared greatly relieved at Vicente's assurance.

"This is Alejandro," Vicente told Race. "He is a member of the Colombian intelligence community, in Medellin. Alejandro is a friend of the Estados Unidos. Is this not so, Alejandro—?"

Alejandro nodded his head vigorously. The man was deeply agitated. He kept glancing back at the door leading to the cafe, making sure it had not opened.

"Can you take me to the Estados Unidos?" the man queried. He was looking closely into Race's face.

"If there is cause," Race answered.

"I cannot go back to Colombia, not after what I have seen."

"What is that, Alejandro?" Vicente asked. "You said only that you wanted to get to the United States. Why can't you go back to Medellin?"

"I saw them—and they know it."

"Saw what, Alejandro—?" Vicente pressed.

"The missiles."

Race was suddenly very attentive. "Missiles in Colombia—?"

"In Colombia, yes," the little man said quickly, "but I know they are in other countries as well."

"How many missiles are we talking about—?" Race asked.

"A great many, senor. A great many."

"How long have they been there?" Vicente queried.

"Just a few days, I think."

"What is the purpose of so many missiles?" Race asked him.

"I don't know that, senor. I heard military officers talking about a scourging—Operation Scourge, is what they called it. They saw me and now they are trying to kill me."

Race frowned at the frightened little man. "Who's trying to kill you, Alejandro?"

"The Brazilians. The agents of Colonel Fariocha."

Race frowned at Vicente. "Who is this Fariocha—?"

"A monster, senor," the little man said, not waiting for Vicente to reply. "A monster who kills and tortures."

Vicente shrugged. "That was one of the things I have to report. Colonel Jorge Fariocha is head of military intelligence in Brazil. His men have been filtering into Mexico City for weeks. Now they are everywhere."

"Does the Mexican government know this?"

Vicente nodded. "The government has given full authority to these CASA agents."

"Did you say CASA—?" Race repeated, remembering who had first mentioned it.

"That's what they call themselves—agents of CASA intelligence. It's not just a Brazilian force. It's a new intelligence unit made up of agents from many Latin countries. That obviously includes Mexico."

"Can you tell us more about these missiles?" Race asked Alejandro. "Are they deployed—are they aimed at a target? Can you tell us anything more about this Operation Scourge?"

Before Alejandro could say anything, the door burst open and two men lunged into the room. Both had pistols in their hands. Both fired at the same time, and bullets thudded into the frightened little man from Colombia. A quick glance told Race that if the bullet in his chest hadn't killed Alejandro, the one in his forehead certainly had.

The concentration on Alejandro cost the Brazilian agents their lives. Before they could shift the muzzles of their guns to target Race and Vicente, both of them were dead.

Vicente motioned to the high window in the restroom. As if they knew what the other was thinking, they reached down and grabbed the smaller of the dead intruders. With a heave, they smashed out the window with his body, letting it drop outside. Each man quickly pulled himself up and through the broken window. In moments, they were fleeing down a narrow alley behind the cafe.

"Were those Fariocha's men?" Race asked, racing close beside Vicente.

Vicente frowned at him. "I thought they were CIA. I swear the one we threw out the window was wearing a false mustache—"

"Very funny," Race panted. "You know where we're going?"

"The embassy sounds good to me," Vicente wheezed between strides. "It won't be healthy around here—"

They burst out of the alley just as a black Mercedes squealed around a corner a few yards ahead of them. Both Race and Vicente realized it was futile to keep running. They turned, and the Mercedes skidded to a stop. The car doors were flung open, flames spitting from gun muzzles as two men jumped out. Both Race and Vicente fired and the two shooters were flung backwards, dead before hitting the pavement.

On the run, Race fired through the open front door of the Mercedes. The driver slumped over the wheel and the horn started blaring.

"Let's go, Vicente," Race said exultantly. "We just got ourselves a taxi—"

Vicente didn't answer. Race looked back over his shoulder and saw Vicente crumpled on the sidewalk. He raced back to the fallen man but it took only a glance to see that Vicente was dead. A bullet had smashed into the middle of his face, ripping out through the top of his skull.

"Sorry, buddy," Race muttered. "Wish you could have made it."

There wasn't time for more. A wolf pack undoubtedly was in pursuit, and Race had to make sure the information the little man from Colombia had given them reached the right ears. Race ran to the car, pulled the dead driver out onto the roadway, then slammed the doors shut and took off with a squeal of tires.

\* \* \*

That same day, just before midnight, China launched its sweep through Asia. Hundreds of thousands of Chinese troops poured across the border into North Viet Nam and began advancing toward Hanoi. There was no opposition.

A surprisingly strong naval force disgorged huge forces into South Viet Nam and overran Ho Chi Minh, the former city of Saigon, without a shot being fired. Troops swarmed inland to Phnum Penh. Cambodia bowed like the others to the awesome tide of armed might.

There was also a twin push into Korea. Troops flooded south across the border toward P'Yongyang as a naval force came ashore at Inch'on, swiftly moving east to Seoul. Again, there was no organized opposition.

Another Chinese naval task force moved in at the same time on Krung Thep, known to westerners as Bangkok. Panic swept through Thailand, although it would be weeks before it fell completely under Chinese control.

It was an incredible show of force that left the world stunned, its leaders incapable of reacting to the enormity of the Chinese aggression. Operation Red Tiger rolled through Asia as swiftly and effortlessly as its planners had envisioned.

As night continued to pull its curtain across the continent, Operation Red Star burst across the former Soviet Union.

Although the preparations for a military takeover of the republics was as carefully planned as the Chinese campaign, fierce fighting flared in almost every region. Coming on top of the eruption across Asia, a shudder of fear swept through the entire world.

\* \* \*

In Washington, Sam Baldwin called an emergency meeting of a select group of his top advisors. They were gathered in the Roosevelt Room, across from the Oval Office, on the main floor of the West Wing. There was Anne Ashford, who had been hurriedly recalled from Utah, James Van Durlin, Duff Jenkins, Admiral Boots Brunswick, Stuart Akker, Quinn Adams, and one other special guest—General Aaron Stark. All were seated around a long table, with Sam Baldwin at the head, his back to the cold fireplace.

"All right," Baldwin growled, "the fat's in the fire. What do we do about it?"

The President's glance swept around the table, settling on the head of the Joint Chiefs. Admiral Brunswick cleared his throat, gathered his thoughts.

"Frankly, Mr. President," Boots finally said, "we're doing just about all that can be done from a military standpoint. We've been flooding Europe and the Pacific with troops, planes and ships since first learning about these operations. We—"

"What about the capacity for nuclear response?" Secretary of State Van Durlin interrupted. "Do we have it, and," he added, his eyes swiveling to Sam Baldwin, "are we prepared to use it?"

Brunswick's brows lifted. "We have it, Mr. Secretary, here and in Europe. But to my knowledge, there have been no reports of direct threats to the West by either the Russians or the Chinese."

"We want to be sure we don't signal any threat on our part, Admiral," Baldwin said quickly. "Especially not involving nuclear weapons. For now, we treat this whole thing as not vital to the interests of the United States."

"There are treaties, Mr. President," Van Durlin murmured.

"We ignore all those treaties for now," Baldwin grunted. "We're sitting between two firestorms and I want to be certain this country isn't trapped in the middle. Any indication that Japan is being threatened?"

"I was informed by the Japanese ambassador, just before coming to this meeting," Van Durlin replied, "that the Chinese have assured them, through official channels, no threat to Japan exists. The Chinese used the phrase, 'peaceful coexistence' in their communique."

"They probably sent the same message to Korea, Viet Nam and all those other countries," Baldwin snorted.

"I doubt that, Mr. President," Van Durlin demurred. "The Chinese and the Russians both appear to be taking great precautions to avoid anything that will automatically trigger a response from us. I don't believe either country wants to provoke us into engagement, not at this stage, at least."

"If not now, when?" Brunswick muttered. "Didn't someone say that once?"

Baldwin switched his attention to Quinn Adams. "You seem to be ahead of the situation, Mr. Adams, judging from the reports on my desk."

"We have begun Condition Two extradition procedures," Quinn replied. "We're moving people and materials to Pyramid Seven—"

"Where is Pyramid Seven?" Brunswick asked.

"The Intermountain West, Admiral."

"Why there?"

"It's boxed in by mountains on all sides," Quinn told him. "From a defensive point of view—"

"Who are you expecting to defend against?" the admiral asked, his tone querulous.

Quinn gave a little lift of his shoulders. "It's called strategic planning, Admiral."

"Nevertheless, Quinn," Akker complained, "your unit is acting very high and mighty. You really should bring the rest of us into closer contact."

"We're not high and mighty, Stu—we're high level security," Quinn answered, his voice remaining calm. "The only way to maintain that security is to keep a tight, small circle. A report to the CIA would be on the front page of the Washington Post the next day."

"You have no right to say that," Akker said angrily.

Quinn's eyebrows raised. "You mean there really are no leaks out of Central Intelligence—?"

"I resent that—"

"No offense intended, Stu," Quinn murmured, "just making a point."

Baldwin interjected himself into the exchange.

"I wish every department of government was as prepared as Mr. Adams to meet this situation. I get the feeling a lot of us are sitting around with our pants down—" He flashed a quick glance at Anne Ashford. "— with all due apologies, Madame Vice President. I know I called you back almost as soon as you got there, Anne, but what is your assessment of the situation in Pyramid Seven?"

"A lot of people are in shock, Mr. President," Anne Ashford replied, "and that's before they have any idea of what's going to hit them."

"Are there any major concerns?"

"Only several hundred," Anne said wryly. "We need an immediate declaration of martial law. We're going to upset everyone's life in that whole region. A strong military presence will help people accept that."

"Keep them calm if you can, Madame Vice President," Baldwin grimaced, "but do what you have to do. Use the full authority of this office."

Baldwin looked at Quinn again. "This might be a good time for you to introduce General Stark. All of us know your reputation, General," he added, nodding at Stark, "and I want to personally thank you for joining the team again. Go ahead, Quinn."

"General Stark has agreed to come out of retirement during this emergency and once again serve as the commander of NECCO forces. As you know, he acted as Supreme Commander of all United States forces during the Eagle Red emergency seven years ago. I add my gratitude to that of President Baldwin for Aaron giving up some great fishing in New England to take on a very formidable task."

Duff Jenkins, the White House chief of staff, lifted a hand in greeting to Stark. "Hope you brought some of those Maine lobsters with you, Aaron. The water around here just might get hot enough to cook them."

Admiral Brunswick stood up and leaned across the table to shake Stark's hand. "I served under you back then, General, and was proud to do it. Glad to have you aboard."

The others in the room added their greetings. Admiral Brunswick gave Stark a quizzical stare.

"Did I understand correctly that you'll be directing the military affairs of this NECCO thing of Mr. Adams?" he asked.

Stark understood what the admiral was really asking.

"My reactivation has nothing to do with the regular military, Admiral. We'll act independently, but hopefully we'll be able to fully cooperate with the other services."

"No one's ever mentioned the size of this NECCO force," Akker said, obviously still angry. "I'll confess to trying to pull some information out of a computer or two, but it seems NECCO keeps its files well protected."

"I assure you, Stu," Quinn said, "that the lack of information about NECCO is not accidental. Nor are our computer locks."

Akker pressed the point. "It still seems advisable that the military, the CIA, and the Bureau—at a bare minimum—be informed of your activities, if we are to achieve the cooperation General Stark mentioned."

President Baldwin cut him off.

"Let me make something clear to everyone. This thing of Mr. Adams, as Boots called it, is the National Emergency Coordinated Command Organization. It is commissioned by presidential authority to do whatever is needed. Should NECCO elevate this or any other emergency to Condition One, requiring only my authority, all military forces, and all government agencies," he added, putting emphasis on the 'all', "will become subject to NECCO direction. That includes the Joint Chiefs, all our regular military forces, the CIA, the FBI, and the Bureau in charge of acquisition of toilet paper. Is that fully understood?"

Akker leaned back in his chair, mouth thinning into a clamped line. He said nothing. Brunswick drummed his fingers for a moment on the table, studying the two NECCO officials sitting across from him. What the president just said left little room for questions.

"I appreciate you clearing up that point, Mr. President. I assure General Stark and Mr. Adams that in the event a Condition One emergency is declared, they will have the full cooperation of the Joint Chiefs."

"Thank you, Boots," the president said quietly. "I would appreciate you passing that down the line." He nodded at Stark. "Any comments on what you've heard so far, General?"

"I fully support the Condition Two alert, and the selection of Pyramid Seven. It has some vulnerabilities, but so does every other relocation site. It will add to the panic that is sure to erupt when the public learns what is happening, but I see no alternative. We must proceed as if Condition One is inevitable."

Stark looked directly at Brunswick. "I particularly appreciate the support of the Joint Chiefs. There are a few questions about the outflow of resources, but I'm sure those can be cleared up once I'm able to study the reports. Incidentally, Admiral Brunswick, I have one request, and though I'm not fully briefed yet, one recommendation."

"Your input is welcome, General," Brunswick said. "What is the request?"

"A report on fleet dispositions. What and where. Atlantic, Pacific, Mediterranean, Indian—wherever. Especially the submarine fleet. I'm sure Mr. Adams has much of the information available, but it would be helpful to have the latest updates."

Brunswick looked hesitant. "That is highly classified information—"

"Admiral," Baldwin said, "Mr. Adams, and now General Stark, have higher security clearances than anyone in this room, including myself—and yourself."

Brunswick nodded. "I understand, Mr. President. I'll have the report in your hands in a couple of hours, General."

"I appreciate that. It's not a capricious request, I assure you, Admiral." He tapped the black file folder in front of him, similar to those everyone had received. It contained a summary of military and Central Intelligence reports dealing with the international activity of the past few hours, and had been hastily prepared for this meeting.

"One other thing, Admiral. I notice we have satellite photos showing the Chinese naval forces involved in their various landing activities."

"Not all of the landings, but most," Brunswick confirmed. "We'll have data from daylight passes processed in a couple of hours. That should provide accurate detail of all their invasion forces."

"I was surprised at the apparent size of their navy," Stark continued. "It appears to have doubled or tripled in an amazingly short space of time."

Brunswick frowned, nodding agreement. "I noticed the same thing, General. There's no way they could have built that much tonnage without us being aware of it."

"So where did all those ships come from?" Baldwin asked.

"Difficult to tell from the night photos, but we're enhancing them and all other pictures taken in later passes. Personally, I believe that many ships could only come from one source—Russia."

Van Durlin was surprised. "The Russians? Surely we would know about such a transaction?"

Stark gave Akker a quick glance. "Not if the ships were covertly detached from the Baltic and Black Sea fleets."

The president didn't glance at the CIA director—he glared at him. "That true, Stu?"

"We can't be sure."

"You can't be sure if the Chinese bought, or stole, half the Russian navy?"

Akker scowled defensively. "There have been reports over the last few months of Russian ships sailing from the Baltic and Black Sea fleets, that's true. They were individual ships, not battle groups, with a lot of widely dispersed destinations. Orders showed they were mostly on sea trials and training missions. Those ships have been tied up in port for several years."

"Well, the Chinese have them now," Baldwin snapped. He opened his copy of the black file and skidded the photos inside it down the table toward the CIA director. "Take another look, Mr. Director. You telling us those ships came from Toys R Us?"

Admiral Brunswick's face showed his anger. "That's a tremendous build-up of Chinese naval power, Mr. Akker. I can't believe the CIA missed it. The military should have been warned."

"You had observers at St. Petersburg and Odessa," Akker snapped. "Your people were in a better position than we were to detect such activities."

"I didn't realize the mission of the CIA had been redefined as a back-up to military intelligence," Brunswick said coldly.

"We haven't got time for this," Baldwin said sharply. He looked over at General Stark. "You mentioned a recommendation, General—"

"Yes, sir," Stark said. Again he directed his attention to Admiral Brunswick. "You will probably consider this presumptuous, Admiral, but I strongly recommend that you immediately put every vessel out to sea that can get underway. That is especially true of all submarines and all carriers."

Brunswick frowned back at him. "Why would you recommend that, General?"

"A lesson taught us over fifty years ago, Admiral, at Pearl Harbor. A ship at anchor is a sitting duck."

"You expect us to come under attack?"

"Not a matter of expectations, Admiral—precautions. We won't be dealing with aircraft this time if an attack does occur. Missiles—possibly nuclear missiles—will be a whole lot more destructive than bombs dropped from Japanese carrier planes."

Baldwin showed his concern. "You really think we could be facing something like that, General?"

"We can't rule it out, Mr. President. That means we must prepare for such a contingency. The best way to do that is scatter our ships out to sea. I'm sure that if a missile attack is planned, now or in the future, every naval port and shipyard will be primary targets."

"Makes sense to me," Baldwin muttered. He glanced at Brunswick. "How do you feel about that, Admiral—?"

"I still feel strongly that neither the Russians or the Chinese plan such an attack, not with all that's occupying them on such broad fronts, but I certainly agree with General Stark that it would be irresponsible to rule out the possibility." He nodded at Stark. "There aren't too many ships ready to put to sea on either coast, but I see the wisdom in your recommendation, sir."

"Get them out of port as soon as possible, Admiral. Worry about readiness later. Use the reserves, even the Sea Scouts if you have to, but we need to change those sitting ducks into birds of prey."

Baldwin looked around the table. "All right, let's sort out some of this crap before we call in the thundering herds of experts—"

# 13

## CONDITION ONE

Race Courtney arrived back in Washington, D.C., two days after the violence in Mexico City. A Marine helicopter, on alert after Quinn's call, whisked Race out of the city minutes after arriving at the embassy in the stolen Mercedes.

The Mercedes was quickly driven away and parked in a part of the city where normally it would be stripped to the chassis minutes after the driver was out of sight. This time, however, the car was stolen intact, repainted, and sold—all in less than twenty-four hours.

Race was flown south to Veracruz, mainly because that would not be an expected flight pattern. A light twin-prop piloted by a man on the CIA payroll took him north up the coast to a private landing strip near Tampico. From there, he crossed the Gulf to Houston in a small business jet painted black with no numbers. The plane, the pilot told him, was normally used on night flights to run drug shipments into Louisiana. The pilot didn't explain his connection with the CIA and Race didn't really want to know. From Houston, a NASA jet flew him to Andrews Air Force Base.

An hour and a half after reaching NECCO headquarters, Race, Quinn and Aaron Stark were admitted into the Oval Office. Baldwin came forward to shake hands with all three men.

"What's this about, Mr. Adams? You made it sound important over the phone—"

"It is, Mr. President," Quinn replied. "Important enough that I recommend we use the quiet room—just the four of us."

Baldwin reached over and punched in a number on his telephone. "Duff—you know who's in here with me. I want to use the downstairs conference room. Make sure we're not disturbed."

Minutes later, they entered a conference room on the basement level of the West Wing that was completely enclosed in lead—walls, ceiling and floor—and defied even the most sophisticated eavesdropping technology. Even the electrical wiring and outlets were encased in lead shields. Whatever was said in this room went no farther than those high security walls. The heavy, electrically operated door closed and double locks slid into place.

"All right, gentlemen," Baldwin said, motioning for them to sit down. "It doesn't get any more secure than this. What's so important—?"

"We're recommending immediate activation of Condition One, Mr. President," Quinn said grimly.

"Something's happened, I take it—"

"Yes, sir. I'll let Race fill you in."

Race quickly repeated what he had learned in Mexico City about missiles in Colombia and other South American countries, the presence of CASA forces, and Operation Scourge.

When Race finished, Baldwin leaned back in his chair and stared at the three men. "What is going on?"

"Difficult to say, Mr. President," Quinn muttered. "Whatever it is, I don't like it."

"Neither do I," Baldwin grated. "Missiles in Colombia? What are they going to do with them?"

"If the Latin countries are working together, and this CASA organization seems to indicate that," Quinn said, "then it's unlikely they're going to shoot at each other. That leaves only one other target, Mr. President."

"Attack the United States?" Baldwin sounded as if the idea was completely incredulous. "That's insane—"

"Nevertheless, Mr. President," Aaron Stark said, "it's difficult to reach any other conclusion."

Baldwin fastened a questioning stare on Race. "You sure about this, Race? Maybe this Colombian was hallucinating on drugs. They have a good supply down there."

"Those CASA men wanted him dead, Mr. President. If they hadn't been so set on that, I might not be sitting here."

"So you believe his story?"

"Absolutely, sir."

"Operation Scourge. Do we know anything about it?" the president asked.

"Just that it exists, Mr. President," Quinn said. "We have our people working on it, but it will take time."

"Call the Israelis," Baldwin growled. "They seem to know everything that's happening everywhere."

"They didn't mention it specifically by name at our last contact, sir," Quinn said, "although they did confirm our own intelligence that strange things are going on down there."

"More than strange, apparently," the president said. He looked at his visitors. "So you're proposing we go to Condition One emergency procedures?"

"Under the circumstances," Quinn replied, "we don't really have an option."

"What exactly will that entail?"

"First thing, sir, is we get you out of Washington. All the key people in government and Congress—you've seen the lists, Mr. President."

"We go to Pyramid Seven, I take it."

"Correct, sir. Then we start doing the same for key people in every occupation—all the brain power from all across the country. We also start moving strategic materials, weapons, military—"

"We'll need to bring the Joint Chiefs in on that," Baldwin interrupted. "The whole military situation is confused right now, with all the deployments abroad."

"If you approve Condition One, Mr. President," Stark said, "I'll meet with them within the hour."

"I'd be more comfortable if the Pentagon remained staffed until an attack actually occurs—if it does." He shook his head in disbelief. "Hard to imagine such a thing happening."

"Let's hope we have time to evacuate if it does," Stark murmured. "I understand your concerns. We can proceed with minimal disturbance to military channels, Mr. President, if that is your wish."

"But you advise against it—"

"I do, Mr. President."

"Well, at least put the Pentagon at the end of the chain. Tell Brunswick to start moving all available men and equipment from the rest of the country into Pyramid Seven. Can it handle an influx like that—?"

"Military locations are selected throughout the intermountain states, Mr. President," Stark assured him. "We can handle everything the Joint Chiefs send."

"Anne Ashford is already there, isn't she?"

"Yes, sir. Up to her neck in arrangements."

"What about you three—?"

"We're moving all of NECCO to Utah," Quinn said. "We're sealing off headquarters here in Virginia. If it should be penetrated—well, there's going to be the mother of all explosions."

"When do you want me to leave—?"

"Immediately, Mr. President."

"Any of you want to ride to Utah with me—?"

"I'll accept that offer, sir," Quinn said, "along with Race. It will give us an opportunity to brief you on problems that will need your immediate attention."

"I'll confer with the Joint Chiefs, push a few buttons, then join you out there," Stark said. "I want to be sure Admiral Brunswick did something about all those sitting ducks—especially knowing what we do now."

"I'll have Duff prepare a declaration of Condition One for me to sign. That will put you officially in command, and you can order the Chiefs to do anything you think is necessary."

"Thank you, Mr. President."

Half an hour after Air Force One lifted off, headed west to Utah, the incredible, the impossible, became grim reality.

Missiles began to rain down from the skies.

# 14

## OPERATION SCOURGE

General Aaron Stark was meeting with the Joint Chiefs at the Pentagon when the missile attack was first reported. At first, there was stunned reluctance to accept the report as factual. Within minutes, however, a steady stream of aides brought updated reports of strikes across the country. The meeting quickly adjourned to the deep level war room. They gathered in the observation level, watching the feverish activity going on the cavernous, computer-filled area below them.

Wall-sized electronic screens of the continental United States were already blinking with red dots as missile strikes were recorded. The military officers stared at it, unwilling to believe what they were seeing.

"There must be hundreds of strikes," Brunswick breathed.

General William Zabriskie, head of Army operations, leaned over a speaker, addressing the duty officer, an Army colonel who seemed almost as mesmerized by the screens as the Joint Chiefs.

"Are those all missile hits, Colonel?" Zabriskie asked.

The colonel looked back at the observation room, saw the assembled power, and nodded. He leaned over the mike in front of him.

"Yes, sir. We're getting at least twenty reports a minute, General."

"Any of them nuclear?" Brunswick asked.

"No, sir. Not that we're aware of."

"Where are they coming from?" Zabriskie growled.

"All from the south, sir."

General Gus Sorenson, of the Marines, leaned over the mike. "What does that mean, Colonel—Alabama?"

"No, sir," the colonel snapped, obviously under tremendous pressure. "It means South America, sir."

"Do we have tracking verification of that—?"

"Not for the first hits, General Sorenson. We're on line now. The missiles are incoming from at least ten locations down there. Some apparently were launched from subs in the Gulf."

The Joint Chiefs stared at each other in disbelief. It became more incredible with every flashing dot.

"Where did they get this kind of firepower?" Brunswick said, not expecting anyone to answer. "And missile submarines—that's unbelievable!"

Aaron Stark spoke into the microphone. "Do we have any reports on casualties, Colonel?"

The Colonel flashed a puzzled look at him, not recognizing who had asked the question. He was with the Joint Chiefs, though, so it must be all right.

"Not yet, General. Probably heavy. Many of the cities have taken a dozen hits or more. No apparent pattern, sir. They just seem to be trying to erase the target."

"Is the frequency of incoming slowing down—?" Stark asked.

"Not really, sir. They seem to be firing in waves. Almost simultaneous hits all over for about ten minutes, maybe a ten minute break, then it starts again. We've seen four waves so far—could be another any minute."

"Looks like our military installations are taking a beating," Zabriskie muttered.

"Every major base throughout the mid-west and the east, sir. We undoubtedly have taken heavy casualties among military personnel."

"Have all the air bases been alerted—?" General Tad Thorne asked.

"Didn't need to alert them, General," the colonel replied. "Base commanders went autonomous when the missiles started coming in. Everything that can fly is already scrambled." He looked up at the window again. "Any orders, Admiral Brunswick—?"

"Keep on it, Colonel. Bring in the whole staff. We need reports and updates as soon as you get them. Get a printout of where those missiles are coming from. You're handling this well, Colonel. Good work."

"Thank you, sir."

The officers took seats along the table fronting the observation room, studying the activity below. It was still a numbing situation, but the years of training and experience of these battle-proven officers was taking over.

Brunswick looked down the line toward General Thorne. "We have planes airborne. Time to return some of that mail, General—"

"That's assuming they're armed and fueled for long-range—which many probably aren't," Thorne muttered.

"What about our missiles?" General Sorenson asked. "Once we pinpoint where this Latin hardware is coming from—"

"Every missile in the system, General, is programmed for a European or Asian target. Nothing is pointed at South America," Thorne replied. His frustration was showing plainly. "It will take time to change those coordinates."

"They've hit all our naval installations on both coasts, it looks like," Brunswick muttered. "However, thanks to the advise of General Stark, a lot of ships put out to sea the last few days. A lot don't have adequate fuel or weapons, and some have only skeleton crews, but at least they're afloat. Talk about Pearl Harbor—this is a thousand times worse."

He looked at Stark. "You're uncanny, General—"

"Anyone care to speculate on what will happen next?" Stark asked, staring at the large wall maps.

"We can't speculate until the missiles stop, can we—?" Admiral Robert Bradshaw of the Coast Guard, replied.

"I think we can, Admiral," Stark said grimly. "It's right up there in front of us."

Brunswick was also staring at the map. "Heavy concentration of targets in the mid-western states, and along the east coast. Looks like only San Diego, San Francisco and Seattle have been hit on the west coast."

"The Gulf ports," Sorenson added, "from Corpus Christi to Pensacola, are also taking a beating. Judging from the number of impacts, that area is taking the heaviest pounding in the whole country."

"What do you think is the reason for that, General Sorenson?" Stark asked.

The Marine general studied the map, came to the same conclusion Stark had already reached. "The bastards are going to invade us—"

"I agree," Stark nodded. "My guess is they'll come ashore in the Gulf area, and push up through the Mississippi valley. They've softened that whole route north—military bases, utilities, industrial sites, all the state capitals. It's going to be difficult to organize effective retaliation, especially if they move fast."

"We must be dealing with that new coalition of South American states," Brunswick said tersely. "None of those countries would dare do something this audacious on their own."

"I don't see how they did it even as a coalition," Zabriskie grated. "They simply do not have the expertise, or the hardware, to do this."

"Well, they're doing it," Brunswick grimaced, "and we're standing here watching it happen. Looks like another wave of incoming just started—"

The screens were showing another forest of red dots.

General Thorne spoke what was in all their minds. "Wonder why we've had no hits here in Washington?"

"I suspect we'll get our turn soon," Stark said somberly. "Which brings us back to Condition One, gentlemen. We need to be on a plane within the next thirty minutes—"

"We can't leave now," Zabriskie snapped angrily. "We're needed here—"

"We're seeing the start of what I suspect is the Operation Scourge that surfaced in Mexico City," Stark said. "It is imperative we all leave Washington. The evacuation to Pyramid Seven has already begun, and with such widespread devastation to the military establishment, it will be vital to regroup quickly. I'm certain we'll be dealing with an invasion force in a matter of hours. Those Latin troops must be stopped before they sweep up the Mississippi valley. Once they do that, we'll be cut in half. We won't be able to stop them spreading toward the Atlantic coast and taking the entire eastern third of the country."

"Even so, we can't just shut down the Pentagon," Zabriskie insisted, "not with all this going on. If they do target the east, it's all the more important we keep this as a base for operations."

"Your decision," Stark shrugged. "Leave it operating, but there are three hundred senior officers who will be evacuated to Pyramid Seven immediately, including yourselves. I don't want to pull rank, gentlemen, but I remind you I am operating under Presidential authority." He glanced at his watch. "NECCO Rangers are waiting for us at Andrews. Your families have probably already left for Pyramid Seven."

"Shutting down the Pentagon is unthinkable—" Zabriskie protested.

"General Zabriskie," Stark said, cutting him off, "the only unthinkable thing here is not performing your sworn duty."

The scene at Andrews Air Force Base had the appearance of panic, but everything actually was remarkably under control. As Stark said, many of the families of those designated for evacuation had already left. A couple of huge stratocruisers lifted off, filled with bewildered officers. More stood in line, waiting for the lines of military personnel to board. The taxi strips were full.

The jumbo Boeing 747 carrying the Joint Chiefs, Aaron Stark, and other top Pentagon officials, was directed to the head of the line and was quickly cleared for takeoff. It was less than ten minutes out of Andrews, still climbing into the western skies, when the plane suddenly was tossed thousands of feet into the air.

The jet twisted and was flung helplessly about for some two minutes, seeming like several lifetimes to the people inside the plane. Finally, control was regained and the plane leveled out.

The pilot's voice, low and stricken, came over the intercom. "They just nuked Washington."

The plane veered right and people crowded to the windows. The sight that greeted them caused the faces of even the most hardened career officer to blanche.

A nuclear mushroom cloud could be seen billowing over the city, now barely visible on the horizon. It was the shock wave from that explosion that had flung the giant plane about like a toy, even at this distance.

Then, to everyone's horror, a blinding flash could be seen over the city. Everyone cried out and covered their eyes, jerking away from the windows. As the brilliant light faded, people came back to the windows in time to see a second mushroom cloud start to form. The first was now grotesquely twisted and dissipating.

The pilot of the 747 pointed the nose of the jumbo jet away from Washington, gave full throttle to the massive engines, and began climbing as steeply as specs would allow. Everyone braced themselves for another cyclonic nuclear shockwave, tears of pain on leathery cheeks.

The world's symbol of democracy and freedom was gone, blasted apart in atomic winds and fury. No one doubted that most, if not all, landmarks and life in the stricken capital were destroyed.

It was all so sudden. So impossible. So numbing.

And so frighteningly real.

# 15

## IN HARM'S WAY

When they left Washington, Stacy and Jill decided to make it a leisurely drive west. There was no reason to hurry, and both women were eager to enjoy the freedom of the road, away from pressures and routines and husbands who were irritatingly absorbed in work these past few weeks.

For two days, they sang songs, played games with Leah, talked and laughed almost incessantly about life in general. The conversation hadn't settled on serious matters until this evening. They were pushing to reach Denver, still several hours away, before stopping for the night. Perhaps it was the sense of pressure again that finally caused Jill to reach down inside and release some of the trouble bottled up inside her. Stacy was driving, keeping the van at seventy-five along an almost deserted freeway. Leah was asleep in the back seat.

Jill slipped off her shoes and pulled her feet up onto the seat, holding her chin on her knees.

"I've been such a brat. I wouldn't blame Quinn if he did hate me."

"I'm relieved to hear that," Stacy said, staring straight ahead. "He told me just before we left that's the way he feels."

Jill stared at her. "Quinn hates me—?" She saw the little smile begin to pull at Stacy's mouth. "Don't tease like that—I'd die if he really did hate me."

"What's the problem between you two, anyway?" Stacy asked. "Everything seemed so peachy keen—then suddenly you're a mess."

"I'm not sure he loves me anymore, Stacy. I hardly ever see him—"

"Quinn and Race are both practically strangers these days. That's because of their jobs—it has nothing to do with their feelings for us."

"It's more than that," Jill muttered. "He's seeing that Israeli woman again—Joanna Shazebak."

"Seeing her—you make it sound like he's dating her. Is he—?"

"I don't know."

"Don't give me that."

"She called him in the middle of the night—"

"And if she hadn't, you'd both be dead."

"She had our private number—"

"She's a spy, Jill. Spies know things like that."

"I think Quinn has been seeing her all along. He told me he spent three days with her in Tel Aviv a week or so ago."

"Spent three days with her—as in having sex?"

"I don't know."

"Yes you do—"

"He denies it. Says it was just business."

"Do you believe him?"

"I don't know."

"Yes you do—"

"All right, I believe him—that time. This woman makes me feel so—well, so totally inadequate. She goes around killing people with her bare hands, and I make dinner."

"You also go to bed with the man."

"She did that, too—"

"In another life. You can't be jealous of what happened years ago. She's a memory, Jill."

"Not just a memory. I was supposed to go to dinner with her a couple of days ago—"

"So what's the rest of it—?"

"The rest of what—?"

"Something is upsetting you—it's not just Joanna. You've been acting strangely ever since the night you and Quinn were targeted by that hit squad."

Jill put her chin back on her knees. She said nothing, just staring out at the road again. Finally she nodded.

"That really did frighten me. All the shooting, and the noise—men were trying to kill us, Stacy. I've never experienced anything like that before."

"You know why that bothers you so much, don't you—"

"No. Why do you think it does?"

"It triggered memories you don't want to deal with again."

"You're talking about Seattle—the men who raped me."

"No. I'm talking about the day you found out there isn't a Santa Claus—of course I'm talking about the rape."

"All that's behind me, Stacy—" she protested.

"No it isn't—just barely pushed down below the conscious. Those men raped you, Jill—brutally and repeatedly. A woman can't ever forget a nightmare like that. Quinn saved you—saved all of us. What happened a few nights ago—the shooting, the killing—brought it all back, didn't it."

Jill nodded again. This time her voice was a whisper. "It's like I wasn't in that hallway—I was back in Seattle. I can't let that become real again."

"You tried blocking it out before, remember. It didn't work then, and it won't now. If those memories are back, you have to deal with them. You're trying to avoid them by fastening on other things—like your husband having an affair with Joanna. Which, incidentally, I don't believe he is."

Jill was silent for a long time. Stacy cast an occasional sidelong glance at her, keeping quiet, knowing her friend was sorting through a parade of terrible pictures in her mind. The brutal rape by four terrorists seven years ago had left deep scars. She finally recovered from the physical abuse, but it had taken much longer to deal with the emotional damage.

Jill suffered a nervous breakdown and her relationship with Quinn was destroyed. Quinn showed understanding and patience, but Jill was unable to deal with any kind of contact with a man.

It took months of therapy but she did finally learn to deal with it. Soon after that, she married Quinn. The dreadful reality of the rape was accepted, memories no longer haunting. Not until the attack in the apartment building brought it all back. It must be devastating, Stacy thought, to relive a horror buried for seven years.

"What do I do, Stacy?" Jill asked, her voice low and trembling. I can't let memories come between us again—his, or mine."

"Therapy worked before. Maybe you should—"

Stacy frowned at what she suddenly saw in the rear view mirror. "Where did they come from?"

Jill looked back, seeing about twenty or more motorbikes roaring close behind the van. She couldn't see faces clearly, because most were wearing helmets and dark glasses, but the beards and leather jackets and the oddly customized handlebars left no doubt this was a gang of hard-core bikers.

"Speed up, Stacy."

"I'm doing seventy-five," Stacy said, studying the bikers in the mirror.

"I'm going to slow down and let them pass."

The van slowed to sixty and about half of the motorcycles moved ahead, yelling and waving at the two women as they passed on both sides.

"Crazy scumbags," Stacy muttered.

The bikers ahead of the van began to slow gradually. Stacy had to slow too, or run into them. She looked down and saw the speedometer had fallen to forty-five. Alarm began to rise in the two women.

"What are they doing?"

"Having fun," Stacy grimaced. "If they don't get out of my way, I'll have fun running over them."

The bikers in the rear roared past and the whole group picked up speed, the distance between them and the van widening. They got about a mile ahead and both women started to relax.

Stacy flexed her hands, which had been tightly gripping the steering wheel. She gave a little shudder of relief.

"Didn't see anyone I'd like to take to the prom, did you?"

Before Jill could answer, they both gasped in alarm. The gang of bikers suddenly swerved, stopped, and spread their machines across the freeway, blocking both lanes and both shoulders. The distance closed rapidly and Stacy began braking.

"Don't stop," Jill gasped. "Go through them—"

"I can't," Stacy said tightly, "not with Leah in the back. I can't risk hurting her. Lock all the doors—"

The van stopped a couple of feet from the nearest bikes. Bearded, grinning faces appeared at every window, hands clawing as if trying to grab the women. Without warning, one of the bikers crashed a heavy chain against the window of the door beside Stacy. It shattered into little pieces. Another chain shattered the window beside Jill. She screamed and covered up her face. Hands reached in and both doors were unlocked and jerked open.

The women fought as they were dragged out of the van, each held between bearded, leather-clad bikers. They all reeked of sweat and foul body odors. Behind them, Leah started to cry. She was standing up in the van, watching as Stacy and Jill struggled to free themselves. Now the seven-year-old started screaming and calling for her mother. One of the bikers grabbed Leah and dragged her out of the van.

A large, muscular man approached. He was dressed in black leather like all the others, had the same full, bushy beard, and smelled just as bad. One thing distinguished him. He was wearing a lion's skin. The top part of the lion's head was fastened onto the top of his helmet, the skin hanging like a cape over his shoulders. It gave the man a fierce look that started new fears tingling inside both Jill and Stacy.

The man stared narrowly at the two women. One was glaring defiantly, eyes bright with anger. The other was about ready to faint. His stare shifted to the little girl kicking and struggling to get free of the grasp of the biker holding her. Leah was beating her little fists against the biker.

The man in the lion's skin grinned. "Feisty, ain't she. You should be glad she ain't a full-grown woman, Turk."

The other bikers laughed. The lion man reached out a hand toward Leah's cheek.

"What's your name, little girl?"

"None of your business," Leah spat back, pushing his hand away. "You leave my mommy alone, and Auntie Jill—"

"Let me have her, Leo," a biker growled.

Stacy kicked out at the biker. "Put one hand on her and I'll kill you—"

The biker leered and looked at the man in the cape, obviously the leader of the gang. The lion king shook his head.

"Put them all in the van. Once we get to camp, we'll decide who gets what. Nobody gets nothing until I say so."

A roaring inside Jill's head threatened to engulf her. She wanted to scream, but couldn't. Sobbing moans were all that would come. She could feel the strength leaving her legs and knew she was close to fainting. She held on to consciousness desperately, wanting somehow to help Stacy and little Leah.

When the man holding Jill let go, she reached out and tore her fingers down his face. The man clenched a fist and clubbed her hard against the side of her head. His eyes glittered with anger.

"You'll pay for that."

Leo, now sitting astride his bike with a black woman straddled behind him, raised his arm in signal. The motorcycle's roared into life, the noise loud as engines were revved. But just then, the noise of the bikes was drowned out by a powerful throbbing sound above them.

They all looked up, startled. Hovering just a few feet above them was a large military helicopter. It seemed to have come from nowhere. No one had seen it approach, nor drop swiftly until it was no more than ten feet off the ground. It hovered there, rotors holding it in place.

Although the unexpected appearance of the helicopter was startling enough, it was the sight of the heavy caliber machine guns pointing down at the bikers that held them transfixed. And the black-uniformed troopers who conveyed, without any need of words, a deadly threat to every bearded biker below them.

A command, issued over a loud speaker, blared down at the bikers.

"Back off from the van. Stop your engines. Put your hands over your head and do not move. Do it now—"

The arms of every biker shot into the air. This was clearly not a situation where anything was in their favor.

The speaker blared again. "Mrs. Adams—Mrs. Courtney. Rangers will be coming down to assist you. You are safe now, ladies."

Moments later, rope ladders were tossed from the helicopter. Four Rangers descended and quickly crossed to the van. Stacy and Leah stepped out to meet them. The first Ranger to reach them was a young-looking major. Stacy saw all of them were from the elite Special Force.

"Can't tell you how glad we are to see you, Major," Stacy told him. "Did you just happen to be passing by—?"

"No, ma'm," the major said. "We came to find the three of you. Our orders are to take you to NECCO headquarters at Hill Air Force Base, ma'm."

Jill stepped forward. "How on earth did you find us, Major?"

"All vehicles of the Pharaoh Force have locator transponders installed, Mrs. Adams. They send out an electronic signal that can be tracked to the vehicle's location. We figured you would be on this freeway, somewhere near Denver—the transponder signal brought us right to you."

"Your timing couldn't be better, Major," Jill breathed.

Stacy was frowning at the Rangers on the ground and in the helicopter, guns still threatening the bikers.

"What's going on, Major—?"

"You haven't been listening to the radio, I take it."

"We came on this trip to listen to each other. What did we miss—?"

"Last night, this country was attacked, ma'm."

Both Stacy and Jill stared at him in disbelief.

"What do you mean—attacked?"

"Missiles, ma'm. There were heavy casualties, civilian and military."

"You said a moment ago you were taking us to NECCO headquarters at Hill Field," Jill frowned. "That's in Utah—"

The major nodded. "That's right, ma'm."

"When we left two days ago, NECCO headquarters was in Washington—"

The major's features hardened. He struggled to keep his voice emotionless.

"Washington was destroyed last night, ma'm. Four direct nuclear hits."

"I can't believe it," Jill breathed. She sat down on the running board of the van, stunned. Then she looked up in alarm. The major knew what she was about to ask.

"Both Mr. Adams and Mr. Courtney are safe at Hill Field. They're waiting for you. We've already radioed in that we've located you."

Suddenly there was a commotion. A beautiful black woman was running toward the Rangers. A howl of anger rose from the biker in the lion's robe.

"Get back here, Candi—"

The black woman ran even faster, heading for the van. She ducked behind the major, who was intent on watching the bikers.

"You're dead, Candi," Leo bellowed.

He pulled a pistol from his waistband and aimed it toward Candi—which meant he was also aiming toward the major. Other bikers grabbed for weapons. Whatever Leo and the others had in mind, other than blind rage, was never known.

The machine guns in the helicopter started spraying a lethal curtain. In less than two minutes, every biker, every companion, was dead. Silence followed.

When the shooting started, the major shoved Jill and Stacy to the ground, picking up Leah and huddling her beneath his own body. Candi was on the ground beside them. When it was over, all of them climbed back onto their feet.

"Everyone all right?" the major asked.

They nodded. Stacy took her daughter from him. Leah was crying, but unhurt.

"Thank you, Major. I won't forget what you just did for my daughter. What is your name, Major?"

"Major Caldwell, ma'm. That's a great little girl you have there. I'm thankful she's safe."

The major turned his attention to the black woman, now also on her feet.

"Do you have an explanation for what just happened, ma'm?"

"It was a chance to get away. I had to take it." She looked over at the dead bikers. "I'm glad Leo's dead. The others weren't much better. You soldiers did the world a favor, Major."

"Why were you trying to get away—?"

"I know things, Major—things they didn't want me to tell."

"Like what, ma'm?" the major pressed. "A lot of people just died—"

The black woman looked at the other two women. "I'm Candi. When I saw these soldiers arrive, I knew you both must be important. I took a chance on you ladies being willing to help me."

"Why should we?" Stacy asked, eyeing the black woman suspiciously. "I saw you on the bike with that Leo—"

The woman called Candi was beautiful. Classical in the fine lines of cheek and chin, with a wide, voluptuous mouth. Dark eyes were wide with the adrenaline of what had just happened. Eyebrows were perfectly arched in a thin line. Her figure was full in breasts and hips, but with no sign of fat or flabbiness. Firm and muscular, Stacy noticed. She was dressed in a low-cut red blouse and a short, black leather skirt that exposed most of her long legs. Stacy apparently showed her surprise at seeing such a beautiful woman in company with Leo and the other biker scumbags.

"I'm not one of them," Candi said firmly. "I came up from California two days ago to deliver—deliver a message. Leo liked what he saw and decided I belonged to him. Now maybe you understand why I'm glad he's dead."

"What was the message, ma'm?" Major Caldwell asked. "What brought you here from California?"

"Drugs, Major," Candi replied. "I work for a syndicate that controls virtually all of the drugs going through California. We were making a distribution deal with Leo and his gang." Her lips twisted into a scowl. "I told my people in California it was a mistake."

Stacy was even more hesitant as she looked at Candi.

"What did you expect to gain by taking this chance?" she asked.

"Get away from Leo, for starters," Candi muttered. "I figured I could make a deal with you people, and end up back to California."

Major Caldwell shook his head. "No chance for that, miss."

"Why not—?"

"California is a red zone. Nobody goes in."

Candi was staring at him, anger showing. "That's crazy, Major. Why can't I go back to California—?"

"You obviously haven't heard either," Major Caldwell said. "We're at war, miss."

"Since when—?" Candi gasped.

"Since last night. California is now a high risk for invasion. However, under the circumstances, we'll take you to the Federal Zone. You must consider yourself under arrest, miss."

He looked over at the other Rangers, who by now had checked all the bodies of the bikers.

"Let's get these four ladies aboard. This freeway is going to be a parking lot before the day's over."

# 16

## THE FEDERAL ZONE

The attack on the United States by the forces of the Coalition of Allied States of the Americas was perfectly timed. The capability of the U.S. military to respond was at its lowest ebb in a decade, the result of the huge numbers of troops, planes, ships and military equipment deployed abroad in the past weeks. Everything was in confusion at overseas bases as NATO defense lines all across Europe were hurriedly reinforced along the borders with former Soviet republics, and every Pacific base scrambled to prepare for attacks that could come from anywhere in Asia.

A mass recall of U.S. forces was out of the question for at least two reasons. It would leave Europe and Asia vulnerable to Soviet and Chinese aggression. The more painful reality was that few, if any, U.S. bases were sufficiently operational to handle a re-deployment back to the States, even if it was ordered. The CASA missile attacks had been deadly accurate.

Army and Air Force Reserve units were also scattered, some already sent overseas, others deployed to bases now in smoking ruin.

Naval and air installations in Panama were pounded out of operation. There was almost total destruction at Guantanamo, in Cuba, with casualties reported at a staggering eighty-five percent. The Cuban army, showing surprising efficiency, overran the base.

The entire network of U.S. defenses was pointed east and west, leaving the underbelly of the Gulf Coast completely vulnerable. The CASA forces were virtually unopposed as they parachuted into Texas, Louisiana, Mississippi, Alabama and northern Florida. At the same time, waves of landing craft brought tens of thousands more troops, armored vehicles and light tanks to U.S. ports along the Gulf. The assault craft emerged from cleverly concealed hiding along the Gulf of Mexico.

The green-uniformed CASA forces moved rapidly inland, pressing north up the Mississippi valley. The swift advance was made easier by a highly organized chain of sabotage at power plants, communication centers, transportation hubs, even police stations. Panic ran out of control among the civilian population as cities were crippled from both missiles and sabotage, leaving them dark and isolated in a flood of terror.

The terror increased with every hour as CASA troops swept through town after town, savagely killing men, women and children. The only ones spared were those of Hispanic or Asian descent. In some smaller communities, not one person was left alive.

The brutality numbed citizens and military alike. Word spread ahead of the invaders that the Latin soldiers were slaughtering every white and black American they found. Horrified citizens listened to the reports of what was happening and made desperate efforts to escape, jamming roads and highways into a grid-lock extending for hundreds of miles.

All of this was being reviewed by General Aaron Stark, meeting with President Baldwin and his select group of top advisors at the new NECCO headquarters at Hill Field, located a few miles north of Salt Lake City.

Stark was standing at one end of a long conference table, the wall behind him covered with large monitors. The screens showed the eastern and western sections of the United States, the Gulf Coast, the Caribbean countries, and the northernmost countries of South America,

Aaron put down the lighted pointer he was using, pausing to study briefly the people seated around the table. He assessed what he saw on each face, not surprised at the shock and disbelief most were feeling.

President Baldwin sat at the opposite end of the table, his expression grim. The chief executive looked like he'd aged ten years in the past three days. Anne Ashford was sitting next to the president, Quinn Adams beside her, then Lincoln Banes. On the other side of the table, Secretary of State James Van Durlin looked somber and deep in thought. Next to him sat Duff Jenkins. Admiral Boots Brunswick was at the end, next to Stark. Brunswick was pale and subdued, the sight of Washington, D.C., disintegrating in those mushroom clouds still horribly fresh in his mind. No one would ever forget that sight.

"Based on the facts presented," Stark summarized, "I am making two suggestions. One, we immediately establish this region as a protected Federal Zone and urge all civilians to get here any way they can."

Duff Jenkins showed a worried frown. "That will bring millions of refugees—"

"You've heard the reports, Duff," Baldwin reminded him. "Those Latin soldiers are committing wholesale murder. I support General Stark's suggestion. Let's broadcast it, drop leaflets — hell, let's do sky writing if that's what it takes. Let the people know they can find safety here."

"Are you sure they can, Mr. President?" Van Durlin asked quietly. "Can we hold this region if the CASA forces attack it—?"

"I'll answer that question, Mr. Secretary," Stark said. "NECCO has put years of planning into this kind of emergency and Pyramid Seven has always been the top selection as a relocation site. That's because we have natural barriers here in the west that make a ground assault potentially too costly to attempt."

"The mountains won't help us against planes, General," Van Durlin responded, "nor against missiles. In fact, it appears to me that the more compressed we become, the more vulnerable we are."

"Sound logic, Mr. Secretary," Stark told him, "but there are contingencies to counter that."

"What contingencies, General?" Brunswick asked, interested in the exchange. "The Secretary makes a very valid point—"

"I'll discuss those in due time, Admiral. Our first priority now is saving lives."

"I'd think it was stopping those Latins from taking the whole country," Jenkins muttered.

"We'll stop them from doing that, Mr. Jenkins," Stark said with quiet assurance. "What we can't stop is the loss of the eastern half of the country. For all practical assessment, that's already happened. I believe Admiral Brunswick will agree, in the face of our losses and the present condition of the military, we must pull back into the strongest defensive position possible."

Brunswick nodded agreement. "Extract all the manpower and materials we can, then regroup. It's all we can do."

"That will leave the civilian population in the east completely unprotected," Baldwin quickly protested. "That is unacceptable—"

"It is unavoidable, Mr. President," Stark replied gravely. "They caught us looking the wrong way. We're paying the price for that."

Baldwin pressed both hands against the sides of his head, grimacing at a headache impervious to medication. He looked at Stark. "You mentioned a second suggestion—"

"This is painful, Mr. President, but in my opinion absolutely essential," Stark said. "We must initiate a scorched earth policy in every area taken by the enemy."

"Details, General—" Baldwin muttered.

"Destroy everything that could possibly be used to aid or succor the enemy. Factories, airports, power grids, certainly any food warehousing that can't be extradited in time to keep it out of their hands. We have to make it impossible for them to live off what they take, sir. I'm sure they're counting on that."

"What makes you so sure, General Stark?" Jenkins asked. "They've surprised us in every area so far. Perhaps they're not planning on living off the land — that would mean we destroyed facilities we will desperately need ourselves once this situation is under control."

"We can't take the risk," Brunswick said, jumping in ahead of Stark. "General Stark is absolutely correct — we must conduct a scorched earth policy. I've issued orders to military units to leave nothing usable behind when they evacuate bases. It only makes sense to extend that policy to civilian facilities."

"We must remember," Quinn said, "that the enemy is ten times stronger than any of us thought possible. Missiles, military hardware, and technical assistance has been poured into those countries, and it's been done very cleverly. We didn't pick up on it at NECCO, and we should have. Neither did the CIA nor anyone else. I hold myself responsible for the lapse at NECCO—"

"Nonsense," Baldwin interrupted. "We'd be bleached bones in Washington if not for what NECCO accomplished. We all owe you, Mr. Adams. The CIA dropped the ball – I don't understand how they could miss anything this massive."

Anne Ashford cast a worried frown at the president. "The governors are not prepared to handle this, Mr. President — not all those refugees and the problems they'll bring. We could be looking at a hundred million people — even a hundred and fifty million — pouring into this region."

"We're now under martial law, Madame Vice President," Lincoln Banes reminded quietly. "The governors must relinquish their authority. Our strategic planning at NECCO took a lot of the problems related to refugees into consideration — although this situation is going to stretch any scenario we projected."

"Plans are in motion for constructing emergency housing, augmenting utilities, sanitation, and other facilities," Quinn added. "Our immediate problem will be feeding all those people, but it's not as impossible as it sounds. We've relocated entire food processing plants to the Zone and they should be in operation within a few days."

"It's a relief to hear that, Quinn, as it will be for the governors," Anne replied.

"The best brains in the country are working on solutions to the problems facing us," Quinn continued. "Every university and college in the region is now functioning as a national research lab, all working the crisis. We've seen some startling results already."

Baldwin tapped his fingers on the table. "So we get everyone possible into the Zone. We abandon – blow up – half the country. Then we regroup the military." The president was looking directly at Stark. "What then, General Stark? How long before we throw these Latins out of our country?"

"Difficult to project, Mr. President," Stark replied. "We need to fully assess the damage, accurately determine our capabilities for launching a counter offensive. Sorry I can't be more specific, Mr. President." He glanced at Admiral Brunswick. "Boots, you have anything to add to that?"

"It won't take long, Mr. President," Brunswick said confidently. "We've suffered heavy losses but we still have tremendous firepower left, more than enough to do the job. The facilities here in the Zone are excellent, thanks to NECCO, We should go on the offensive very soon, sir."

"What about retaliation for firing those missiles?" Baldwin growled. "I want those countries on the receiving end."

"We've identified twenty launch sites, Mr. President," Brunswick said, "in ten countries."

"Which countries?"

"Venezuela. Colombia. Guyana. Costa Rica. Honduras. Nicaragua. Guatamala. Mexico — apparently only from the Yucatan peninsula. Missiles were also launched from Cuba and the Dominican Republic. We believe some came from submarines offshore in the Gulf."

"Where did the nuclear missiles come from—?"

Brunswick gave a little shake of his head. "We can't be sure, Mr. President. Best guess is Colombia, but they could have come from Venezuela. There were so many incoming, it was difficult to pinpoint the nuclear source."

"Nuclear missiles hit only Washington, right?"

"That's correct, sir."

"It was Colombia," Baldwin grated. "Feel it in my bones. Some drug lord with a score to settle."

"Very possible, sir."

Baldwin looked at Quinn. "Find out, Quinn. Get me proof of where those nuclear missiles came from. I want those people to pay for every body and every building they destroyed."

"Will do, Mr. President," Quinn murmured.

"I want them all to pay," Baldwin said angrily. "I want their capitals in ruins, just like they did to us."

Stark spoke up quickly. "We all want that, Mr. President, but right now, our primary consideration is gaining a military advantage, not just vengeance."

"I want those Latins to suffer—"

"They will, sir. I have a plan, Mr. President, but this is not the time to present it," Stark said. "First, we must get our military in fighting order."

"He's right, sir," Brunswick added. "It's essential we regroup before launching any offensive action."

Baldwin looked again at Quinn. "You haven't said much, Mr. Adams. Do you agree with the assessments—?"

"I do, Mr. President, though it looks pretty bleak at the moment," Quinn said. "The situation is thoroughly covered, it seems. The generals will concentrate on military preparedness. NECCO will handle the evacuations and establishing the new Federal Zone. Madame Vice President," Quinn added, "has the unenviable task of coordinating with local governments."

"With a great deal of help from your organization, Quinn, I hope," Anne Ashford said, flashing him a worried look.

"We're in this together, Anne," Quinn assured her. "It's vital we keep public confidence, assure them the situation is under control. There will be huge construction projects starting, and enormous challenges in coping with social, medical, and welfare problems. We'll need special regulations drawn up to deal with price gouging, rent controls, black markets, and the like."

"Let's not forget about crime," Jenkins added. "This whole region is likely to become a cesspool if we're not careful." He looked at the president. "It will require emergency powers for law enforcement to deal with it, Mr. President."

"What about Stu Akker and Norm Dean?" Jenkins asked the president. "Shall I brief them on this meeting—?"

"No. I'm ticked off at both of them," Baldwin grunted. "Get Akker into my office later this evening. Remind Dean the FBI jumps whenever NECCO or Madame Vice President snaps a finger. Tell them they won't be attending any policy meetings until they plug the leaks in their organizations."

The meeting broke up shortly after that, each person heading for their individual mountain of responsibilities. The President drew Quinn aside and asked him to remain. When they were alone, Baldwin put an arm solicitously around Quinn's shoulder.

"What's this I hear about Jill and Stacy — are they missing?"

Quinn gave him a smile of relief. "Not any more, sir. The Rangers located them about an hour ago, just east of Denver. They should be arriving here at Hill any minute."

"That's great news. Glad to hear it, Quinn."

"So am I, sir—"

# 17

## THE BEIJING WEB

"I want them executed!"

The thin face of Chen Xingtao, Premier of the Chinese People's Republic, was flushed with anger. The long, stringy goatee hanging from the Premier's delicate chin shook as he slapped a hand angrily against his thigh.

The Premier was glaring at General Wang Jingwei, chairman of the Central Military Commission. The general, sitting straight and stiff across from him in one of the five large, silk brocaded chairs forming a circle about the Premier, looked very uncomfortable.

"Those responsible are being sought—" General Wang began, but the Premier waved his hand angrily.

"That is not satisfactory. Such a thing must not happen again. Who is the commander overseeing Operation Scourge?"

"General Wu Zhenkang. He has done an excellent job in forming the coalition of the Latin countries, and in putting the operation together."

"He has put the future of the People's Republic into jeopardy," the Premier snapped. "How could he allow this to happen?"

"Strict orders were issued—"

"—and disobeyed. General Wu has failed to assert his authority."

"The men responsible are drug lords, outside the control of the CASA forces, Premier Chen. General Wu has determined the nuclear missiles were fired from northern Colombia."

"Strictly forbidden in all our planning," Premier Chen reminded sharply. "I trust those nuclear missiles did not come from the People's Republic. There must be no possible connection to our country."

"No connection, Premier Chen. It is believed the drug lords obtained the missiles from Iran."

"Have the Colombians responsible been identified?"

"General Wu reports the people are known and their capture is imminent. The missiles were fired from portable launchers north of Medellin."

"Those people must be executed," Chen repeated. "General Wu is not personally participating, I trust?"

"He is still in Brazil. The assault upon the criminals is being directed by a Colonel Fariocha, the director of CASA intelligence."

"Our nation must not be involved."

General Wang shook his head. "A report will reach the Americans placing blame upon the drug lords and identifying Iran as the source of the missiles. There will be no cause for the United States to connect the People's Republic with the incident, or with Operation Scourge."

"We do not want the Americans retaliating with nuclear weapons upon the Latin hemisphere – and certainly not upon our land."

"That is the wish of all of us, Premier Chen."

The Premier leaned back, black eyes looking around the circle of chairs. A uniformed and be-medalled general of the PLA sat in each chair. None had interrupted during the exchange between the Premier and General Wang. Sitting silently when the Premier was angry was the higher course of wisdom.

Among these silent witnesses were General Chang Kuoseng, director of the powerful Political Department of the People's Liberation Army, General Yan Ming Hua, commander of the western theater of military operations, General Zuo Qichen, commander of the eastern theater, and General Pu Te-huai, commander of the southern theater.

The Premier again turned his attention back to General Wang. "Is Operation Scourge proceeding according to plan?"

"Better than all expectations. The CASA forces are meeting almost no opposition. The American military is completely disrupted, as we planned. The policy of extermination has frightened the civilian population so much they also pose little threat. The occupation of America is going very well, Premier Chen."

"It will please the Council to hear that. General Zuo, your report, please."

The commander of the eastern theater straightened in his chair, a difficult thing to do because of the bulging stomach that seemed about to pop the buttons on his uniform. His round, flabby face broke into a beaming smile.

"Operation Red Tiger is going very well, Premier Chen," the general said. "We had a few problems with South Korea. Some politicians had difficulty accepting the wisdom, and the inevitability, of their country being united once again with the North and with the People's Republic."

"Has the matter been settled?" Premier Chen frowned.

General Zuo nodded quickly. "The trouble-makers are dealt with. The people of both the North and the South are pleased to become part of our great nation."

"What about the Japanese? All this happening around them must have caused alarm—"

General Chang Kuoseng interjected. "We reassured the Japanese government they have nothing to fear, Premier Chen. A delegation headed by Vice Premier Tian Zimying leaves for Tokyo tomorrow. They will again assure the Japanese we do not intend any action against them."

"Be sure they are convinced," the Premier frowned. "We do not want the Americans using a threat against Japan as an excuse to begin military action against the People's Republic."

"It will be made very clear, Premier Chen."

The Premier looked again at General Zuo. "What about the rest of the front—?"

The general's face broke into a beaming smile again. "Vietnam is once again united. There has been full cooperation in Hanoi and Ho Chi Minh — but that was certain even before Red Tiger began. Laos also has accepted our hand of friendship. The People's Liberation Army is in complete control. We have experienced almost no casualties."

"Excellent. General Pu — are things going as well in the southern theater?"

"Yes, Premier Chen. Cambodia has acknowledged the People's Republic as its sovereign. Thailand has officially capitulated, although we expect some problems in the northern provinces. Malasia has welcomed our soldiers. There is some fighting in Myanmar, but our forces have advanced north from Krung Thep almost to Mandalay. We expect a formal surrender within a few days. As you are aware, the liberation of Indonesia, the Philippines, and the territories west of Myanmar, falls into the second phase of operations. The planning of the Council was divinely guided, Premier Chen."

Chen nodded, accepting the implication that he was part of the divine power. "Very good, General Pu. How is Red Star progressing in the west, General Yan?"

"Unfortunately not as well as those operations under the direct control of the People's Liberation Army, Premier Chen," the commander said sadly. "It was agreed to let the Soviet generals conduct their own campaign, but there are problems. Much more resistance to a central military command has been encountered than the generals anticipated."

"Is the success of Red Star in danger—?"

General Yan quickly shook his head. "The generals will succeed in taking over control, but it is more difficult, and taking more time, than projected. The Soviet military will be a unified power again very soon, Premier Chen."

"We do not want them to become too powerful," General Chang reminded him. The political strategist frowned at General Yan. "The old Soviet Union must never be restored. That is an important consideration of the Great Plan."

"No political unification of the republics will be attempted by the generals — it could not be accomplished again even if they tried. But our objective of a single military chain of command will soon be a reality."

Premier Chen started nodding his head repeatedly, obviously pleased. "Excellent. Excellent. You have all done well. I will inform the Council that the Great Plan is progressing on schedule."

The chairman of the political affairs department raised a hand deferentially. Premier Chen nodded toward him. "Yes, General Chang. You have something to add?"

"With all respect, Premier Chen," the general said, "I notice there has been no mention of Operation Desert Sword. Is there a change in timing for this?"

"If I recall correctly, General Chang, it was your suggestion to wait until the successful completion of the invasion of the United States. Are you having new thoughts on this matter?"

"It might be wise to consider accelerating that timetable," General Chang responded. "With the successes of Red Tiger and Red Star, and the invasion of the United States proceeding so well, there are advantages in having Desert Sword get underway."

"What advantages, General Chang?" the Premier asked.

"The participants will feel very confident in their ability to succeed," Chang replied. "They now see the forces of the United States tied up abroad and suffering huge losses in the defeat of their homeland. If the Desert Sword coalition strikes now, there is virtually no chance the Americans will interfere."

Premier Chen was frowning in thought. "And if we wait—?"

"The Americans fell into our traps and the CASA attacks caught them by surprise," Chang replied. "However, they will fight ferociously to overcome these setbacks. They are second only to ourselves in military power — we cannot rule out the possibility the Americans will reverse the tide, Premier Chen, if given enough time. Strike now with Desert Sword and we give an advantage to the enemies of Israel."

"Is Desert Sword ready?"

"The alliance is not complete, but many seeds are planted. With the permission of the Council, I will take personal charge, Premier Chen. Desert Sword will be ready to initiate within a matter of weeks."

"Your words have wisdom, General Chang," the Premier said. "Perhaps it is wise to move up the timetable, place a sense of urgency upon it." He glanced around the circle of generals. "Does anyone have a comment on this matter?"

General Zuo spoke up. "The Eastern Command will be ready to provide support if needed. Our objectives will be fully achieved by then."

General Wang shook his head in disapproval. "We must not weaken the eastern front, General Zuo. It is important to keep the United States fearing the possibility of an attack upon their western coastline."

"The Southern Command will also be able to provide some support," General Pu said. "It will depend on how long the opposition in Myanmar continues, and the reaction of neighboring countries."

The premier raised a hand to cut off further comment. "Desert Sword must be carried out independent of aid from the People's Republic," he said firmly, "or it will not succeed."

"Do you believe the Arabs – all Muslims – can join together in this?" General Zuo asked. "It will be alliance of bitter enemies."

"All share a hatred greater than their jealousies," General Chang replied. "They will eagerly seize the opportunity to erase Israel from the face of the earth, especially when they do not have to contend with the American satan."

General Yan spoke softly. "It will not end with the death of the Israelis. The Muslims will fight amongst themselves with even greater fury over the spoils."

"Perhaps the time for the Arabs to disappear from this earth also approaches," the Premier murmured. "General Chang, talk to those involved. Remember Iraq and Iran cannot be trusted to follow a coordinated battle plan, not even with other Arabs. They must be carefully watched. It will be a great temptation for them, since they hate the Israelis so deeply, to use nuclear weapons. That must not occur. Report back to me on your progress, General Chang. I will bring the matter before the Council."

"Thank you, Premier Chen."

"The prospect of an early start to Desert Sword is pleasing. The Great Plan will then almost be complete."

The next day, Colonel Nia Yao Gui, serving on the Central Military Commission staff of General Wang, was among a five-member delegation sent by the People's Republic to Tokyo. Their mission was to reassure the Japanese once again that no military action was intended against them, despite the massive operations underway throughout the Far East.

On the second day, Colonel Nia did not show up for the scheduled morning meeting. He had not slept in his room the previous night but no one was unduly alarmed. Nia Yao Gui was single and it was supposed that a combination of saki and sex was probably responsible. However, when he did not report all that day, nor show up again that night, an alarm was sounded.

It was a futile search. Colonel Nia had slipped into the U.S. embassy the night before and by morning, when he was first missed, was already on his way to the United States.

He was flown from Tokyo to Guam, from there to Hawaii, and on to San Francisco. By the time a full search for the missing aide was begun in Tokyo, Colonel Nia was being admitted to the office of Quinn Adams in the temporary headquarters of NECCO at Hill Field. He was accompanied by Race Courtney, his immediate superior in the intelligence unit in which he'd served for the past ten years.

Quinn greeted the agent from Beijing, now dressed comfortably in slacks and sports jacket, with a warm smile. "Yao Gui. This is a pleasant surprise. After not hearing from you for nearly two months, we were worried about you."

"It is unfortunate I had to come out. Incredible things are happening in Beijing. It was not an easy decision."

"You wouldn't be here if it wasn't the right thing to do," Quinn said, motioning for the two men to sit down. "You've been in deep cover a long time, Yao Gui, and I respect your judgement. Obviously something important happened."

"I didn't risk sending out word about Red Tiger and Red Star. I knew the Israelis were aware of them and assumed the Mossad would brief you," Yao Gui said. "Unfortunately, Operation Scourge was so secret that even I didn't know about it until a few hours before the attack. It was too late to send a warning."

Quinn showed his surprise. "You knew in advance about Operation Scourge?"

"It's a Chinese operation, part of their Great Plan."

Quinn and Race exchanged startled glances.

"Unbelievable," Race breathed.

"Are Chinese troops involved?" Quinn asked. "Is that where they got all that hardware?"

"No troops," Yao Gui replied. "Not even the missiles or the other weapons, not directly, at least."

"I don't follow."

"Nearly everything was smuggled into the Latin countries by the Russians, at the request of the People's Republic."

"The Russian government is in on this?"

"No. The Russian military. A group of dissident generals who made a deal with Beijing. Nearly everything used in the attack was removed covertly from hidden Russian arsenals. Only a few at the top know how much Soviet weaponry is stashed away, and where. I found out the stuff has been siphoned off in deals made with the old Soviet military heirarchy over at least the last three years."

"And none of our people picked up on it," Race muttered, still shaking his head in disbelief. "You need a new director of intelligence, Quinn. I'm obviously incompetent."

"You're not the CIA, Race," Quinn said. "Your responsibility was intelligence related to NECCO operations here in the United States. We weren't geared for worldwide espionage." A little grin tweaked his mouth. "We did our share, of course, but it was never our mission. We covered as many hot spots as we could with a handful of people like Yao Gui here, and Vicente Cabrillo, only because we couldn't trust the CIA to do its job."

"How is Vicente? Yao Gui asked.

"Dead," Race said quietly. "Died saving my life, He gave us our first lead on Operation Scourge. We thought maybe you were dead, too."

"I knew my silence would be troubling, but I couldn't risk being uncovered, not with so much happening. Security in Beijing has been unbelievably tight. But there was another break two days ago – three days, now. That's when I decided to come in."

"Do they know you've been a mole?" Quinn asked.

"I doubt it. They'll probably assume I was murdered in some bar or whorehouse, and disposed of. I was assigned to the Tokyo delegation a week ago, so it provided an opportunity to run without arousing suspicion."

"I'm not sure I want to know what this new development is," Quinn muttered. "If Red Tiger and Red Star didn't drag you out, this must be a doozy."

"Our friends in the Mossad will think so," Yao Gui replied. "I only have bare details, but I know General Chang himself is now involved in bringing it to operational status as quickly as possible."

"What are we talking about?" Race asked, leaning forward in his chair.

"Another part of the web the People's Republic has been weaving. This ties all the operations together and opens the whole world to Chinese domination."

Quinn frowned. "What ties them together, Yao Gui?"

"Operation Desert Sword."

# 18

## RETRIBUTION IN MEDELLIN

Colonel Jorge Fariocha crouched low in the shadows against the walls surrounding the sprawling mountain-top estate. More than three hundred soldiers, half of them members of the Colonel's own elite corp from Brazil, crowded those shadows, completely encircling the retreat of one of Colombia's most notorious drug lords.

Fariocha glanced at the luminous hands on his watch. Twenty-five seconds to go. He had no doubt the attack would go precisely as planned. All those who had attended the briefing five hours ago in Medellin knew what the price would be for not following orders to the second.

Fariocha looked at the watch again, then nodded to the officer beside him. A red flare shot skyward, the signal to unleash a deadly frenzy of activity.

Helicopters rose out of nowhere, four of them swooping over the lighted compound before the red glow from the flare faded. The gunships, their searchlights pinpointing targets, began firing at gun emplacements on the grounds, blasting away the steel-reinforced gates, gouging huge holes in the thick walls of the main house. The gunships spread a withering hail of death and destruction for exactly two minutes.

The helicopters stopped firing, hovering overhead to bathe the grounds in light. Explosives blasted away the remnants of the outer gates and CASA troops poured into the compound. They were followed by a convoy of trucks that roared around a curve in the road as soon as the attack began. All three hundred CASA troops were inside the compound on schedule with twelve seconds to spare.

From that point, it was a massacre. Intelligence units had reported earlier about one hundred and fifty members of the drug lord's personal army were inside the compound. It proved to be fairly accurate. One hundred and sixty-two bodies by actual count.

Only fifteen minutes lapsed from that first red flare until Colonel Fariocha entered the large living room of the house. Members of his own elite First Military District force were holding ten people at gunpoint, six men and four women.

Fariocha recognized four of the men from the files he had studied. They were the four this whole operation was designed to catch.

Enrique Ortiz. Ruben Echevalla. Lorenzo Perrez. Luis Camarena.

Four of the most powerful men in Colombia — more powerful than anyone in the government. Four of the wealthiest men — wealthy enough to privately fund a nuclear attack on the United States. Four ruthless drug barons who recognized no authority but their own — until they looked into the face of Colonel Jorge Fariocha.

Fariocha stared at the group contemptuously, though he felt a cold sense of satisfaction. Success always felt much better than failure.

"I am Colonel Fariocha, of the united CASA forces." He pointed at the four women. "Who are these—?"

There were assorted, mumbled responses. Two apparently were mistresses, the others whores bought for the night. Fariocha nodded to one of his officers. The women were taken away. The colonel looked at the two men he had not recognized.

"Is there any reason I should not kill you both—?"

The two frightened men, standing with arms raised, looked at each other. There was silence for a few seconds as each tried to think of the best reason for staying alive.

They took too long. Fariocha raised the automatic in his hand and fired twice, casually, almost not looking. Both men slumped to the floor.

"I have questions to ask you others," the colonel said coldly, fastening his eyes on the remaining four prisoners. "You may put down your hands, but don't make any other movement."

The four most powerful men in Colombia slowly lowered their arms, none of them taking their eyes from the officer with the gun. They stood beside each other without moving.

"Now," Fariocha asked, "which of you is considered the leader?"

No one answered.

"Very well," the colonel said, "which of you owns this estate?"

Enrique Ortiz spoke. "It is my home, Colonel."

"Thank you," Fariocha said politely. He raised the gun and shot Ortiz dead.

"Now there are only three of you to answer my questions," the colonel said coldly. "One more will die every time any of you tells me a lie. I am very good at knowing when someone is not telling the truth. Do you understand—?"

All three nodded at the same time.

"You are responsible for launching the nuclear missiles against the United States—?"

Again the men nodded in unison.

"Where did these nuclear missiles come from—?"

"From Iraq," Ruben Echevallo said. The others nodded again.

"From secret arsenals the Iraqi government has kept hidden from the West," Lorenzo Perrez added.

"Iraq produced these missiles—?"

"They were manufactured in Pakistan," Luis Camarena explained, anxious to prove how ready he also was to be truthful. "They were bought by Iran but stolen by rebels and sold to Iraq several years ago. We were told the Iraqis would sell if the price was right."

"Did your government know about your plan—?"

All three heads shook in unison.

"We knew about Operation Scourge," Luis told Fariocha. "We planned our attack to coincide with it."

"Who programmed the missiles—?"

"We hired four Russians to do it. We were told they were experts in aiming missiles at the United States."

"They were. Washington was destroyed."

Fariocha paused, studying the three men. They were telling him the truth, he knew. They were even becoming a little relaxed. He raised the automatic and fired. Ruben Echevallo looked a little surprised as he dropped dead.

The surviving two men stared down at Echevallo in horror. They were no longer relaxed.

"We are telling the truth, Colonel," Camarena cried.

"Good. I was beginning to wonder if you were. Why did you do this thing? You must have known the use of nuclear weapons was strictly forbidden."

"We had a score to settle with the Americans. They killed members of our families, pressured our government, made it difficult for thousands of Colombians to make an honest living."

"You mean growing and producing drugs."

"We supply what people want," Perrez shrugged. He glanced at

Camarena, then back to Fariocha. "If you are interested, Colonel, we can offer you a very profitable arrangement—"

Fariocha raised the gun and fired twice more. He looked down at the last two of the most powerful men in Colombia, now dead.

"Not interested," the colonel said softly. He glanced at his watch, looked at his officers. "I'm going back to Medellin. Leave a message here. Hang these four where they can be seen, and burn everything else. Be sure photographs are taken — I want proof of what was done here."

Fariocha turned and started from the room. He looked back and gave the officers a thin smile. "No need to hurry. The interrogation went ahead of schedule."

# 19

## PENSACOLA SURPRISE

General Carlos Barboza watched the large silver jet, with its green CASA insignias on sides and tail, touch down smoothly at the Pensacola Air Base, on the edge of Florida's western extension along the Gulf Coast.

The commander of CASA's invasion forces was not smiling as the jet's engines shut down and a ramp was hurriedly pushed into place. General Barboza and the two officers with him moved toward the plane. All three were wearing green fatigues, clean but badly wrinkled.

The door of the jet opened and four dark-suited men hurried down and fanned out at the bottom of the steps. They eyed Barboza and the two other officers suspiciously as they approached. People in the security forces always eyed other people suspiciously, the general reminded himself. It was their job, but Barboza found himself irritated by it today. The three officers stopped near the bottom of the ladder.

The general was five feet five inches tall in the shower, but stood two inches taller now in his elevated army boots. It was a source of annoyance to Barboza that even with those elevated heels, he still looked shorter than he was. That was mostly due to the two hundred and forty-five pounds he carried, much of it packed firmly around his stomach.

The sun overhead wasn't particularly hot, certainly not when compared with the temperatures he was accustomed to enduring in his home country of Brazil, but General Barboza was starting to sweat profusely. Little rivulets began trickling down each side of his face, down the ridge of his nose, down into matted eyebrows. Barboza knew this was not going to be a pleasant meeting, and without any direct orders, his brain was preparing the rest of his body for tension.

A man in a cream colored business suit appeared in the doorway of the plane. Fernando Francisco de Branca always looked cool and immaculate. Barboza couldn't remember a time when the chairman of the Governing Council of CASA had not looked completely at ease and completely in control. The silk suit did not appear to have a wrinkle on it. A warm smile of greeting was on the man's face now as he waved down at the waiting officers.

The sweat on Barboza's face increased from trickles to streams. It wasn't because Francisco de Branca was a fearsome person, like Colonel Fariocha of the intelligence unit. Just the opposite, in fact. Francisco de Branca was more like an affable playboy, exuding personality, well-liked by the people, a soft-spoken, friendly person. It was the man's power that was making Barboza break out in sweat. The Chairman had more power than any other man on the Governing Council. The thought of that power, and what it could do to Barboza, made the general's uniform soak up dark circles around the collar and under the arms.

After handshakes were exchanged, Barboza led the newcomer toward two waiting automobiles. A young CASA lieutenant, also dressed in fatigues, opened the door of a white Lincoln limousine and Barboza and the Director got in. The other officers and the security men climbed into a black Cadillac limousine parked behind the Lincoln.

The two cars left the military base and drove only a short distance before turning into the grounds of a luxurious hotel. The main building was only three stories high, but it was surrounded by a maze of secluded bungalows hidden amid a verdant jungle of palms and shrubbery.

"I have arranged for you to stay here, Mr. Chairman," Barboza said. "The accommodations are much better than any of those at Pensacola."

"Where do you stay, General?"

"Most of the time I'm at the base," Barboza replied. "However, I do have quarters reserved here for when I can get away."

"Most pleasant," Francisco de Branca murmured. He turned his head to look at three young women wearing scanty bikinis who came out of the lobby of the main building. A car drove up and three CASA officers got out. All six went into the hotel, the women giggling and laughing as the officers stroked familiar places.

"One would hardly believe we are at war in enemy territory," the man in the cream suit said softly. He looked questioningly at Barboza. "We are still at war, aren't we, General? I mean, it seems so — so pleasant here."

"It wasn't that way two weeks ago, Mr. Chairman," Barboza answered defensively. "We have advanced swiftly since our landing here. Our forces are now fighting several hundred miles to the north, and some have pushed east to the Atlantic coast. In a few days, I expect to move our headquarters to Chicago."

"I'm glad to hear that, General. I'm looking forward to a detailed report. The members of the Governing Council are concerned that we do not have a full grasp of the situation here in the United States."

The lieutenant came around and opened the door. The two men got out and entered the hotel. Minutes later, after being shown to one of the bungalows located on a hillock that provided a view of the Gulf, Barboza offered the chairman a drink from the wet bar.

"Thank you, General, but no. I prefer we talk."

Barboza put down the drink he'd poured for himself, leaving it on the bar. Francisco de Branca went out onto the veranda of the bungalow. It offered a view of a large swimming pool, crowded with people laughing and splashing and enjoying themselves.

"Those are your men, I take it, General?"

The sweat was tracking down Barboza's face again. "This hotel is designated as a rest area for our officers, sir."

"I'm surprised so many need rest after such a short time. Especially when, according to your reports, General, very little fighting is being done."

"Overrunning the enemy should not be confused with not fighting," Barboza said stiffly. "We have met with incredible success, sir. The men that come here have earned a right to relax. It is a matter of morale—"

"Morale must be very good in a place like this. I commend you, General."

Barboza was well aware of the brittle edge to the man's voice. The chairman was not pleased with what he was seeing. Barboza decided it was time to bring up matters that would not appear so pleasant. He started to speak, then accepted the chairman's waved invitation to sit at one of the umbrella tables on the patio.

"My reports have been somewhat vague because the situation changes with every day," Barboza began, "lately, for the worse."

"Why is that, General?"

"The Americans are conducting a scorched earth policy. When we drive them out of an area, they leave nothing behind. Buildings are blown up. Utilities are destroyed. There is no food or electricity or water for our troops. We are advancing even faster than planned, but that only increases our problems. We cannot live off the land, as we thought. Our own supplies are dwindling, even as the distances increase."

"What about casualties? Your reports indicate they are very light."

"They are. The American soldiers retreat without any real opposition. They appear to be engaging only in delaying tactics."

"If they are not fighting, what are they doing?"

"An evacuation is underway to what they call the Federal Zone. That's a large area in the western region encompassing several states and located between two mountain ranges. They believe it will be very difficult to drive them out of this Zone."

A frown gathered across the brow of Francisco de Branca. "I don't understand, General. From what you are saying, the Americans are slipping through your fingers. I'm not a military tactician, but it appears obvious even to me that once established in this protected zone, they will reorganize and launch a counter offensive."

"I'm sure that is their plan, Mr. Chairman." A smile spread across Barboza's face. "However, I have something different in mind."

"What is that, General—?"

"The Americans are doing us a great favor. When their retreat into the Zone is complete, total victory will be in our grasp."

"I'm not following you. You have a plan—?"

"Total saturation with our missiles. Total destruction of their military. And an enormous loss of civilian life — which is according to plan. They are squeezing themselves into a death trap, Mr. Chairman."

Francisco de Branca stared thoughtfully at the general, seeing the pleased expression on the man's face. Barboza obviously believed what he was saying. The Chairman stood up and leaned on the railing of the terrace, looking for a weakness in Barboza's plan. Finally he turned.

"Surely the Americans are aware of the danger they are placing themselves in—"

"Perhaps yes – I'm not sure. They believe we will be fully occupied in the eastern portion of the country, consolidating our gains against a counter offensive. They will be completely vulnerable. Once we launch our missiles into the Zone, Operation Scourge will come to a quick and successful conclusion."

A telephone rang in the suite behind them. An aide to Barboza answered it. Moments later, he came out on the terrace and extended a portable phone toward Francisco de Branca.

"It's for you, Mr. Chairman."

The Chairman frowned at Barboza. "Who knows I'm here—?"

The general wore a blank expression. "No one — at least, I thought no one did. I made the arrangements myself in complete secrecy."

The Chairman took the phone. "This is Fernando Francisco de Branca—"

It was a woman's voice on the other end. "This is Anne Ashford, Vice President of the United States. Welcome to America, Mr. Chairman."

The look on the face of the man from Brazil was one of total shock. He said nothing for a moment, wondering if this was some kind of a prank.

"Are you there, Mr. Chairman?" Anne Ashford asked.

"Yes." Still in shock, he couldn't think of anything else to say.

"I am calling to suggest a meeting between our two governments," the Vice President continued. "We have important matters to discuss."

"I agree," Francisco de Branca replied, regaining some of his composure. "I am pleased you called, Madame Vice President — and of course, a little surprised. It's been less than an hour since I arrived in your country."

General Barboza had stiffened in disbelief as he heard the identity of the caller. He looked around, as if expecting to see someone nearby with a telephone.

"We saw you arrive, Mr. Chairman," Anne Ashford said matter of factly. "We could have shot down your plane, but it's better that we talk. Besides, it's such a beautiful day in Pensacola, isn't it."

"A day of surprises, certainly. What do you wish to talk about, Madame Vice President?"

"That should be obvious, Mr. Chairman."

"Where do you suggest this meeting take place?"

"On neutral ground."

"Is there such a place—?"

"You have shown no intent to attack Canada. Is that a proper reading?"

"It is. A meeting in Canada would be acceptable to us, Madame Vice President. Whereabouts in Canada?"

"May I suggest Vancouver. That's in the western province of British—"

"I've visited the city several times, Madame Vice President. Very beautiful."

"Of course, we'll consider any alternate location if Vancouver is not satisfactory."

"I will confer with General Barboza—"

"He might not be receptive to such a meeting. I certainly hope your Governing Council will, however. As I said, this meeting is very important to both our countries."

"What size of delegation do you have in mind?"

"We prefer it be very limited. That way, points can be communicated clearly by both sides in a much shorter period of time. For our part, we will limit attendees to myself, our military commanding officer, General Aaron Stark, and one recording technician. We feel an appropriate roster on behalf of CASA would be yourself and General Barboza, and someone to record the meeting."

"It appears you have a limited agenda, Madame."

"Very limited. One or two matters connected to Operation Scourge and our mutual friends across the Pacific. I expect our views can be exchanged in less than an hour. Is this acceptable to you, Mr. Chairman? If so, I will make preliminary arrangements with the Canadians and pass them along for your approval."

"Acceptable, Madame Vice President. A pleasure talking to you."

"The same, Mr. Chairman. I'll be in touch shortly."

General Barboza pushed to his feet as the chairman hung up the phone, staring in disbelief. "Was that the Vice President of the United States—?"

"I can only assume it was," Francisco de Branca replied. "I've never met her, but I've seen her picture. She's a very attractive woman."

"How could she reach you?" Barboza asked in amazement. "How did she know you were at this hotel? How did she know you were even in this country—?"

"Excellent questions, General," Francisco de Branca said quietly. "Even more interesting, what does she know about 'mutual friends across the Pacific'? I suggest you get some of those men down by the pool back in uniform, General. Your security obviously is not very secure."

The barb registered but Barboza's thoughts were racing in other directions. "Do you think the Americans will make an offer of surrender?"

The Chairman shrugged. "It's possible, of course, but I don't see that happening this soon. More likely, they want to negotiate — perhaps ask us not to interfere with people evacuating to the western zone."

"I wouldn't oppose that," Barboza smiled. "Their fate will be the same, anyway."

The chairman frowned at Barboza. "Put me in touch with General Fariocha. He's back in Rio, I believe. This lapse in security may be more serious than I like to think about."

In the small conference room at NECCO headquarters, Anne Ashford hung up the phone and looked around, a pleased smile tugging at her lips. With her in the room was Quinn, Race, Aaron, and Yao Gui.

"That was one surprised hombre," she murmured. Her glance settled on Yao Gui. "Your information is dead-on. I could tell he thought I either had a crystal ball or was hiding in his bathroom."

Yao Gui smiled. "The Chinese inner circle will be devastated when they learn America is aware of the connection between China and CASA."

Anne looked at Race Courtney. "You sure we didn't put your people in jeopardy? CASA will know we have people in the area."

"That was the last report from Pensacola," Race told her. "Our people are gone by now."

"I'd like to have seen their faces," Anne smiled. "General Barboza in particular. They tell me he sweats a lot."

Quinn looked questioningly at Aaron Stark. "The ball's in your court, Aaron. You ready for this—?"

Aaron let a satisfied smile crease his face. "Ready and able. Received confirmation a couple hours ago that everything is in place. We still have the President's approval on this, I take it—?"

Anne Ashford nodded. "This is what he wanted. He's not completely comfortable with it, though, especially Phase One. This is what you call grim reality."

"Each phase is dependent on the other," Stark said. "Besides, they brought this on themselves."

"The President knows that," Anne said. "You have his complete support, General."

"I wish I could be at that meeting," Quinn grinned. "I'd like to watch you two hammer in the stake."

"I understand both you and Race are going to Vancouver," Anne said.

"Not for your meeting. We're meeting with the Mossad – probably Joanna Shazebak and whomever else they send. Yao Gui is going along, too. We'll be discussing Operation Desert Sword. The Israelis will be coming in through Greenland and Canada. The timing worked out well for both meetings."

"Are the Canadians willing to let us meet in Vancouver for this?" Yao Gui asked.

Anne nodded. "I cleared it earlier, although they're very uneasy about being involved in anything that might endanger their neutrality."

"If we don't stop CASA," Quinn muttered, "Canada will have to worry about existing, not being neutral."

# 20

## CHECKMATE

Three days later, the U.S. delegation and the CASA delegation arrived in Vancouver, B.C.. It was agreed that only the two principals from each side would be directly involved, but two additional people could be included for recording and note taking purposes, along with a security force of not more than twelve military personnel.

The CASA delegation arrived in Vancouver a day early. They flew north to Winnipeg, in the Canadian province of Manitoba, and transferred to a Canadian Air Force plane which flew them directly to Vancouver, arriving in the early afternoon. A hotel near the airport was reserved for their exclusive use.

At nine o'clock the next morning, two large Canadian Air Force helicopters picked up the delegation and flew them across Vancouver to the heliport near Gastown, on the edge of the city's waterfront. They were escorted a short distance from there to the SeaBus terminal.

Vancouver's SeaBus system linked the city across the Burrard Inlet to North Vancouver. The small ferries were a busy link to the bedrooms and amenities of North Vancouver and a unique attraction to visitors. Today, however, all service was suspended in deference to the visiting foreigners.

Three of the busses were already at anchor in the middle of the harbor, tied side-by-side. The CASA people entered a fourth SeaBus and proceeded to the mid-channel rendezvous. The Canadians suggested this arrangement because it offered maximum security for all parties concerned. Small Canadian warships ringed the group of ferries, making sure there was no interference by sea. The CASA ferry pulled alongside the three moored vessels and waited for the arrival of the Americans.

Anne Ashford and Aaron Stark, with the other members of the U.S. delegation, flew from Hill Field to McChord Air Base, just south of Seattle. They transferred to waiting Canadian military helicopters and were flown a little over a hundred miles north to the heliport in Gastown. Schedules were carefully arranged to make sure they arrived ten minutes after the CASA delegation boarded their SeaBus.

Minutes later, the U.S. delegation arrived at the ferries in mid-channel, tying up on the far side, away from the CASA delegation. Each side then sent its technicians to electronically sweep the three central busses. Satisfied the meeting would be conducted in privacy, the two parties of chief negotiators met in the center SeaBus.

Security forces remained in the outer boats. The two adjacent ferries remained empty. Seats in the center SeaBus were replaced with a small conference table and chairs. The two parties stood facing each other, the two principals in the center, flanked on each side by the recording secretaries.

Anne Ashford found herself scrutinizing the man across from her even before introductions were made. Francisco de Branca was somewhere in his middle forties, she guessed. She was startled that the man was — well, so pleasant looking. He was actually handsome, she admitted reluctantly to herself. Dark wavy hair, white teeth that flashed brightly against a deeply tanned complexion. She noticed the man's eyes were surprisingly warm and friendly. Quite tall, he was lean and appeared physically fit. The athletic type, not the typical over-weight power politician. She interrupted her appraisal with a guilty start. She was not here to date the man. He was an enemy. An attractive enemy perhaps, but still a man she should feel nothing but loathing toward.

Francisco de Branca was trying not to let similar thoughts of admiration distract him. He'd seen photos of the Vice President but she was much more vivacious than they conveyed. Short, curly hair that looked naturally blonde, styled in a young, bouncy cut. She was wearing a plain dark blue suit that was expensively, and tastefully, tailored. The skirt was shorter than he would have expected, showing very attractive legs. Her eyes were blue and sparkling, the mouth full — bordering on sensuous, he thought. He guessed that this woman, removed from the formality of a political meeting, would be very pleasant company. He imagined she had a quick smile, one that easily broke into laughter. Anne Ashford was not at all what he had expected to find in a Vice President of the United States.

Francisco de Branca brought his thoughts back to the reason they were all standing here in a SeaBus in the middle of Vancouver harbor.

"I am Fernando Francisco de Branca, Chairman of the Governing Council of the Coalition of Allied States of the Americas." He extended his hand over the table toward Anne Ashford. "It is a pleasure to meet you, Madame Vice President."

"Thank you, Mr. Chairman," Anne responded. His hand was pleasantly warm, like his smile. She glanced at the general standing beside him. "I presume this is General Carlos Barboza, commander of your military forces."

Barboza bent his head in a stiff bow. "Madame Vice President." It was Barboza's turn to stare at the uniformed general standing across from him. "I have not had the pleasure, General—"

"General Aaron Stark," Anne said. "He is the commanding general of the United States unified military forces."

"Shall we sit down and get to the business at hand," Francisco de Branca suggested, flashing another of those disturbing smiles in the direction of Anne Ashford. "Since this meeting is at your request, Madame Vice President, the opening statement should be yours."

"This meeting will be short, gentlemen," Anne began, "for reasons that will become very clear. General Stark will present our terms and conditions."

Barboza's heavy eyebrows gathered into a frown. "Terms and conditions—?"

Anne Ashford seemed not to hear him, continuing unbroken in her statement. "First, however, I must formally protest in the strongest terms the unprovoked attack by your coalition forces upon the sovereign territory of the United States."

Francisco de Branca gave a brief nod. "The protest is noted, Madame Vice President."

"And I must warn you, Mr. Chairman, that the cruel and barbaric actions of CASA troops against citizens of the United States demand the harshest response. No excuse can be accepted for the wholesale slaughter your forces have inflicted upon our people. I warn you, there will be consequences, Mr. Chairman."

Barboza half rose out of his seat, his face angry. "You seem to forget the position the United States is in, Madame—"

"Sit down, General," Stark growled. He glanced at Anne Ashford. "No sense in prolonging this discussion. With your permission, Madame Vice President—?"

Anne nodded. "Please lay out the facts for these gentlemen, General Stark."

Barboza was glaring across the table. "I resent your attitude, Madame, and yours, General—"

"You'll resent them much more, General Barboza," Anne said coldly, "when you hear what General Stark has to say."

Barboza pushed back from the table and stood up. "We are not here to be insulted." He looked over at Francisco de Branca. "Mr. Chairman, I suggest we conclude this meeting."

Stark pointed a finger at him, his voice cold and threatening.

"And I suggest you sit your ass down, General, and listen carefully." Anne looked at Francisco de Branca, sitting with almost no expression showing on his face.

"Mr. Chairman, let me assure you it is in your interest to hear us out," she said. "We are talking about hundreds of thousands of your people losing their lives. Every minute wasted here lessens their chance of survival."

"Sit down, General Barboza," Francisco de Branca said softly. "I wish to hear what the general has to say."

Barboza sat down, glaring angrily at both Stark and Anne Ashford.

"Thank you, Mr. Chairman," Anne said. "General Stark, please continue."

"The coalition of governments you represent, Mr. Chairman, has conducted missile attacks upon nearly sixty of our cities, resulting in hundreds of thousands of dead and injured. The brutality of your troops since landing on our shores offends the entire civilized world," Stark declared quietly and solemnly. "The time has come, Mr. Chairman, for retribution for these acts."

"May I remind you, General," Barboza growled, "you are not in a position to make threats."

"We are not threatening you, General. I am officially informing you that the United States plans to retaliate upon the countries of the coalition."

Francisco de Branca's voice remained quiet but his demeanor had grown tense. "In what way do you plan to retaliate, General Stark?"

"There are two phases to our response, Mr. Chairman," Stark replied. "Phase One will begin at three o'clock this afternoon, Mountain Standard Time. That is just slightly under four hours away, sir."

"And what may we expect in the way of retaliation, General—?"

"Missiles will be launched upon those countries involved in launching missiles against us," Stark said grimly. "There are twenty major cities and ports, in ten of your countries, targeted for destruction in Phase One."

Both of the CASA officials appeared stunned. This was a far cry from the talk of surrender they had hoped would be the topic of this meeting.

Twenty cities targeted for destruction.

"Why are you telling us this, General?" Francisco de Branca asked, still managing to keep any clear sign of distress out of his voice.

"For two reasons, Mr. Chairman," Stark replied. "We do not wish civilians to be killed in the wholesale manner that resulted from your sneak attacks. Four hours warning is not much, but it is more than you gave us. At least your governments will have time to evacuate some of the civilians from the cities targeted."

"I cannot believe the audacity of this," Barboza snapped. "If such an attack is launched, we will simply reduce more of your cities to rubble—"

"You will not, General Barboza," Stark told him, "because after those initial attacks, you will be facing Phase Two of our planned response."

"And what would that be—?" Barboza demanded.

"Complete nuclear obliteration of every major city and port in South America," Stark said quietly. "The entire continent will be turned into a wasteland."

Francisco de Branca's face suddenly was tight, his color paler. "That is barbaric, sir. I can't believe the United States would consider such an act."

"No more barbaric than your attack upon our country, Mr. Chairman," Anne Ashford responded.

"But nuclear weapons—"

"May I remind you, sir, that nuclear missiles have already been used against our country," the Vice President replied, displaying a flash of temper. "Our national Capital, one of our most priceless treasures, is in ruin and will probably remain so for generations. It was destroyed with nuclear weapons."

"That attack was not sanctioned or conducted by the Coalition, Madame—"

The protest was dismissed in another flash of temper. "Nevertheless, a nuclear precedent is set. The United States has absolutely no compunction about retaliating in kind."

"You are bluffing," Barboza said harshly. "You don't have the capability for such a monstrous assault—"

"This is no bluff, General," Stark warned. "Phase One will speak for itself in four hours — nothing agreed to here will stop that. Phase Two is equally indefensible. The United States has the mightiest navy in the world, General, and your sneak attack did not accomplish the same result as the one on Pearl Harbor. As we speak, there are over three hundred submarines on station off your Atlantic and Pacific coastlines. On signal, they will fire nuclear missiles at every major city and port from Mexico to Cape Horn. The continent will be rendered uninhabitable."

Francisco de Branca stared at Stark in disbelief as the general quietly and dispassionately pronounced a death sentence upon all of South America.

"You appear to be serious in this threat, General Stark," he said at last.

"Deadly serious, sir. Phase Two is not a threat — it is a planned and approved military operation."

"I assume that the fact we are talking means there is something in this that is negotiable—"

Anne Ashford spoke up. "General Stark has proposed an alternative to Phase Two — at least, a temporary one. It is the heartfelt wish of the president of the United States that you accept it without discussion or delay, Mr. Chairman. If you do not, Phase Two will be initiated. That will bring death on a scale none of us wish to contemplate."

"What is this alternative proposal, General Stark?" the Chairman asked. This time the pressure in him could be heard, as well as seen.

"First, let me repeat that Phase One will occur regardless of whether you accept or reject the proposal," Stark said. "However, we will not initiate Phase Two if the Coalition agrees to a temporary truce."

"What do you mean by a truce?" Barboza asked suspiciously.

"Your forces hold in place. You do not occupy any new territory. There is to be no more fighting between us, and absolutely no more atrocities committed on the civilian population."

"How long a period of time are you contemplating?" Francisco de Branca asked.

"Until a satisfactory solution to this matter can be found," Anne Ashford answered. "I hope that can be a political solution. Few will be left alive to enjoy a victory by either side if the choice is renewed military conflict."

"They're stalling," Barboza grated, looking at the Chairman. "If they attack our continent, we will turn the United States into a graveyard."

"After Phase Two you will not have the capability to start a bonfire, General Barboza," Stark interrupted. "We, on the other hand, have the firepower to do exactly what we have outlined."

"A stand-off?" Francisco de Branca asked. "We call a halt to the fighting and our governments discuss a political solution—"

"That is our offer, Mr. Chairman," Anne replied.

"I wish to make one stipulation very clear," Stark added. "Should one missile be fired into our western Federal Zone, we will immediately activate Phase Two."

"Do you understand that, General Barboza?" Anne asked.

The Latin general glared from Stark to the Vice President, then to Francisco de Branca. The Chairman answered for him.

"General Barboza understands completely, Madame Vice President."

"What is your answer, Mr. Chairman," Anne queried, fastening the Chairman with a penetrating stare.

Something deep inside her wanted to feel sorry for the man. She could see the crushing defeat in his eyes. Instead, she pressed the point.

"The President is waiting to hear your decision, Mr. Chairman. He does not want to initiate Phase Two but let me assure you, he will do it if the Coalition does not agree to a truce, or violates it in any way."

Francisco de Branca did not even look at Barboza. "I agree to your terms and conditions, Madame Vice President. I am sure I speak for the entire Governing Council."

Both Anne and General Stark stood up. "We will be in contact, Mr. Chairman. Right now, I suggest you warn the cities on this list."

She handed him a piece of paper with the names of twenty cities on it. Francisco de Branca's eyes quickly scanned down the list.

Mexico City, Merida, Campeche, Villahermosa, in Mexico. Havana, Cuba. Santo Domingo, Dominican Republic. Caracas, Maracaibo, Cumana, Valencia, in Venezuela. Bogota, Medellin, Cartagena, Barranquilla, in Colombia. Georgetown, Guyana. Paramaribo, Suriname. San Jose, Costa Rica. Managua, Nicaragua. Tegucigalpa, Honduras. Guatemala City, Guatemala.

The list was accurate. Every country from which missiles were fired against the United States was included. And apparently weighted. More cities targeted for destruction in those countries from which a greater number of missiles were launched.

Francisco de Branca felt a painful knot growing in his stomach. It was a death list no one expected to be issued. Or perhaps it was not so unexpected by some. For one fleeting moment, he wondered if perhaps this development was secretly anticipated by those who created the Great Plan.

"I sincerely regret what is about to happen, Mr. Chairman," Anne Ashford said quietly, her voice clearly communicating the sincerity of her feelings. "Tens of thousands of innocent civilians will die this afternoon – their blood is not on our hands, but on those who ordered the attack on our country. I hope agreements can be found that will make further bloodshed unnecessary. We do not want to activate Phase Two – but make no mistake, we will do it if there is no other alternative."

Four hours later, the United States initiated Phase One of General Stark's plan.

Twenty cities were destroyed in the space of thirty minutes. The devastation caused by the missiles, all fired from ships at sea, all with conventional warheads, all having the deadly accuracy of U.S. technology, was complete. Waves of high-level bombers dispatched from bases in the west were recalled.

Satellite photos showed there was nothing left to bomb.

# 21

## FRIENDS IN A BOTTLE

Joann Shazebak and her brother Dovid flew from Tel Aviv to London on Israeli passports. From London, they flew on British passports to Montreal and westward across Canada to Vancouver. They arrived the same day as the CASA delegation but stayed the night in a suite of rooms at a downtown hotel. Officially, they were traveling as sales representatives for a new line of British woolen goods.

When the helicopters carrying the U.S. delegation landed at Gastown the next day, three men in the contingent did not accompany the others to the waiting SeaBus. They went to the restroom in the terminal, waited a few minutes, then left by a side door and caught a taxi. Ten minutes later, Quinn, Race and Yao Gui were admitted to the Shazebak suite.

After greetings were exchanged and Yao Gui was introduced, they settled down in the tiny sitting room that separated the two bedrooms.

"This is one you owe us, friend," Dovid Shazebak grinned. "It was your turn to play frequent flyer."

"Appreciate it," Quinn retorted. "This isn't exactly a slow time for us."

The Israelis were well aware of the meeting between the U.S. and the CASA officials that was just getting underway in mid-channel. Joanna gave Quinn a quizzical look.

"They won't go away happy, I trust."

"Extremely unhappy," Quinn answered.

Dovid was studying Yao Gui. "I suppose you're the reason we're here, Yao Gui. I hope you aren't going to spoil our day."

"I'm afraid I am, sir," Yao Gui said apologetically. "The information I bring from Beijing is not good news for Israel."

"You don't mind if we tape this, do you?" Joanna asked, producing a small tape recorder. "If it's important enough to bring us all the way here, our people will undoubtedly appreciate hearing some of it first-hand."

"Everyone be sure no names are mentioned from this point," Quinn replied. "We'll rely on you to edit any slip-ups, Joanna."

Yao Gui began to tell the Israelis all he knew about Operation Desert Sword. It didn't take long, because there weren't that many details. What there was, however, left deep frowns of concern on the faces of both Dovid and Joanna.

"Operation Desert Sword," Dovid muttered. "We suspected something was going on but had no idea it was this far along in planning. This is why the Arabs have been so unusually quiet."

Joanna flashed a quick smile at Quinn. "So this time you beat the Mossad. I suppose it has to happen every now and then, even with you Americans."

"I wasn't going to mention it," Quinn grinned, "but I'm glad you did."

Dovid frowned. "You say the People's Republic is moving up the timetable, Yao Gui?"

"Under the personal direction of General Chang Kuoseng, the director of the PLA's political department — which I'm sure you know is a lot more than its name implies," Yao Gui answered. "He seems to think he can pull this coalition together in a matter of weeks."

"Is there a list of the countries involved?" Joanna asked.

Yao Gui shook his head. "All of the Arab countries, of course. I got the impression they were going farther afield than that, though. Turkey, some of the African countries, Muslim-dominated republics from the former Soviet Union. I understand Pakistan and India pledged weapons and supplies — part of a non-aggression pact the People's Republic is offering them."

Dovid glanced at his sister, seeing her concern matched his own. "If they pull together a coalition that powerful, Israel can't possibly survive."

"The Chinese are right in figuring the United States won't be able to intervene," Quinn added, "not while we have this Latin coalition to deal with."

"General Chang plans to make that a persuasive part of his negotiations with the coalition countries," Yao Gui agreed. "It is the main reason for accelerating the timetable."

"You have to hand it to Beijing," Race said with grudging admiration. "Their Great Plan rips up the world then puts it back together the way the Chinese want it."

"With the United States crippled, they are convinced nothing can stop them," Yao Gui added. "They believe their Great Plan is divinely sanctioned."

"This explains the attack on you, Quinn," Joanna said. "By eliminating you, they hoped to disrupt NECCO operations."

"Then why was it such a sloppy operation—?"

"The Chinese insisted on being completely out of the picture," Yao Gui said. "They left it to the Coalition. The Latins obviously didn't understand how important NECCO was to the United States' response to Operation Scourge."

"Which doesn't change the fact I'm sitting here alive because of you, Joanna." Quinn reached over and clasped her hand. "My thanks again."

"We should start back," Dovid said, standing up. "There is much to be done. We will pray your eagle soon soars free again, my friends. We need it to cast fear into those who would destroy Israel."

* * *

Quinn and Race lived in the same community of apartments and townhouses, built on base about a mile from NECCO headquarters. When Quinn arrived home, he found the townhouse dark and cold. At first, he thought Jill wasn't home. He reached for the light switch but Jill called out from the living room.

"Don't turn on the lights, please."

He saw her then, a dark shadow sitting in a chair near the window. He saw something else; the silhouettes of two bottles on the lamp table directly in front of the window. As he came into the room, Jill reached over and set a glass down beside the bottles.

"You're home early," she said. "It's not midnight yet, is it?"

"Sorry. Had to meet with the President after we got back from Canada. I got away as soon as I could."

"No need to apologize. I should though — I didn't fix dinner."

"Not hungry," Quinn said. He squatted down beside his wife, putting his hand on hers, peering at her anxiously. "You all right—?"

She pulled her hand away, not angrily but obviously. "I'm fine. Are you all right—?"

"I'm fine, too." He stood up and reached over to pick up one of the bottles. Vodka had been in it but it was empty now. He saw the second bottle was half empty. "This is something new, isn't it?"

"Vodka—? No, the Russians have been drinking it for centuries."

"But you haven't. When did you start — drinking vodka, and drinking alone?"

"I haven't been alone all the time – Candi left not too long ago. And I started after our little experience in Denver. I needed comfort, Quinn, and you were never here. I discovered there was a friend inside every Vodka bottle, so I've been opening as many as I can. They make good company."

Quinn squatted down beside her again, putting his hand back on hers. "Jill — this isn't you. What's going on—?"

"I'm relaxing. That's what you and the doctors told me to do, remember. Relax, and I'll be perfectly all right again. I took the pills — all of them. Thirty days worth just this week. Only you know what, Quinn, I'm still not relaxed. Not even with the help of my friends here," she said, gripping one of the vodka bottles. "I think I have a serious problem but my dear husband already has a full load of those, don't you?"

Quinn squeezed her hand hard. "I'm sorry, Jill. I didn't know you were in pain like this."

"I'm surprised you even knew I was home," Jill muttered, once again withdrawing her hand. "Thank goodness for Candi."

In the darkness, Quinn frowned. "You want candy?"

"Candi – with an i," Jill corrected.

"Jill, you're not making sense."

"Yes I am. You just don't understand me. That's our problem, Quinn — you don't understand me anymore."

"Let me get you into bed—"

Jill gave a sharp, almost hysterical laugh. "You'd like that, wouldn't you. Let's get Jill into bed. It's the story of my life."

"You're drunk, Jill. I'll sleep out here. I'll stay home tomorrow and we'll talk."

"Go to work. I've got Candi to talk to. Candi with a capital c and an i. Candi, my friend."

"Who is this Candi?"

"Leo's girlfriend – but you never met Leo, did you. You never even asked me about Leo."

"You are definitely drunk. Get some sleep and we'll talk about this in the morning. I'm sorry, Jill – I really am."

"Were you really in Canada today?"

"I was. I was in a meeting in Vancouver."

"Was Joanna there?"

Quinn remembered what happened the last time he told the truth. "No," he lied.

"You took a couple seconds too long. You're lying to me. See, I'm getting pretty good at this spy stuff."

"We'll talk about it tomorrow."

Jill giggled. "You sound like Scarlet O'Hara."

"I feel more like Alice in Wonderland," Quinn muttered. He helped his wife to her feet. He started to help her across the room but she shook off his hands and walked unsteadily toward the bedroom by herself. He watched her until she closed the door.

Leaning over, he clicked on the lamp beside the chair where Jill had been sitting. Now he could see an ashtray on the table, a half dozen or more cigarette butts crushed in it. All had lipstick on them, he noted. There was another glass, too. So there was a Candi, with a capital c and an i. He went into his study and dialed the number of Frank Kantros.

"Sorry to call this late, Frank. I know this is probably in a report somewhere on my desk, but I need your help. Can you brief me on a woman named Candi – capital c and an i. I think she might have been part of that biker gang my wife and sister ran into—."

# 22

## THE CANDI SHOP

Lincoln Banes, briefcase in hand, tried to move past his wife. Cora blocked his way, her arms folded, a firm set to her face. In his professional football days, Linc was famous for brushing aside three hundred pound tackles, but he had seen that look on his wife's face before. No sense even trying. He stood in the hallway.

"What—?"

"We can talk here or we can go into the bedroom and close the door. I strongly recommend the latter," Cora said.

Inside the bedroom, Linc put down the briefcase and sat on the edge of the bed. He looked at his wife, a little smile on his face. Cora had remained slim through almost thirty years of marriage. He thought she was beautiful that first day he'd seen her on campus, and she still was. A few extra pounds here and there, a few gray streaks in her hair, but he still appreciated the fact that he had shared the companionship all these years of an intelligent, compassionate, and passionate, woman. No man could ask for a better wife, no son for a better mother. But when she showed this side, Linc knew it was time to listen.

"I take it something is troubling you, woman."

"Candi is troubling me. That woman is troubling me a lot. I don't suppose she's troubling you at all."

"Now why say something like that?" Linc protested.

"Because I can't remember any man being troubled by having a beautiful young woman flouncing herself in front of him."

"You're not going to accuse me of—"

"No, I'm not. Unless you want to confess to something I don't know."

Linc smiled at her. "You're all the woman I can handle, sugar."

"I wouldn't want to put that to a test," Cora said, raising an eyebrow. "It's not you that's got me worried — it's Luther."

"Luther — and Candi?"

"Don't give me that surprised look. Of course Luther. He's seventeen, and big enough to be twenty-five. I've seen the way that boy looks at her — and I've seen the way she looks back. We got to get that woman out of the house."

"Candi seems nice enough from what I've noticed," Linc murmured.

"What you've noticed is exactly why she has to go," Cora snapped. "Our son is noticing it too — every time she walks down the hall, or sits and crosses her legs. That woman has a very appropriate name — Candi. Our Luther is developing a sweet tooth."

The Banes had taken Candi into their home when the woman reached the Zone with Stacy and Jill. They offered to do it as a favor, to show appreciation for Candi's cooperation in giving information over the past two weeks that already had brought arrests of nine major drug dealers in the Zone. Her knowledge of the drug pipelines out of California were proving invaluable.

Candi was refined and intelligent – an honors graduate from Stanford, she told them. She seemed genuinely appreciative of being invited into the Banes home. She appeared anxious to start over here in the Zone, talked of getting a job as quickly as possible. Cora helped her look for a place of her own, although in these days when hundreds of thousands of people were pouring into the Zone every day, it was usually death that created a vacancy – and that was always filled in a few hours.

But something changed. Thinking back, Cora thought it started when Candi received a phone call that really excited her. It was a man calling about a job, she said, but she never did say what the job was. After that, Candi began to show a hardness, an unsavory side kept hidden before. For the first time, Cora saw glimpses of the woman who had lived in California's elite drug circles. Cora did not want any of that hardness rubbing off onto her son, who was difficult enough just being seventeen.

"What can I do?" Linc Banes asked. "You can't blame Candi because Luther likes the way she wiggles—"

"So you have been noticing," Cora said quickly. "Forget Luther. Let's concentrate on you—"

A grin spread across Linc's face. "All right. I'll check around for a place. We've got all the records at NECCO. I'll come up with something."

"Soon," Cora stressed. "And from now on, you just watch my behind."

Candi moved out the next day. She got a job with a public relations firm, she told them, and they had helped locate a place to live. She was very excited about it. Her apartment was on the west side of the Salt Lake valley. As she described it to Cora, the place was unbelievably large, comfortably furnished, with two bedrooms and two baths.

Cora was relieved, as was Linc when his wife called and told him. Even Luther seemed pleased for Candi, and Cora was doubly happy about that.

She wouldn't have been, however, if she'd known her son left school early that day and an hour later was knocking on the door of Candi's new apartment.

Candi opened the door, smiling as she invited Luther inside. She showed him around the place, making the last stop her bedroom. Luther looked around curiously, noticing the bed was king-sized.

"I got the word today, Luther," Candi said softly. "You're in, if you want to be."

"That's great, Candi," Luther said excitedly. "I really appreciate it."

"You're in on the ground floor. This is going to be a great opportunity for you, Luther. You'll be running with the power, man."

Luther grinned. "The New Brotherhood – even sounds powerful."

"The most powerful organization in the history of crime," Candi told him. "Every minority will be represented, everybody works together. Whatever comes down from the Supreme Council is the law. And guess who's the top dog on that council, Luther—"

Luther's eyes widened. "You—?"

Candi nodded. "You'll be my main man, Luther, especially when it comes to working with the brothers."

"Geez, Candi. I really owe you—"

Candi took his hand and pulled him into the bedroom. "You can pay me on the installment plan," she smiled.

\* \* \*

There had been some anxious moments at NECCO headquarters as officials waited to see how the CASA leaders would react following the destruction caused by Phase One. If CASA refused to accept the truce, contingency plans were ready. Everyone, especially President Baldwin, had heaved deep sighs of relief when it became evident General Stark's plan was working. There were no attacks on U.S. positions these past two weeks, and aerial reconnaissance photos showed the CASA advance had indeed stopped in its tracks.

The threat of total nuclear destruction, backed up by the terrible show of force against the countries from which missiles had been fired, made it clear to the Coalition leaders the United States was not bluffing. Reassessment was clearly called for.

With the immediate military crisis on hold, Quinn Adams and the others in NECCO turned their attention again to the overwhelming problems piling up on the civilian front. Hundreds of thousands of refugees poured into the Federal Zone daily, placing enormous stresses upon facilities for feeding and housing and other facilities needed by the millions of people now crowded into the Zone.

People registered and were quickly processed out into the camps and towns burgeoning throughout the Intermountain West. Factories and manufacturing plants, extradited from areas under siege, were reassembled in an amazingly short time. Wells were sunk throughout the Zone, power lines strung, power diverted from other cities along the west coast and bought from a reluctant Canada. Oil and natural gas fields went into maximum production, keeping pipelines filled, supplying the vast new needs. Time after time, planners in NECCO faced seemingly overwhelming challenges, and came through in ways that could only be described as miraculous.

Quinn and Race spent time whenever they could trying to figure out their wives and sisters. It was frustrating for both of them. The one thing both Stacy and Jill needed most — time with their husbands — they couldn't provide. Not until the flow of refugees stopped, not before the staggering supply systems were in place.

Days passed, then weeks. The truce still held, easing a lot of pressure. There were many days, however, when neither Quinn nor Race left the NECCO complex.

Stacy seemed to be managing, partly because she had Leah to occupy her thoughts and take up her time.

Quinn tried to get close to Jill but she became more and more distant, showing alarming signs of increasing agitation. She seemed to resent his efforts to reach her. She was drinking heavily now, and apparently was spending a lot of time with her friend Candi.

This evening, Jill was dressed to go out. Quinn, of course, was not home — had not been home for the past three days. She picked up the phone and dialed Candi's number.

Candi answered.

"I'm on my way," Jill said, her voice tight.

"It's too early, girlfriend — not even six o'clock. We said eight, remember—"

"I can't wait that long, Candi."

"You sound strung out. You already used up all that stuff I gave you—?"

"This morning. I can't wait another two hours, Candi. I'm coming over."

"You must be hitting it heavy, baby. That should have lasted you another two weeks. Maybe you should slow down—"

"I need a hit, Candi — now."

There was a pause. "Okay. Settle down, girlfriend. I'll fix you up as soon as you get here."

Jill drew in a deep, thankful breath, clasping her hands tightly together to control the shaking.

"I'm on my way. I'm okay – I'm under control. Just have it ready—"

# 23

## DEEP CRISIS

Quinn returned home early that night — ten o'clock could be considered early, compared to his almost round-the-clock schedule recently. Jill was not home, and there was no note. He called Stacy, wondering if Jill had gone over there. He was surprised by the hesitancy he heard in his sister's voice.

"No — I don't know where she is, Quinn."

"You say that like you know but don't want to tell me," Quinn said.

"Nothing like that," Stacy said quickly. "I'm really not sure."

"Take a guess. I'm worried about her, Stacy."

Another long, hesitant pause. "I think she's with Candi."

Quinn was surprised. "Candi—?"

"I think they were going out somewhere for a drink. You know how she's been lately—"

"Maybe if I called Linc—"

"Not a good idea. Candi doesn't live there, hasn't for weeks. She has her own place somewhere out on the west side. Besides, Candi is not a welcome topic of conversation for Cora or Linc."

"Why not—?"

"Didn't Linc tell you? Luther has moved in with her."

Quinn was aghast. "Luther and Candi — I don't believe it."

"It's true. Cora is devastated. Luther just turned eighteen, so there isn't much they can do about it."

"Does Jill figure into any of this—?"

"No - not in that part, at least. She just hangs out a lot with Candi - relies on her to — well, help her out."

"Like how—?"

"She's your wife, brother. She made it abundantly clear she doesn't want me interfering."

"Is Jill on drugs—?"

"Talk to her, Quinn. If I do hear from her – and I assure you I won't–I'll call you."

The phone clicked and Quinn stared at it, trying to define what he had heard in his sister's voice, what she had communicated but not said. One message was loud and clear; Jill's life was terribly mixed up.

He couldn't help remembering the nightmare of her breakdown seven years ago. He knew the recent attempt on their lives had brought back some of the terror suffered after she was raped. The incident with the bikers on the Denver freeway had undoubtedly added to her stress. Now alcohol and drugs. There must be something he could do.

Quinn tried to stay awake but exhaustion took its toll and he fell asleep in the chair. He was awakened abruptly by the sound of keys fumbling in the lock of the front door. He sprang across the room and flung it open.

Jill stared at him, dropped the keys and gave a surprised giggle. She was being supported between Luther Banes and Candi. Jill was so drunk she couldn't stand up without their help.

Quinn lifted her and carried her to their bedroom. He put her down on the bed and came back. The front door was still open but Luther and Candi were gone. He considered going after them, but decided it was more important to care for Jill. He picked up the keys and closed the door.

Jill was already asleep when he returned to the bedroom, sprawled out across the bed where Quinn had dropped her. He sat her up, started trying to undress her. She opened her eyes, frowning to focus them. Quinn had looked into eyes like that before. A sick knot tightened in his stomach. Jill wasn't just drunk. She was floating in a fog of drugs.

She flopped back, eyes closing. He picked up her arm and pushed back the long sleeve of her blouse, exposing a tell-tale line of needle pricks. All those tracks in such a short space of time told him his wife was using heavily. Quinn stared down at her, feeling pain, and anger. He glanced at his watch. It was a quarter to four. He switched off the light and left the room.

The phone rang at seven-thirty. Quinn groggily got up from the couch and answered it. It was Anne Ashford.

"Sorry to call so early, Quinn. The President would like to see you, General Stark, and myself in an hour. Can you be at the heliport in half that—?"

"We're going flying—?"

"Not far. You sound awful. Are you all right—?"

"I'm fine, or I will be when my body wakes up. I'll be there."

"See you then."

Quinn glanced in at his wife, saw she was still sprawled on the bed. It appeared she hadn't moved all night. She was breathing heavily in deep sleep. He closed the door and called his sister.

"She's home—?" Stacy asked.

"About four this morning. Can you come over and babysit — I have to meet with the President. She's still out, probably will be for a long time."

"She's more than just tired, I take it—"

"So drunk she couldn't stand. And I know now what you didn't want to tell me. She's definitely on drugs – a heavy user, by the looks of her arms."

"I wasn't absolutely sure, Quinn. I didn't want to hurt you if it wasn't true."

"Appreciate that, sis. Can you come over — she's going to hate life when she wakes up."

"Be there in a few minutes."

"Thanks."

"Go see the President. Gee, it's so nice having an important brother—"

The helicopter carrying Anne Ashford, Quinn, and Aaron Stark took off and headed south toward Salt Lake City. The city sat at the head of a mountainous 'u' shape, the downtown area and the state capital building nestled against the slopes at the northern end of the 'u', with two parallel ranges of mountains stretching to the south. The Wasatch range ran along the east, the Oquirrh mountains along the west.

The valley between the ranges, once arid desert, was now a solid mass of residential communities and businesses, some fifteen miles wide and reaching some twenty-five miles south to the Point of the Mountain. This wind-blown promontory marked the line between the Salt Lake valley, and the Provo valley beyond.

The copter flew past Salt Lake and on down the valley, suddenly veering 90 degrees east and heading into the wild beauty of Little Cottonwood Canyon.

Little Cottonwood wound steeply up into the Wasatch, finally widening out into a huge basin containing some of the finest ski resorts in North America. Unfortunately, these recreational facilities were blocked from the general public now by a huge concrete gateway complex at the mouth of the canyon, controlled by unsmiling, alert Rangers of the NECCO force.

Not even tanks could get through those gates without permission.

Clearance for the copter to enter Little Cottonwood was arranged. Without that clearance, no plane could make it through the curtain of ground-to-air missiles that would be launched against them.

The NECCO copter went only a couple of miles into the canyon before it veered off to the left, away from the narrow, twisting canyon roadway. It landed on a large, paved pad in an area blasted and leveled at the foot of one of the towering canyon peaks.

"We're meeting the President here at Granite Mountain?" Quinn asked, surprised.

Anne Ashford nodded. "Don't ask me why. He just said be there."

Granite Mountain was indeed a surprising place for a meeting with the President of the United States. Some thirty years ago, officials of the Mormon church began excavating a tunnel system into the solid granite bowels of the mountain. It was from this same mountain that huge blocks of granite were carved a hundred and fifty years earlier for the construction of the striking Mormon temple in Salt Lake City.

The church used the tunnels to store its vast accumulation of genealogical records compiled world-wide and put onto microfilm. It was a unique storage system, naturally temperature controlled, safe even from a direct nuclear hit.

Over the years, local, state and even federal agencies were granted permission to use the vaults for special needs. This arrangement was broadened under the powers of NECCO, and the complex was now under total federal control — more specifically, under NECCO control. It was here in Granite Mountain that the priceless national treasures from Washington, D.C., and many other locations, were secreted. Local residents complained bitterly about the closure of the canyon but had no idea why such tight security was imposed by the military.

The three passengers stepped from the helicopter and hurried toward the entrance to the complex. There were several layers of security procedures, despite the fact that the three visitors were almost as well known as Santa Claus. Finally, they were admitted into the brightly lit interior.

Under NECCO control, the labyrnth of granite tunnels was greatly enlarged. Not only did these tunnels contain such treasures as the original Constitution, the Bill of Rights, and many of the most priceless art treasures from national museums, they also were now the resting place of the nation's entire gold reserve. Added to that was the gold being held by the United States for many other countries, along with monetary reserves of many of the world's largest banking systems. The gold "vein" inside

Granite Mountain was undoubtedly the richest in the entire world.

President Baldwin was waiting for them, sitting in an electric cart. He waved a hand in greeting.

"Climb in. I'm driving — this is the only place I get to do that."

They started whirring through what seemed like miles of tunneling, passing row after row after row of files and vaults. It was staggering to see such vast storage of records, most of it now federal statistics. The cart twisted and turned down one corridor after another, the President keeping the accelerator to the floor, a happy grin on his face. Following behind them, of course, were two other carts, each containing four unsmiling Secret Service men.

President Baldwin finally stopped in front of a small ante-room blasted out of the granite. Beyond the ante-room, which contained five more unsmiling men of the Secret Service, was a metal door. It was painted black, with a presidential seal emblazoned on it in gold leaf.

"Welcome to my retreat," Baldwin grinned, stepping out of the cart. "Or should I say, to my deep retreat. And believe me, folks, this is deep."

One of the waiting agents opened the door as they followed the President into his underground office. It actually was a very elegant suite of living quarters. The office was large, richly paneled and luxuriously furnished. There was an adjoining communications room, which somehow worked despite being buried deep in granite. There was a bedroom beyond that, complete with separate dressing room, shower, and an oversized whirlpool tub. The living quarters also contained a kitchen and a well-stocked, walk-in pantry.

The President sat down behind his desk, motioning for the others to also sit. He got right to the point of the meeting.

"Secretary Van Durlin was notified last night that the Israelis have appointed a Special Ambassador to the United States. Dovid Shazebak. I know you've worked with him for years, Quinn—"

"As a Mossad agent," Quinn smiled, "not as a politician."

"I suspect he's still a little of both," Baldwin said. "No matter. I know the Israelis are very concerned about this Operation Desert Sword. He'll arrive here in the Zone in a few days, accompanied by his wife and sister. You also know both of them, Quinn—"

"His wife looks like Sophia Loren but can be as scary as Attila the Hun. She's a great lady," Quinn nodded. "Joanna and I go back a long ways."

"Dovid Shazebak has requested a meeting with me the same day he's scheduled to arrive. I think I know why he wants that meeting. I talked to the Israeli president this morning. He didn't say anything, but only an idiot wouldn't understand what he wasn't saying."

"You have our full attention, Mr. President," Anne said, a half-smile twitching at her mouth. "I suppose that what he didn't say is the reason for this meeting—"

"And I certainly hope, Mr. President," Quinn added, "that you are not going to not say what the Israeli president didn't say—"

"Strip away the political double-talk and the message is clear," Baldwin grunted. "Before I get into that, however, I want to show you people something. Let's take another ride. Better grab a parka on the way out — it gets pretty chilly where we're going."

They got back into the electric cart and once again the President floored the pedal. Behind them, the two cart loads of Secret Service kept a respectful distance.

"Feels good to be behind the wheel," Baldwin told his passengers, "even if it is only a golf cart."

The wheels of the cart actually squealed a couple of times as he negotiated sharp turns in the maze of corridors. The others were amazed that he knew where he was going — except Quinn. He knew exactly where the President was heading. Quinn had helped lay out this route.

Baldwin braked as the cart approached a mass of flashing red warning lights and a steel barricade manned by NECCO Rangers. Behind the Rangers were two large steel doors, blocking an entrance some fifteen feet square.

The soldiers were respectful of their visitors, but still looked ready to shoot down even these people.

"Your Rangers take this seriously, Quinn," Baldwin said, as he got out of the cart. "Always get the feeling they're trying to decide if they should shoot me."

"They're paid to look that way, sir," Quinn responded. "It's part of the training — scare people."

Identities were closely checked by the lieutenant in charge. Baldwin looked over at Quinn. "I'm the President. What do I do if some day they won't let me in—?"

"If they won't, sir, it isn't you," Quinn grinned.

The steel doors slid open and the four people entered. Almost instantly, the doors closed again. They rolled so smoothly that only the hum of electric motors could be heard, followed by faint clicking of locks falling into place.

They were now in a huge vault, at least thirty feet high. The walls could not be seen. That was because of the endless rows of gold bullion bars neatly stacked and glistening under a flood of brilliant overhead lights. The entire chamber was full of gold, as far as the eye could see. It was a breathtaking sight.

"There are two more vaults just like this one," Baldwin said, having difficulty taking his own eyes off the incredible mountain of wealth. "You could sum it up by saying there's a lot of gold in Granite Mountain."

"Simply overwhelms the mind," Anne Ashford breathed. "Are we allowed to take home samples, Mr. President—"

"Touch one of those bars," Quinn grinned, "and you'll unleash the banshees from hell."

"It's impressive," Baldwin muttered, "but it isn't what I brought you here to see. Follow me, please — and like Quinn said, don't even touch any of those bars. We'll all be deaf for life."

The President walked ahead of them toward another steel door at the far side of the vault. He reached toward the handle but Quinn called a soft warning.

"The code, Mr. President. You need to punch in the code — the systems on this door are a little more deadly."

"Thank you, Quinn. Nearly forgot."

He punched in a five-digit code on the small panel to the right of the door. There was a sound of motors again, then five clicks as metal locking rods withdrew. Baldwin glanced at Quinn questioningly.

"It's safe to proceed, sir."

Baldwin grasped the handle and opened the heavy door. The vault beyond was much smaller than the one containing the bullion and was empty except for two metal cases sitting on their own tables. They were large but less than a foot high. Each was hermetically sealed, and bound with four steel bands. Each band had its own lock, attached to a cylinder. Baldwin waited until Quinn, who was the last person to enter, closed the door.

"I suppose you can guess what these cases contain," Baldwin said soberly.

General Stark was staring at the steel containers. "The Constitution of the United States—"

"—and the Bill of Rights," Anne Ashford finished.

"Correct," Baldwin said. "I don't know about you, but when I stand beside these documents, I get a feeling that I can't experience any other way. We are standing in the presence of the heart and soul of this nation. There is not a doubt in my mind that these two documents were written under divine inspiration. I believe that God, or somebody from the heavens, sat with the men who wrote those words, helped them put the very essence of freedom down on paper so the whole world could understand what this nation stands for. The rights guaranteed by those declarations must never be lost."

No one said anything, each feeling the awe of just being in the same room with these two documents.

"This is what everything is about," the President said quietly. "This is what we who serve this nation are all about."

Tears started running down the cheeks of Anne Ashford. She made no attempt to brush them away. "I wish every American could feel their power. We'd be a different nation, a different society."

"I brought the three of you here because I want your advise, and I want you to give it with these two documents in front of you. Unless I'm completely wrong, we will be asked soon to do something in direct violation of the spirit and the laws of this land. Despite that, it may also be the right thing to do."

"You're talking about the Israelis, aren't you," Aaron Stark said.

"Correct, General. I think Dovid Shazebak will present an official request for the immediate repatriation of all American Jews to Israel. That's what the President wasn't telling me this morning."

"A voluntary repatriation, of course," Anne said.

"I don't think so. All Jews go back to Israel, like it or not."

"We can't do that, Mr. President," Anne said quickly.

"Deporting citizens of this country without legal cause, or without their consent, is clearly against the law."

"But is it against the heart and soul of the law?" Baldwin asked quietly. "Is right always right, and wrong always wrong?"

"Are you seriously considering ordering a mass exodus of all Jews. Mr. President," Anne queried, "even against the will of the individual?"

"Ask the question that way, and it puts it into one light," Baldwin replied. "Ask it the way I'm sure the Israelis will put it, and there's a different light."

"In what way, sir?" Aaron Stark asked.

"A matter of survival. Send them enough manpower and military support to defeat the coalition against them, and we not only preserve the state of Israel, we protect our own vital interests in that part of the world."

"It would be a simple matter to resolve if we had the manpower and resources to send, Mr. President," Stark said. "Unfortunately, we're not in that position at the moment."

Baldwin nodded agreement.

"Israel is a strategic buffer for this nation. If it's destroyed by the Arabs, and the Chinese become the dominant power in that part of the world, we're completely cut off from most of the world's oil reserves."

"It seems we're dealing with a double edged sword, Mr. President," Anne Ashford frowned. "Do we abrogate an individual's rights and preserve the Union, or do we put Constitutional rights ahead of the national welfare?"

"We may face that choice, Anne. All I want you three to do for the present is think about it," Baldwin said. "Not only the Constitutional dilemma. General Stark, what happens to our military strength if we lose millions of our Jewish people? If we send manpower without sufficient military hardware to support them, are we just sending more Jews for the Arabs to kill? Do we have enough military hardware to spare in quantities meaningful in a conflict like the Israelis will be facing?"

Stark grimaced. "Not easy questions, sir,"

"That's not the whole dilemma either. What happens from the standpoint of brain power and recovery, Quinn?" the President added. "How many Jewish people are in key positions of leadership, and can we afford to lose them?"

"No sir, we can't," Quinn answered unhesitatingly. "Our human resources would be seriously damaged, sir. We can make adjustments, of course, but many of the top men we depend on are of Jewish heritage."

"So there we are," Baldwin sighed. "Rocks and hard places. Hopefully, I've misread what the Israelis will request — but don't count on it."

The President's face grew even more serious. He looked from one to the other, seeming to be looking for words to express his thoughts.

"There's another reason I brought all of you here," he said finally. He looked again at the two metal cases. "Those documents are already in serious jeopardy. General Stark, you've worked out a good stand-off with the Latins. Sooner or later, though, that's going to break down. I know what we've threatened to do, but I can't see us actually doing it. Not killing millions of innocent civilians who don't have a thing to do with what's happened. So I'm asking the three of you to come up with a permanent peace plan. I realize you're all carrying full loads as it is, but this must become your highest priority. I can't give this to the politicians or the diplomats – they'll never find a light at the end of the tunnel. They'll take years to decide who should go into the tunnel first. We need a fresh approach to end this stalemate, and we need it before both continents — millions of our people, and theirs — are destroyed in a nuclear holocaust."

"Do you have any guidelines, Mr. President?" Anne Ashford asked, her voice lowered by the heavy responsibility just placed on three people.

"None," Baldwin said. "I'm in the same boat as State and the Congress. We've been trained to think in channels. This will take imagination, innovation, the same boldness General Stark used in getting us this reprieve. I'm absolutely convinced that you three, working together, are the best hope we have of making sure this nation, these documents, endure beyond this crisis. We need a solution that settles the military dilemma, the political dilemma, and the social dilemma. Use whatever resources you need, do whatever has to be done, but do it."

He looked at them, his expression grave. They could tell he was under tremendous strain.

"I'll be praying you receive the same divine inspiration and guidance as the men who wrote these documents."

# 24

# A High Price

The Shazebaks arrived at the Salt Lake International Airport four days later. They were met by Vice President Anne Ashford, an unusual gesture of respect that showed the Israelis the United States was giving their mission high priority.

They were escorted to a downtown luxury hotel reserved exclusively for the use of foreign dignitaries. Anne chatted with them for a few minutes then left. Later, a message arrived from Quinn Adams, inviting the three of them to dinner that night at NECCO headquarters. Shortly after, Dovid Shazebak was taken to the State Capital building, now taken over by the federal government, for a meeting with President Baldwin and Anne Ashford.

It was now almost nine in the evening, and Quinn and Race were already seated at a table set for six in one of the private dining rooms at the main NECCO restaurant. These special rooms, which could accommodate up to a dozen guests, were regularly swept electronically to be sure all discussions were indeed conducted in privacy.

Stacy was shown into the room and both men rose as she sat down at the table. She fluttered a hand in front of her face.

"My, my, gentlemen," she said, feigning a Southern drawl, "Ah haven't seen such chivalry since ah left our plantation in Georgia."

"I thought Jill was coming with you," Quinn said.

Stacy shrugged and shook her head. "She won't come, brother. I tried, but she's determined not to sit at the same table with your lover."

"Joanna is not my lover."

"Lover — ex-lover. It's the same thing in Jill's mind."

"That's ridiculous—" Quinn said, exasperated.

"Did you ever meet a woman who was completely understanding about ex-lovers?"

Quinn stood up. "I'll call. Maybe she'll change her mind."

He used the telephone in the room. It rang until the message machine turned on. "Jill, if you're there, please pick up the phone—"

Nothing. He dialed again and this time left a message asking her to join them, no matter how late it was. He returned to the table.

"I don't know how to deal with this," he muttered. "It's not about Joanna. Jill has flipped out."

"She needs help," Stacy agreed. "Someone besides Candi."

"She refuses to go to a doctor, won't even discuss seeing a psychiatrist," Quinn said. "Between the drinking and the drugs, I don't know her anymore."

"How about getting her into rehab?" Race suggested. "It would at least get her back to being rational—"

Quinn shook his head. "Not a chance. She's firmly in denial. In her mind, the only problem she has is me."

"One thing's for sure," Stacy said, a worried frown on her face, "you have to get her away from Candi. That woman is up to something. I have no idea what it is, but Candi is a loose cannon. Race, why don't you start digging into that woman — and I do mean figuratively. She's doing too well, too soon."

"Good idea," Race said. "Something's going on in the Zone. A lot of bad guys from the old days are popping up dead."

"You're right, Stacy," Quinn agreed. "We need to give Candi another check. I doubt if the FBI will come up with anything – they didn't the last time. Put some of your men on it, Race."

A few minutes later, the Shazebaks were admitted to the dining room. Quinn introduced everyone. Race had met Joanna in Washington, and later in Vancouver with her brother. This was his first time to meet Sophia, however. Stacy hadn't met any of the Shazebaks. Quinn couldn't help noticing his sister giving Joanna a close scrutiny.

As usual, both Sophia and Joanna looked stylish and beautiful. Dovid looked like he was not a particularly happy man, despite efforts to conceal it.

"I take it things didn't go well with the President," Quinn said, as they all sat down.

Dovid shot him a quick smile. "It makes me nervous when someone knows me well enough to see inside me."

"Been a lot of years, buddy," Quinn smiled back. "Although this is the first time I've sat across from Special Ambassador Shazebak. Is that for real—?"

Dovid nodded. "I'm officially a politician. No longer do you see a Mossad agent."

"Except for Sophia and Joanna," Quinn grinned, looking over at them. "Ladies, you both look ravishing, as usual. And as for you, dear Dovid, no appointment will ever take the Mossad out of your soul."

Dovid grinned agreement. "Too many good parties to remember."

"So, back to your meeting with the President. Can you tell us anything about it?"

"I gather you already know about our request—"

"President Baldwin mentioned what he expected you were going to ask. I've already briefed Race."

"It was exactly what he expected," Dovid said wryly. "He turned us down."

"Flatly — no options?"

"No options. Not for the present at least."

"I can tell you, that wasn't an easy decision for him."

"I gathered that. I couldn't really argue with his reasoning. He has to put his own country first, but it leaves a devastating problem for us."

"Well," Quinn said, picking up his menu, "let's order dinner and talk it through. Maybe we'll come up with a solution before dessert."

Joanna looked at him. "Isn't your wife joining us—?"

"She sends her regrets," Quinn smiled. "She's under the weather and I agreed it would be best if she stayed home. Maybe next time—"

They all enjoyed an excellent dinner, discussed the problems facing the Israelis in attempting to deal with the threats of Operation Desert Sword, and found no solutions. The conversation after dessert turned to the invasion by the CASA forces, how the government was coping with the devastation caused by the Latins, and the myriad of problems facing the government in the Federal Zone.

"This gives me a better understanding of why President Baldwin made the decision he did," Dovid said. "Sounds like a nightmare."

"It is," Race agreed, "but we're working through it."

"You mentioned the research being done at your special centers," Joanna said. "Sounds like you're getting exciting results—"

"Unbelievable is a better word," Quinn said. "How would the three of you like to visit a couple of the centers tomorrow?"

"Wonderful," Dovid said quickly, "if it's permissible."

"I'll give you clearance," Quinn smiled. "It will be helpful for you to see some of this. Technology may be the only thing we can send to Israel for awhile. You'll find it tremendously interesting."

The conversation at the dinner party continued for the next couple of hours, drifting pleasantly back and forth between the problems of today, the hopes for tomorrow, and the memories of yesterday.

While this was going on, Jill was driving to Candi's house. She was out of drugs again and desperately needed relief. The door was opened by Luther, who gave an understanding grin.

"Looks like you need a fix, Jill."

"Desperately. Is Candi here—?"

Candi came down the hallway, buttoning her blouse. She tugged at her skirt, straightening it, then brushed a hand at her hair, which was tousled and out of place. She gave Jill an angry frown.

"You need to call before you come over, girlfriend."

"Sorry," Jill said, pushing past Luther and coming toward her. "I'm in need, Candi—"

"Well, some of us have other needs," Candi said. She shot a quick look at Luther. "We finish that later, Luther—"

Luther grinned. "I'm ready—"

"You're always ready," Candi murmured. "That's what I like about you, boy."

"Candi – can't all this wait," Jill said, grabbing Candi's arm. "I'm going out of my mind—"

Candi looked at her. Jill was too far gone to see the disgust on her face.

"You're getting to be more trouble than you're worth, girlfriend. I think we have to do something about that." She nodded at Luther. "Give her a shot. Make it a good one, and put her down to sleep it off. Then I want to talk to you—"

Luther was grinning again. "Talk—?"

A few minutes later, Luther joined her in the bedroom. She was sitting on the edge of the bed, staring thoughtfully at the telephone. Luther sat beside her, waiting.

"I was hoping she would be of some use to us," Candi said finally. "Married to the big honcho Pharaoh man and all — a pipeline right into headquarters. It's not working out – she's a wreck. Nobody tells her anything. Didn't know at the time how much baggage she's carrying around. She's hitting the stuff so hard now, I'm worried she'll do anything for a fix."

"How much does she know about the Brotherhood?" Luther asked.

"Don't know," Candi frowned, "but she's seen more than I'm comfortable with. I think it's time to help poor little Jill solve her problems. You're my man, Luther. I got a job you're going to like—"

# 25

## SERENDIPITY

Early the next morning, a twin-engine NECCO jet sliced through the air at high speed as it headed south toward St. George, in southern Utah. The plane frequently dropped to a thousand feet as Quinn pointed out one bustling center of activity after another where just a few months ago there had been only empty desert. There was almost a continual line of new towns and industrial complexes all the way down through the state.

Quinn, Dovid, Sophia and Joanna were in the main cabin, with two NECCO pilots up front at the controls.

"All the tent cities are gone, except for a few in northern Idaho and Wyoming," Quinn told his passengers. "Some of our most important breakthroughs have come in the areas of construction."

"I can't believe you've accomplished all this in such a short span of time," Dovid said, looking down at another town under development in the desert below them. "It's amazing."

"I'll show you one of our secrets when we get to St. George," Quinn smiled. "Although I'm not sure we should share this one with you."

"Why not—?" Sophia asked.

"Because in a month, there won't be a square inch on the West Bank without a housing development," Quinn smiled.

"It's already headed that way," Dovid said. "Remind me to show you around next time you're in our part of the world."

"No thanks. Not until you Jews and Palestinians learn how to all kneel on the same prayer blanket."

"Not in your lifetime," Sophia murmured.

They landed at St. George, the visitors from Israel already impressed with what they had seen from the air. The progress in resettling the hundreds of thousands of refugees was truly startling. In a matter of months, St. George had grown from a small town into a large city. It was difficult to visualize the same thing happening throughout the entire Intermountain region.

A limo was waiting for them, the air conditioned interior welcome, for it was hot here in Utah's Dixie. As they approached a fenced-off cluster of buildings, with military guards at the gate, Quinn continued to brief the Shazebaks. Some of the things he was about to show them were indeed important discoveries that could be vital to the survival of Israel.

"We concentrated our brain trust efforts down here on five major areas of development," Quinn explained. "Food supply. Housing. Industrial capacity. Energy. Mining technologies. In some of those areas, we've done only cranial theory — think tanks coming up with ideas that hopefully will work beyond theory. We have already achieved practical applications in some of them."

Identities were carefully checked, then they headed off toward the buildings in the distance. On the way, they passed several huge earth movers, busily digging into the ground.

"See the strange scoops on those earth movers," Quinn pointed out. "They have retractable steel corkscrews with built-in lasers. They can move as much earth in an hour as it took a whole day before. Some test models are already strip mining in central and eastern Utah — there are enormous coal deposits in those parts of the state. These new machines should open the fields for efficient mining. That in turn, of course, will provide huge quantities of energy."

They drove on, and Quinn next pointed to a large building off to their right. Thick, light colored smoke was belching from two tall stacks above the building. As they approached, the limo's air conditioning unit picked up a strong, acrid odor from outside.

"Don't tell me," Sophia said, scrunching up her nose. "This is a factory producing men's deodorant—"

Quinn grinned. "We're doing chemical fertilizer research here. Stinks, doesn't it. We won't go in—"

"— for which you have my eternal gratitude," Sophia grimaced.

"They have some new formulas cooking in there," Quinn continued, "that are making plants grow so fast they're almost jumping out of the ground. The scientists are projecting as many as four to six harvests a year on some crops."

"Amazing. Simply amazing," Dovid breathed. "Do you know what that would do for Israel—"

"Not as much as what's going on in the next building," Quinn replied. "That's where we're conducting research on biological bacteria — the good kind. Just sprinkle the bacteria on the ground and it grows into high-nutritional food by itself. Crazy stuff—"

"How can you accomplish all this?" Dovid said, shaking his head. "This is like seeing a Jules Verne novel come to life."

"No," Quinn corrected, "it's seeing what the collective brains of some of the greatest scientists in the world can accomplish. We simply put them together in teams, gave them a crisis and a deadline. You can literally feel all that brain power churning. And it's producing results that no genius by himself probably could have imagined."

"Makes you wonder if all the problems in the world could be solved by this approach, doesn't it," Joanna said, looking around at the nearby fields, all green with young crops.

The limo pulled up in front of a long building. Attached to the building was one greenhouse after another, stretching for at least a mile. Quinn opened the door.

"This is worth seeing. Time to stretch, anyway."

They again passed through security, then Quinn led them out into the vast lines of greenhouses. From where they stood near the front, they couldn't see an end to them at the back or on the far side. It was hot and very humid. There was row after row of small plants, sitting on tables in long, shallow aluminum troughs.

"This is our seed research center," Quinn began, pointing at the thousands of rows of plants. "We brought the best brains out of every agricultural college in the country here. They've already come up with hundreds of fast-growing strains."

He walked closer to a row of plants, and pointed. "See anything significant about these plants—?"

"There's no earth," Sophia said quickly. "Just water—"

"You're witnessing one of the more remarkable achievements of this team," Quinn said proudly. "These plants are hygroscopic — they soak up moisture. Our scientists have developed a root system with strong hydrophilic tendencies—" He could see he had left Sophia and Joanna back on hygroscopic. "These plants don't need soil to grow. They feed on nutrient-loaded water that turns them into Jack's beanstalks. You don't even have to plant these babies — they just drink and grow by themselves. In a controlled climate, like this, they'll grow all year round. It's not a new technique, of course, to grow plants in only water, but it sure is improved."

"I feel like I just stepped into the next century," Sophia muttered.

"We have," Dovid nodded. "This is incredible."

"Let's get back to the car," Quinn said. "There's one more thing I want to show you."

This time the limo took them to a cluster of buildings that looked busier than any of the others they had visited. Scores of workers could be seen bustling around, trucks were being loaded, smoke was belching from a score of stacks. Some of them looked like furnace stacks, and they could see heat writhing out of them.

"It's like this round the clock," Quinn told them as they got out of the car. He pointed to some slabs of what appeared to be concrete leaning against one of the buildings.

"This is what I wanted to show you," he told Dovid. He glanced at Joanna and Sophia. "I think you ladies will find this interesting, too."

They walked toward the slabs, and as they got closer, could see the slabs definitely were not concrete, as they had appeared at a distance. In fact, the panels appeared to be almost translucent.

Quinn reached out and rapped one of the panels. It sounded hard, but the others saw it vibrate slightly. This was surprising, for the panel was several inches thick and ten or twelve feet square. One would have thought that a blow from a sledgehammer wouldn't cause it to vibrate.

"We sort of stumbled onto this," Quinn grinned. "We were fiddling with a combination process involving rock, sand, and lasers, trying to come up with something that could be produced in a hurry and used in industrial plant construction. There was a mix-up — a happy mistake. The result was this."

He motioned toward Dovid. "Go ahead. See if you can move it."

"This would not be a good time to get a hernia," Sophia warned her husband. "I'm considering this trip the honeymoon we didn't get."

"Trust me, Sophia," Quinn grinned. "Your husband won't suffer any damage — to anything."

Dovid stepped forward and gripped one end of the large slab with both hands. He found it was hot to the touch.

"Is it supposed to be hot?" he asked Quinn.

"Just been out in the sun. Give it a try — but be careful."

"Now he's saying be careful," Sophia said quickly, with mock concern. "Don't you strain anything, Dovid—"

Dovid set his feet and gave the slab a heave. It tipped up on one end and almost flew out of his grasp. The panel could not have weighed more than a hundred pounds, if that. Dovid set it down again, stepping back with a look of wonder on his face.

"That is amazing," Dovid breathed. "I could carry that whole slab by myself. What is it—?"

"We're still perfecting it, so it doesn't have a name yet. But it is incredible, isn't it."

Dovid turned to his sister. "You try it, Joanna—"

"Don't be silly. I'm a woman."

Dovid snorted. "Don't give me that woman stuff. I've seen you throw a full-grown man over your head. Go ahead and try it — both of you."

Reluctantly, the two woman walked over to the slab. Joanna tried to lift it first, and gasped in surprise as almost the same thing happened to her that had happened to her brother. She set it down and Sophia stepped up. The same results. It was no more difficult than lifting a couple of automatic assault rifles.

"That is incredible," Sophia muttered. "What on earth is it made of? It looks almost like clear plastic, but much lighter."

"It is a plastic — although something totally new in concept. There are some chemicals in there — that's where the original accident occurred — and some special heating processes applied. So far as we can tell, the slabs are virtually indestructible."

Dovid was leaning close, peering at the slab. "I see a lot of flecks in there — they look like silver. And here, along the edges — those are computer chips, aren't they—?"

"We think we've hit the jackpot with this," Quinn said quietly. "That's why I wanted you to see it. The brain trust thinks it has come up with a new wrinkle on solar energy. I can't explain it scientifically — it's way over my head. But our people believe this slab, and hopefully millions like it, will change the entire construction industry. This stuff is highly malleable while being produced, is virtually impervious to deterioration, and contains its own solar energy plant. It collects and stores solar power."

"If that's true," Dovid said, "the possibilities are staggering."

"It's true," Quinn assured him. "They're working now on completing a reverse application — making the heating system become its own cooling system, too. That's tied in with the computer chips you noticed. If it works as they are convinced it will, these slabs will be indestructible, contain their own lighting system inside and out, and function as a self-contained air conditioning unit. A city built of this material would need no street lights, no electrical power plants, no wiring inside a house. All a homeowner would need is a remote control unit. That's where my mind blanks out."

"Absolutely fantastic," Dovid breathed again, touching the slab with his fingers. "This will indeed revolutionize all building techniques."

"Just think what would happen if highways were paved with this stuff," Quinn added. "You'd have built-in street lighting, snow removal would be a thing of the past, because heat would melt it." He shook his head. "Thinking of the possibilities makes my head ache. And remember, this is just one of a score of research centers we've set up."

"Thank goodness the Chinese nor the Latins had any inkling of what NECCO could accomplish," Joanna said, taking hold of Quinn's arm. "If they had, they would have sent a regiment to kill you, instead of a squad of amateurs."

"I can't take credit for any of this," Quinn protested. "All I do is move pegs and push buttons."

"So remind me never to get into a game of Chinese checkers with you," Joanna smiled, squeezing his arm. There was a warm glow of pride in her eyes that she didn't try to hide.

The plane returned to Hill Field later that afternoon. The Shazebaks were driven back to their hotel, and Quinn decided to go home rather than return to the office. Race had promised to contact him if any new emergencies came up, and since he hadn't, Quinn assumed none had.

# 26

## LOVE LOST

When he let himself into the apartment, Quinn felt a twinge of guilt. Last night after dinner, he called Jill several times. There was no answer so he assumed his wife had gone out again. Not wanting to deal with another confrontation, he went back to his office and worked on the stacks of information and satellite photos on his desk. Finally, with only a few hours before he was to meet the Shazebaks for the trip to St. George, he fell asleep on the couch in his office.

He called home again before leaving, but there was still no answer. He had mixed feelings as he closed the door and called out to Jill.

Once again, no answer.

He went into the bedroom and saw his wife sprawled on the bed. She apparently had tried to undress, for her blouse and brassiere were off, and her skirt was pulled up around her hips. Her panties were on the floor, along with her shoes. She must have passed out then, for she had made no attempt to cover herself with sheet or blanket.

Shaking his head, Quinn crossed and started to pull a blanket over her. His hand touched her bare shoulder and a shock wave rammed through him. His wife's flesh was stone cold. He fought what his brain started screaming.

Jill was dead.

Quickly, he felt her neck for a pulse. There was none. She was so cold he knew she'd been dead for a long time. Guilt poured hotly through him. Had she been lying here, dying, when he called yesterday? If he'd come home, would she still be alive? He sat on the bed beside her, overcome with guilt and a crushing sadness.

They were once so much in love. The years with her had been so good. It was only these past few months she'd changed, and he couldn't rid himself of the feeling that if he'd tried harder, if he'd insisted she get help, if he'd recognized the signs of breakdown earlier—

All too late now. He took hold of her cold hand and squeezed it. She was gone. It was a reality difficult to accept.

Finally, he called Race. This had happened on base, and he would rather have the investigation handled by NECCO than regular military police. In minutes, the townhouse was crowded with people.

Stacy came over and stayed with Quinn in the guest bedroom while all the activity was going on. She couldn't hold back her tears, for Jill had been her best friend since childhood. They were close all through their marriages, the two of them taking turns consoling and offering advice and keeping laughter in their lives. Her death was tough for Stacy to accept. It was more Quinn comforting his sister than the other way around.

Race took personal charge of the investigation, required whenever there was an unattended death. His own appraisal of the death scene left him disturbed. The doctor, one of the highly skilled members of a NECCO special team, completed his examination and motioned for Race to step outside with him.

"There's a lot not right about this," the doctor said, speaking in a low voice so that only Race could hear. "She's obviously been using narcotics. I suspect the cause of death is an overdose, but I'll need to conduct an autopsy to be sure of that."

"Anything else—?"

The doctor nodded. "Plenty. She apparently took a severe beating. She's bruised all over her body. She was raped, too — there's semen on the sheet."

Race scowled angrily. "Jill was murdered – are you sure?"

"I will be after I conduct the autopsy. There's no way this was accidental."

"Is it possible she died from the beating?"

"Possible, but I'm reasonably certain it was an overdose. She shows all the signs."

"Keep this between us for now," Race said quietly. "Quinn is going through enough just with losing her. Complete that autopsy as quickly as you can. I want to know details. By the way, when did this happen?"

"She's been dead between twelve and eighteen hours."

Jill's funeral was held three days later. She was buried in a pleasant setting in a cemetery in the southern end of the Salt Lake valley. It was a short ceremony, attended by a small group of people. Among those who stood beside Quinn at the graveside was President Baldwin.

Later, family and friends met at the apartment of Race and Stacy. Quinn didn't want to go back yet to the place where Jill died. He held up fairly well through the ordeal, until he saw his wife's body being lowered into the ground. He fell apart then. Race helped him back to the limousine.

It was another three days before Quinn showed up at his office. President Baldwin ordered him not to come back before then. Still, Quinn knew the work was piling up and finally felt worse about that than staying alone with his grief.

The day after his return, Race dropped into his office and closed the door.

"We need to talk, Quinn."

Quinn motioned toward a chair. "Judging by your face, it's serious."

Race nodded. "Don't want to do this, buddy, but we have to talk about Jill's death."

Quinn drew in a sharp breath. "I know. I saw the bruises, and I saw the semen. I just didn't want to face anything that ugly right then. I'm glad you're digging into it. What have you found—?"

"She died from an overdose — almost pure stuff. We found some syringes and a few ounces of heroin in the house, but nothing of the lethal grade the doctor found in her system."

"She took the overdose somewhere else—?"

Race nodded again. "Trouble with that is, she couldn't walk ten feet with that much stuff in her."

Quinn thought about that. "Someone brought her home, probably after she was dead."

"More likely, she was still alive. There's that semen on the bed sheet — I'm sorry, Quinn. I know it must hurt to talk about this."

Quinn shook his head. "We have to get at the truth. What do you think happened?"

"She was beaten and raped, we know that. It appears that happened in the house."

"What did the autopsy show—?"

"Cause of death was a drug overdose – almost pure stuff. She almost certainly didn't administer it herself."

"The beating—"

"Brutal, but not lethal – on the surface, at least."

"So she was beaten and raped, then someone administered a lethal dose and took the evidence with them."

"That's the way it looks, Quinn. I wish I didn't have to dump this on you, but like you said, you need to know."

"Any leads—?"

"I think so. At least on the person who brought her back to the house."

"That would be the one who killed her."

"That's the logical conclusion."

Quinn stared at his friend. "You're being evasive, Race. Are you protecting this bastard—?"

"If I was sure, I'd kill him myself. She was my sister, don't forget."

"Who is it? Has there been an arrest—?"

"Not yet. Salt Lake detectives are staking out the place where he lives."

"What's his name, Race?"

"Luther. Luther Banes."

Shock pulled the color out of Quinn's face. "Luther—?"

"Nothing is certain — not yet. His fingerprints were found in the bedroom and a couple other places. Has he ever been in your house before—?"

Quinn still looked dazed. "No — that is, he could have. He was bringing Jill home that first night, with Candi. Maybe he brought her home other times, too."

"Well, let's not jump to conclusions. We'll get at the truth once he's picked up."

"This is going to kill Linc and Cora," Quinn muttered. "They're already in deep pain over that kid."

When Cora Banes got the telephone call from the Salt Lake police department, she became hysterical. She had difficulty dialing her husband's number at NECCO. When Linc answered, all she could do was cry. Linc heard her wracking sobs and was instantly concerned.

"Tell me what happened, Cora," he told her for the fourth time. "Why are you so upset—?"

"Come home, Linc—" It was all she could get out. She hung up the phone.

By the time Linc got to their house, Cora was composed enough to tell him about the phone call from the police. Luther was in custody, was all the man said. Both Linc and Cora were to come down to Salt Lake police headquarters as soon as possible. Linc called, but they would tell him nothing more over the phone. Their son was being held for questioning. They would be told the charge when they arrived at police headquarters. It was a serious matter. Moments later, Linc was driving at high speed down the freeway toward Salt Lake, his wife crying beside him.

At police headquarters, they were shown into a small interrogation room. Luther was already there, sitting at a table, smoking a cigarette. He crushed it out when his parents walked in. Cora ran forward and put her arms around him, once again starting to cry. Linc pulled her back and had her sit in a chair opposite their son.

"Guess we need to talk, son," Linc said quietly.

"I didn't do anything," Luther said, looking at his father defiantly. "Whatever they say I did, I didn't do it."

"They say you killed a woman, Luther—"

"That's crazy."

"They don't think so."

"So who are you going to believe — them or me?"

"Aren't you curious about who they say you killed—?"

"No. I didn't kill anybody."

"Jill Adams. The police say you killed Jill Adams—"

"They're full of crap."

"But you know she's dead—"

"Sure. It was in the papers."

"Do you know how she died—?"

"A drug overdose."

"That wasn't in the papers."

Luther shrugged. "It's on the street. A lot of people knew she was a heavy user."

"Did you see her that night—?"

"No. I told you."

"You said you didn't kill her. You didn't say you hadn't seen her."

"What is this — you putting me on trial? I'm not charged with diddly-squat. You two come in here and start questioning me about a murder I had nothing to do with. How am I supposed to act when my own parents accuse me of something I didn't do."

"We're not accusing you, son," Linc said. "We just want to get the truth. The police say they have evidence you were in her house."

"Sure I was in her house," Luther snapped. "Several times. Just the day before she was killed, if you want to know. What does that prove—?"

"Why were in her house, son?" Cora asked.

"I dumped her off. When she passed out in taverns. Candi would call me and I'd come and pick her up. Mrs. Adams was hitting it hard — booze and drugs. She couldn't handle it. I'd carry her into the house — she gave Candi a key. I'd dump her on the bed then leave. They should be giving me a medal, instead of trying to pin a bum wrap on me."

"Did you ever touch anything in the house, Luther. Think about it for a minute. Did you ever stay after you put her on the bed—?"

"No — well, yes. The last time — the day before she got killed. She wasn't completely out, like she usually was. She asked me to get her some pills. I looked in the drawer of the table beside her bed but couldn't find any. So I went into the bathroom and looked in the cabinets. Nothing there, either. So I got her a glass of water, put it on the table beside her, and split. I only did that once, because she was out of it all the other times."

Cora leaned forward and took her son's hands in a tight grasp. "Luther, I know things are all upset since we moved out here. I've said things that hurt you, but it was only because I love you. Nothing can change that — your father and I will always love you. Tell me honestly, Luther — did you do anything to Jill Adams? Any of those dreadful things the police are accusing you of doing—?"

Luther looked his mother in the eyes. "I didn't hurt her, mother. I was there the night before, bringing her home, but not the night she died. That's the truth."

In the small room behind the mirror, Quinn and Race looked at each other.

"Either he's very clever, or he really is telling the truth," Race muttered.

One of the detectives standing behind them gave a grunt of disgust. "He's a lying punk. He must know we have his prints on the bed table and in the bathroom. He just gave himself an alibi for them being there."

"You think he knows we're watching him—?"

"Sure he does," the detective said sourly. "These guys take courses in being interrogated."

"Have we got anything to hold him on?" Quinn asked. "Any hard evidence?"

"Just the prints and the semen on the sheet — not enough to hold him very long. We're getting a court order for a DNA sample. If his semen matches what we've got, he's toast."

Race turned to him. "I want him transferred to federal jurisdiction. That will keep him on ice a little longer – and it won't take so much red tape to get that DNA sample."

"It takes three or four weeks to run DNA tests that hold up in court."

"Can we hold him that long," Quinn asked, "without hard evidence?"

"I'll confine him to base," Race said. "He'll be under military jurisdiction there. We're under martial law, don't forget. That means we can make it tougher on the bad guys."

"Let's do it." Quinn turned to the Salt Lake detectives. "You gentlemen have any problem with us taking him off your hands?"

"Be our guest," the detective in charge growled. "Maybe his mother buys his story but that kid is guilty. I got twenty-eight years on the force that says I'm right."

Linc and Cora were asked to leave, then Luther was interrogated for several hours by Salt Lake detectives. They got nothing more than what Luther told his parents. Both Race and Quinn declined to participate in the questioning, knowing they both were too closely involved.

After the interrogation was completed, Luther was placed in chains and put into a police van for transportation to Hill Air Force Base, or more specifically, the NECCO section of the base.

The van was several miles north of Salt Lake when a convoy of three mini vans pulled alongside. One positioned itself just ahead of the police van, one alongside, and one to the rear. The sliding door of the center van opened and an automatic rifle began spraying the tires of the police van. Both left tires were shot out and the police vehicle started weaving.

The driver of the lead van suddenly veered in front of the police vehicle. The policeman driving tried to brake but couldn't avoid crashing into the vehicle ahead of him. All the vehicles came to a stop in a cloud of gravel and dust.

Men in hoods jumped out of the third van in the convoy, ran to the police vehicle and shot through the windows of both doors, killing the two policemen in the front seat. Others shot off the lock on the back doors of the van and jerked them open. Another officer was crouched on his knees inside, his pistol at the ready. He only squeezed off one round before falling.

From inside the van, Luther called out. He was huddled on the floor, his hands protecting his head.

"Careful — you nearly shot me too."

Moments later, two of the vans sped away from the scene of death, Luther inside one of them congratulating his rescuers. The third van was left mangled in the collision with the police van. It was clean and contained no prints that might identify the occupants. Police identification of the owner was not a problem. The van was stolen just a couple of hours earlier.

# 27

## THE PHOENIX PLAN

President Sam Baldwin looked at the three-inch-thick report Anne Ashford had just put on his desk. The report was fastened in a black leather binder, the cover stamped with gold foil. It read:

THE
PHOENIX
PLAN

\* \* \*

TOP SECRET

\* \* \*

The President looked up at his Vice President. "Is this what I think it is—?"

"It is, Mr. President," Anne replied. "A draft, at least."

Quinn Adams and General Aaron Stark had accompanied the Vice President into the office. Baldwin tried to read their faces but all three wore noncommittal expressions.

"Well," Baldwin growled impatiently, "do we have a solution or don't we—?"

"We do, Mr. President," Anne said. A little smile tugged at her mouth. "A very good solution, sir."

Baldwin slapped a hand excitedly on the cover of the report. "I knew you could do it—"

"It wasn't just us, sir," Anne said quickly. "We each hand-picked a brain-trust team to work with us in solving the problems in our individual areas. Then we put them together. The result is the Phoenix Plan in front of you, sir."

"Am I going to like it—?"

"Mr. President," Anne smiled, "you're gonna love it."

"Great," Baldwin beamed. "Madame Vice President, give me an overview, will you. Then each of you expand on it." He waved an arm toward them. "Sit. Spout—"

All three sat in front of his desk, each holding their own copy of the black leather report. Anne glanced at her companions, then began her explanation to the President.

"The plan is divided into three primary sections, as you suggested, sir. Military. Political. Social. There are a lot of sub-sections, but everything is covered under those three major headings. We wanted to keep it as simple as possible—"

"Glad to hear that," Baldwin interrupted, "because you're probably going to have to explain this a couple hundred times before you get through."

"The objective for everything was the same — get us through the present military stalemate and on a path of recovery. We were seeking solutions that cost the minimum loss of life and provided the maximum amount of security for the future, not only for ourselves but for countries of Central and South America as well."

Baldwin tapped the bound report. "Good. Does this plan accomplish those objectives, Anne—?"

"I believe it does, sir."

Baldwin leaned back and gave a deep sigh of relief. "Those are very sweet words to hear, Madame Vice President. Please proceed."

"There was one major requirement. All policies and procedures included in the plan must adhere to the rights and freedoms guaranteed under the Constitution of the United States."

"Nothing could be more important than that," Baldwin agreed softly. "That's why I called the meeting in Granite Mountain — I wanted this project started with those rights fresh in your minds."

"It accomplished that, Mr. President. Perhaps I should begin the review with a look at the recommendations in the political section."

"If it satisfies the politicians, we're nine tenths home," Baldwin grunted.

Anne Ashford didn't even glance down at the document on her lap.

This had become a part of her being these last weeks. The text was clearly written word for word in her mind.

"The basic assumption in this arena was that both sides must be willing to cooperate and compromise. Since both sides are looking at a doomsday alternative, that shouldn't be as difficult to achieve as it sounds.

"Obviously, control and authority become the central issue. We propose establishing a joint governing body for both hemispheres—"

The President frowned. "Does that mean surrendering our sovereign right to govern ourselves—?"

"No, sir," Anne explained. "That would be unacceptable to us, and probably everyone else. What we're proposing is in essence a second body of governmental authority, whose membership comprises all sovereign states, which will guarantee that no act or policy by one member violates the rights of any other member state."

"We seem to be talking along the lines of an American hemisphere United Nations—"

"Exactly, sir. We have even proposed a name for this governing body — the United Sovereign States of the Americas. To reduce that to an acronym — the USSA."

Baldwin let a smile flicker across his face. "That sounds vaguely familiar—"

"The difference being the Constitution of the United States, Mr. President," Anne said quickly. "That must be accepted by all countries involved as the governing principle."

"That won't be easy—"

"Again, in our opinion not as difficult as it sounds," Anne continued. "There are very few countries in the world who wouldn't be eager to have that protection — the general populations, at least. No doubt a lot of politicians will fight it, especially those who are making a mockery of democratic rule, but we have to remember that the alternative is clearly unacceptable."

"So this — this USSA — primarily acts as an oversight committee—?"

"Basically, yes, but with greater power to regulate. The only people who could object to that are those who intend to violate the principles of the agreement."

"Is there a structural proposal in the plan—?" the President asked.

"No, sir. We thought that should be worked out between the parties involved. You mentioned the United Nations — developing an organization along those lines might be a good starting point."

Baldwin rubbed his chin thoughtfully. "It sounds plausible," he nodded. "Gives us all a chance to discuss our problems on common ground."

"There are a thousand details to work out," Anne said, "but our objective here is come up with a framework on which to build. We believe the concept of a United Sovereign States of the Americas provides that platform, Mr. President."

Quinn Adams picked up the conversation. "It also gives us a base from which to develop the social programs all countries will need."

He saw the quizzical lifting of a Presidential eyebrow and continued. "Looking at our own problems first, sir, they divide into three major categories, all equally critical.

"The problems we are facing here in the Zone — an exploding refugee population, the shortages in food, housing, public facilities, education — too many more to enumerate. Also, a tremendous increase in all types of crime and drug abuse."

"Sorry to interrupt, Quinn," Baldwin said, "but you mentioned a new mafia organization in your earlier reports. Have you made any progress in identifying it—?"

"Yes, sir. It's an organization of young, ruthless thugs — even worse than the older crime organizations they've been eliminating."

"How much do we know about them?"

"Not a lot. Informants have a habit of dying. The organization seems to represent all of the ethnic groups. Well organized apparently, and rapidly assuming total control in the underworld."

"Are we moving to stop them?"

"We just recently managed to plant one of our men into their inner circle," Quinn replied. "He's a good operative. He'll be a valuable source of information."

"What about Norm Dean and the FBI—"

"They're pretty busy with all that's going on—"

"In other words, they're not doing anything," Baldwin growled.

"They have their priorities, sir."

"I'll talk to Dean. I don't want your people tied up with what clearly should be a top priority for the FBI. Anyway, let's get back to the Phoenix Plan. You were talking about the problems here in the Zone as the first category—"

"The second one is the problems in the occupied sections of the nation. We know the CASA forces have been committing wholesale murder, keeping civilians imprisoned in camps worse than any of the World War 11 concentration camps in Nazi Europe, and are forcing thousands of women and girls into providing sex. It's painful to even think about what those people are going through, Mr. President."

"Surely we can provide some relief—" Baldwin exclaimed.

"Not without violating the truce," Quinn said grimly. "And if we do that, we risk causing even greater slaughter."

"You mentioned a third category—"

"The people isolated in areas that were not occupied in that first push by the CASA forces, but are now cut off from escape. We're doing what we can with airlifts of food and medical supplies but there are too many cities and towns — and too few supplies."

"You paint a bleak picture—"

"It is bleak, Mr. President."

"Are you telling me nothing can be done—?"

"Not individually — not without a high risk of making things worse for them. But an approach is outlined here in the Phoenix Plan that we believe will provide a solution to help everyone. It will even help the Latin people."

"I'd definitely call that a miracle."

"Just cooperation between people, Mr. President," Quinn replied. "The main thrust of Phoenix in this area is for the government — all governments — to spearhead a massive recovery program. Here in the U.S., we form a volunteer corp of hundreds of thousands to start rebuilding and putting the country back into operation. The scorched earth policy achieved its objective, sir, of leaving the CASA forces unable to live off the land, but it also left our farms and factories and power systems badly damaged."

The President was frowning again. "Do I understand you are recommending the recovery be a total federal project, Mr. Adams—? Perhaps I got those initials wrong — did you say USSA or USSR?"

"We can't get choked in red tape, sir. In this case, that means civil squabbling over everything from ownership of land and factories, responsibility for damages, labor unions, minority rights — heaven on earth for attorneys, Mr. President. The national recovery will be tied up for years while people with the most money and the best lawyers prove they have the most power. We can't allow that to happen, sir."

"I could sign an executive order making it illegal to be an attorney," Baldwin murmured, only half facetiously.

"Once the country is running again, once the objectives of the Phoenix Plan have been achieved, we go back to the private enterprise system," Quinn continued. "We're only talking about a few months. Then all those people with their writs and gripes and fancy lawyers can have their day in court. Until then, yes — it's communism, if you want to call it that. Or you could say we're temporarily expanding the welfare system to include all citizens. It doesn't matter — just so long as we get a united, coordinated effort to get this country back on its feet."

"We could call it a revitalized, temporary communist concept in an abridged democratic form," Anne Ashford murmured, "designed to increase the rights and freedoms of all peoples in both the northern and southern hemispheres. I think we could say that—"

"The lawyers and the courts will take years to figure that explanation out," the President grinned.

"We won't need that long, Mr. President," Anne smiled back.

"We start rebuilding in one or two locations, then expand to more, until we're back into full production," Quinn continued. "In the interim, we allocate harvests and production to those people most in need."

"What are the Latins doing all this time?" Baldwin asked. "Beating their weapons into plowshares and cheering us on—?"

"Working beside us, sir."

"Why would they do that—?"

"Because under the Phoenix Plan, they get a share of our national production."

"Seems to me you're expanding communism, not shrinking it," the President snorted.

"No, sir. We work together, we share the fruits of that labor. It's a two-way street, north and south."

"Do you have a formula for that—?"

"One of the details to be worked out, Mr. President," Anne Ashford said, "but it certainly can be formulized on an equitable basis."

Baldwin leaned back, clasping both hands behind his head. He stared silently at the three people in front of him.

"I like it," he said finally. "I'm trying to poke holes in it, but you've convinced me it's a solid platform. I agree that details can be worked out later." He looked at Aaron Stark. "Where does this leave the military situation, General?"

"I'd say in an excellent position, Mr. President. If the Governing Council of CASA, or whatever they call themselves, accept the principles of the Phoenix Plan, the military situation will be relatively simple to resolve. Mostly a matter of how many of them stay in the United States, if any, and where. I think it would be good to have some degree of interchange take place between the military. Our people will have a lot of anger about what's happened, but if we take it slowly—"

"You really think it will be that easy—?" the President queried.

"Not easy, Mr. President," Stark corrected, "but it can be done."

"They're going to demand you drop the nuclear threat—"

Stark smiled coldly. "Be happy to do that, sir. We'll drop the threats, but we won't allow them to track our ships and submarines. That way, they'll never really know what we're doing. You could look on it as an incentive to toe the line, Mr. President."

The President looked down again at the report in front of him, drumming his fingers on the black leather. He reached a decision.

"All right. Let's run this by State, and the leaders of Congress. I really don't care if they like it or not — I'm sure someone will propose taking a year or two to study it. Anne, I want you to contact that Francisco de Branca fellow and set up a full presentation of the Phoenix Plan to their Governing Council. That's where the rubber will hit the road."

"They'll probably insist I go to Brazil—"

"Don't go alone. You and Quinn, and a detachment of those NECCO rangers. Not sure I trust you with all those handsome Latin men—"

Anne felt a stirring of guilt. For a flashing moment, she had a vivid recall of Fernando Francisco de Branca. An enemy, Anne, she reminded herself sternly. She felt annoyed she could even think of this man as attractive.

# 28

## The Israeli Dilemma

Dovid Shazebak stepped out of the limo and entered the Z House — that was the name given to the temporary residence of President Sam Baldwin on the NECCO compound. Like the former residence, it also served as a complex of offices for high ranking administration officials.

There was no resemblance to the now destroyed White House in Washington, D.C. The large, two-storied concrete and steel structure — actually there were several underground floors — was painted in camouflage colors that made it almost invisible against the background of the Wasatch mountains, despite its size. The President frequently held meetings in the State Capital in Salt Lake, but this was where the real work of governing was done.

The Israeli Special Ambassador was quickly admitted to the office of Sam Baldwin. The President got up from his desk and came forward to shake hands.

"Glad you could stop by," Baldwin said. He motioned for Dovid to sit in one of the armchairs, then sat across from him. "I understand you're going back to Israel today. You've been here, what—"

"About ten days, Mr. President. We stayed for the funeral, then there have been several important briefings arranged for us. Those have been very helpful, and we appreciate it. Now we need to get back. The threat of Desert Sword becomes greater every day. May I say it is always an honor to meet with you, Mr. President."

"Sorry I had to be so firm the other day—"

"We understand your position completely, Mr. President. It's not what we wanted to hear, of course."

"Has Quinn briefed you on the Phoenix Plan?"

Dovid shook his head. "No, sir."

"Well, you Israelis need to know what's in the wind. I'll get hold of him—"

"I'll be seeing him in a few minutes," Dovid said. "He's going to accompany us to the plane."

"Good. This Phoenix Plan could change a lot of things — including the matter you and I discussed."

"That's the best news I've had in a long time, Mr. President—"

"Can't promise anything specific at this stage of the game," Baldwin continued, "but I see the possibility of meeting your request at least part way. That is, if the Phoenix Plan is accepted by the Latins. Quinn will explain that."

"What should I tell my people, Mr. President—?"

"Tell them I am seriously considering allowing a voluntary exodus to Israel of those Americans who request it. The first step would be an application, and that would have to be screened and approved. A great number of Jewish people are in vital positions in both government and industry. We can't risk crippling any programs by losing too many of them. And of course, we will never consider involuntary repatriation."

Dovid let a deep breath of relief escape him. He reached across the space between them and grasped the President's hand in both of his.

"I cannot express the gratitude of our nation enough, Mr. President," he said quietly. Baldwin could tell how much emotion was behind the words. "Without the open backing of the United States, we have no chance against the huge enemy force being assembled against us."

"We didn't have any choice when we talked before," Baldwin said solemnly. "We were in deep kimchi ourselves. Now at least there's a hope, if this Phoenix Plan is accepted."

"You know Israel will do anything it can—"

Baldwin stood up. "This is one helluva time, isn't it, Mr. Shazebak."

"It certainly is, sir," Dovid smiled, also now standing. He shook the President's outstretched hand again. "May God be with both our countries."

When Dovid left Z House, the limousine pulled up again and he got in. Sophia, Joanna, and Quinn were already inside.

"What did he want?" Sophia asked anxiously.

"Good news," Dovid said quietly. "The President said he would consider allowing an exodus of our people to Israel."

Sophia clasped her arms excitedly around his neck. "That's wonderful!"

Joanna also was smiling in pleasure at the news, but she knew her brother well enough to detect there was more to the meeting. She could read it in the little crinkles around his eyes.

"There were strings?" she asked.

Dovid shrugged. "Not strings exactly – a few conditions. If it happens, it will be voluntary. And there will be screening to protect U.S. national interests."

"Not everyone can go, then?"

"The only ones stopped from going will be those that people like Quinn say can't go."

"Wait a minute," Quinn protested, "how did I get into this?"

"More important, what have you been holding back from us, my dear and trusted friend?"

"For a short meeting, you and the President seem to have covered a lot of ground."

Dovid grinned. "Just giving you a bad time. The President said he was going to contact you about—"

As if on cue, the cellular phone in Quinn's jacket pocket buzzed. He took it out.

"Quinn Adams here."

It was a patch-through from the President. Quinn listened for a minute or so, then smiled. "Yes, Mr. President. Be happy to do that."

He put the phone back in his pocket, flashing a brief grin at Dovid. "You realize this is going to delay your flight."

"What's going to delay us?" Sophia asked, a puzzled look on her face.

"A little story about a bird who died," Quinn told her, "and came back to life out of its own ashes."

"That was the phoenix, wasn't it—?"

"An Egyptian legend about a centuries old bird who burned itself to death, then came back as a beautiful young thing," Joanna added. "It always sounded like such a great thing to do when you get old and wrinkled."

"Always the complete woman," Quinn murmured. He leaned over and gave her a light kiss on the cheek. "I'm going to miss you, Miss Shazebak."

"I certainly hope so," Joanna smiled, giving him a pat on the cheek.

They had an early lunch in one of the private dining rooms at the NECCO complex. Quinn briefed them on the Phoenix Plan, adding that he was flying to Brazil with Anne Ashford in two days to present it to the Governing Council of the new Latin government.

"You think they'll go for it?" Dovid asked, when Quinn finished.

"It sure beats the options," Quinn said grimly. "The way things stand, sooner or later the situation will get out of hand and those buttons will get pushed. When that happens, Central and South America will become one big graveyard."

"You think the United States would do that?" Sophia asked.

"If it was the only way for us to survive," Quinn replied.

"Well, the survival of Israel will depend on you doing a good selling job, Quinn," Dovid said. "You'll have our prayers with you, and those of the whole Knesset."

"I'll let you know how it goes as soon as I get back," Quinn promised.

Soon after, they were back in the limousine and headed for the Salt Lake airport where the Israeli jet was waiting. Little was said, for there was a lot to think about. The Israeli plane was parked away from the terminal and they drove onto the taxi way. Steps to the door were already in place. Quinn hugged both Dovid and Sophia.

"Go with God, my friends," Quinn murmured.

Dovid and Sophia entered the plane. Quinn stood staring at Joanna.

"I don't want you to go, Joanna," he said softly. "Guess I shouldn't say that so soon after—" He paused, then grasped her shoulders and kissed her, full on the mouth, but gently. Joanna looked up at him without saying anything, then turned and started up the steps. She didn't want him to see the tears starting to fall.

Quinn reached out and took her arm. He pulled her back onto the tarmac.

"How essential are you these days to the Mossad?" he asked.

She gave a puzzled frown, then shrugged. "You know how that goes. You're essential until you're not there."

"That's nowhere near how essential you are to me," he said huskily. "I can't let you go again, Joanna. It's killing me to think I might never see you again."

"We've managed three times in the last few months," she smiled.

"Joanna, marry me — right now, while Dovid and Sophia are still here. They can leave tomorrow, tonight even, but I don't want to make the same mistake again. Joanna, I never want us to be apart again."

Joanna looked up at him, staring deep into his eyes. She flung herself into her arms.

"I didn't know how I was going to make it up those steps," she whispered.

"Is that a yes?"

She kissed him, long and passionately. "I love you so much, Quinn Adams—"

# 29

## BETRAYAL IN BRAZILIA

"An excellent presentation, Madame Vice President," Fernando Francisco de Branca said. "You and Mr. Adams have made a strong case for your Phoenix Plan."

Anne Ashford, standing at the head of the long table before the charts and graphs she and Quinn used in presenting the details of Phoenix, let her glance take in the serious expressions of the others in the room before responding.

There were fifteen Governing Council members present. Either some chose not to attend, or not all countries in the hemisphere warranted membership on the Council. A leather-bound copy of the Phoenix Plan was in front of each man. Anne had quickly noticed there were no women on the council.

Anne looked at Quinn. He was very persuasive in outlining the benefits of the social and military aspects of the plan. And very diplomatic in touching on the consequences both hemispheres would face if some type of agreement was not reached. Anne swung her eyes back to Francisco de Branca.

"I appreciate your comment, Mr. Chairman. I hope we conveyed our sincere belief that within this plan is a solution acceptable to all parties."

"You did indeed, Madame Vice President," Artur Mennaros, one of the council members, said. "It's been a long day, but I hope you and Mr. Adams will accept at least a few more questions—?"

"That's why we're here in Brazilia, Senor Mennaros," Anne replied graciously. "Every possible question and suggestion should be dealt with."

Each of the members of the council were introduced at the start of the morning session, and in front of each person at the table was a large nameplate. Both Anne and Quinn were grateful for that help in identifying the people who questioned them during both the four-hour morning session and this afternoon session, which already had lasted over five hours.

"I am interested in the timeline your country proposes for the initiation of this plan?" Mennaros asked.

"We are ready to initiate joint planning as soon as an agreement is signed by both parties."

"Are you asking us to believe the United States would be willing to switch overnight from a state of war, in which we have both suffered great losses, to one of peaceful co-existence—?"

"I'm not asking you to believe anything, Senor Mennaros," Anne said steadily. "I am stating my government is willing to begin immediately to work with the Coalition of Allied States of the Americas to formulate conditions of our mutual responsibilities under the Phoenix Plan. If you don't have sufficient trust to believe that statement, I hold little hope for the future."

Mennaros raised his hands quickly. "Please, Madame Vice President, do not misunderstand the intent of my question. It's just that the generosity of the United States seems overwhelming in the face of what has happened."

Quinn glanced at Anne. "May I offer a comment, Madame Vice President?"

Anne quickly nodded. Quinn took a step forward. There was a polite smile on his face, but his eyes were boring into Mennaros.

"Senor Mennaros, please understand that my country is not being generous in making this offer. If anything, we are being selfish. We want an end to hostilities between us, because a continuation can only bring death and greater disaster to hundreds of thousands more on each side. We intend to end the military stalemate one way or another. I don't say that in a threatening way. We must agree — or disagree. Too many people are suffering and dying for this situation to remain in limbo much longer."

"Are you saying that if we don't agree to this Phoenix Plan, fighting will be renewed between our forces, Mr. Adams?"

"I'm saying we need to find a solution, Senor Mennaros. A peaceful one, if humanly possible. If it isn't, we all know the present truce will end disastrously sooner or later, most likely with neither of our governments responsible. Tensions will boil over somewhere and fighting will resume."

"And the consequences of that, Mr. Adams—?" asked Floriano Paranais, a council member seated next to Mennaros.

"We will each attempt to achieve victory," Quinn said quietly. "Gentlemen, please do not construe that as even a veiled threat. We are looking raw truth in the face. The government of the United States wants the Phoenix Plan to work. We believe a stronger, better American hemisphere will emerge. We believe that forming the United Sovereign States of the Americas will start all of our countries on a path to peace and prosperity."

At the opposite end of the table, Francisco de Branca stood up.

"Gentlemen, we have much to consider. I appreciate your candor, Mr. Adams. It is indeed time to be frank with each other. I too believe it will be disastrous for all of us if we cannot come together in a peaceful solution. The Phoenix Plan, as it is outlined, sounds like an excellent place to start."

He looked down the table, seeing heads nodding in agreement. Francisco de Branca smiled at Anne Ashford and Quinn Adams.

"The members of the council will discuss this tonight. Accommodations are arranged for both of you, and your military escort. The top two floors of one of our finest hotels here in Brazilia are at your disposal. If agreeable, let us meet again in the morning — say about ten o'clock. We will convey our decision at that time."

Twelve members of NECCO'S elite Rangers had accompanied Anne Ashford and Quinn to Brazilia, the capital city of Brazil. Although no one really expected trouble, the Rangers were to maintain round-the-clock guard duty, six at a time. This four hours on, four off, rotation was rigorous but these Rangers could stay alert for weeks on such a schedule.

At the hotel, two Rangers remained in the hallway on the top floor outside the suites provided for Anne and Quinn. Two more Rangers were stationed at stairwells at each end of the floor. The remaining two Rangers on duty were positioned on the floor below, where the others slept. Trouble would have a hard time getting past those seasoned Rangers.

The night passed without incident. Quinn and Anne both slept soundly. At Anne's invitation, Quinn joined her in her suite at eight o'clock the next morning, and they ate breakfast together. They were speculating on what the reaction of the Council would be when the telephone rang. It was Francisco de Branca, wondering if he might join them for a few minutes.

Shortly after, Francisco de Branca was admitted to the suite by one of the Rangers. The Brazilian shook hands and accepted an offer to sit beside Anne on the sofa.

"I hope you both got more sleep than the members of the Council did," he smiled. "Our discussions went until four this morning."

"Does that mean a lot of problems surfaced?" Anne inquired.

"Not the kind of problems that affect the primary purpose of your visit," Francisco de Branca replied. "You will both be pleased to know it took less than an hour's discussion to reach a unanimous acceptance of the basic terms of the Phoenix Plan — well, almost unanimous."

"Almost unanimous—?" Quinn said.

The Brazilian shrugged. "Representatives of two smaller countries could not envision the hemispheric benefits being more important than their own selfish interests." He smiled again. "What they saw clearly, however, was an end to their personal abuse of power."

"What took so long to decide?" Anne asked.

"Our own participation in the plan, how we could allocate percentages of contributions and benefits fairly. Should it be determined on territorial size, national income, population — we probably never will completely agree. That is the Latin way, I suppose."

"But an agreement was reached to accept the Phoenix Plan as outlined—?" Anne questioned again.

"Voted upon and accepted," Francisco de Branca assured her. "We are ready to sign Articles of Intent as soon as they are prepared."

Both Anne and Quinn were smiling in relief. "That is excellent news, Mr. Chairman," Anne said. "The President will be happy to hear of your decision."

"How do you propose we accomplish the next step?" Francisco de Branca asked. "Do you have a draft agreement?"

"We thought it appropriate to wait until a basic agreement on principle was reached," Anne replied. "It won't take long to draft, however. The best approach would be for both parties to share in the preparation."

"I agree. As Chairman of the Council, I am assigned to that duty. Who will be representing the United States—?'

"I suppose I will," Anne said. "That's the wish of the President, I believe."

Francisco de Branca looked at Quinn. "Will you also be participating, Mr. Adams?"

Quinn shook his head. "Too many preparations at home. I'll be busy with those. Madame Vice President knows more about what needs to be included in the Articles of Intent than I do, in any case."

The Brazilian looked again at Anne. "May I offer a suggestion— would you consider remaining in Brazilia long enough to work up a draft of these articles with me? That way, you could take a signed agreement back with you."

Anne frowned. The frown was to cover up any possible showing of anything else on her face. Working closely with this handsome Brazilian for a week or more was a prospect that set something churning inside her. Was it a good something — or a silly something that should have left her after graduating from high school?

"That makes a great deal of sense," she heard herself saying. "The faster we can draw up a document to sign, the better for everyone."

"You won't change your mind, Mr. Adams?" the Chairman asked. "Your input would be valuable—"

"I'll look forward to working with you on the full plan." Quinn flashed a wry little smile. "Besides, I was married three — no, five days ago — and I haven't spent as much as an afternoon with my bride. All my time was spent getting ready for this presentation."

Anne Ashford, among the few invited guests at the hurried ceremony before Dovid and Sophia left to fly back to Israel, patted Quinn's shoulder.

"Get back to your bride," she said. "She seems like such a lovely person."

"I'm impressed," Francisco de Branca added. "Few men would make such a sacrifice for their country."

Quinn did not have a chance to respond. At that moment, the door to the suite was thrown open. Two men entered, one of them pointing an assault rifle fitted with a silencer at the three startled occupants of the room.

Quinn tensed, but instantly realized he would not be able to close the distance between himself and the man with the gun without getting shot. There was a tight knot in his stomach as he realized the presence of the two men meant there were dead Rangers in the hallway.

Both of the men were in civilian attire, the one with the assault rifle shorter and heavier than the other. The taller man had the haughty manner of accustomed authority. A pistol hung loosely in his right hand, pointed at no one. It also had a silencer attached.

Evidently Francisco de Branca knew him. "Colonel Fariocha — what is the meaning of this?"

Colonel Jorge Fariocha, formerly the head of military intelligence of Brazil's First Military District but now in charge of the Coalition's joint intelligence service, gave a flinty smile.

"Please forgive the intrusion, Mr. Chairman. Circumstances did not permit a more formal entrance."

Quinn's attention was riveted on the man with the assault rifle, who kept moving the muzzle in a short arc. That was surprising, Quinn thought, because he was including Francisco de Branca along with Anne and himself in the threatening sweep of the weapon. Francisco de Branca noticed it too.

"Is your man threatening me, Colonel Fariocha?" he asked harshly.

"Yes, Mr. Chairman, he is. He has orders to kill all three of you."

"Are you insane, Colonel—?"

"In my business, no one can be completely sure, one way or the other."

"Your orders are to kill me and these Americans—?"

Fariocha nodded. "Issued to me personally by General Wu Zhenkang."

"You are taking orders from the Chinese? That is treason, Colonel—"

"We are all taking orders from the Chinese, including yourself, Mr. Chairman. I simply get mine through more direct channels."

"Is the military attempting a coup to overthrow the Governing Council—?"

"No, sir. You are the only member I've been ordered to kill."

"Why do the Chinese want me dead—?"

Fariocha shrugged again. "I'm really not sure — possibly as a lesson to the others. I am told you strongly advocated acceptance of this Phoenix Plan. I do know these Americans are to die to make sure there will be no such alliance." He eyed Quinn coldly. "I don't know who you are or why your death is important, but the rape and murder of the vice president of the United States certainly will end negotiations for peace between the two hemispheres, don't you think?"

"You can't do this, Colonel," Francisco de Branca grated. "The United States will retaliate. You are condemning millions of our own people to death—"

Fariocha unscrewed the silencer and put it and the pistol into the pocket of his jacket. "Such matters are not my concern. That is for politicians to worry about, isn't it. Now the time for talk is over—"

Quinn stepped over to place himself in front of Anne Ashford. "You're not getting the picture, Colonel. If you kill this lady, the United States will retaliate with nuclear strikes against every city in this hemisphere. That is very much your problem, since you will be one of those millions who die—"

"Perhaps," Fariocha said. "However, your appointment with death is more immediate, Mr. Adams."

Anne Ashford moved from behind Quinn, stepping toward a small table where her purse sat. The assault rifle swung to follow her. She looked at Fariocha, ignoring the gun.

"I'd like a cigarette — one of my own brand. I don't mind being shot, if that is inevitable. It's the other part you mentioned that's making me a little nervous."

Fariocha smiled, motioning for the gunman to relax. "I wasn't sure it had registered, Madame Vice President. It is most definitely on my mind."

Anne picked up her purse, opened it and reached inside. Quinn didn't look at her, but he was tensed and ready. He was the only other one in the room who knew Anne Ashford didn't smoke.

The bullet, fired through the purse without Anne ever taking out the small pistol inside, caught the gunman in the face, just below the right eye. He screamed, dropped the rifle, and clutched both hands to his face. Blood started streaming over his fingers.

Quinn jumped forward and threw himself heavily against Fariocha, making the colonel stumble sideways. Quinn lunged for the assault rifle. He fired a short burst into the screaming gunman, ending his misery. Then he dropped to the floor, rolled over and pointed the rifle into the hallway.

The silencer muffled the sound of the shots fired from the rifle but the noise of the single shot from Anne's pistol brought two men running into sight. Quinn fired two more bursts. Both men staggered backwards, falling dead.

Fariocha regained his balance and was tearing a pistol from his pocket. He started to lift it and Francisco de Branca gave a curdling yell, launching himself into the air feet first, soccer style, toward the colonel. There was a snapping sound as his feet delivered a hard kick to Fariocha's head. The colonel went flying backwards into the large window. It shattered and Fariocha disappeared from view.

It was fifteen stories down but the fall didn't hurt the colonel. The soccer kick by Francisco de Branca broke his neck.

None of this was seen by Quinn. After shooting the assassin, he rolled out into the corridor. In one sweeping glance, he saw four Rangers sprawled on the carpet. The two nearest him had died from a bullet in the brain. He had no doubt the two at the ends of the hallway were killed in similar fashion.

Three men in civilian clothes came running toward the suite of rooms. Two were on the left end of the hallway, one on the right. He took out the two on the left first, rolled again, and fired another burst into the remaining civilian. He didn't need to check; they were dead before any of them hit the carpet.

Quinn leapt to his feet, bounding back into the room. Francisco de Branca was looking out the shattered window. He turned back to the two Americans.

"I am grateful to you both."

"That was fancy kicking—" Anne told him.

"I was on Brazil's national championship soccer team — about fifteen years ago. That was fancy shooting, Madame Vice President."

Anne put the purse on the table. "Thanks to my good friend Sam Baldwin, who insisted I accept a little present. The measurement 'thirty-eight' will always have new meaning for me."

Francisco de Branca glanced out into the hall. "Your men—?"

"Dead."

"I'm sorry. The ones off duty—?"

"Also dead, I'm afraid. If they were alive, they'd be here."

"There's probably more of Fariocha's men on the next floor—"

"Could be, but I suspect they're gone. One look at Fariocha splattered on the sidewalk, and they'd run."

Francisco de Branca reached for the telephone. "I'll call for security — men we can trust. I suggest we remain in this room until we make sure all is secure."

"I'll check on my men and collect some of the weapons," Quinn said grimly.

"What about you, Mr. Chairman—" Anne asked.

"Please," Francisco de Branca said. "After what we just shared, I think we should all be on a first name basis. Call me Fernando—"

"Anne—"

"Quinn—"

"You were saying, Anne—?"

"Killing this colonel will not end the threat to yourself, not if the order really came from the Chinese."

"There are very few like Fariocha. Most of our people have a deep sense of patriotism. The rest have a deep sense of survival."

"Will this change the decision of the council regarding the Phoenix Plan—?"

"If anything, it will make them more determined to see it implemented," Fernando said firmly. "This oversteps any agreement reached with the People's Republic."

"May I suggest a slight change in plans. If might be better for all concerned if you accompany us back to the United States, Fernando." Anne said. "We can complete the document there. It is important you stay alive."

Fernando fastened her with a look that was both puzzling and unsettling. "I hope you share in that concern, Anne."

She was suddenly flustered. "Of course I do—"

"You have not yet used my name—" Again there was that direct stare.

"Fernando." She smiled, hoping it did not show the stressful flow of emotions inside her. "Fernando. I like it. It sounds so — so Latin."

# 30

## HEART STRINGS

In the darkness of the bedroom, Joanna snuggled tightly against her husband. Her heart was full, her thoughts racing. They were naked and she let the warmth of his flesh warm herself. The smell of him stirred excitement, even after making love several times since going to bed. She could feel the gentle expelling of his breath as he breathed softly and regularly in sleep. For a moment, there was an unreasoning fear this was not real.

Yet it was. She was finally married to the man she had loved for so many years. Even in the unreality of the times they shared together, amid shadowy uncertainties and violence and intrigue, deep in her heart she had longed for just this sense of peace and fulfillment. It was a dream she long ago accepted as having no chance to become real, convincing herself it was best to treasure such thoughts in the mind, where they could be protected from the ugliness of the real world. Dreams were sometimes better left as dreams. Not this one, though.

Her hand reached for his, clasping it tightly. This was real, she told herself again. Thank you, dear God. Thank you for letting me know such happiness.

Quinn stirred. She waited, wondering if he would awaken. The regular breathing started again. Still, she was too filled with the wonder of lying here as husband and wife to not reach out.

"Are you awake—?" she whispered. She knew he wasn't but she also had seen him come wide awake at a silent footfall. Something about the senses of a person trained to live with danger overcame the normal drug of sleepiness.

"I am now," Quinn murmured. His arms tightened around her. "Is this really you—?"

"I was lying here thinking the same thing." She rolled over, pressing herself against him. "I needed to tell you how much I love you—"

"My lovely Joanna," Quinn breathed softly. "Do you realize we have the rest of our lives to spend like this—"

"I can't really believe it yet. I have to keep fighting those old memories. The days of ending. The times we were forced to say good-bye. Those terrible fears we would never see each other again—"

"I was a fool—"

"No more than I. It was the times, the shadows we lived in. We didn't expect a normal life."

"And yet here we are, in worse times, in darker shadows. We create our own reality — we should have known that."

She kissed him lightly on the mouth. "Do you think I'm too old to have a baby—?"

He pulled his head back and grinned at her. "Where did that come from—?"

"From my heart," she whispered. "I want your child, Quinn. I want us to be a family—"

"White house and picket fence—?"

"Not **the** White House. But a dog, too."

"Can you stand being that normal?"

"You're holding a changed woman, my love."

He kissed her hard. "You'll make a wonderful mother."

She returned his kiss passionately.

\* \* \*

Anne Ashford and Fernando Francisco de Branca were at that moment in one of the conference rooms of Z House, the administration complex adjacent to NECCO headquarters. The table at which they sat was littered with papers. Two computer terminals and a high-speed laser printer were at one end of the room, an overflowing wastebasket beside them showing the activity of the marathon session just concluded. The coffee table between the two sofas, with its remnants of snacks and sandwiches, also attested to how long these two had worked.

Anne glanced at her watch. "Do you know it's almost three in the morning—?"

"But it's done," Fernando sighed, stretching his arms. "You are an amazing woman, Anne. You have an uncanny grasp of communicating the essentials in a way my people will understand." He gave her a quizzical smile. "Are you sure your parents are not Latin—?"

That smile was still disturbing Anne. It was incredible how white and even his teeth were, how positively charming the smile. It was four or five days now — they had both lost track of time — since they started drafting the Articles of Intent. She simply could not stop being attracted more and more to this man.

"You realize we've gone beyond our original intent," Fernando said. "Thanks to the input from your NECCO organization, and your vision of the plan, we have succeeded in producing a document that spells out a comprehensive implementation agreement between our hemispheres. I am very pleased, Anne — and very impressed."

Anne went over to the sofas. "Also very tired, probably," she smiled. "I know I am. But very pleased, like you. If everyone agrees with the principles of this document, we will be able to initiate the Phoenix Plan without delay." She picked up the coffee pot from the table. "Another cup—?"

Fernando nodded and sat down across from her. He accepted the drink and leaned back. "I feel very privileged to have this opportunity of working with you, Anne. I mean that."

"I've enjoyed it too," Anne said. She took several sips of the coffee, suddenly completely at a loss for words.

"You never asked about what Colonel Fariocha said to me — that I was taking orders, even if indirectly, from the Chinese. Is there a reason for not doing that—?"

"I figured there would be a time and place," Anne replied. "I'm more than curious, of course. It's something that has to be talked about, because we must know if this Chinese connection will affect our agreement."

"Are you up to talking about it now, or are you too tired—?"

"Now would be a good time. I need to know before presenting the details of the agreement to the President tomorrow — today," she corrected herself, smiling.

"You have a lovely smile, Anne. I hope you don't find that rude or offensive. I noticed it the first day we met and I just couldn't wait any longer to tell you."

"I don't find it at all rude or offensive," Anne said, smiling again. "I'm flattered." She tried to be outwardly calm, not betraying the hammering that had started inside her. This was ridiculous, she told herself, letting herself be so emotionally vulnerable. "Of course, you Latin men have a reputation for saying things a lady likes to hear."

"That's not why I said it, Anne," Fernando said quietly. His eyes were searching hers. "It is only one of the things I'm beginning to realize I admire about you—"

"Are you trying to change the subject?" Anne asked lightly. She hoped she wasn't showing the increase in body temperature she was feeling. Totally, absolutely ridiculous. "We were discussing how the People's Republic is involved with the Coalition of Allied States of the Americas—"

Francisco de Branca scrubbed at his face. Anne noticed the stubble of whiskers he had grown over the past twelve hours spent completing the agreement. Ordinarily, she didn't like beards or unshaven men. Rather than macho, it made them look sleazy and unclean, in her opinion. It annoyed her that the stubble on the man across from her aroused a completely different reaction. It made Fernando look even more handsome, she thought, gave him a definite masculine charm. Perhaps it was because the silver streaks in his hair contrasted so sharply with the dark whiskers. She caught her thoughts and brought them sharply back.

"Are we talking about the Chinese government, or a group of individuals?" she asked.

"It's a confusing story, and even I don't know the full details," Francisco de Branca began. "It began over twelve years ago—"

"That far back—?" Anne said, surprised.

"Possibly even farther than that. It apparently started with an economic cartel — a powerful, world-wide group of financiers, dominated and controlled by an inner circle of Chinese. Some say it was a Chinese crime organization. There is no way of knowing. Personally, I think it was more legitimate than that. The objective at that time seemed to be gaining control of world economics."

"The objective changed—?"

"About five years ago, the Chinese began influencing political affairs in some of the smaller countries in our hemisphere. Unlike here in your country, there are always groups of dissidents willing to resort to military force to put themselves into power."

"Was that when the plan to attack the United States came into existence—?"

"I'm sure it was part of the Chinese plan a long time before that," Fernando said. "First, they proposed helping to establish the coalition. It was shortly after the birth of CASA that Operation Scourge surfaced."

Anne frowned and shook her head. "I simply can't understand how you people could go along with it—"

"Millions of our people live in abject poverty, with no hope of ever bettering themselves. Many of them feel deep jealousy and resentment toward you rich gringos in the United States. It's not hard to feed the rage of desperate people. One by one the countries agreed to the Chinese plan, until it became a mandate to the Governing Council."

Once again Francisco de Branca scrubbed his face. "I'm not trying to excuse our actions, Anne. We went along willingly and eagerly. The Chinese offered to supply arms, equipment, and strategic planning for the invasion. They saw to it the United States was diverted, its military resources committed to other fronts. Before anyone realized it, Operation Scourge was an express train that couldn't be stopped."

"So now the People's Republic want the Phoenix Plan derailed — they want leaders like you killed," Anne said soberly. "I'm sure their agenda goes beyond the United States being taken over by the Coalition. Sooner or later, the Chinese will assume control."

"I'm sure you're right," Fernando nodded. "None of us really looked beyond the promises, the spoils of victory."

"That was what really kept you up all night back in Brazilia, wasn't it," Anne said. "Deciding whether or not to break away from the Chinese."

"Deciding whether or not it was possible," Fernando corrected.

"Is it—?"

"Yes — if the United States becomes a partner, rather than an enemy. The People's Republic have made it very clear they don't want a direct confrontation with your country."

"So you believe the Phoenix Plan has an honest chance of working—?"

"It will work. Perhaps now you can understand why we agreed so quickly to accept it. It offers great hope for the future, but even more importantly, it provides an opportunity to break away from the death-grip the Chinese have on us."

Anne studied him intently. There was no doubting the sincerity of what he was saying. And it was all believable. The Latin countries had become expendable pawns in a great Chinese game of chess. Anne saw that Fernando was genuinely suffering from what he'd just told her. It undoubtedly was difficult, letting an enemy know how easily CASA had fallen into the Chinese trap. Suddenly she wanted to reassure this man that she was not his enemy. Instead, she changed the subject.

"What about your own safety? Will there be others like Colonel Fariocha seeking to kill you—?"

"Perhaps. I briefed the Council before I left. I didn't need to tell them the killing probably wouldn't stop with me. By this time, General Wu Zhenkang is in custody — or dead. He is the man who directed operations for the Chinese. Now that the Council has made the decision to go along with the Phoenix Plan, we can move openly against the Chinese power structure in the hemisphere."

"So you personally feel safe now—?"

Fernando grinned briefly. "The taxis in Rio are always a threat. But yes, I doubt if there will be any more assassination attempts. Thank you for your concern, Anne."

Anne stood up. "I appreciate your openness, Fernando, in telling me all this. I can't speak for the President, but I know he's as anxious as I am for the Phoenix Plan to work."

Fernando also stood up. He fastened Anne with a serious look.

"This is completely out of line, but I'll probably be going back to Brazil in a few hours. Do you suppose, after the agreements are signed and we are no longer on opposite sides, you would allow me to call on you socially—?"

For some inexplicable reason, Anne was no longer flustered. The schoolgirl tingling was gone. She looked at Fernando Francisco de Branca and saw a handsome man. She saw qualities she had come to admire. She saw a man who aroused womanly instincts in her, a man who obviously was interested in her. And she suddenly felt comfortable with herself, accepting the attraction between them. She smiled and offered her hand.

"I would be most pleased to have you call on me, Fernando. I would have been disappointed if you hadn't asked."

# 31

## RED TIGER, RED BEAR

Premier Chen Xingtao's normally placid face was flushed with anger. He held up a sheaf of papers in one hand and with the other, stabbed a finger at the man standing in front of him. General Wang Jingwei, chairman of the Central Military Commission, had never felt more uncomfortable in his entire life.

"This is unacceptable, General Wang. Completely unacceptable—"

"I am sorry, Premier Chen."

"That too is unacceptable." The Premier waved the papers angrily. "We have planned this for over twenty years. We have spent billions of dollars setting it up. Now you tell me it is falling apart — that Operation Scourge is threatened with failure. I will not accept that, General Wang."

"We could not anticipate the Americans developing this Phoenix Plan—"

"You gave me your assurances that all contingencies were anticipated and prepared for, General. I, in turn, gave those assurances to the Council. I will not lose face like this, General Wang."

"I will personally go to South America to assess the problems, Premier Chen."

"What of this General Wu — how can he have failed so miserably? Where is he now—?"

"He has not been seen or heard from for over a week. We must assume he is dead."

"He deserves to die. If he is not dead, execute him. No — bring him here to Beijing and let the Council witness his death."

"As you say, Premier Chen."

"Is there nothing that can be done—?"

"The betrayal has been complete. The entire Governing Council has turned against us."

"It makes no sense," the Chinese leader said angrily. "We gave them the United States — a gift of the richest country on earth. How can they not bow in gratitude before us—?"

"The Americans were quick to counter the military offensive. Their threat to destroy the entire southern hemisphere with a nuclear assault brought an unexpected end to the invasion."

"Unexpected — unexpected," Premier Chen shouted angrily. "How many more things were not taken into account. Two moves by the Americans and everything we planned for a quarter of a century is destroyed. It is unforgivable, General Wang."

General Wang bowed his head. "I am dishonored, Premier Chen. Do you wish me to step down?"

"I wish you to bring Operation Scourge back to life. I don't care how you do it, but this peace accord between the north and the south must be destroyed. That is an order, General Wang. Make no mistake about this — your honor and your life depend on you accomplishing this."

General Wang's head remained bowed. He did not dare meet the flaming eyes of the Premier. "I am your servant, Premier Chen. I will do as you wish, or die by my own hand."

\* \* \*

News of the impending signing of a peace treaty between the United States and the invading Latin countries quickly reached across Europe. It brought a tremendous sense of relief to most governments, for the threat of an attack by the new Soviet military junta was growing daily. Peace in the Americas meant the United States would be able to fulfill its treaty obligations to the NATO alliance.

It was not good news for the three military leaders of the new Military Union of Soviet Independent Republics, meeting in the resplendent office of General Victor Kuchakov in the Kremlin, overlooking the huge square that was the military heart of Moscow. The name of the new military organization did not particularly please anyone — it was felt that the acronym MUSIR did not communicate a needed sense of power — but it was accepted out of the necessities of political compromise. The independent republics, forced under pressure to accept the military alliance, insisted there be no hint of a political union.

General Kuchakov was puffing on a huge cigar, a gift from Cuba's new military commander. So were the other two men in the room, General Sergei Yazenko, of the Republic of Belarus, and Admiral Andrei Chekonovich, of the Republic of Ukraine. They were sitting in front of a roaring fire, which was not needed but which General Kuchakov insisted on having every day, winter and summer. It still helped to burn away memories of those bleak days of banishment to Leningrad.

"So we do not agree," Kuchakov grunted. He reached over to a nearby table and poured himself a glass of vodka. He held the bottle up questioningly to the others, but both men still had almost full glasses. "The three of us should be united before we bring this to the full Commission."

"It is madness to attack Europe under the present circumstances," Admiral Chekonovich muttered. "Even if we hide it from the others, we must be honest with ourselves. We are not prepared to conduct such a campaign."

"Especially now that the United States has made peace with the Latin coalition," General Yazenko added. "The Americans will intervene—"

"You talk like frightened children," Kuchakov snorted angrily. "With all the destruction the coalition caused, the Americans will not open a new front. All their resources will be needed to rebuild their own country."

"You're wrong, Viktor," Checkonovich said firmly. "They will not abandon Great Britain."

"Then we will not attack Great Britain."

"And they will not abandon their defense treaties with the other NATO countries," Checkonovich continued. "We are not strong enough to risk attacking Europe — not without the full political support of all the republics."

"Which we do not have," Yazenko reminded, "and will not get. At least, not in the immediate future. If there is any hope of success in attacking Europe, it must be done immediately."

"That is what I am saying," Kuchakov snapped. "Attack now, before the United States has time to rebuild its military power."

"You are forgetting the People's Republic, Victor," Chekonovich reminded. "They warned us they will intervene if we attack Europe."

"The Chinese do not want to confront the United States—"

"They will not be confronting them," Chekonovich said. "They will become an ally of the United States fighting against us. We will be fighting on two fronts, east and west — a nightmare that is no stranger to any of us."

"You forget, Viktor, that the United States sent a large military force to Europe before it was invaded. They undoubtedly have, and are prepared to use, nuclear weapons. We can't do this, Viktor."

"Then what do we do—? This great new military power we have created — how do we stop it from once again being destroyed by the politicians?"

"We wait, Viktor," Sergei Yazenko said. "We wait, and we build more power. We make the new military union indispensable to every republic. We make the politicians rely on us, become the answer to their problems. Our time will come."

"Sergei is right," Chekonovich muttered, taking a long drag on his cigar. "Our own phoenix bird is rising from its ashes. One day we will see who is the most powerful—"

# 32

## THE NEW BROTHERHOOD

Luther Banes peered anxiously through the windshield of the black Cadillac, staring up at the sky. He pushed the button to roll down the heavily-tinted window and looked again. Dusk would soon darken into night. He looked at Candi, sitting in the front passenger seat beside him.

"Do you think he'll show—?"

"These Orientals work on precise schedules. There's still fifteen minutes before he's due to arrive. My guess is, he'll be exactly on time."

The Cadillac was parked alongside an abandoned private air strip in open desert country on the west side of Utah Lake, close to the foothills and some forty-five miles south of Salt Lake City. The strip was once used by a mining company but was abandoned over twenty years ago. The runway had recently been graded and leveled, weeds and brush cleared, potholes filled in. Generator-powered lights were added to each side of the landing strip, which was long enough to accommodate twin-engine prop planes. The strip now served as a private, uncharted airfield for the New Brotherhood.

Luther rolled the window back up. He half-turned in the seat and looked admiringly at Candi. He still couldn't believe he was living with her. Every time they made love, and that was often, she was fiercely passionate. It was exhilarating having a woman like her. He wished he could tell his high school buddies how different it was with a mature, beautiful woman than those quickie conquests in the back seat.

"Candi, why are you doing this for me?" Luther asked. "I keep telling myself I can't really be this lucky – I'm just a kid."

"You're a man, Luther."

"How come you're so smart, Candi?" Luther said, genuine awe in his voice. "All the guys respect you, and no one ever questions you heading the New Brotherhood. I know everybody on the Supreme Council is supposed to be equal, but they all do whatever you say."

"I grew up with power, Luther. My daddy was a big man in the black power circles," Candi said softly, allowing thoughts to drift back. "He was one of the biggest drug dealers in all of Southern California — even the Mexicans and the Colombians respected him. My daddy had the power of life and death — and used it."

"I like the way you talk, Candi," Luther said admiringly. "You're smooth — you must be real educated."

"Graduated with honors from Stanford. Double majors — business and political science. That was where I learned what sex could do. It gives you the power."

"All I know, sex with you is powerful good," Luther grinned. "Is your father still in California—?"

Candi's face clouded over. "He's dead. The Asians tried to move into our territory. I was a full partner then, and they wanted both of us out."

"What happened—?"

"They set us up — a phony drug meet. My daddy tried to save me. He got out of the car with his hands up, but they blasted him anyway."

"How did you get away?"

"I was driving. When the shooting started, I jammed the Mazeratti into reverse and tore out of there. Last thing I saw was those slant-eyed gooks standing over my daddy, still shooting. I won't ever forget that. That's why I'm having a tough time with this meet. I keep telling myself to stay cool — this Chinese dude we're meeting has nothing to do with the Japanese yakusa who gunned down my daddy – but it's not easy to see any difference between them."

"Who is this guy?"

"Colonel P'eng Songlin. He's somebody big in the Chinese military. Don't know any more about him than that."

"Why's he coming here? Sounds pretty risky to fly into the Zone—"

"Guess we'll soon find out," Candi murmured, pointing up into the sky. "That must be his plane." She glanced at her wristwatch and smiled. "He's touching down right on the minute."

Fifteen minutes later, the plane was pushed to the side, covered with camouflage netting from a nearby shack, and the Cadillac was heading north in a trail of dust, racing along dirt roads toward the distant freeway. Candi turned and smiled at the lone passenger in the rear seat.

"Our people are waiting to meet with you, Colonel Songlin."

"It is Colonel P'eng," the man corrected in an unfriendly voice. "May I ask what your position is in this organization — the Brothers, isn't it?"

"The New Brotherhood," Candi replied, trying to ignore his coldness and keep her own voice friendly. "It includes all factions, all minorities. We don't use the term brothers any more."

"And what position does a black woman like yourself hold?" He managed to make it sound demeaning to be even talking to her. "I was told someone in authority would be meeting me—"

Candi looked at Luther. "Stop the car."

The Cadillac stopped in a swirl of dust as Luther jammed on the brakes.

Candi swiveled around, so she could face the man in the back more directly. Her voice now was openly hostile.

"This black woman is the chairwoman of the Supreme Council, Colonel. I am also head of the Black Brotherhood — the largest and most powerful group in the organization. And this is not China. You may be important there, but here you're just a yellow piece of crap who's come crawling for a favor. You will show me respect, Colonel, or get back on your plane — that's if I don't decide to kill you."

Colonel P'eng said nothing. He just stared back at Candi with what was truly an inscrutable expression. Finally he gave a slight nod of his head.

"My apologies. It was a clumsy mistake. How should I address you—?"

"Candi. Just Candi." She stared at him for several more moments, then motioned to Luther. "You can go now—"

Luther put the car in gear, smiling to himself. Candi didn't take any crap from anyone.

The Supreme Council was already assembled when they arrived. All were gathered around a table in what was formerly the basement recreation room of a ten-story brick apartment building. The remodeled building now provided luxury suites for the leaders of the nine factions, The basement served as headquarters for the organization. Candi introduced Colonel P'eng and had him sit at one end of the table. She took her place at the other end.

"Colonel P'eng has come a long way. I'm sure what he has to say will be of interest to all of us." She nodded at the colonel, her manner still frosty. She wasn't sure about doing business with this man. In her mind, she could see her daddy lying on the ground, his body jerking as bullets tore into him. Colonel P'eng had no idea how close he was to joining his ancestors.

The man from Beijing studied the faces around the table. The contempt he was feeling did not show on his face. These people represented all that was evil and corrupt. In China, they would all be shot. The black woman, Candi — he could not allow himself to dwell on the anger seething inside him when he looked at her. One day, she would pay for her insulting arrogance.

He saw there were three Asian groups represented. Chinese. Japanese. Vietnamese. The others were easy to place. Arab. Philippino. Nigerian. Haitiian. Hispanic — he couldn't tell if the man was Cuban or Mexican. The thick-set, stony-faced man at the other end of the table looked Russian.

Suddenly his glance shot back to the Chinese member. There was something familiar about him. He studied the man. Candi noticed his suddenly sharpened attention.

"Something wrong, Colonel P'eng?" she asked.

P'eng pointed a finger at the man from China. "This man — what is your name?"

"Lin Shangli."

"No it isn't," the colonel said sharply. "Nia — Nia Yao Gui. I know you from Beijing. We were told you were killed in Tokyo."

Candi's stare also fastened on the man she knew as Lin Shangli. "Is he telling the truth — are you this other man, Shangli?"

Nia Yao Gui leaned back in the swivel chair, a thin smile coming to his face. "I was once known as Nia Yao Gui, yes. And I did know this man in Beijing. We both served in the General Political Department of the People's Liberation Army, under General Wang Jingwei. We were both colonels, in fact."

"This man is a traitor," Colonel P'eng shouted.

"And this man is full of crap," Yao Gui replied evenly. He looked at Candi. "My death was faked so I could come to the United States. I was to enter the Zone and learn all I could. I have friends in the Chinese communities both in Los Angeles and San Francisco, and they gave me the recommendations I presented to you. I am not a traitor, nor a spy. I am here merely to observe. When this new development occurred between the American government and the South American coalition, I reported it to Beijing. I recommended they contact this organization because it had the brains and the power to accomplish some very important objectives of the People's Republic. They sent Colonel P'eng, but obviously did not tell him about me. I'm sure they simply wanted to protect me."

Candi, along with every other member of the council, was staring at Yao Gui. He seemed unperturbed, even faintly amused.

"Truth is," she said, "you lied to us, Shangli — or whatever your name is. I don't trust liars—"

Yao Gui gave a short laugh. "Come on, Candi — look around you. Show me one of us who hasn't lied his way to hell and back. That's how we all survive."

Despite herself, Candi let a smile flicker across her face. "Can't argue with that, Shangli — what is your name, really?"

"Yao Gui — Nia Yao Gui. At least," he added with a smile of his own," it's the one I used in Beijing. I'm not sure I know what my real name is any more."

"You recommended this meet to the Chinese—?"

"Yes. Both sides can do each other big favors."

"What do they want from us—?"

"I suggest we let Colonel P'eng explain that. The council can then set its price."

Candi looked down the table to P'eng. "That okay with you, Colonel?"

"I do not trust this man. My superiors in Beijing would have told me—"

Yao Gui interrupted. "I am sure General Wang will have something to say to you, Colonel P'eng, when I tell him how you have bungled this whole assignment. This not a council of peasants, Colonel. You are being arrogant and insolent, and threaten the success of your mission. I suggest you show a little humility and proceed before you must report complete failure to General Wang – from the grave."

It was all a bluff. The whole thing. But Yao Gui could tell it was working. Even Colonel P'eng had suddenly backed down at the mention of General Wang and failure in the same sentence. At the worst, Yao Gui reasoned, the council would think he was being devious — but that was a position familiar to all of them. Whatever the truth was, it appeared to offer benefits to the council. He just might get out of this room alive, Yao Gui told himself.

"What this man has said is true," Colonel P'eng said.

Though he said it reluctantly, it increased Yao Gui's chances, for the others simply heard confirmation of what Shangli — or Yao Gui — had told them.

"I bring you an offer from the People's Republic, that I am sure you will find—"

Candi interrupted him. "There are three things to consider, Colonel. Investment. Risk. Return. Cut the crap and get to the facts."

P'eng took a deep breath, again bringing his anger under control. This black woman must somehow pay for her insolence. But Yao Gui was right — the success of the mission came before anything else.

"We want you to disrupt the upcoming signing of the peace treaty between the United States and the Coalition," he said. "Not just disrupt it — we want all trust between the two parties destroyed. We want the fighting to begin again, until one or the other is defeated."

Candi stared at him with narrowed eyes. "Let me get this straight, Colonel. You're asking us to make sure the fighting starts again." She glanced around the table. "We're not pillars of patriotism, but we're not stupid either. This country goes down, we go down with it."

P'eng quickly shook his head. "There is no question of the United States losing. It will win the conflict — there has never been any doubt of that."

"Then why bother—?"

"We do not want hostilities stopped so soon. That will affect other plans. We will give you any assistance needed to delay the peace accord."

"We just bust up the signing ceremony—?"

"More than that will be needed."

"What exactly?"

"There are plans to rebuild destroyed sections of your country. It is to begin in Kansas City, I understand."

"Seems like you got a good pipeline, Colonel," Candi said. "What about this reconstruction—?"

"It must not happen, not for many more months anyway. You will destroy the supplies, stop the convoys, kill as many as it takes to keep people from volunteering to go to Kansas City."

"Is that all?" the representative of the Hispanic brotherhood sneered. "You're crazy, man. We're big and we're tight, but we ain't no army."

"We will give all the help you need," Colonel P'eng said quickly. "Men and weapons."

"We'll do our own recruiting, Colonel, if that becomes necessary," Candi said coldly.

"Nevertheless, we have already arranged for a force of South American soldiers to attack the convoys both en route to Missouri, and to continue to harass them during the reconstruction efforts."

Yao Gui frowned questioningly. "Are you planning on breaking the truce?"

"We would like that, of course," the colonel replied, "but we do not expect that to happen. The soldiers I am talking about are renegades. They have already broken away from army control. Nothing more than bandits now, but they will serve the purpose."

"Since you seem to know so much about it," Candi asked, "how many people are going to be in this reconstruction group going to Missouri?"

"We have been told the first convoy will number about a million volunteers."

Candi's eyes widened. "A million people—?"

"Those are civilian volunteers. I am sure there will be a significant number of military forces accompanying them."

The Hispanic man threw both arms in the air. "Dude, you're really out of it. We can't go against numbers like that—"

"All you have to do is disrupt, cause damage, instill fear. Destroy their morale."

"We've covered the investment," Candi said, staring speculatively at P'eng, "and it's not hard to figure the risk – just this side of impossible. What's our return—?"

"My government is prepared to meet any reasonable requirement," P'eng said firmly. "This is very important to us."

"As important as a billion dollars?"

Candi was watching the colonel closely. She wanted to see what that amount of money did to his eyes. Maybe they narrowed — who could tell?

"That is more than expected—"

Candi noticed he didn't say 'much' more.

"We also want drugs – an open pipeline. We get as much as we want, free for the first year, negotiable after that. Weapons. And a steady supply of Asian girls – guys really get off on how young they look."

"Your price is high—"

"Our risk is high. Our return should be high, too. What do you say, Colonel — will your people in Beijing go for that?"

"Can you guarantee you will accomplish all that is asked—?"

"Absolutely. If we fail, all it'll cost you is the billion dollars you put up front."

Colonel P'eng's eyes clearly narrowed this time. "My superiors will never agree to that."

"Sure they will, Colonel. Because we don't do a thing until we get the money. I don't need to remind you, we're the only game in town."

Colonel P'eng studied the woman at the opposite end of the table. She was not bluffing, he knew. General Wang had said to accomplish his mission at any cost. His stare slid to Nia Yao Gui. Was this man truly an operative for General Wang, as he said. P'eng could not bring himself to completely believe that.

Yao Gui sensed the man's thoughts. "They can do it, Colonel. They can blow hell out of this peace business for you. We both know the importance of that, not only to General Wang, but to Premier Chen and the Council — to the whole future of the People's Republic. As I see it, you really don't have any options. Such a sum is readily available in California. I know these people of the New Brotherhood, Colonel. They can get half that much from the United States government just for turning you over to them — with no risk involved."

"Not a bad idea, Shangli," Candi muttered.

"I must talk to General Wang—"

Yao Gui shook his head. "You have full authority to close the deal, Colonel. Talk to your people in California, no one else — and talk only about money."

"One billion dollars – cash, diamonds, or gold. No securities," Candi added. "As soon as you deliver, we start throwing a treaty signing party — - one that the People's Republic will like."

Colonel P'eng hesitated for only a moment longer. He would do his part. If the government wanted to change the agreement with this cesspool of criminals later, he would welcome it. He would urge it.

"Remember, much will be required for such a high price," he told Candi. "There is one thing that might be helpful. We have learned that Fernando Francisco de Branca, head of the Governing Council of CASA, appears to have become enamored with your vice president, Madame Anne Ashford."

"That for real?" Candi frowned. "Is she hot for him, or is this one way?"

"We understand both feel the same attraction. If this is true, and it went as far as marriage, it would be disastrous for our purposes. An emotional linkage between the two continents — we do not want that to happen."

"How far do we go—?"

"Hopefully, events will make such a union impossible. I mention it only so you will be aware of it. A wedding – even a formal engagement –must not happen. Now I will make that call to California—"

Unfortunately for Colonel P'eng, things did not work out quite as planned. He made the phone call to Los Angeles, short and in Chinese, monitored closely by Yao Gui. The details of the agreement would get back to General Wang almost immediately, Yao Gui knew, but there would be no mention of a man who had not died in Tokyo as reported.

Two days later, the money arrived in three planes at the desert airstrip, carrying cash, diamonds and bullion as requested. After being unloaded and refueled, the planes returned to California.

The next day, Candi and Luther drove Colonel P'eng to the strip where his own plane had remained concealed by camouflage. The plane took off with no good-byes exchanged.

Candi and Luther were back in the car when they heard an explosion. They jumped out in time to see the colonel's plane spiraling earthward in a ball of flame. They watched it crash in yet another explosion several miles away in the desert.

"Crap," Luther muttered, "what happened?"

"The colonel's plane blew up," Candi said, showing no emotion. "Don't ask me how, because I don't know. Let's get out of here."

Two miles away, behind a finger of foothill where they could not be seen from the airstrip, a NECCO Ranger tapped his buddy on the helmet as the man lowered the stinger missile launcher from his shoulder..

"Good shooting, Buck. Instead of two billion, two hundred million Chinese, now there's only two billion, one hundred and ninety-nine million, nine hundred and ninety-nine thousand, nine hundred and ninety-nine."

# 33

## Attack on Phoenix

Only one person did not show up at the emergency meeting of the Supreme Council called by Candi as soon as she and Luther got back into the city.

Nia Yao Gui. Or Lin Shangli.

When it became evident he wasn't just late, but wasn't going to show, Candi's face set into a hard mask.

"He was double talking us," she said angrily. "He's probably the one who arranged the colonel's little plane accident."

"Maybe the colonel did him in," one of the group muttered, "or maybe Shangli just took off—"

"And maybe I'm the tooth fairy," Candi said. "We can't count on it. I want everybody out of here in fifteen minutes. Only take records and files. Move everything out of the warehouses too. There's a new location we haven't used before. I was saving it for bigger and better things — and I think a billion dollars satisfies that criteria."

Luther, who did not normally attend the council meetings, this time was standing near Candi. He leaned over and muttered into her ear. She nodded and Luther quickly left the room.

Moments later, Cora Banes answered the telephone. She almost dropped it when she heard her son's voice.

"Luther — where are you? Are you all right? Everybody is looking for you—"

"I'm fine, mother," Luther said, trying to calm his mother. "Is dad there?"

"No. He's at the office. Are you sure you're all right, son. I've been worried sick about you—"

"I'm fine, mother. Something happened a little while ago—"

"Are you in more trouble?"

"No, mother. I was just about to clear myself, to prove I had nothing to do with Jill Adam's death."

"Can you do that? You really didn't do it—?"

"I told you I didn't, mother. I was to meet a guy who could prove it, but he didn't show up for our meeting."

"Who is it — can I help find him? Can your father help—?"

"That's why I'm calling. Dad might know him. He's Chinese. In his early thirties. I think his name is Nia Yao Gui, or something like that. He had something to do with intelligence work—"

Cora gasped excitedly. "I talked to your father earlier today and he mentioned something about a man like that. I didn't pay any attention to the name — don't even remember if your father mentioned it. He just said he was going to be late because he had a meeting with Quinn and Race and a Chinese man—"

"Thanks, mother," Luther interrupted. "Got to go. I'll be in touch."

"Do you want me to have your father see if he can put this man in touch with you. If he can prove you didn't have anything to do with Jill's death—"

"I know how to get in touch with him now. Thanks."

Luther came back into the room and again whispered into Candi's ear. She clenched her fists for a moment, then looked at the others around the table.

"Shangli was a plant – he works for NECCO intelligence. Luther just confirmed it."

"What about the money—?"

"It's safe. Everybody move out – now!"

Forty-five minutes later, Candi, Luther and four members of the Supreme Council watched in the darkness from the roof of a building two blocks away from their headquarters. Salt Lake blocks were twice as long as those in other cities, but there was no difficulty seeing the scores of flashing lights from the police cars now surrounding the headquarters building. Three helicopters began circling the area, bathing the building and surrounding areas in brilliant light. The people on the roof automatically crouched down.

"This wrecks the plan, doesn't it?" one of the men muttered. "Shangli knows we're going to blow up the Delta Center during the signing ceremonies—"

"Not any more." Candi hissed. "We'll let them worry about it, though, while we cook up a little surprise."

"What you got in mind, Candi—?"

"Something I'm going to enjoy. Let's get out of here."

Back at NECCO headquarters, six people were seated around a table, frowning in deep concentration. There was Quinn, Linc, Race, Yao Gui, Aaron Stark and Frank Kantros. The signing ceremony was scheduled in six days, the entire Governing Council of the Coalition due to arrive in five. The raid on the headquarters of the New Brotherhood had netted nothing of any value. The warehouses Yao Gui had known about were emptied before NECCO forces got there. In reality, nothing tangible had been achieved by the raids on the brotherhood.

"I should have stayed longer," Yao Gui muttered. "Me not being there sounded the alarm."

"I ordered you out, Yao Gui," Quinn reminded him. "You did all you could. No one was going to trust you after that colonel blew the whistle."

"Incidentally," Race asked, "how did you come up with a story like that on the spur of the moment—?"

"An old Chinese proverb — necessity is mother of invention," Yao Gui smiled. "At the time, I felt an extreme necessity to be inventive."

"What do we do now?" Linc asked. "Do we call off the ceremonies?"

"We can't," Quinn said, "not now. We just have to make sure nothing happens."

Frank Kantros shrugged. "If they're planning on using explosives, like Yao Gui says, we can seal off a square mile and sniff it clean."

"That wouldn't stop a rocket attack, or some other type of missiles," Aaron Stark said, shaking his head. "I agree with Linc — I don't see how we can risk it, Quinn. We're talking about the heads of state of over a score of Latin countries, not to mention our own President and Vice President, and the leaders of Congress."

"Let's not forget about worldwide television coverage," Quinn snapped. He scrubbed both hands in his hair. "Sorry, gentlemen. Everything that's been said is valid. But cancel the ceremonies because of a threat by a gang of punks – that's unthinkable. We're smarter than they are — we have to outthink them."

"We probably should bring Francisco de Branca in on this," Linc said. "He flew in today ahead of the others."

"I suggest we have a plan of action before doing that," Race countered. "He might do exactly what the brotherhood wants — call off the signing ceremony."

Quinn stood up and paced around the room. "We know they planned to blow up the Delta Center and everyone in it. They know Yao Gui has told us that. We can't ignore the possibility they'll still try it, but it's more likely they'll come up with a different plan of attack. They haven't got much time. Yao Gui, how many punks are in the brotherhood?"

Yao Gui pursed his lips thoughtfully. "A thousand – maybe fifteen hundred."

Race whistled his surprise. "I would have guessed half that."

"Don't forget these people have no compunction about killing. Self preservation is all that counts with them."

"I could throw a cordon about the whole area," Frank Kantros grunted, "that theoretically an ant couldn't get through. But one always does."

"The same thing for air cover," Aaron said. "It's not possible to make an area completely penetration-proof."

"So what do we do—?" Race grimaced.

Quinn drew in a deep breath. "They're probably asking the same question. Let's all get a few hours sleep. We need to be sharp and I'm feeling fuzzy. Let's meet back here in four hours."

They all stood up. Race clapped a hand on Quinn's shoulder.

"Let me tell you, buddy — your fuzziness is in a whole lot better shape than my fuzziness."

\* \* \*

Anne Ashford was feeling excited. Fernando called after arriving in Salt Lake this afternoon and arranged for them to meet for dinner. With all the conferences with state officials these past few weeks, and getting ready for the international signing ceremonies, Anne moved from her quarters at Hill to a downtown hotel reserved for dignitaries. Fernando was in the same hotel, though three floors lower.

There was a light tap on the door and Anne crossed to open it. A maid was outside, with one of those large linen carriers. She was holding a bundle of towels.

"I'm sorry to interrupt, Madame Vice President," the maid smiled, "but our records show you did not receive fresh towels today."

Anne smiled back. "I did, but there are some soiled ones now if you'd like to change them."

"Thank you, Madame," the maid said. "I'll just be a moment. I'll turn down the bed while I'm here."

Anne turned and started back toward the bedroom. She heard the maid close behind her and swung around, startled. The woman was holding a can of spray of some kind. Anne saw the spray coming toward her face and tried to leap back, but not in time. There was a sharp pain in her skull as she breathed the spray, then sudden and complete darkness. As she slumped to the floor, the maid put the canister back into the towels.

"So sorry, Madame," Candi murmured, looking down at Anne. "We won't bother with turning down the bed. You won't be spending the night here."

Luther, dressed in hotel uniform, entered the room dragging the unconscious figure of the Secret Service agent assigned to Anne Ashford's suite, another victim of the gas. Candi wheeled the laundry cart in and closed the door. She produced two rolls of gray tape from the cart and tossed one to Luther.

"You know what to do—"

Luther quickly taped the Secret Service agent while Candi taped Anne's mouth, wrists and feet. Then they bent her legs up until her knees were pressed against her stomach. Luther bound her that way, taping completely around her body. She was still unconscious as they lifted her into the linen basket and piled some sheets and towels on top of her. Moments later, they wheeled the basket down the hallway.

\* \* \*

Francisco de Branca got out of the shower, shaved and dressed, keeping a watchful eye on the time. He tried to control his impatience but the eager anticipation of his meeting with Anne grew with every minute. He had not stopped thinking about Anne Ashford since returning to Brazil. How did she feel? Was she looking forward to this evening as much as he was? She had sounded polite on the phone — no, there was more than politeness. Not quite eagerness, but he knew she'd welcomed his call. The telephone rang and he crossed swiftly to answer it.

"Fernando—?"

He frowned. It was a woman's voice, but not Anne's. Who in the United States knew him well enough to call him by his first name?

"This is Fernando—"

"You don't know me, Fernando, but we have a mutual friend. Anne Ashford—"

His interest quickened. "Yes—"

"I'm sad to tell you Anne is not feeling well, Fernando. Not well at all."

"What's wrong—?"

"She's all bound up."

Francisco de Branca frowned. This was not something strangers talked about to each other. "I'm not sure I understand—"

"Anne is bound up, Fernando. Hands and feet. I'd let you talk to her but her mouth is all bound up too."

Alarm shot through him. "Who is this—? What are you saying—?"

"I'm saying that Anne Ashford is my prisoner, Fernando. I'm saying that unless you follow my instructions," Candi added, her tone hardening,— "I will kill her in one hour."

"Is this some kind of joke—?"

"No joke, Fernando. Your little sweetie will be dead meat in an hour unless you do exactly as I tell you."

Francisco de Branca's mouth was suddenly dry. This woman was not joking. Anne was in danger — serious danger.

"What do you want—?"

Candi smiled. She had him — she could tell it in the change in his voice.

"I want you to leave the hotel without any escort. I know you have your own men, and also some NECCO Rangers assigned. I'll be watching. If you don't leave alone, forget it. Madame Vice President dies."

"I'll do it," he told her. "What then—? If you want money, I didn't bring much with me. I can get more—"

"I don't want your money, Fernando," Candi said quietly. "There will be a black Cadillac limousine waiting just north of the side entrance to the hotel. Not the main entrance — the entrance on the west side of the building. Do you understand—?"

"I understand."

"The rear door will be open and there will be a black man in chauffeur uniform waiting. Get in and you will soon be with little Annie. That depends, of course, on you leaving the hotel without being followed. Is all this clear to you, Fernando—?"

"Perfectly clear."

"Good. The limo is already waiting. Don't do anything foolish. I'll know if you do, and I promise you, you will cause Anne Ashford to die very unpleasantly."

Francisco de Branca made an excuse to the NECCO Ranger, dressed in civilian clothes, stationed outside his suite. He told him he was just going down to the lobby bookstore and would be back in a minute. He got off the elevator on the mezzanine, walked to the west end of the building and took the stairs down to the lobby, away from the crowded area about the elevators. Then he was outside.

He saw the limousine a short distance from the entrance to the hotel, a uniformed chauffeur beside it. He walked to the car, got in and the chauffeur closed the door. The chauffeur went around the car and got in behind the wheel. Moments later, the Cadillac pulled away from the curb.

Just as the chauffeur closed the door for Fernando de Branca, a NECCO Ranger appeared in the hotel entrance behind him. The Ranger had caught the next elevator after the Brazilian official left, going down to discreetly check the bookstore in the hotel lobby. Seeing that the Brazilian was not there, he jumped on a table and checked the crowd. He spotted Francisco de Branca just as he left through the side entrance. Rushing across the lobby, the Ranger looked right and left without seeing his man.

Something jerked his attention back to the black Cadillac parked a short distance from the entrance. He had not seen who got into the car and only caught a flashing glimpse of the driver, but as the car pulled away, recognition clicked. He reached for the radio in his pocket.

"All points emergency. I just lost the Brazilian—"

"How did it happen?" a voice asked.

"He tried to slip out. I'm sure he got into a Cadillac limousine parked outside the hotel."

"Can you give us a license number—"

"Didn't see it — the light was out."

"Are you sure Francisco de Branca was in the car—?"

"No. Couldn't see inside."

"What makes you think he's in the car—?"

"I recognized the chauffeur. It was Luther Banes — Lincoln Banes' son."

In the back seat, Fernando felt the weight of the pistol in his jacket pocket and was tempted to take it out and shove it against the head of the driver. But he realized that wouldn't help Anne.

Of course, there was the chance he'd been duped, that Anne's name was used only to draw him into a trap. He realized he hadn't even called her room to check on that possibility. There was something in the voice of the woman on the phone, however, that told him this was no bluff. They had Anne. He needed to be patient, watch for whatever opportunity presented itself after he was with her.

For a dreadful moment, the thought flashed through his mind that Anne might already be dead. He refused to accept that, pushed it away. She was alive, and somehow they both would come through this.

# 34

## HUNT AND KILL

"I want her found Quinn, and brought back safe." "So do I, Mr. President. We all want that, sir." "How does it look—?" "No clear leads, but we'll find her. We're pretty sure she's still somewhere in the area."

"Nothing more than that—?"

"Why don't I get back to you, sir. I don't mean to be rude, but we're pretty busy at the moment."

"I want you to—"

Quinn hung up the phone. Race stared at him.

"You just hung up on the President of the United States, buddy. You planning on early retirement—?"

"I love the guy, but right now he's a distraction I don't need," Quinn grunted. "Let's get back to some productive thinking."

In his office were Race, Yao Gui and Joanna. His wife had dropped by to check on him, since she hadn't seen or heard from him in a couple of days. On an impulse, Quinn asked her to stay and participate in the think session. There wasn't anyone in the world he trusted more in sorting out little scraps of information that turned alphabet soup into a clear message.

Joanna picked up the threads again. "We must assume they knew about Anne and Fernando being attracted to each other. That wasn't common knowledge. How did they find out—?"

"I should have mentioned that," Yao Gui said guiltily. "Colonel P'eng told them."

"And there's not much left of him left to question," Race muttered.

"He had to be stopped," Quinn said. "How did P'eng know—?"

"Had to be someone on the Governing Council of CASA," Yao Gui answered.

Quinn nodded. "Fernando said there were two who opposed the Phoenix Plan. It would be logical for them to leak to the Chinese."

"So we're back to the burning question," Race grimaced.

"Where did all the punks go—?"

"Is there anything, Yao Gui," Joanna asked again, "that might give us a lead? Something you overheard, something that didn't register, something that didn't make sense at the time. Some isolated scrap of information someone dropped—"

Yao Gui locked his hands behind his head and closed his eyes. The others also sank into deep thought. There were several minutes of silence.

"Are there any hangouts of the New Brotherhood we don't know about?" Race questioned. "A club or a social hall. Maybe some place just the black brothers hung out with Candi and Luther—"

Yao Gui's eyes popped open. "That's it," he said excitedly. "You just triggered it—"

"Some club—?" Race asked.

"No. Black brothers. Luther mentioned it about a month ago. Made a joke about it—"

"Think back—" Joanna urged. "Can you remember the joke?"

Yao Gui closed his eyes again, searching back for recall.

"Give yourself time," Joanna said soothingly. "Go back to Luther. Who was he talking to — where were you?"

"It was outside their headquarters. He was talking to Candi. They stopped when I came up, but I heard something—"

"Keep the picture in your mind—" Quinn said quietly.

Yao Gui's eyes snapped open again. "A building. They were talking about some building. That's it — the Black Brothers. That was the name of the building—or something like that. That's why they were joking about it."

Race was already reaching for the phone. He snapped a few quick orders then hung up. "They're checking. If it's in Salt Lake county, we'll know in a few minutes. If it's somewhere in Utah, or some other state, we'll track it down."

"Let's see what we have," Quinn said. "Luther and Candi were talking about a building, possibly a building the brotherhood owned—"

"That's my impression," Yao Gui cautioned. "I'm not sure though."

"None of the buildings and warehouses we've checked so far has a name like that," Race frowned.

"So it's been kept secret, probably for future use," Quinn continued. "We know they left in a hurry. They knew Yao Gui would finger every place he knew about. Since he didn't know about this one, odds are pretty good that's where they went."

"Wherever it is, they need a lot of warehousing space," Race said. "We're probably not looking at an apartment complex."

"They didn't take the freeways, because a caravan of cars and trucks that size would have been noticed," Joanna said. "That means it can't be too far away — at least, it can be reached by county roads."

"The area north of Salt Lake is jammed with housing and established production plants," Race said. "I like the south part of the county. Even with all the influx of refugees, there's still a lot of undeveloped space in that part of the valley."

"We have to assume that, whatever their reason for taking Anne and Fernando hostage," Joanna added grimly, "they don't plan on letting them live to a ripe old age. Time is our enemy."

"I say we roll the dice," Quinn muttered. "Race, move your people down into the south part of the county. Get hold of Frank Kantros and have him do the same thing with the Rangers. Notify Aaron. There's a National Guard headquarters down in the south end of the county – Draper, I think. Tell him to assemble a helicopter assault force. If we go in, I want those punks to think another World War just started." He looked around at the others. "If we're right, we save precious minutes. If we're wrong — well, we lose some."

Race left the office.

Yao Gui sighed nervously. "Maybe this Black thing doesn't lead anywhere. Maybe I just heard the last part of an old joke—"

"It's the best lead we have," Quinn assured him. "I have a good feeling about it."

The telephone rang a few minutes later. Quinn answered it and they could see satisfaction crowd onto his face as he wrote down an address. He hung up the phone and looked triumphantly at Joanna and Yao Gui.

"There is a Black Brothers Warehousing and Storage company in Granger, formerly the Granger Storage. That's in the south end of the county. The registered new owner is a Mrs. Candi Black."

Yao Gui clenched both fists and gave a yell of satisfaction. "Yeeess!"

Quinn was reaching for the phone to call Race when the office door opened and he burst into the room. He was holding a piece of paper in his hand.

"A Salt Lake County sheriff's report, received just a few minutes ago."

He held up the paper. "A Mrs. Lois Jenkins, an old lady who lives alone, called in to complain about a lot of lights and traffic in a warehouse she claims has been empty for years. She's worried that drug dealers are moving into her neighborhood."

"I bet Mrs. Jenkins lives in Granger," Quinn smiled.

A grin spread across Race's face. "You got the address—"

"In Granger. Obviously right across the street from Mrs. Jenkins. Let's go get 'em."

Joanna grabbed his arm. "You're not leaving me here."

It wasn't a question. Quinn hesitated. This was the woman who had been beside him in most of the covert operations in those years in the CIA, and later, on NECCO assignments. No one was better in a fight.

"Promise me one thing," he said. "You won't take chances. Leave the rough stuff to the Rangers."

"I will if you will."

He looked into her eyes, reached out and gave her a kiss. "I know you're tough, but you're not bullet proof. And I can't lose you now. Be careful."

"I'll be watching your back."

An assault helicopter was already waiting for Quinn, Joanna and Race. Yao Gui, who was not experienced in this kind of combat mission, was ordered to remain at NECCO headquarters, in the communication center. Just as they were boarding, Lincoln Banes ran across the tarmac toward them. He looked up at Quinn.

"Let me go with you, Quinn—"

Quinn shook his head. "You're not trained for this kind of stuff, Linc. We need you here."

"I have to go. No matter what he's done, Luther's my son."

"Another reason not to go, Linc," Quinn said, raising his voice to make himself heard over the rotors. "Luther's in a lot of trouble — no telling what he'll do. He might not come out alive."

"That's why I need to go. I'll stay back — stay in the helicopter, if you want — but take me along, Quinn."

Quinn could see the pain on Linc's face.

"All right," he said reluctantly, "but do just what you said — stay in the helicopter. Stay out of the action."

Linc clambered aboard and the helicopter lifted off. As they flew southward from Hill, the four of them changed into battle fatigues, donned protective vests, and checked weapons. Quinn leaned over and tapped Linc on the chest.

"Remember. You stay here. I'm letting you put on this stuff so you won't catch a stray. It's not your ticket to combat—"

Linc nodded. "I understand."

Quinn looked down at the automatic rifle Linc was holding. "Do you remember how to use that thing—?"

"Sure do."

"Well, use it if you have to—"

The pilot's voice came over the radio in each of their helmets.

"Estimate eight minutes to target."

\* \* \*

Candi was holding an impromptu meeting with the members of the Supreme Council in an upstairs office of the main building of the warehouse complex. They had all received assignments, each of the brotherhoods responsible for a particular phase of the campaign of terror.

"Any questions?" Candi asked. No one raised a hand. "Then get ready to raise hell. Every city hall. The airports. The bus stations. Hospitals. Schools. Radio and television stations. Newspapers. I want people too scared to go out on the streets. I want those Latin bigshots too scared to leave South America. Those of you who have assignments in other cities, better get moving. Use the local brotherhoods. I want this whole Federal Zone in flames come tomorrow night. Do a good job of this. The Chinese are a little unhappy about their man being barbecued, so we want them to see we're keeping our end of the deal. After all, this party is costing them a billion bucks."

She added one final warning. "Don't go near the military bases. We don't have firepower or manpower to take them on. Give them lots of fires and explosions to go see. Above all, don't anybody lead them back here. If you get caught, don't talk. The military or the cops show up, whoever is responsible is dead."

The meeting broke up and Candi motioned to Luther to accompany her. They went to one of the back rooms on the administration level. The room was empty but Luther went to a door at the far end, opened it and flicked on the light inside.

The large closet area, designed to hold files, was empty except for the two figures bound back-to-back lying on a small, twin-sized mattress. They were lying on their sides but both Anne and Fernando turned their heads to stare at Candi and Luther as they entered. Both hostages were squinting from the harsh light above them.

Candi smiled at them. "You two haven't been doing anything naughty lying here in the dark, have you?" She looked over at Luther. "Luther, did you forget to untie these nice people—? Shame on you. Untie them — and take that tape off their mouths. I'm sure they would appreciate being able to talk to each other."

She waited while Luther cut the tape. Both Anne and Fernando stretched painfully.

"Luther, you watch Fernando. Let him stretch, but if he tries to stand up, shoot him." Candi reached down and helped Anne onto her feet. "I'll bet our Vice President has to pee. There's a portable pottie over in the corner, but why don't you come with me to the ladies room, Anne. I'm sure you'd appreciate some privacy."

Anne could hardly walk so Candi put an arm around her and helped her hobble across the hall to the restroom. Luther watched as Francisco de Branca stretched arms and legs, groaning as circulation returned. When Candi and Anne returned, Luther grinned down at him.

"How about you, Mister Bigshot — you need to go potty?"

Fernando shook his head. Luther raised his eyebrows. "Good bladder, but if I was you, I'd go. It might be a long time before you get another chance."

Fernando pushed against the wall and forced himself to stand up. Luther stayed a cautious distance behind as Fernando haltingly walked toward the restrooms.

"Just empty your bladder, Fernando," Candi called out to him. "No way you're in shape to take Luther. Besides, I'll shoot the lady if you try anything."

With both Anne and Fernando back in the small room, Candi flashed another smile at them.

"Now it gets fun. Both of you take off your clothes."

They stared at each other, then back to Candi.

"I won't do that," Anne told her.

"Either you do it, or Luther will do it for you." She looked at Luther, standing in the doorway near her. "You'd be willing to do that, wouldn't you, Luther—?"

"You bet I would," Luther grinned.

Anne began to undress, turning away from Fernando. Candi waved the gun in her hand toward the Brazilian.

"You too, handsome. All the way down to the skin."

They both stopped when they had stripped to their underwear. Candi pointed the gun again.

"Naked. Both of you."

The two hostages slowly complied with her order, carefully avoiding looking at each other.

Luther gathered up the clothing, taking the opportunity to leer at Anne. Candi gave them instructions.

"The pottie's in that corner. There's nutritional bars and bottled water in this corner. Better memorize it, because the lights go out and stay out."

"How long are you planning to keep us here?" Fernando asked angrily.

"You better hope for a long time," Candi told him, "because next time I visit, it will be to kill you. That shouldn't be for at least a couple of days — but there are no guarantees. You shouldn't waste any time."

"What do you mean?" Anne asked.

"Sex, lady. You don't have much time – might as well enjoy it while you can."

"You are a terrible person," Anne spat.

Candi laughed again. "Take out that light bulb, Luther. By the way," she added, "I don't think I mentioned that this cozy little room was once a vault for the company safe. Steel reinforced walls, floor, and ceiling. Steel door, too. You'll only get bloody knuckles if you try to bust out."

"You can't leave her like this," Fernando grated. "At least give the lady a blanket. It's cold in here—"

"Do your thing, Fernando," Candi smiled. "Keep the lady warm."

The door to the vault banged shut. Luther sprawled out in a chair and looked questioningly at Candi.

"What happens now—?" he asked. "We just going to leave them there?"

"Only until nature takes its course," Candi replied.

"You mean until they—"

"That's exactly what I mean."

"Wouldn't take me long," Luther grinned.

"It's going to take our gentleman from Brazil a little longer."

"What happens after that?"

"Once the act is completed, we stage a little Greek tragedy."

Luther was puzzled. "Greeks? Ain't no Greeks in the Brotherhood—"

"It's a college thing," Candi smiled. "We make it look like Fernando raped her, killed her, then in a fit of remorse, killed himself."

"I thought we grabbed them to get a payoff—"

"We're getting one, Luther. A billion dollars. Trust me, our little tragedy will make our Chinese friends very happy."

"How do we know when it happens—?"

"There's a video camera concealed in another of those corners, trained on the mattress. It's got a night-vision lens, so you keep checking. You can see them, but they can't even see themselves."

That was when all hell broke loose. A battering, deafening sound of helicopters descended upon the sprawling warehouse complex. The buildings and parking lot areas were suddenly bathed in brilliant light. People on the ground began running in startled confusion. A crescendo of automatic weapon fire turned the scene into a nightmare.

Luther ran to the window. He saw helicopters everywhere, in the air, on the ground. Soldiers were pouring out and running toward the buildings, weapons chattering death.

"We're in trouble, Candi—"

Candi was grabbing weapons and ammunition off a shelf in the office.

"Kill the lights, Luther—"

They ran from the office and started toward the stairs, stopping abruptly as they heard footsteps pounding up toward them. Candi pointed back toward the room they had just left. They ran back and slammed the door shut. Light was streaming through the window from all the flares and searchlights outside. They backed toward the small room where Anne and Fernando were imprisoned, keeping their weapons trained on the door leading to the hallway.

Suddenly the door was flung open. Lights from the hallway illuminated the outlines of two Rangers as they burst into the room. Both Candi and Luther opened fire at the same time. Both Rangers jerked from the bursts of automatic fire, then both slumped to the floor.

"Get those two out here," Candi hissed. "Don't kill them — we need them alive."

Luther hurriedly unlocked the door. Seconds later, Anne was shoved out into the grasp of Candi. Luther appeared moments later with Fernando in his grasp. Luther's eyes were wide with fear.

"Just stay cool, Luther," Candi told him. "We got us some high-price insurance."

The lights in the room clicked on. Two more Rangers in battle fatigues came rolling through the door, too fast for Candi or Luther to follow them, hampered as they were with holding the hostages. The two lay prone on the floor, weapons trained on the four people in front of them. Both Candi and Luther now had pistols pressed to the heads of their captives.

"Put down your guns, or they're dead," Luther cried hoarsely.

"It's not going to happen, Luther," Quinn answered from his position on the floor. "We better all talk about this."

Quinn and Joanna climbed slowly to their feet, never letting their weapons waver from Candi and Luther. Anne and Fernando, though naked, appeared unhurt.

"You two all right?" Quinn asked.

Both of them nodded.

"You must be Candi," Joanna said. She felt high, the adrenaline pumping. It was good to be in action again. "I've heard a lot about you. Pleased to make your acquaintance."

"Cut the crap," Candi spat. "Do we make this a bloodbath, or do you listen to reason—?"

"We're listening," Quinn said, his voice low and calm. "You want out. We want your hostages. How do we both get happy—?"

"One of those helicopters — and a pilot. Someone with a wife and kids, who won't try to be a hero."

"That can be arranged. We want your hostages more than you, Candi. When do you let them go—?"

"They come with us in the chopper—"

Quinn shook his head. "Can't agree to that. We could talk trading hostages, perhaps—"

"Sure, me and Luther in a chopper full of Rangers. Sounds good to me—"

"What do you suggest? There's no way you're leaving with those two."

Candi thought for a moment. "Okay. You give us two choppers. Me and Luther, and any of my top men still alive. We keep our weapons. Two of your Rangers, unarmed, in each chopper, plus the pilot. Nobody follows. You get these two as soon as your men and mine are ready for takeoff."

"And the Rangers—?"

"They'll be released when we land the choppers and take off for parts unknown."

"Alive—?"

"If they don't give us trouble, all they get is taped up."

Quinn stared thoughtfully at her. It wouldn't work out that way, none of it. It wasn't possible to let these two go. But it sounded good enough to get past the present impasse.

"Deal," Quinn said.

"Too fast, Adams. You got something up your sleeve."

"Not with those guns to their heads. I want them alive. Seems a fair enough trade."

From the doorway, Lincoln Banes' heavy voice rumbled out at his son.

"Put the gun down, Luther. Let those people go—"

Luther stared angrily at his father. "Why did you come?"

"I'm your father."

"Who gives a crap. This ain't no truancy gig. This is big time."

"We'll get you a good lawyer. If you're innocent—"

Luther laughed. "Forget innocent, dad. I did it."

"You killed Jill Adams—?"

"I brought her home, did her, then gave her the big trip. That's the way it went down."

Quinn was having a difficult time controlling himself. His finger tightened around the trigger. Joanna was watching him, knowing the pain that was cutting through him. She could see his finger tighten on the trigger.

"Not here, Quinn," she said softly. "Not now—"

Francisco de Branca was watching Lincoln Banes' eyes, seeing the darkening. He also was aware that the muzzle of the automatic pistol Luther was holding to his head had wavered during the conversation. Fernando suddenly lunged to one side, doubling over and rolling away.

Luther snarled and swiveled the gun. From the doorway, Linc raised the automatic rifle and fired. At least a dozen bullets smashed into his son. Luther stared at his father, a bewildered expression on his face.

"I'm your son—" he gasped.

"Who gives a crap," Linc muttered.

Candi pulled back when the bullets started slamming into Luther. Anne jerked aside, leaving Candi exposed. It was Joanna who emptied a long burst into her. Candi stared down at the red stains spreading across her chest and stomach. She looked genuinely surprised. Then she folded over and died.

# 35

## THE PHOENIX RISES

Anne and Fernando were sitting on the rear step of an ambulance. Someone had found their clothes, so they were dressed and beginning to feel warm again under the blankets tucked around their shoulders. There was a lot of activity going on around them, but the shooting had stopped.

Sirens sounded frequently as vans were loaded with prisoners and left for the state prison, a few miles farther south. It was decided to take the members of the brotherhoods there temporarily, rather than putting them in less secure county jails that were already crowded.

A white-coated doctor approached Anne and Fernando.

"We're about ready to take you two to the hospital—"

"I appreciate the concern, doctor," Anne said, "but there is nothing wrong with me and I would much prefer to spend the night in my bed at the hotel. That will be the best medicine for me."

"I feel the same way," Fernando added. "I would make a very bad patient."

The doctor shrugged. "I have no medical grounds to keep you. You both came through this amazingly well. If that is your wish, Madame Vice President—"

"It is, doctor," Anne said, giving him an appreciative smile. "Thank you for being so considerate."

The doctor left. Anne gave a weary sigh as she looked at Fernando.

"It's been quite an evening."

"Our times together certainly are not dull," Fernando said. "First in my country, now in yours. It wouldn't surprise me if an earthquake struck this very minute and split the ground between us."

Anne laughed. "Things do seem to happen when we're together, don't they."

"In case that does happen, and even if the timing is terrible, I must tell you what I am feeling." He reached over and took her hand. "I was going to wait until after the signing ceremony, but I can't wait even that long. I've fallen in love with you, Anne. You are a beautiful, amazing, intelligent, compassionate, understanding woman. I've never met anyone like you."

Anne reached up and put a finger against his lips. "You'll have me blushing, Fernando. It wouldn't be proper for the Vice President of the United States to be seen blushing like a schoolgirl."

"You're not the Vice President to me. You're the woman I want to marry."

"You could be influenced by the fact that we just spent some time naked together," Anne murmured.

"You know that isn't true. Even if this is a bad time, I must ask this. Do you think you could ever love me?"

"I'm afraid it's too late, Fernando."

"But why—?"

She smiled at him. "It's already happened. Weeks ago, when we were working together. Even before that, when I wouldn't allow myself to be attracted to you. You're looking at a fallen woman, Fernando."

Fernando reached over and drew her to him. They were still holding each other tightly when Quinn and Joanna approached.

"This looks serious," Joanna murmured.

"It most definitely is," Anne smiled.

"Wonderful," Joanna exclaimed. "I'm happy for both of you. But then, I think love is grand."

"It's symbolic," Quinn grinned. "They'll be chiseling your faces on Mount Rushmore one of these days."

"Could you give us a ride back to Salt Lake," Anne asked. "They keep wanting to take us to a hospital, and we both just want to get back to our rooms."

"That's why we came over," Quinn said. "We're taking Linc Banes back — he needs to be with Cora. We can drop you off at the hotel — there's a heliport on the roof. And this time, there'll be enough guards to keep the boogie men away."

"It's pretty much over, isn't it?" Fernando said, looking around. Lines of bodies kept growing longer as more dead members of the brotherhoods were brought out of the buildings.

"I hope so," Quinn said grimly. "It's a clean sweep here. With Candi dead, the others will talk. We should wipe out this cancer from the whole Zone."

A short while later, Anne Ashford and Fernando Francisco de Branca were dropped off at the downtown hotel, where they were met by a dozen guards. Then the helicopter continued on to NECCO headquarters at Hill Field.

Linc hurried off to bring the news about their son to Cora. Quinn offered to do that for him, knowing how hard it would be for Linc to tell his wife how Luther died, but Linc declined, feeling it was necessary for him to deal with it.

Not long afterwards, Quinn and Joanna drove up to their own quarters, one of the few single dwelling houses on the base. Quinn suggested dropping in at his office for a quick check, but Joanna was firm. As she was unlocking the front door, another NECCO sedan drove up. A man got out and hurried toward them.

"Mr. Adams, sir. There's been another emergency—"

Quinn frowned, realizing he didn't know the man. He was about to ask for credentials when the gas blasted into his face. Joanna had time only for one cry of alarm before she too slumped unconscious to the ground.

\* \* \*

A faint throbbing of engines brought Quinn back to consciousness. He was lying on a bunk, in a small bedroom. He thought of Joanna and alarm shivered through his system. He rolled out of the bunk and stood up. A dizzying head rush hit him and he grabbed for support. When the dizziness cleared, he realized he was holding onto another bunk, above the one he had just left. He saw Joanna, stirring fitfully, and felt a tremendous sense of relief.

She opened her eyes, looked around at the strange surroundings, then saw Quinn. She reached out to him and he took her hand. She raised up on an elbow, studying the room.

"You know what this is, of course," she muttered.

"A submarine," Quinn replied. "What I don't know is why we're on it."

Joanna had him help her down. She also swayed for a moment under an attack of dizziness.

"What was that stuff—?" she asked, frowning.

Quinn shook his head. "Whatever it was, it worked fast."

"Did you just come out of it?"

Quinn nodded.

She studied his face. "When did you shave last?"

"The morning of the day Anne and Fernando were grabbed. Why—?"

"That's a good two-day beard you're sporting."

"So we've been bye-bye for awhile."

"Do you also realize we are standing here in our underwear—"

Quinn smiled. "I did notice that."

"Do you suppose I've been violated?"

"Not by me."

"That doesn't necessarily make me feel better."

There was a soft knock on the door. Quinn answered it. An officer in a Chinese naval uniform was outside in the small corridor. He bowed politely.

"It is the wish of General Wang that both of you join him in half an hour," the officer said. "Would that be agreeable—?"

"General Wang — General Wang Jingwei?"

The officer nodded. "Yes, sir."

"Tell him we will be pleased to accept his invitation."

"Thank you, sir." The officer bowed again and left.

Quinn closed the door and looked at his wife. "Just don't ask me to explain this, okay?"

Quinn and Joanna found their fatigues on a chair, washed and pressed. There were tooth brushes in the sink, even American tooth paste. They washed up. Joanna tried fussing with her hair but quickly realized it was on an independent streak. Quinn assured her she looked charming any way it decided to go.

Half an hour later, they were shown into the officers' wardroom. There were two men waiting in the room, and both stood up as they entered. Quinn instantly recognized General Wang Jingwei from NECCO intelligence files. The other man, older, was not familiar.

"I am General Wang Jingwei," the general said, a smile beaming on his face. He looked at Quinn. "I am told you already were aware of my name."

"And the fact that you are Chairman of the Central Military Commission of the People's Liberation Army," Quinn nodded. "It is a pleasure to meet you, General. May I introduce my wife, Joanna Adams—"

"Until recently, Joanna Shazebak, a very highly placed member of Israel's Mossad," General Wang added. He extended his hand. "I have followed your career for some time, Mrs. Adams. You have my utmost respect."

"Thank you, General Wang," Joanna smiled. "I'm both surprised, and flattered."

The general now motioned respectfully to the man beside him. While the general was wearing his uniform, this other man was dressed in a simple, black kimono-like robe.

"It is my extreme pleasure to introduce you to Premier Chen Xingtao, of the People's Republic."

Both Quinn and Joanna bowed deeply to the man.

"This is an honor, Premier Chen," Quinn said, his attitude conveying the sincerity of the compliment. "My wife and I are most grateful for this opportunity." He glanced over at General Wang. "At the same time, we are most curious why this meeting is taking place—"

Premier Chen motioned for them to sit down. They squeezed behind the table, making themselves as comfortable as possible. Premier Chen sat at the head of the table, General Wang beside him.

"You have caused our government great distress, Mr. Adams," Premier Chen began. "I hope you will understand it is nothing personal when I say it was unfortunate that the attempt to assassinate you failed."

Quinn flashed a brief smile. "It seemed very personal at the time, Premier Chen."

"It should not," Chen said matter-of-factly. "People have tried to assassinate me on several occasions. Like your would-be assassins, Mr. Adams, they are all dead, so it is no longer of any consequence."

"A fatalistic way of looking at it, I suppose."

Joanna spoke up quietly. "I cannot help but be concerned over the possibility of more attempts on my husband's life—"

"We have no intention of posing such a threat, Mrs. Adams. You can be assured of that," Cheng replied. He studied Quinn closely, saying nothing for a moment. "At last we meet, Mr. Adams. Your exploits over the years have been very costly to my country."

"Over the years—?"

"Since before you became one of the Pharoahs in charge of your country's emergency command organization."

"That's over ten years ago—"

Chen nodded. "Your operations in the Mediterranean — accompanied by this charming lady who is now your wife — cost the Corporation several billion dollars. You brought us down, Mr. Adams — something no one thought possible."

Quinn's eyes narrowed. "The Corporation—?"

"Yes. I was personally very disappointed, Mr. Adams, when you turned down our invitation seven years ago to join our organization."

Quinn stared at him with open surprise. "Seven years. The Omega

Corporation. Your people were behind that—?"

"It was a different organization then. Broader in membership — a world-wide cartel. We have refined it during these past years, centralized operations and control. We were sincerely sorry you took the actions that you did."

Quinn knew what the man was referring to. Those actions had been sealed from the American public for seven years, and would be for forty-three more. But Premier Chen obviously knew what only a half dozen people in the United States knew. Suddenly Quinn understood the power of the force he was fighting in those days.

"I would make the same choices today, Premier Chen," he told the man.

The Premier nodded. "I know you would, Mr. Adams. I respect a man of your integrity. I am making no new offers."

Joanna was looking from one to the other. She knew important things were being left unsaid. Well, if they were things she should know, Quinn would tell her. The fact that he hadn't, however, told her he probably wouldn't.

"The reason for this meeting, Mr. Adams," Chen said slowly, "is to discuss the Phoenix Plan."

Quinn tried to read Chen's face, but that was impossible. "What is it about the plan that interests the People's Republic?"

"It seems there will be no stopping this Phoenix Plan from joining the two American hemispheres together."

"I assume you know I am aware of the mission of Colonel P'eng Songlin — and the billion dollar offer made by the People's Republic."

"As we are aware of the failure of that mission, Mr. Adams — and the probable loss of that billion dollars."

"Then we can speak frankly between us."

"That is my wish. This Phoenix Plan has many aspects that interest my country, Mr. Adams."

"You realize it was created as an answer to the attempt by the People's Republic to take over the United States. Not a direct attempt, of course, but we both know the coalition of the southern countries was also the brainchild of the People's Republic."

General Wang looked uneasily at Quinn. "You speak very bluntly, Mr. Adams."

"I can be even blunter, General Wang. This is the second attempt by the People's Republic to overthrow the United States' government in the past seven years. That makes me very cautious in evaluating any new interest you have in my country."

Premier Chen nodded slowly, raising a hand to stop any further comment from Wang. "Let me remind you, Mr. Adams, that both attempts failed. And you played a very significant role in causing those failures. You have my word, Mr. Adams, that the People's Republic will make no more such attempts." A thin smile flashed across his face. "At least, not for another hundred years."

"I respect your word, Premier Chen, and accept it. The President will be most happy to hear this."

"This Phoenix Plan — do you think it could be expanded to world-wide use?"

Quinn was surprised. He thought for several moments before answering. "Theoretically, it could. From a practical point of view, however, I doubt it very much."

"Why is that—?"

"Simply facing the realities of human nature. The Phoenix Plan calls for a high degree of trust among those participating. It calls for honesty and fair dealing between all peoples involved. Do you think that is possible on a world-wide scale, Premier Chen?"

"I appreciate the point. On the other hand, it is close to the principles of communism the People's Republic already embrace."

"Close, yet significantly different. To be honest, Premier Chen, I don't think you could make the Phoenix Plan work in China. Not for any reason other than you have over two billion people who must voluntarily, and willingly, work cooperatively together, yet still keep alive the rights and freedoms of the individual. Not having those freedoms means you have no incentive. The Phoenix Plan is designed to elevate people, Premier Chen, not governments."

There was a long silence this time from the Premier. He stared off into space with his eyes closed, so long that Joanna began to wonder if he might have dozed off. He suddenly opened his eyes and looked at Quinn.

"You are right, Mr. Adams. There are deeper problems with this plan than I realized. However, I would like to make an offer for you — and Madame Anne Ashford — to come to Beijing and plant the seeds of this idea in the minds of my people, just as you did for the Coalition."

"That would be an honor, Premier Chen," Quinn replied."I am sure President Baldwin will be pleased to accept the offer."

The premier looked at Joanna. "May I extend the hospitality of the People's Republic to you and your husband. We would be most happy to have you spend as long as you wish in our country, as our guests. We have caused your husband a great deal of pain and trouble over the years. It would please me to have you see the great sights and beauties of the People's Republic. Consider it a wedding gift — a small gesture of friendship."

Joanna gave her husband her a startled look. Quinn smiled and nodded.

"We would be most pleased to accept your offer, Premier Chen," she replied. "The timing of our visit, of course, will depend on many things."

"Thank you, Mrs. Adams." The Premier stood up and reached over to shake hands with Quinn. "I had hoped we could make more definitive progress, Mr. Adams. But we are a patient people."

General Wang also stood up. "We are a little more than twenty miles off San Francisco. We will return you immediately."

It was a strange end to an even stranger meeting. There was no doubt the People's Republic felt it was important to hold it. Premier Chen had not left his homeland in over fifty years, if reports were to be believed. And General Wang almost as rarely appeared to foreigners in his official capacity. Was it just the expressed interest in the Phoenix Plan, or did it go deeper? Quinn was troubled by a suspicion that despite what was said, he had been approached in some way he did not yet realize.

Back in the stateroom, Joanna gave her husband a quizzical stare.

"What was that all about—?"

"Don't know," Quinn shrugged. "Whatever he was going to say, I think he decided not to say it."

"Are we going to get out of this?"

"Yes. Whatever else he wants, I think Premier Chen wants me alive."

"So we still have a chance to live happily ever after?"

"Absolutely."

She came forward and wrapped her arms around him.

"Who said being married was going to be dull. I didn't have this much fun in the company."

Quinn grinned at her. "Looks like we may get that little white house with the picket fence—"

She looked up. "I never said I wanted a little house. I want a big one – but we should re-think the fence. Forget the pickets. I'm seeing a ten-foot, high voltage electric jobbie—"

*  *  *

The signing ceremonies went off without a single disturbance. The next day Anne and Fernando were married in a ceremony that outshone any wedding of royalty in its splendor, dignity and guest list. It was a magnificent affair. Anne was positively radiant, and the women in attendance were convinced there never was a more dashing, desirable groom.

The wedding was sudden, but the opportunity to emphasize the new link between north and south was too important to miss. Besides, both Anne and Fernando were more than willing to cooperate.

The Phoenix Plan progressed smoothly. Most of the Latin troops were withdrawn to their homelands. All countries cooperated in establishing the new policies, which in effect controlled the hemisphere's economic and trade policies so that all contributed to production and shared in profits on an equitable basis. It resulted in an almost immediate improvement in living standards for millions of Latin Americans, as well as millions of citizens of the United States.

The massive exodus to start the rebuilding of areas destroyed in the invasion began on schedule, with a million civilian volunteers leaving the Federal Zone in the first wave. Kansas City was decided upon as the place to begin the massive reconstruction. That was partly because of its central location in the country, and partly as an acknowledgment of the vital contributions of the leaders of the dominent Mormon church in the Zone. The genesis of the whole Phoenix Plan had originated with them, and they were insistent on the importance of the Missouri location.

With Washington uninhabitable because of radiation, the national capitol was officially relocated to the Missouri site. Almost overnight, the city of New Washington rose from the ruins of Kansas City.

When finished, New Washington was an awesome sight, drawing visitors and dignitaries from around the world. The new solar panels proved even more effective than hoped, and the entire city literally blazed with light after dark, every wall inside and out illuminated by the stored energy. Even the streets were paved with the new materials, eliminating any need for other lighting. A new national capital was built, a new White House, a new, more efficient system of connected government buildings. No one could deny that New Washington was a bright star the whole world admired.

Another city was built adjoining New Washington on the north. This had a huge commerce of its own, but it was primarily a bedroom community for the millions of people now living in the area. It was called New Jerusalem by the religious leaders who had provided the money to construct it. Most of the structures were high-rise towers of apartments and condominiums, all built with the amazing solar panels The twin cities set the skies ablaze at night, giving a glow that could be seen for hundreds of miles.

Secretly, a new NECCO headquarters was built in New Washington and Quinn and Joanna moved from the Federal Zone to the new capital. The old nerve center at Hill was kept on line, but it now served as a regional headquarters.

In an amazingly short span of time, the whole country was reborn. Bright new cities rose from the ashes of the old ones. These were such a vast improvement that even cities not destroyed in the occupation of the CASA troops underwent extensive renovations, just to compete in the startling new worlds of industry and commerce. A new society took form, and life began to be normal again for millions who had feared it never would.

The People's Republic quietly disengaged from its plan of conquest. Military troops were withdrawn from occupied countries, although political dominance continued. The bamboo curtain dropped once again, even more impenetrable than before.

The Russians made it clear they had no intentions of anything but consolidating a united military organization. Each republic was to maintain its political sovereignty and the military machine was simply for the good of all.

No one believed it, especially the republics, but it seemed unlikely the generals would dare go beyond their stated objectives — at least, not until something changed.

Radiation levels dropped much faster than expected in the old Washington, D.C. It was decided to leave the ruins as a huge memorial. The city, with its shattered monolithic buildings and broken memorials of democracy, became a world-wide symbol of the horrors of nuclear destruction. Millions visited it and went away with the grim conviction that it must never happen to any other city in the world.

With the Phoenix Plan working effectively on both continents, another massive signing ceremony was held. This one was in Brazilia, and it marked the official birth of the United Sovereign States of the Americas — the USSA.

Two more years passed. Quinn retired from NECCO and he and Joanna built their white house on the Oregon coast. It was on a cliff with a magnificent view of the Pacific ocean. It had a picket fence – with an intricate alarm system. There was even a dog — a gentle-natured, lovable female collie they named Israel.

They never accepted Premier Chen's offer of a honeymoon in China. Quinn couldn't shake the conviction there were doors in the People's Republic he never wanted to open.

Aaron Stark went back into retirement in New England. Frank Kantros remained as head of the NECCO special forces. Race Courtney became head of NECCO. He and Stacy were frequent visitors to Oregon and they bought an adjacent lot, looking toward the day they too would build on that beautiful hillside.

Anne Ashford Francisco de Branca completed her term and reluctantly bowed to pressure to run with Sam Baldwin again. It was a sweeping victory. She and Fernando bought a home in New Washington. Fernando kept his palatial mansion in Rio de Janeiro and the couple visited Brazil whenever possible. That was quite frequently, because Anne was given the permanent assignment of being the country's representative on the joint administrative council, which alternated meeting venues between New Washington and Brazilia.

With life so normal once again, Quinn was surprised when Race and Stacy showed up unexpectedly one day. He could tell immediately that Race was not his usual calm self. After a few minutes of conversation about life in general, Race asked Quinn if he could visit with him in his study.

They settled down in soft leather chairs. Race hardly looked at the expanse of ocean outside, one of his favorite views. He pulled a file from his briefcase.

"You remember Jules Henshaw, of course—"

"Good man."

"His staff has been concentrating recently on worldwide weather analysis and natural phenomenon. Three days ago, Jules gave me this report," he said, handing it to his brother-in-law.

"I don't like the look on your face—"

"It's scary, Quinn. If what's in that report is true, this country is facing the worst disaster it has ever known — and there doesn't appear to be anything we can do about it."

"Maybe you haven't noticed, but I haven't been in my office for a couple of years—"

"Read it, Quinn. Then we'll talk."

Race left and Quinn started to read the report. He read it, then read it again. Finally he put it down and stared out across the ocean.

Race hadn't overstated a thing. If Jules Henshaw was correct, life might well never be the same for anyone on earth.

# THE MOMENTUM FACTOR

## PART THREE

# 36

## Grim Outlook

"We are all familiar with El Nino, hot spots in the Pacific ocean which have spawned one disaster after another these last few years. The El Nino of late1997 had the energy of a million atomic bombs like the one dropped on Hiroshima. In eight months, it killed over two thousand people and caused over thirty billion dollars in damage. Sea life was devastated."

Jules Henshaw adjusted his spectacles, pushing them back on his nose.

"We now have conclusive evidence that a possibly far more destructive disturbance is being spawned at this moment in the western Pacific."

Henshaw looked at the people sitting around the long conference table, seeing he had their full attention.

"La Nina – unusually cold ocean water which pushes in after the hot spots dissipate – is responsible for just as much disturbance in global weather patterns and can cause as much damage as El Nino."

For a moment, his glance slid to the man at the far end of the table. Sam Baldwin, President of the United States. Henshaw always felt uncomfortable in Baldwin's presence. The man seemed able to know what he was going to say before he said it. He could tell the President was concentrating intently on his report.

"These two phenomenon will impact both North and South America but can also be expected to produce world-wide havoc. Atmospheric pressures completely thrown off normalcy, higher or lower. I won't take time here to review all the reversals in normal weather patterns these past few years, but they are all related to changes in the direction of upper air streams. That is a direct result of these unusual ocean temperatures."

Quinn Adams, sitting at the far end of the table next to Sam Baldwin, interrupted with a question.

"As I understand it, Jules," Quinn said, "there isn't much we can do about this brother and sister act, is there?"

"That's correct, One—" Henshaw stopped, looking at Race Courtney sitting beside Quinn Adams. "Sorry, Race – force of habit, I'm afraid."

Quinn had returned to New Washington only yesterday, and for Henshaw, he was Pharaoh One. Race Adams grinned, waving a hand in dismissal of the apology.

"He's still Pharaoh One to me too, Jules."

"Well," Henshaw continued, "the basic cause of all this upheaval is the Japanese current, which has been dramatically changing its flow patterns around the Pacific, sometimes moving at twice its normal speed. Like you say, One, we just can't control that."

"You're saying we should expect more bad weather," Baldwin said. "I hope not like this past year — it's been a nightmare."

"Much worse, Mr. President," Henshaw said. "More extremes, more reversals of normal patterns."

"Can you be specific—?"

"We can expect unusually heavy rain and snowfall – that almost certainly will cause destructive mud slides and avalanches. Not to mention floods, hailstorms, tornadoes, hurricanes, severe drought, massive wildfires – it will all get worse. Hotter, drier summers around the world, and much more severe winter storms. The weather will be ugly and very unpredictable, I'm afraid."

There was an outbreak of conversation around the table. Gathered in the room were all of the Pharaohs of NECCO, along with the President and Vice President, and Quinn. This emergency meeting was called to discuss Jules Henshaw's report, indicating the world faced imminent danger of catastrophic natural disasters. It was that report that had brought Quinn back to New Washington.

"Gentlemen – and Madam Vice President — if I may continue," Henshaw called, his adam's apple bobbing nervously. "As bad as the weather outlook may appear, it is not the major reason for this meeting."

Silence fell along both sides of the table as all eyes fastened again on the scientist.

"Our data indicates," Henshaw said quietly, "there is a major possibility of worldwide volcanic activity, possibly coinciding with a devastating series of earthquakes. Strange things are happening deep inside the earth's crust. We don't know what's causing it, or what it means, but we anticipate an outbreak of major natural disasters—possibly very soon."

Baldwin was peering intently at him.

"Volcanic activity – does that mean major eruptions?" he asked.

Henshaw nodded. "Here on our continent, Mr. President, and around the world."

Baldwin glanced at Race and Quinn. "Is NECCO prepared to handle volcanic emergencies?"

Race nodded. "We are, Mr. President. All known sites for potential volcanic eruptions were identified long ago – there's a frightening number of those, incidentally. Evacuation plans are in place. However, as we saw in the cataclysmic 1980 eruption of Mount St. Helens in Washington State, we really can't predict all the problems that might arise after the initial eruption. A cloud of volcanic ash several miles wide circled the earth that time, if you remember. If a dozen Mount St. Helens were to explode at the same time—"

"Mind boggling," the President muttered. He was studying Henshaw again. "I gather there's more, Jules—"

There it was again, Henshaw thought. The President's uncanny ability to see into his brain.

"Perhaps not any more important on a disaster scale, Mr. President," Henshaw nodded, "but certainly of more immediate concern."

"What would that be—?"

"California's San Andreas fault, sir."

"Crap. That's all we need."

A map of California and the Pacific appeared on a screen behind Henshaw. He looked up at it, studying the hundreds of red dots and red lines zig-zagging across the ocean and along the Asian coastline.

"As you can see, gentlemen," he said, clearing his throat and again pushing at his glasses, "the Pacific tectonic plate has been a trouble zone for many years. Every one of those dots – and there are hundreds of them – mark a recorded earthquake in recent times. There has been a marked increase in activity along the entire Asian edge of that plate in the past few months. Scores of earthquakes, all minor so far, have been recorded in Russia, China, Japan, and on down to New Zealand and beyond. Some violent underwater earthquakes have occurred along the entire Ring of Fire – the Kufil Trench off Siberia, the Japan, Bonin, Mariana, New Guinea, New Hebrides, and the Kermadek faults are all involved in this new activity."

"What's the significance for us?" Baldwin asked.

"The eastern edge of the Pacific plate, which runs down our entire western coastline, is affected. The main concern is the underwater crust that rises up and breaks along the California coast – the main fracture being the San Andreas fault. There's been alarming activity along that entire fault line these past weeks. Small tremors, but frequent. We normally record three to six tremors in the region every day. For the past two weeks, that has increased to more than twenty a day."

"What conclusions—?" the president asked.

"Nothing definite, sir. But it is a major concern that in the past few days, the tremors have stopped."

"Sounds like good news to me," Baldwin said.

"No, sir," Henshaw told him. "Very bad news. Everything has jammed tight. Pressure readings are increasing. With no movement, there's no release for that pressure."

"And that means—?"

"A major earthquake can be expected in California at any time, Mr. President."

"They've been expecting that for a hundred years—"

"This time it's going to happen, sir."

"Exactly where does that San Andreas fault run?"

Henshaw lifted a lighted pointer to the map on the screen.

A dotted line stretched along the California coastline, marking the path of the fault. It reached from San Diego up past San Francisco and disappeared into the sea again.

"Basically, from the Salton Sea north to Mendocina, Mr. President. You can see many smaller fault lines would also be involved in a massive San Andreas slippage. The Hayward and the Calaveras faults off San Francisco, The Puente Hills fault in Los Angeles – that's a vertical fault, meaning slippage would occur up and down, not sideways like most of the other faults. In an event of this magnitude it won't make any difference. The Elsinore, the San Jacinta, and the Imperial faults, all east of San Diego, would undoubtedly become involved, running that close to the San Andreas."

"Are you telling us that whole fault line could give way – that we're expecting an earthquake big enough to wipe out every major population center in California?"

"It is a definite possibility, Mr. President."

Baldwin was shaking his head, trying to deal with the enormity of such a catastrophic event.

"If it happened, how would Portland and Seattle be affected?"

"Hard to predict, sir. At the northern end of the San Andreas – at Mendocino – there's what we call a Triple Junction. The North American plate, the Pacific plate, and the Gorda plate all meet at that point. Impossible to even guess what will happen."

"You think Portland and Seattle could be destroyed—?"

"I seriously doubt it, sir," Henshaw said, his brow furrowed in thought. "There's been a lot of volcanic activity in that area for many years, but this would be vastly different. The Northwest has an off-shore fault system, but quakes are usually minor. That's primarily because of the liquifaction factor—"

"That something new?" the president asked.

Henshaw shook his head. "Liquifaction is basically an interaction between water and ground vibrations – like shaking a bowl of jello, sir. The ground sort of melts. The same thing will be seen – might be seen — in San Francisco bay. Portland and Seattle, I believe, might not feel anything more than a shockwave. Salt Lake City would probably feel it a lot more. We're talking of an earthquake of such magnitude, however, that anything is possible."

"You've never stuck your neck out like this before."

"The data gathered in the last few days, Mr. President, has never been so overwhelming. We will get a massive earthquake in California very soon, sir. And we can expect similar massive earthquakes to occur at any time along a dozen other major fault lines around the world. I wish I could sound uncertain, sir, but as a scientist I must warn you that our data shows this earth is going to go crazy in the very near future."

* * *

Quinn and Joanna stepped out of the elevator on the fifty-ninth floor of the Ashford Tower. Race and Stacy were waiting for them in the foyer, both smiling broadly as Race handed Quinn a set of keys.

"Welcome back to New Washington, buddy," Race grinned.

"You got our old place back," Joanna gasped.

She rushed through the open door of the condominium, going from room to room. They could hear her exclaiming in pleasure as she threw open the double doors that led out onto the balcony. Stacy came out to join her.

"How on earth did you manage it?" Joanna asked excitedly. "This is wonderful, Stacy—"

"If you want the truth," Stacy muttered, her voice falling so the men inside couldn't hear, "it's been empty ever since you went to Oregon. Race kept saying you'd be back. It's been used for special guests on occasion, but it's remained on a reserved status all this time." She smiled and gave Joanna a hug. "I'm so happy you're back."

Quinn and Race joined them.

"Had a hard time not taking this for ourselves," Race told them. "A view like that is very special now to Stacy and me."

The view he was referring to stretched out below them, a huge park-like setting that was really the new Temple Square constructed by the Mormon church. The mile-square park was dominated by the twenty-four main temple buildings, all joined by a system of high arches lifting over a central court. Although neither Quinn nor Joanna were members of the church, they thoroughly enjoyed looking out over the serenity and beauty of the square.

Quinn looked questioningly at his friend. "Why is it so special now—?"

Stacy answered for him. "Things have been so crazy the last couple of times we were together, we didn't get a chance to tell you. Race has been a Mormon all his life, although he's been completely inactive since his parents died — what was that, about twenty-five years ago? Anyway, last year – mainly because of Austin and Vanessa – we started going to church. To cut a long story short, I was baptized a little over a year ago, and last month, Race and I were married in the temple."

Joanna gave her a long hug. "I don't understand what that means, but I know it's very important to every Mormon. I'm happy for you, Stacy."

"What does it mean?" Quinn asked. "Wondered about it for years, but never got around to asking anybody—"

"Put simply, so your feeble mind can understand it," Race grinned, "it means Stacy and I are married for time and eternity."

"We'll be married in the next life, as well as here on earth," Stacy added.

"The next life—?" Quinn gave a wry shake of his head. "Seems like we've got enough on our hands getting through this one."

"Think about it, buddy," Race said, suddenly serious. "I know how much you love Joanna. Wouldn't it be nice to be married to her forever—?"

"Seems like forever already," Quinn grinned. He ducked to avoid the arm his wife swung at him. "But yes, if I really believed there was a forever, I'd want to share it with Joanna."

Joanna came over and put her arms around his waist. "Maybe we should look into this, Quinn. Sounds pretty good to me. I already believe there's a life after this one."

"Well, let's first deal with what we're going to do about Jules Henshaw's report. We'll invite the Wells over later."

Joanna reached up and gave him a quick kiss.

They all went back inside. The men made themselves comfortable in the living room while Joanna and Stacy went into the kitchen. Quinn could tell by the delighted squeal from his wife that the refrigerator was well stocked. That would be Stacy's doing.

Quinn clasped his hands behind his head, staring thoughtfully at the ceiling.

"Why did Jules underplay the scariest part of his report?" he asked.

"I told him to do it."

"Why? That's what brought me out of retirement. This whole world is threatened."

"I know," Race said, "but I wanted everyone to concentrate on dealing with California, and all the other places in our own country that are threatened. What Jules is predicting is so enormous that we can't afford to worry about those other countries – not until we've got our own act together."

"That's pretty cold."

"It's putting our own people first, Quinn. You think I'm wrong—?"

Quinn sat up, shaking his head. "No. I'd have done the same thing."

"Talking about our problems," Race muttered, "I don't know where to start myself. I'm not sure what we can do about any of it."

"That was heavy stuff this afternoon," Quinn agreed. "We obviously can't do anything about Jules' predictions. Those things will happen, or they won't. Personally, he convinced me."

"So what now?"

"Let's assume everything he said is going to happen. That paints a pretty bleak picture, but it gives us a place to start."

"Going over every emergency procedure," Race nodded. "Accepting the fact there will be little left in California but casualties, we establish a perimeter to get out survivors. Military airlifts. Lots of helicopters, because if it's anywhere near the size of catastrophe Jules is expecting, there won't be many highways or airports left. Emergency hospital sites. We'll need food and clothing—just put everything on the list."

"A declaration of martial law should be ready for the President to sign. You know we'll have a looting problem. National Guard units in nearby states must be put on alert, ready to fly rescue missions and control refugees."

The two men stopped, looking at each other.

"Do you believe what we're saying, buddy?" Race grimaced.

"I hope it happens only in California, and we don't have to deal with similar disasters all across the country. Or all around the world. And I also hope," he added. "that our house on the Oregon coast doesn't slide into the sea—"

# 37

## SAN ANDREAS ISLAND

It was the most massive quake ever recorded on the North American continent – 9.3 on the Richter scale. It struck at 5:14 a.m. on Tuesday, only three weeks after Jules Henshaw warned it was coming.

The quake flung people out of bed as far north as Seattle, and on up into Vancouver, British Columbia. It shook the entire western United States, savagely rattling Boise, Salt Lake City, Reno, Las Vegas and Phoenix. Only in Nevada and Arizona, however, was serious damage reported.

Nearly thirty minutes passed in confusion before the grim truth became known. The desperate plea of a ham radio operator was the first word out of California.

"Emergency! Emergency! We're sinking. Los Angeles is gone — the whole state is in the sea. God have mercy on us!"

Thirty minutes later, two Boeing 747's, designated Command One and Two, were airborne. These were communication centers always ready for instant take-off in the event of an emergency situation. The delay in getting into the air was caused by waiting for shocked officials to reach Stark Air Force Base.

A primary group of observers, including President Baldwin, Race, Quinn, Jules Henshaw and a number of top military brass, were aboard Command One as it streaked to 45,000 feet and headed for California. Command Two, with Vice President Ashford aboard, was only two minutes behind it.

After crossing the Sierra Nevada mountains, both planes dropped to fifteen thousand feet. Billowing clouds of steam and smoke made it unsafe to go lower, but the view from this altitude was numbing. All conversation stilled as people stared down at the incredible devastation below them.

Wherever a town could be seen, there was nothing but ruin. Crumbled buildings, fires raging through whole communities, evidences of explosions, bodies everywhere. Some survivors could be seen among the rubble, but very few.

Everyone crowded to the windows of the plane as Los Angeles appeared on the horizon. As they got closer, the destruction appeared to be total. It was as if some giant sweeping hand had laid the city waste. Everything broken, flattened. Mile after mile of smoking devastation. Freeway interchanges shattered and collapsed, huge concrete blocks thrusting up from roadbeds twisted into grotesque shapes.

The quake had ripped open several channels into the city from the coastline. The largest and deepest of these started just south of Santa Monica and gouged its way into the downtown area. Huge waves foamed angrily into these new inlets, crashing and spewing sea water into a downtown in which not a single high-rise structure was still standing. Vast tide pools inundated huge areas surrounding the new channels, creating mosaics of floating debris and tiled squares of roof. Much of the city was under water, the flooding worsened by the enormous tidal waves battering the coast incessantly since the initial shock.

As Command One circled the city, they could see another frightening tsunami forming about two miles offshore. They watched helplessly as the wave rose to what must have been thirty or forty feet high – it was difficult to tell exactly from fifteen thousand feet. Finally the tsunami smashed inland along a front that stretched a dozen miles or more. Again the gaping rifts foamed and flooded. Debris swirled and tossed and broke into smaller pieces. More of the tiled roof mosaic disappeared under the pounding seas.

It was the mountains, though, that most clearly showed the force of the quake. New cliffs dropped sheer for a hundred feet or more, as if sliced by some enormous cleaver. Twisted highways that had climbed out of the city toward the canyons now ended abruptly before solid, impenetrable faces of rock. The canyons, and the rest of the roadways, could be seen fifty feet or more to the south. It was chilling, graphic evidence of how far the Pacific coastal plate had jumped when it finally wrenched free of the pressures jamming it against the North American continental plate.

There was little sign of human life in the devastated city below. Casualties in some areas must have reached one hundred percent. Fortunately, warnings broadcast these last weeks about scientific evidence predicting a major quake had caused millions to flee the area. If they had gone far enough, they would be alive.

After viewing the stricken Los Angeles, Command One veered south to San Diego. The same appalling scene of destruction greeted them there. The San Andreas fault here in the south swung a considerable distance inland, reaching almost to the corner where California, Arizona and Mexico met, but San Diego had not escaped its fury. A large part of the city was also under foaming seas. Ships that had been at anchor at naval installations were tossed a half mile inland by the giant tidal waves that followed the violent movement of the earth.

Baldwin visibly paled as he viewed all the devastation. He finally ordered Command One to proceed north up the California coastline – or what had been the coastline. It was no longer recognizable, for huge chunks of land had been swallowed into the sea.

As they flew along the line of the San Andreas fault, it looked as if pieces of a vast jigsaw puzzle had been torn loose, no longer fitting together as before. The ugly gash of the fault had cut fresh, deep scars for hundreds of miles through mountains and valleys.

Henshaw was shaken by the display of forces unleashed in the most violent upheaval on this continent in modern times. He nearly shoved his balding pate through the plane window when he suddenly spotted another shuddering, rumpling movement of the hills below.

It was a violent after-shock, taking place at that very moment. People in the plane could see the terrain lifting, trees falling, even the spectacular splitting of a line of hills into fresh, raw escarpments.

"Did you see that—?" Henshaw cried, not taking his eyes from the window. "Did you see it jump—?" He was shaking his head in disbelief. "Those hills must have been shoved another twenty-five feet north. That's incredible. It seems impossible there could be enough energy left in the fault—"

Henshaw was so excited he had difficulty speaking. "We just saw a delayed realignment, a local jamming along the fault that suddenly broke loose. Absolutely spectacular – do you realize that mankind has witnessed an upheaval like that only a few times in the history of this planet!"

"I'm not a scientist, Jules," Baldwin said wearily. "It just looked to me like a lot more death and destruction we don't need."

"You'll probably never see anything like that again in your lifetime—"

"I sincerely hope not," Baldwin muttered.

The plane continued north and suddenly everyone realized the true enormity of what had happened.

A huge section of California was no longer attached to the mainland.

The bulge that stretched from Santa Barbara all the way up to Monterey Bay had been broken off along the San Andreas fault line. It was now separated from the rest of California by a churning, quarter-mile wide channel.

Baldwin was shocked. "It's an island—"

"San Andreas Island," Henshaw murmured, the words barely audible. He knew he never would see the birth of an island again.

Command One circled the new island several times. It appeared to be over a hundred and fifty miles long and some fifty miles wide. No sign of life could be seen, though the ruins of a few small communities were visible along the western coastline. No one could even imagine the horror that must have accompanied such a violent relocation.

"It's a good name, Jules," Baldwin muttered. "San Andreas Island it is. May God help anyone still alive."

Finally, Command One turned northward again. Long before they could actually make out any details, they knew San Francisco was not far ahead. A pall of dark smoke rose high into the sky. Sam Baldwin ordered the pilot to descend as low as he felt it was safe. Their approach was bringing them over the lower peninsula. Quinn was familiar with this part of the country, and was shocked by what he saw on the ground.

The waters of the southern end of San Francisco bay were dark and muddied, bubbling and roiling violently. Huge sections of land around the east and west sides of the bay had disappeared.

Race was also staring down at the bay. "It's almost twice as wide as it was—"

"Undoubtedly liquifaction," Henshaw said, studying the scene intently. "All the land built up from tidal deposits over hundreds of years just dissolved back into the bay as mud."

The erosion had eaten inland along the peninsula until the bay waters now boiled against the ruins of cities sprawled on the higher ridges. Palo Alto, Redwood City, San Carlos, San Mateo, Burlingame – all lay in flaming destruction.

There was no San Bruno, nor a San Francisco International airport. The San Andreas fault ran roughly up the middle of the peninsula, cutting down into the sea west of, and almost opposite, Daly City, adjoining the southern edge of San Francisco. The sliding Pacific plate had broken free with demonic power, ripping the upper portion of the peninsula apart like a wishbone, all the way down to where San Bruno had stood. At this point, the rift veered sharply eastward. Now a half-mile wide sea channel gouged across the peninsula and out into the bay.

Either the snarling fury of the Pacific ocean slashing through the channel, or the violent shaking of the inner bay flatlands, had caused the airport to disintegrate. No trace of it could be seen from above.

The savage rifting of the peninsula now completely isolated the city of San Francisco. It had become another island, lashed on all sides by furious seas. The buckled towers of the Golden Gate bridge sagged into the bay. The bridge had folded in upon itself, dumping the huge span into deep waters. The Oakland bridge also had collapsed. There was no land access to San Francisco.

The city was engulfed in flames. The proud hotels and commercial towers were heaped in ruin upon each other, rubble piled several stories high in downtown streets. Even buildings touted to withstand any quake had crumpled in the unprecedented violence of this superquake.

Unlike Los Angeles, thousands of people could be seen amid the smoking, flaming ruins of San Francisco. Baldwin pointed them out to Quinn and Race.

"We've got to get those people out of there—"

"Rescue operations are in place, Mr. President," Race assured him. "We have ground troops and helicopters alerted in five states. Orders have already been sent. They should be here very soon, sir. We'll get everyone out that we can."

"Get them all out," Baldwin snapped, tension in his voice. "That must be pure hell down there."

Baldwin turned away from the window, shutting his eyes and putting both hands to his temples.

"Have you seen enough, gentlemen?" he grunted. "I don't think I can take any more of this."

Henshaw had shifted to the other side of the plane, staring from a window to see the cities lining the eastern side of the bay more clearly. A cry of dismay broke from him.

"Oh, dear. The Hayward fault went too."

The others came over to peer down. It was true. More savage evidence of the fury of the quake. Oakland was shattered. Looking north, Berkeley and Richmond lay in a haze of smoke. It was the same scene of devastation to the south. San Leandro. Hayward. Union City. Newark. Fremont. All concealed in billowing, ruddy smoke. The loss of life on this east side must also be staggering.

Baldwin sank back in his seat. "Get us out of here."

Command Two, on orders from Baldwin in Command One, made a detailed inspection of the lower half of the state.

Baja California, which millions of years ago had split apart from the mainland in a similar upheaval, was drastically changed. The quake had jerked the Baja leg wider apart, splitting Mexico farther north and allowing the Gulf to spill into parts of the Imperial valley. The Imperial fault had indeed rifted as a result of the San Andreas movement.

Anne Ashford and the other observers in Command Two could easily trace the torn San Andreas up from the Salton Sea, along the Chocolate mountains, and up along the San Bernadino range. It then ripped west along the crest of the Gabriels, activating the Elsinore and the San Jacinto faults. Luckily, the San Joachin and Sacramento valleys fared better than expected. Silence fell over the occupants of Command Two as they headed north and the new island came into view. There were no words to express the agony in every heart.

In Command One, now on a course back to Stark Air Force Base in Missouri, Baldwin got up and went to sit beside Jules Henshaw. He gave the scientist a worried stare.

"Is it over, Jules?"

"The worst of it, sir. At least, in California."

"Can we expect more quakes there – will rescue operations put more people in danger?"

Henshaw shook his head. "There almost certainly will be heavy aftershocks, Mr. President, but nothing like what just happened. California should remain quiet for a long time – unless the tectonic plates are moving faster than we think."

Baldwin glanced across the aisle at Quinn. "Get an estimate of casualties as soon as you can – although I don't know how that will help."

"The rush to get out of the area this last couple of weeks probably saved millions of lives, Mr. President. We'll do what we can, but we might never get an accurate count of the dead."

# 38

## THE ALEUTIAN BRIDGE

The wrenching of California claimed a staggering toll in lives. It was impossible to know for sure how many died. In the days following the quake, people responded to pleas to report those known dead or missing, but the results were too fragmented and incomplete to provide a reliable count. The number of dead was finally estimated between ten and fifteen million. As rescue operations proceeded, California became an empty state. With no services or facilities, people had no choice but to join the evacuation.

Operations in NECCO headquarters ran at a feverish level, trying to restore order out of the chaos. Just relocating the millions of survivors, and providing food and shelter for them, taxed all systems to the limit. It was what the National Emergency Coordinated Command Organization was created to do, however, and it was performing well. But the enormous magnitude of the disaster stretched every person and resource to the limit—and beyond.

Quinn and Joanna were summoned to the White House—a new edifice, of course, in the new national capitol. The architecture of the old White House in Washington, D.C., had been kept, mainly because it was recognized world-wide as the symbol of democracy. The amazing new solar panel construction was incorporated, however, and the light that emanated from it night and day put new emphasis on the 'White'.

Sam Baldwin rose from behind his desk in the new Oval Office to greet them. Race was already there, and one other individual. A broad smile of pleasure came to Quinn's face and he crossed to throw his arms around the uniformed general.

"Aaron—as I live and breath," Quinn exclaimed. "There's no one in the whole wide world I'd rather see. I hope this means you've accepted the offer to join us again—"

Aaron Stark, the commanding general who twice had headed the combined military forces of the United States in grim struggles for survival, nodded.

"I figured if it was important enough to drag you and Joanna out of Oregon, it had to be something I wouldn't want to miss."

They all exchanged greetings, Joanna giving Aaron a delighted hug, then sat in a semi-circle in front of the President's desk. Baldwin took a moment to study them, obviously pleased, but showing the deep concern he was feeling, too. "You are indeed most welcome, General Stark," the President told him. "I wish the circumstances were different, but your country needs you once again, sir. I thank you for responding so promptly and so willingly."

"I suppose this has something to do with the disaster in California," Stark said.

The President shook his head.

"It doesn't, Aaron. You'll be informed of why you were summoned out of retirement in just a moment, but first I want to clear up an order of business."

Baldwin switched his stare to Quinn.

"Race and I have talked this through, Quinn. It was his suggestion, and I approve completely."

Quinn had no idea what the president was talking about. He glanced at Race, saw only a grin on his friend's face.

"Mr. President—?"

"I know you came back to work the problems in Jules Henshaw's report—" He saw the surprise flit across Quinn's face and nodded. "I've read it, Quinn. I'm well aware Jules soft-pedaled the most explosive parts. I agree with Race, the California situation was top priority at the time—but not now."

"What was Race's suggestion, Mr. President? He has a fairly devious mind, so whatever it was—"

"We both want you to take over again as Pharaoh One, Quinn."

Quinn stared from one to the other of them.

"Race is Pharaoh One now—"

"And you were the head of NECCO almost since its inception. Race is right, there needs to be one person in charge, and you're it. At least until you and Aaron get us out of this mess and you both go back into retirement—which," he added with a smile, "can't be too soon for me. It's a Presidential order, Quinn. Live with it."

Race leaned over and grasped Quinn's hand.

"We need your leadership, Quinn. Like the President says, I'll take the mantle back as soon as you get us out of this mess."

Aaron Stark was looking on. His eyebrows raised as he glanced curiously at the president.

"Am I right in assuming we're looking at a fair-sized mess here, Mr. President?"

"Biggest pile of crap you've ever stepped in."

"Bigger than the Latin affair?"

Baldwin nodded.

"That was up to your knees. I'd say this one is about neck high."

The president looked at Joanna.

"Joanna, your expertise is very important in all this. Particularly your grasp of affairs in the eastern countries. You'll be logging quite a few air miles, but that will include a good deal of time in Israel."

"Always a pleasure, Mr. President," she murmured. She glanced at Quinn. "It's not going home any more—that's with my husband, in Oregon—but a large part of my heart will always be in Israel."

"Sounds like we're not dealing with a purely domestic situation," Stark said quietly.

"The real trouble is," Baldwin frowned, "we don't know what we're dealing with. A big part of me doesn't want to find out, either."

For the next three hours they probed and analyzed the situation that was facing the United States. The heart of the problem was Jules Henshaw's predictions that cataclysmic disasters like the one that had just struck California would inevitably occur in other parts of the world, and soon. That brought up not only how such disasters might affect those countries, and the United States, but also focused attention on the explosive political situation throughout the world.

The recent attempt by the Chinese government to take over all of Asia, and the harsh campaigns by the Russian military to once again seize power in the former Soviet countries, had shattered stability in virtually every government on all continents, with the exception of the two American hemispheres.

With the rule of law so fragile in so many countries, it was of deep concern to the United States what would happen if those nations faced sudden and massive natural disasters, beyond their ability to cope with. In most cases, the disaster wouldn't have to be very massive to put governments in smaller, poorer countries out of control. Some Eastern European governments had already folded during the Chinese crisis. These lands now were virtual feudal domains, with no central government and no cohesion between tribes or sections of the countries affected.

If chaos became wide-spread, and central governments began to fail, what responsibility did the United States have, and what should it do about it?

More importantly, if world-wide de-stabilization became even a possibility, what actions would that spark from power-hungry countries eager to devour a helpless neighbor? That would present a whole new set of problems for the United States.

The trigger, of course, was Henshaw's predictions. He had been deadly accurate about California. Would similar disastrous events break out around the world? No one in the Oval Office was prepared to discount Jules Henshaw and his scientific data.

The meeting broke up, but quickly began again back at NECCO headquarters. This time, Jules was a part of the group, and no one felt worse than he did about the calculations that presented such a grim outlook of global chaos.

They were still meeting when it happened.

The whole NECCO headquarters building swayed violently. It continued for at least two minutes. Everyone held on to the table, staring at each other in disbelief.

"What's going on, Jules—" Joanna gasped.

Henshaw jumped up and ran out of the room.

Five minutes later, all the top officers of the Pharaoh Force gathered in the main conference room. Moments later, Jules entered, clutching a handful of computer readouts, his face flushed, eyes bulging with excitement.

"You have something for us, Jules—?" Quinn asked.

"It was an earthquake, of course," Jules said, hurrying to the front of the room. He held up the readouts in his hand. "A really big one."

"Not California again—"

Jules shook his head. "Somewhere in the Aleutians—don't have exact data yet. It was enormous, I can tell you—bigger than the one in California. That registered 9.3 on the Richter scale. Preliminary readouts indicate this was 9.5—and that's a lot more powerful than those two additional tenths indicate."

"Reports on damage?" Race asked.

"None so far." Jules looked around the room, his face suddenly sober. "A quake of that magnitude, wherever it happened, caused massive damage."

Jules left to gather more data. The closest NECCO station was in Anchorage. The Pharaoh in charge of the Alaska region tried to reach Anchorage but couldn't get through. Phones. Radio. Not even satellite. It was completely blacked out—an ominous sign. There was nothing anyone could do but wait for Jules to return.

He did, clutching more papers, but this time it was clear he was highly agitated. He punched in the large central viewing screen and everyone stared at the map of the Pacific ocean that appeared, showing both the American side and the long line of Asian countries to the east. Everyone realized they were looking at a familiar map—this was the deadly Ring of Fire.

Henshaw used a pointer to trace the western edge of the massive Pacific tectonic plate.

"This is the villain," Henshaw told them. His voice was so hushed, he had to switch on the small microphone in front of him. "Ever since breaking away along the San Andreas, it's been ramming with increasing pressure against the Asian plate."

He stopped, his adam's apple bobbling several times as he stretched his neck and swallowed nervously. His expression was almost sad, and the people in the room could detect a higher-than-normal pitch in his voice. He looked up again at the large map on the screen.

"The extent of the event we just experienced is far greater than first reports indicated," he told the men around the conference table. "I'll attempt to give some idea of what just happened—although it is far too early to know much of anything."

"Our sensors have recorded another giant superquake. The newest data indicates it registered 9.7 on the Richter scale, not 9.5 as I reported a few minutes ago. That is unprecedented in modern times, gentlemen."

The lighted pointer centered on the Bering Sea area.

"The quake appears to have struck along the entire Aleutian chain, which sits on the edge of the deep Aleutian trench. This trench is one of the—the slots—under which the Pacific tectonic plate slips back into the bowels of the earth's core. If you remember, concerns were expressed at the time of the breakaway from the San Andreas, that the Pacific plate might move westward at a rate faster than it could subduct under the Aleutian trench. Apparently those concerns were well founded. Running fast and loose, in geological terms, after the break from our American plate in California, the Pacific plate simply rammed into opposing plates along its western edge. The force of that collision, again in geological terms, was gigantic."

Quinn had to clear his throat, finding his throat had gone dry. "Do we know how widespread the damage is, Jules? We can't get through to Alaska—"

"We don't know where damage occurred, One. We should be getting satellite photos in a few minutes, but they might not show us much. I've ordered new pass coordinates, but those will take a few hours to give us more detailed photographs. However, we can expect a lot of damage."

He stared at them for a moment, then lifted the pointer toward the Japanese islands.

"The quake was so violent, we missed what actually happened. Our seismographs couldn't handle all the data and stress. We now know, however, that a series of enormous quakes struck at the same time along the entire western edge of the Pacific plate."

"Involving what countries, Jules?" Race asked, his voice also hushed by the news.

"We can't be sure, not until we get information from the satellites. Our international center in Colorado, however, shows Japan is a major concern. Data indicates it may have been hit by the worst earthquake in its history—and Japan has seen some bad ones."

"I take it there's no direct communication with the Japanese," Quinn said.

"The Colorado center tried, but got no response. The force of the quake in the islands was recorded at 9.0 Richter. Given the terrain and dense population concentrations, there is a possibility of –" he choked, swallowed again, "of total destruction. That is pure speculation, based on preliminary data, but it is within the realm of possibility that the loss of life in Japan alone could run into the tens of millions. We'll have a more accurate assessment when we receive satellite photos."

Quinn glanced over at Aaron Stark, sitting as grim faced as everyone else in the room.

"Aaron, let's get aerial reconnaissance going immediately. We need close-up photos. Alaska. The Aleutians. Japan too, if that's possible. Scramble anything that will get us hard information."

Aaron got up, nodding. "They'll be airborne in ten minutes."

Henshaw continued his report, moving the pointer down the map.

"Colorado center, and our own sensors, report enormously powerful earthquakes also occurred in the Philippines—here in New Guinea—along the south Pacific island chains—and here in New Zealand. What just happened is cataclysmic, gentlemen—utterly, completely cataclysmic."

The room suddenly swayed again. Not as violently, but enough to make people grip the edge of the table.

Henshaw regained his balance. The pain on his face was suddenly replaced by pure astonishment.

"This is historic," he breathed. "The shaking we are experiencing irrefutably confirms the geo-physical theories of Wegener, the findings of modern paleomagnetic research, even the primeval existence of Laurasia and Gondwana—"

"Non-scientific, Jules," Race said sharply. "We're still shaking. What's happening—in plain language. Are we heading for a quake here in Missouri—?"

"No, sir," Jules said. He looked flustered, trying to assess scientific implications and at the same time explain what was happening so the men in the room could understand. "We're creeping again."

"Explain that, Jules." Race grimaced.

"It's really continental drift—on an unbelievable scale. It's difficult to put such complex scientific theories into plain English, but simply put, the whole American continent is moving westward at an accelerated rate."

"So where are we going?" one of the Pharaohs asked, It brought a few tight chuckles.

"As little as eighty million years ago," Jules began, "scientists believe our North American continent was still part of Europe. They figure South America broke off from Africa about 135 million years ago, and began drifting across the Atlantic to where it is today. We followed a few million years later."

"Are we still moving—?"

"Normally, about two inches a year to the west. However, since California broke loose, we've already moved that much—a whole year's creep in a few days. And it's obviously still going on—that's why we're shaking. Gentlemen, this is truly historic—"

"I'd say it's more frightening than historic," Quinn grunted.

The first satellite photos arrived a few minutes later. They were disappointing, showing only boiling, impenetrable cloud masses over what was believed to be the quake area in the Aleutian Islands. All they could do was wait for the next pass.

The reconnaissance planes Aaron Stark ordered into the air produced the next set of photographs, however. These prints were blown up to enhance the detail. The changes that occurred in the Aleutians in those few minutes of violence were unbelievable.

The entire crustal shelf of the Aleutian island chain was shoved violently upward by the subducting edge of the Pacific plate. Instead of a chain of volcanic islands curving across the Bering Sea, there now was a continuous bridge of lifeless land. It came heaving up out of the sea, the result of plates colliding with such gigantic force it was impossible to comprehend.

The Bering Sea was now isolated from the Pacific ocean, cut off by smoking black stretches of rock thrust up above the ocean surface. The new landscape was dotted by a series of peaks rising several thousand feet into the air. Some of these were the islands that had formed the Aleutian chain before the eruption.

The new bridge stretched from the mainland of Russia all the way to the Alaskan peninsula, connecting continent to continent.

Alaska was devastated. There was no way to send relief, for heaving seas made it impossible for any kind of vessel to navigate. Airports were demolished. Distances were too great to mount any kind of helicopter rescue endeavor. The only thing that could be done was drop food and medical supplies from low-flying aircraft. The first ground rescue missions did not reach Alaska until three weeks later. By then, the dead were dead, the survivors had survived by themselves.

In Japan, it was the worst natural disaster known to mankind. The islands were utterly desolated. It was now a land of death. The initial quake was followed by towering tsunamis. The ocean was carpeted with bodies. No one ever knew how many millions actually died. There was not one habitable city left standing. A civilized order of existence ceased throughout the islands.

It was much the same in the other stricken areas along the smoking western rim of fire. Death and devastation everywhere.

Little could be done for those who survived, because a few hours after the western Pacific disasters, as Henshaw predicted, havoc piled up around the world.

A shocked Pharaoh Force remained on duty through that first night as the reports came in. It was mind-numbing.

Deadly quakes struck in South America, in Italy, in Greece, in Turkey. China was wrenched by a score of earthquakes, but as usual, no one knew how many died.

Reports gave details of shattering quakes in the Himalayan belt, shaking Pakistan and Afghanistan into ruin.

In one of the night briefings, Henshaw showed on the wall screens how scientific theory was being proved deadly accurate.

Scientists believed, Henshaw told the grim-faced Pharaohs, that about one hundred and thirty-five million years ago a single land mass violently split apart into two sections, north and south. About that same time, India was attached to the lower eastern part of the great African continent, as South America was attached to its western edge. In a cataclysmic event, both India and South America broke off from Africa.

The South American continent began drifting westward, while the huge island of India literally raced northward. It traveled some five thousand miles until, about sixty-five million years ago, it rammed into the Eurasian plate with such staggering force that the collision formed the Himalayan mountain range. It was about this time, Henshaw explained, that scientists believe the North American continent broke loose from the European mainland and began drifting westward.

Talking about this world-wide trauma of earth changes, both now and millions of years ago, left Henshaw deeply moved, and his audience of Pharaohs deeply confused. Even for their brilliant minds, the visions of a world land mass splitting apart millions of years ago was difficult to comprehend. No one doubted, however, that earth today was unleashing a titanic shudder.

Shocks struck again and again for days. Volcanoes spewed billions of tons of debris into the atmosphere, darkening skies for thousands of miles. Aftershocks jarred the earth for another week of terror, but with diminishing power. When the earth's crust finally ended its grinding fury, it was estimated that nearly four hundred million people had died. The actual death toll probably was at least twice that many.

# 39

## Rampage

The worldwide wrenching of the earth's crust was the beginning of a nightmare. The gigantic earthquakes, the volcanic eruptions, the rending of the ocean floors, all signaled the start of a series of bizarre phenomenons.

Nature seemed thrown off balance, its order upset. Jules Henshaw and his fellow scientists on the Pharaoh Force, along with what was left of the world's scientific community, scrambled desperately to connect what happened in the next few months into some logical sequence. Nature tossed the measured course of centuries aside. It became willful, determined to awe and destroy.

Immense storms swept across the shattered continents in the wake of those first weeks of violence. Heavy deluges of rain, endless days and nights of howling winds, frightening periods of angry lightning and ear-splitting thunderstorms. It made the task of rescue amid the wreckage of the quakes almost impossible.

The seas, their normal worldwide patterns of current flow totally disrupted, became foaming, destructive mountains. Nothing made by man could survive above or below the raging seas. Ships and submarines scurried toward sheltered harbors but those too far from shore disappeared in the storms. Cross-currents ripped in every direction, some surging down into the deepest depths in sudden great sucking rivers that flowed in the midst of the oceans.

Air currents, always at the whim of the oceans, were thrown into similar distortions. Violent maelstroms of wind rushed for thousands of miles at speeds of two hundred miles an hour and higher. Boiling clouds covered most of the surface of the earth, banging together in savage electrical jousts, sucking up moisture and depositing it in turbulent fury. No planes flew. Even the satellites in space were affected.

The days themselves, in the aftermath of this natural violence, were darker. It was caused partially by the globe-circling storm clouds, but mostly by the billions of tons of dust and debris hurled high into the atmosphere by the quakes and volcanic eruptions.

Then, as winds and storms gradually abated, the world went into fearful shock. People swore they heard voices in the heavens.

Strange sounds were indeed coming from somewhere in the skies, and at times, they did sound strangely like moans and groans. Many claimed the sounds formed words—heavenly warnings of even more dire things to come. When these sounds were first detected over the lessening winds and storms, shivers of apprehension went through the world.

Quinn summoned Jules Henshaw to his office and the scientist was soon settling into a chair in front of him. Jules looked tired, and nervous.

"What's going on, Jules?" Quinn asked. "The whole world is talking about voices from heaven. All I'm hearing is a very frightening noise, but maybe I'm not tuned in—"

Jules swallowed, the apple moving up and down in his long, thin neck. A frown flitted across his face.

"It's mass hysteria," he muttered. "There are no voices. It's a logical sequence of atmospheric cause and effect."

"Explain it to me, Jules," Quinn said wearily, "so I can explain it to just about everyone from President Baldwin on down."

"Well," Jules began, his eyes fastening thoughtfully on a point on the wall behind Quinn, "the upper atmosphere is in turmoil, as you know. It's affected by the upheavals of the lower air masses. The recent volcanic activity tossed vast quantities of fine rock particles into our circling stratospheric bands. I am convinced, as is virtually the entire scientific community, that the sounds are a result of the constant grinding of these volcanic particles against each other. All that dust is trapped between layers of the atmosphere and moving at cyclonic speeds."

"I might be able to explain that," Quinn grimaced, "but not until I understand it."

"Look at it this way," Jules continued, shifting from the spot on the wall to look directly at Quinn. "It's like being locked inside a giant cement mixer. Sounds are bounced around and amplified. People can imagine anything they want, but the noise is a logical, natural phenomenon, not a manifestation of heavenly beings. The noise will end as the dust particles escape from those stratospheric traps and filter back to earth."

Quinn expelled a long breath. "The sounds do seem to be getting weaker—"

"And soon they'll be gone, at least on an auditory level," Jules assured him. "People will settle down."

Quinn flashed him a grin. "I can safely tell them this isn't the end of the world—?"

Jules nodded soberly, not picking up on the humor behind the question. "That is a completely illogical conclusion, One."

As Jules said, the sounds in the skies did begin to diminish and people were eager to accept scientific logic over the dire predictions of religious fanatics.

The storms ended and the clouds dissipated. Once again there was sun overhead—but it brought no relief. The sun now was an eerie orange glow, diffused and intensified by debris still blocking and hazing the upper atmosphere. It created an oven, in which heat radiated and increased, but could not dissipate. From cold, savage storms, people around the world now began to endure suffocating, unending heat.

Nothing could be done to ease the searing temperatures. Range lands withered and burned, forests in every part of the world burst into flame.

In the United States, all reconstruction work came to a halt. People simply couldn't work in such intense heat. It was difficult to breathe, and hospitals became crowded. People and animals dropped dead as they walked, or died in their sleep. Motors burned up, generators failed, public utilities went out of service. The crisis became desperate.

Once again Quinn sat facing Jules Henshaw.

"Is anything ever going to be normal again, Jules—?"

"The whole earth has just gone through an enormous cataclysm," Jules responded. "It's going to take time."

"How much time?" Quinn asked. "People are dying. We don't have resources to fight this heat—"

"It won't last, One," Jules said solemnly. "I'm getting data from stations all around the world. This inversion is weakening—"

"So are we all, Jules."

Then, a few weeks later and for no apparent reason, nature did indeed relent, just as Henshaw had predicted.

Winds began to blow, the skies began to clear and become blue again, temperatures dropped. One day, the sun was a bright ball overhead, doing what man expected it to do.

Damage from those weeks of intense heat was enormous. Forest fires still raged in the United States and throughout the world, causing more ash to accumulate in the atmosphere. Far worse was the stench of unburied millions of dead animals and people, victims of the recent earthquakes. A horrible odor wafted over Asia and Europe.

Though the terrible heat was gone, it was responsible for a fearful aftermath that now struck the shores of every land. A red tide seeped along the coasts of the continents, streaking ominous red fingers into the mouths of rivers. In oceans and seas where warm currents naturally flowed, the water turned bright red for hundreds of miles.

Red tides were not new to the world, of course, but the recent prolonged period of heat damaged the balance of microscopic life in the seas. Deadly toxin organisms bloomed and multiplied into densities never before recorded in the oceans, fatally contaminating marine life.

The planktonic blooms were frightening to watch. From horizon to horizon, seas dashed and foamed in eerie crimson. No one ventured into the fearful red water, the widely broadcast warnings not really needed. Along coastlines around the world, thousands of miles of beaches stood empty in the summer sun.

This time, Quinn strode into the huge lab where Jules Henshaw was working with at least a score of fellow scientists. Machines were clacking, needles waggling back and forth, and men scurried about the lab without seeming to notice that Pharaoh One was present. Henshaw finally did, crossing to greet Quinn with an apologetic smile.

"Didn't see you come in, One," Jules said. He looked around, evidently looking for a chair, but there wasn't one in sight. Everyone was standing in front of a machine or scurrying to another one. "There's a chair in my office—"

Quinn shook his head. "Just stopped by to get the latest on this red tide. What can we do—?"

"Can't stop it," Henshaw said quickly. "Nature's in control. Main thing to do is warn people how dangerous it is."

"I take it this isn't a normal red tide—"

"Far from it, One." Jules stopped for a moment to study a read-out coming in on a machine beside him. He looked back at Quinn. "People must be warned against eating—or even touching—anything from the sea. We must assume all seafood, especially shell fish, have been contaminated. The toxins involved in this red tide are very virulent."

"What happens if people ignore the warnings—?"

"They'll wish they hadn't," Jules said grimly. "These are poisonous organisms we're dealing with. People who ingest contaminated seafood can come down with paralytic poisoning."

"Are the symptoms easily recognizable," Quinn frowned. "I mean, can people get an early warning that they need medical care?"

"They'll suffer symptoms ranging from tingling numbness and painful aches throughout their body, to fatal paralysis," Henshaw answered. "Even if they don't eat contaminated seafood, they can be infected by just going into the water. Or they can contract serious respiratory illnesses simply by breathing toxic organisms sprayed into the winds by the surf. This is a worrisome situation, One."

Soon millions upon millions of fish floated dead in rivers and seas. The stench became almost as fearful as that from the rotting bodies in Europe and Asia. The stinking flotsam was washed onto beaches and huge bonfires burned up and down both seaboards as people continually scraped the dead fish into piles and burned them, the beaches filling again with each tide.

After a few weeks of normal temperatures, the oceans began to clear. Nature restored its balance. Rivers and seas stopped the deadly blooming and the red organisms were drawn out to sea into colder water to die. People still were reluctant to walk along beaches or go into the water, fearful that some lingering, unseen poison was still there.

The red tides were a deadly blow to fishermen. Now able to brave seas still violent but at least navigable, fishermen found the plankton had ruined fishing grounds and destroyed harvests. In all, thirty percent of ocean fisheries were estimated lost during those weeks of creeping red death.

Nature had yet another cruel trick to play in its wild, capricious spree.

Clouds sucked up moisture from contaminated oceans, then dumped poisoned, bitter rains onto a parched earth. The contamination would not affect crops, scientists decided after frantic testing, but the rains were considered dangerous for direct human intake.

The entire group of Pharaohs was assembled to hear the latest report by the scientific community. Henshaw showed some slides of where the problem was the worst, and that of course, was in the poorest and most devastated countries.

"This doesn't pose a major problem in the United States," Henshaw explained, "because reservoirs and water systems are regularly treated and purified. Many other countries, however, are still shattered by war and the recent natural disasters. Most of them have no central water distribution systems working—if they ever had them. People in these countries are struggling to survive and with only poisoned water to drink—

well, gentlemen," Henshaw said quietly, "the death toll could be staggering."

In these ravaged countries, people could only collect and drink the rainwater, either directly from the skies or from the rivers, for there was no other supply source. The bitter water was particularly deadly for children, the elderly, and those weakened by hunger and lingering illness. Many thousands died, for there was no way to help them.

Perhaps it was a veiled blessing from the god of heaven, some muttered. For many, death was preferable to living.

With the seas fully cleared of all traces of the red tide, the rains soon sweetened. For weeks, nothing unnatural happened. No more tantrums. People began to believe the terrible chain of disasters had at last been broken.

They were wrong.

The worst was yet to come.

A loathsome new scourge swept through the shattered lands of Europe, striking dazed, weary people already numbed by the struggle of surviving wars, earthquakes, erupting volcanoes, and the frightening series of natural calamities.

At first, it was thought a deadly new strain of influenza virus had emerged, seemingly more contagious and virulent than any previous epidemic. Hundreds of thousands were afflicted almost at the same time, in widely separated sections of Europe. All victims showed the same symptoms. Dizziness. High fever. Acute muscle pains. Then severe vomiting and diarrhea.

The symptoms quickly grew worse. Realization came that this sickness sweeping the continent was not influenza, nor anything seen before. After the first two or three days, victims began breaking out in huge, puss-filled sores that spread rapidly to cover every part of the body.

Then something far more horrifying. Out of the oozing sores came wriggling thousands of tiny maggots. Spawned from the raw flesh and the matter in the sores, the maggots bored back under healthy skin, growing, multiplying, literally consuming flesh off bones.

Death from the maggots came agonizingly slow. Victims went mad from fever, pain, and the sight of seeing themselves being eaten alive by the swarming, crawling masses of maggots.

In a matter of days, similar outbreaks were reported throughout Asia, and then on the African continent. It was dubbed the Omega virus, for death was a certain end to the torment of its victims.

Fear shuddered throughout the world.

In the United States, NECCO hurriedly assembled an emergency medical task force. No outbreaks of the disease so far were reported anywhere on the American continents. Teams of specialists were sent to Europe and they quickly determined they were not dealing with a disease at all. The reason for the epidemics was as horrifying as the symptoms.

Once again the Pharaohs were gathered, along with President Baldwin and Vice President Anne Ashford. All eyes were fixed on Jules Henshaw as he held up a sealed glass jar. There was something on the bottom, but it was too small for anyone to make it out. Henshaw tapped the jar with a finger, a bleak expression on his face.

"This is what we are dealing with," he grimaced. "A fly—a new breed of fly, to be precise. And one of the most revolting insects you will ever see."

He put the jar down on the table in front of him, staring at the contents with disgust. Apparently the fly inside the jar was dead, for it didn't move.

"This fly, and billions like it, has been traced to the decayed remains of dead people lying unburied all across Europe and Asia. This new species fed and bred in the hundreds of mounds of rotting flesh. We surmise it underwent fearsome incubation change, probably starting during the recent heat wave."

Jules went on to explain that the insects had formed in dark, buzzing clouds above the piles of death, multiplying into billions. Hunger for flesh took them to the living. It was the bite of these flies, and the larvae deposited under a layer of skin, that marked a person for the nightmare of being self-consumed.

Sam Baldwin gave Henshaw a penetrating stare. "You got a way to exterminate these little bastards, Jules?"

"Not yet, sir," Henshaw replied, "but we will."

"Can't think of a higher priority," Baldwin grunted. "Personally, I'm not going anywhere without a can of bug spray."

"Won't work on these, sir," Henshaw told him, "but I recommend you carry it anyway—"

With the problem identified, and thousands of the killer flies brought back to tightly sealed laboratories in the United States, a frantic effort was launched to stem the rising toll of death and insanity and suicide, for many chose to die by their own hand as soon as maggots erupted from the sores.

The first concern was finding a vaccine for those already infected, then developing chemicals and insecticides to eliminate the deadly fly population. An immediate assault was mounted to get rid of the rotting piles of bodies in which the flies spawned. Chemicals were used to create searing, incinerating pyres. The smell across Europe became unbearable and no one went without a mask to protect from the revolting clouds of ash billowing across the lands.

On the steppes of Asia, it was found that the flesh-eating traits had passed to a new strain of grasshoppers, bred in the same manner from unburied dead. It was impossible to tell whether it was more horrifying to fight off swarms of infected flies, or find oneself covered with clicking, biting grasshoppers that within hours produced the same symptoms, and finally the internal hordes of maggots.

With this latest outburst, nature seemed to satiate its anger.

Weather cycles returned to normalcy. The fight against the maggot horror continued with slow success.

# 40

## THE SIBERIANS

"Quinn, have you seen this latest batch of reconnaissance photos out of the Aleutians—?" "I sent them to you, Mr. President."

"Am I seeing what I think I'm seeing?"

"If you're referring to about a million people, you are, sir."

"Where did they come from?"

"Don't know, Mr. President, but they're certainly headed our way."

There was little more to add and the conversation ended a couple of minutes later. Quinn was staring at the same batch of photographs that had been dropped on President Baldwin's desk. Aaron Stark had delivered them personally to Quinn about two hours ago. The photographs were taken an hour earlier on a routine reconnaissance sweep over the new land bridge that had erupted along the southern edge of the Bering Sea. There was nothing routine about what the photographs showed, however.

The barren, rocky curve of land that had been pushed up out of the sea during the recent violent outbreak of earthquakes might be barren but it was no longer bare.

The photographs showed a huge column of people marching across it, stretching for several hundred miles already. Some of the photographs showed a vast number of people massed on the Siberian side, evidently waiting their turn to start the crossing. There must be a million people all told, Quinn guessed.

Quinn's own reaction upon seeing the photographs for the first time had mirrored that of President Baldwin.

Where had they all come from?

He looked up, saw Race and Aaron approaching his office. He

motioned them inside. As he pointed at the photographs, his expression bordered on bewilderment.

"The President just asked me where all those people came from. I didn't know what to tell him."

Race shook his head. "Me neither. I didn't think that many people lived in Siberia—"

"They don't," Aaron grunted. "At least, they didn't. These people must have—well, let's face it, I don't know either."

"Of immediate concern, of course," Race said, "is what are we going to do about them? I have an uneasy feeling those pilgrims aren't planning on homesteading in Alaska."

Aaron Stark opened his own file of photographs, studying them with a puzzled frown.

"These people are moving fast. Photographs didn't even show them a few days ago."

"Photographs didn't show much of anything, remember." Race said. "Heavy clouds have covered that region every day since the land bridge popped out of the ocean."

"It's not a rag-tag column," Aaron muttered, almost thinking to himself. "It looks organized and controlled. I don't think it's military, but you can see people out on point. No uniforms or weapons that I can make out—but these pictures were taken from thirty thousand feet. The pilot wasn't sure what he'd stumbled onto, so he stayed up out of sight."

"Do you have any suggestions?" Quinn asked.

"Move troops into Washington State immediately. If those Siberians are planning on entering the lower Forty-eight—and I agree with Race, that's the only logical conclusion—we'll need to stop them before they flood down unchecked. Best place would be in Canada, just north of Vancouver. Mountains form a natural bottle-neck there. I think the Canadians will cooperate—they'll be more nervous than we are when they see these photos."

"What about intercepting them in Alaska?" Quinn asked.

"Alaska is pretty well torn up," Aaron said doubtfully. "No way to move in by land—all the cross-country highways are gone. Still no airports in operation capable of handling military transports."

"I'm thinking of just a small group," Quinn said. "Make contact and get an idea of what these people have in mind."

"That could be done," Aaron agreed. "We can put our people into Anchorage by a small jet, and ferry in a large helicopter from Seattle. The ocean is calm enough now to set up refueling relays. We airlift our group to meet the Siberians in the Aleutians."

"I don't think it should be Aaron's people," Race interjected. "A military delegation will undoubtedly alarm them. Let's use civilians. An appropriate response can be initiated after we know what to expect."

Quinn and Aaron were both nodding agreement.

"I'm thinking a deputy secretary from State, and a couple of our NECCO people," Quinn said. "And I have this clear vision of you being in charge, Race—"

When the small group of civilians left for the Aleutians, one more person was added. Austin Wells was one of the prominent leaders of the Mormon church in New Jerusalem and had been heavily involved in putting the Phoenix Plan together. He was included after President Baldwin received a special request from Mormon authorities. It seemed the church had an unusual interest in this huge influx of people from Siberia, or wherever they were coming from.

Four days passed before Quinn was notified that Race Courtney wanted to talk to him by satellite relay. He went into his office and shut the door.

"Quinn Adams here—"

"Tell Stacy I won't be home for dinner will you, buddy—"

"Cut the clowning, you idiot. Where are you—?"

"In a very cold and wet place. I think they call it the Aleutians."

"Have you met with the Siberians yet—?"

"Spent several hours with them this morning—that's afternoon to you, of course. The top man is called Abraham. Take twenty years off Fidel Castro, keep the beard, and you've got Abraham. I think the others were speaking some dialect of Russian, but our man couldn't figure it out. Fortunately, Abraham speaks English fluently."

"And—"

"Nice person. Strange—but no Ghengis Khan."

"They're peaceful—?"

"Wouldn't go quite that far. Let's say they're determined."

"Do I have to drag this out of you—?"

"Actually, I'm just putting my notes in order. I'm ready to report now, sir."

"Please do."

"First off," Race began, "I'm still not sure where they came from. They kept telling us Siberia, then pointing off somewhere in the north and mentioning some other place. None of us could get the name, and they didn't spell it. Whatever it was, and wherever it is, no one in our group has ever heard of it."

"What are their intentions?" Quinn asked.

"Seems they heard the good old United States was wiped out in the quakes. Don't ask me where it came from—a nasty rumor put out by the Russian military, I suspect. An America in ruin still sounded better to them than Siberia in any condition, When God provided a highway especially for them—Abraham's words, not mine—they took off. Quite an act of faith, actually. Abraham said they had no idea if God had finished the project all the way to America. They were very relieved to learn they wouldn't have to swim part of the way."

"How many people are in this exodus?"

"Abraham didn't know. I don't think anybody does."

"Why not?"

"These people, wherever they come from, apparently are from different tribes. Seems like they keep in close contact, but each tribe rules itself."

"How many tribes are there?"

"This might sound funny, but I swear it's what Abraham said. There are ten of them, buddy."

Quinn stared at the phone.

"Ten tribes—?"

"Sounds familiar, doesn't it. Especially coming out of the north. I swear I read about that someplace—"

"I'll let you tell the President."

"Anyway," Race continued, "the meeting went well. They were nervous that we were going to order them to turn around. Trust me, buddy, after meeting with them I can firmly tell you that is not an option."

"How did they react when you told them the United States is alive and well—sort of."

"So much the better, as far as they're concerned. They seem anxious to be good neighbors. The subject of hot dogs and hamburgers came up."

"So we're getting a million new immigrants, like it or not—"

"No doubt in my mind. We either accept them, or kill them. If we choose the latter, I get the feeling they're determined to take a lot of us with them."

"Overall impression, Race—can we make this work peacefully?"

"Convinced of it. These people are just looking for a better life and they think we're it. They don't want trouble. I suggest you start thinking about a place for our ten tribes to settle down."

"Can't recall if we have a housing development big enough for a million people—"

"Well, be sure and order a lot of hot dogs. We're scheduled to meet again this evening. I'll report back tomorrow. Got to go, buddy—I think I'm frozen in place."

\* \* \*

There were some minor clashes as the Siberians passed through Alaska, some of the fiercely independent local citizens determined to protect families and communities from what they clearly perceived was an invasion by foreigners—Russians, and that made it worse. The fighting was sporadic, and the Siberians did everything they could to show peaceful intentions. In most cases, clashes stopped when it was discovered that the Siberians apparently were a very wealthy people, and eager to pay for food and inconvenience. Besides, most of the Alaskans were weary of struggling, still devastated by the quakes that had seen the bridge from Siberia come into being.

The same thing happened in Canada as the Siberians passed through, but once again, the offer to pay well for their passage changed most defenders into greeters.

After lengthy discussions with the Siberian leaders, U.S. officials decided there was no need to send troops to meet them. Instead, NECCO set up a series of processing centers in Washington State to get as much information as possible on each individual, and give them medical checkups. In general, the immigrants were found to be in amazingly good health. Most were strong and in good physical shape, even the elderly. Doctors attributed a lot of that to simple diets, hard work, and living in what apparently was a very cold and severe environment. Processing that many people took a long time, but there were no signs of impatience on the part of the Siberians.

Race was correct in his first report about the tribal system of government. Each tribe was provided its own group of processing centers. When registration was completed, the immigrants were shuttled to McChord Air Force Base just south of Seattle, where they boarded military transports and were flown to their assigned areas.

All of the Siberians were settled in Iowa and eastern Illinois. New factories and power plants were established to produce materials needed for the massive building projects that sprang up in country that was either sparsely settled previously, or had suffered extreme damage during the invasion of the Latin forces. It was amazing how fast the immigrants learned new skills, and how quickly that part of the country was given new life.

The Siberians had a governing council, with each of the ten tribes represented according to the number of people in the tribe, very similar to the way the size of the House of Representatives was decided in the United States. Abrahim was council chairman, and obviously highly respected by the other members.

In the months that followed, the Siberians formed a warm friendship with the Mormon church. Huge numbers of Mormon missionaries were sent into Siberian communities in Iowa and Illinois, and it was evident the two groups found much in common, if not in beliefs, at least in understanding of events long past.

No one was surprised when DNA tests proved beyond doubt that the Siberians were definitely connected, however long ago, to the people of Israel. Skeptics abounded, but as far as the Mormons were concerned, the lost Ten Tribes were no longer lost. It was hard to dispute that conclusion.

Officials in New Washington were delighted at the way the immigrants were being helped to integrate into their new world in America. These newcomers, though coming from a world that apparently had little connection with modern times and technology, proved gifted and adaptable. The most startling change could be seen in the young Siberians. A new generation of American teenagers emerged, fortunately incorporating the best of the old and the new. It was almost pleasant to be around them.

Things were not going well in the rest of the world, however. The destruction caused by the recent Chinese gambit for world domination, the savagery of the Russian campaigns, and now this most recent devastation left by the worldwide upheaval of the earth's crust, and the deadly natural phenomena that followed, all combined to tear the fabrics of society into shreds.

President Baldwin helicoptered into NECCO headquarters this afternoon, a thick file of papers in his briefcase, a deep frown on his face. He was sitting now in a conference room with Anne Ashford, Aaron Stark, Race, Quinn and Joanna. Everyone in the room knew what was causing that furrowed brow.

"Somebody tell me the world hasn't gone to hell."

Baldwin looked around the table. There was no response.

"Then somebody tell me what we can do about it."

Quinn leaned forward, clasping his hands on the table as he peered down at the president.

"Hard to know which priority is the highest, Mr. President," he said quietly. "Politically, every country in the world, with the exception of ourselves and Israel, is in shambles. China and Russia still have a pretty tight grip, but hardly any other government is now able to control events within their own borders."

"Is it possible to prop any of them up—help them regain control?" Baldwin asked.

Quinn shook his head, a weary expression on his face. "We've examined every option, sir. My own opinion—it can't be done. Things are too far gone."

It didn't seem possible, but the frown on Baldwin's face deepened.

"I find it difficult to accept such a pessimistic outlook—"

"I find it difficult to express it, sir."

Baldwin glared around the table, fastening on Aaron Stark.

"General, you've always found solutions to impossible situations. What are your feelings—can we get this crazy world back to anywhere near normal?"

"This lastest round of natural disasters was too much, Mr. President. Governments were shaky before, but they're ripped apart now. The sad truth is, Mr. President, we don't have a civilized world any more."

Baldwin scrubbed both hands through his hair, staring down unseeingly at the papers spread out in front of him.

"Can we do anything militarily?" he asked, again looking at Stark. "If we went in and took over some of those countries, if we were able to restore some kind of order—"

Stark was shaking his head. "Won't work, sir. Not without supply lines and support facilities—and none of those are left. Besides, we wouldn't be welcome, sir—not anywhere."

Joanna spoke up. "The situation in most of those countries, Mr. President," she said, her voice low, "is beyond repair. That's difficult for any of us to accept, sir, but it's reality. Europe and most of Asia is little more than a collection of feudal states, controlled by whoever is the most ruthless and unprincipled. The Arab countries are less affected only because they have lived for centuries in a system controlled by royal families and dictators—just another form of feudalism."

Anne Ashford was staring thoughtfully. "You're saying that even if it were possible to help some of these people, there's no one in authority to deal with."

"That's correct, Anne. No one reliable, at least. We can't expect that situation to change in the near future. There is even the frightening possibility it will never change."

Baldwin was struggling against the hopelessness of what he was hearing.

"The Israelis aren't in this situation—"

"Israel has a lot of problems, sir," Joanna answered, "but they escaped most of the recent natural disasters—as did most of the Arab countries. Not many crustal fault lines in that part of the world."

The president drew in a deep breath, shaking his head in frustration.

"So much upheaval. So many dead. So much chaos—"

"It may not sound right, Mr. President, particularly to anyone from California," Race muttered, "but I can't help feeling grateful this country came through it as well as we have, sir."

"I'm grateful too, Race," Baldwin sighed, "but it doesn't make anything sit better."

"I'm leaving for Israel in the morning, Mr. President," Joanna said. "There are indications the Israelis are facing serious trouble in the near future. They want informal talks before sending an official delegation to New Washington."

"Don't like the sound of that, Joanna—"

"I don't think any of us will, Mr. President."

Sam Baldwin left to return to the White House, accompanied by Anne Ashford. There was a huge list of domestic problems that needed attention, along with trying to find some solution to the chaos raging throughout the world.

After the President left, the others started to get up from the table but Quinn motioned them to sit down again.

"I didn't think there was a need to burden the President with this, but I'd like you all to stay. Austin Wells is waiting to meet with us, and he's brought Abraham with him. I understand they have a special request to make."

He pushed a button under the table and a few minutes later, Austin Wells and Abraham were shown into the conference room. All eyes fastened on the imposing figure of the Siberian leader.

Abraham was about six feet tall, sturdily built, looked lean and healthy. He was dressed plainly in a black suit. Instead of the traditional white shirt and tie, he wore a white silk shirt with no collar, fastened at the throat by two black buttons. There was no tie. He looked surprisingly stylish, although he gave the definite impression he was not attempting to look anything but comfortable and relaxed. His face was covered by a bushy, neatly trimmed beard, the cheeks above it looking tanned and weathered. It was difficult to tell how old the man was, but the beard and his hair were graying. He was probably somewhere in his fifties, although he projected the vitality of a man younger than that. He went around the table, exchanging handshakes with each person in the room.

Austin Wells was well known to all of them, had worked closely with them during the years of putting the Phoenix Plan together, the subsequent massive exodus out of the Federal Zone here to Missouri, and the planning of the twin cities. The two new arrivals sat down and everyone looked expectantly at them.

"Whenever you're ready, Austin—" Quinn told him.

Austin looked very much the dignified church leader that he was, also dressed in a black suit, but unlike Abrahim, wearing a white shirt and subdued tie. He was tall, probably two or three inches over six feet, and thin. Austin was probably in his early sixties. He spared a quick smile at his nephew, Race, then fastened his attention on the rest of them.

"Abrahim has asked me to present his request, but will answer any questions you may have," Wells began. "It is really very simple. He is asking that he be allowed to visit Israel, and would like me to accompany him. Race mentioned that planes are flying between the two countries fairly frequently, so we are asking to hitch a ride, whenever that is convenient."

"Your timing is excellent, Austin," Joanna smiled. "I'm leaving for Israel in the morning." She looked at Quinn. "What do you think, Quinn. Any problems with this—?"

"Are you planning on making this an official visit, Austin?" Quinn asked. "The Israeli agenda is very crowded these days—"

Austin quickly shook his head. "We have talked so much about Israel, that Abrahim is anxious to see this land of his forefathers. A short courtesy meeting with an Israeli official, perhaps, but nothing official. Our own people will provide transportation and shelter while we're there."

Quinn looked at the Siberian.

"Your request is understandable, Abrahim, and I see no problem with you and Austin going along with Joanna tomorrow. Does that meet with your schedule?"

Abrahim smiled back, white teeth showing between the beard.

"I am most grateful, Mr. Adams." His accent was thick, but the words very clear. "As you know, my people share a blood connection with these modern Israelis. I am very anxious to visit them, and walk the streets of Jerusalem."

Joanna was frowning. "I should warn you that there is no set time to return. This visit could last a few days, or it could be a couple of weeks."

Abrahim nodded respectfully. "I shall appreciate every moment there, Mrs. Adams."

# 41

## CLOUDS OF WAR

Joanna was sitting out on the patio of her brother's home in Tel Aviv. She and Sophia were sipping iced lemonade, waiting for Dovid to arrive. The sun was warm, birds were twittering in nearby trees, and the sky was cloudless. It would have been very peaceful if not for the churning going on inside Joanna. Sophia had told her nothing about the reason for this sudden summons back to Israel, but that spoke volumes. She and Sophie were too close, knew each other too well, for Joanna not to recognize that her friend was deliberately reminiscing about trivial things in order to avoid more important subjects.

"You know I'm babbling, of course," Sophie murmured. "Dovid asked me to say nothing until he gets here—which hopefully will be any moment now. He had a meeting in the Knesset—" She looked over at Joanna. "Did you know your brother became Prime Minister of Israel yesterday?"

Joanna's eyes widened. "Dovid—? That's a shocker."

"He probably wanted to tell you himself, but I can't sit here any longer and pretend we just invited you over for dinner. Too much is happening—"

"What will this do to your life?" Joanna asked. "You planning on being the politician's dutiful wife—?"

"No thanks. I'd go crazy. I'm staying with the company. One of us has to keep in touch with reality—that's something the politicians have a hard time doing. They act like everything is a simple game of chess. The objective, of course, is never to become a pawn."

"My brother—Prime Minister," Joanna mused. "Never thought I'd see this day."

"He'll do a good job, of course—he's good at everything he does. He didn't expect it, and he certainly didn't want it. This is not a good time to be Prime Minister of Israel."

Dovid came walking out onto the patio. He saw the expresson on his sister's face and looked accusingly at his wife.

"Couldn't wait, could you." He leaned over and gave Sophia a kiss on the mouth. He turned, planting a friendly kiss on his sister's forehead. "Appreciate you coming on such short notice, Joanna. How much has my wife told you—?"

"Only that my brother has shed his skin. From Mossad agent to politician—"

"You make it sound like getting leprosy."

"There was a time you agreed with that assessment."

"That was then. I'm far from comfortable with it, but I don't have much choice. Besides, don't forget our father was once Prime Minister too—"

"I also can't forget that's why we both decided to go into the Mossad."

Sophia poured him a glass of lemonade. He sat down and took a long drink, leaning his head back and closing his eyes.

"You want to go inside—?" Sophia asked.

Dovid's study was soundproofed. Not even electronics could probe inside it. He thought for a moment, then shook his head.

"We're not talking state secrets. Joanna is likely the only person in Israel who doesn't know already."

"Know what—?"

"We've become a target again. A coalition is planning to remove Israel from the face of the earth."

"That's been tried before," Joanna muttered.

"This time it's not just Arabs. It just might succeed."

She was frowning at him, trying to read his face. "Never seen you so down before. This must be serious—"

"I wouldn't drag you over here if it wasn't. Our country's existence has never been more threatened, Joanna."

"Tell me about it—"

"We have solid intel. It's basically the old Operation Desert Sword the Chinese came up with a few years ago. That faded away when the Chinese went back behind the bamboo curtain, but someone has dusted off the cobwebs and put it back into operation."

"Do we know who's involved—?"

"The Arabs finally got together. I'm sure all the havoc caused by those earthquakes is behind the timing. The whole world's in a mess and they believe the United States is too concerned with its own wounds to care much about what happens in this part of the world."

"That's not true—"

"We know that," Dovid shrugged, "but they don't."

"Who are we dealing with besides the Arabs?"

"The coalition is loose, but large. We've pinpointed thirteen countries—I'm sure more will come out of the closet when the attack starts. Arabs. Muslims. Africans. Anybody who despises the Jews. Everybody who hates the Great Satan—destroying Israel is one way, they believe, to humiliate America."

"But no direct assault on the United States—"

"No military attack. The plan calls for an all-out terrorist campaign, however. I got the impression it's designed principally to keep the U.S. occupied—keep them from interfering in Israel. No specific targets listed, but we can probably get them."

"Terrorist attacks—that's going to make President Baldwin very happy."

"Might as well accept the fact you can't stop all of them."

"Any Chinese involvement behind the scenes?"

"Apparently not, neither directly nor indirectly. That's not saying they won't jump in once it starts."

"How imminent is the danger?" Joanna asked.

"We have a copy of the Arab battle plan. They plan on a four-month build-up, then another month of camouflaged massing along our borders—they must think we're pretty stupid not to detect that. Then a simultaneous drive into Israel from all directions."

"Do you expect nuclear attack—?"

"Absolutely. Nuclear and biological missiles. Anti-personnel field neutrons. It's going to be real ugly, Joanna. We know it's coming—we just don't know how to stop it."

"Where are they getting these nuclear missiles?"

"China. Russia. Those two are probably hoping both sides will wipe each other out. They'd probably sell us warheads if we offered enough cash. The biological stuff is stockpiled mostly in Iraq and Libya. Our Sayeret Matkal units are planning to substantially reduce that inventory in the very near future."

The Matkal were elite, highly secret commando attack units that were feared and respected in every country that knew about them.

"Certainly sounds like the old Operation Desert Sword. Any chance the Arabs might speed up the timeline?"

"It could happen, of course. The best thing we have working for us is the disruption of central control and the power squabbles going on in most of the non-Arab countries involved. That could slow things down considerably. I seriously doubt their timetable can be accelerated."

"Is there an estimate of numbers?"

"No way of knowing, but I suspect it will be a million at least. Most of these people are starving in their own countries. Joining the army to get food and clothing is an incentive, but that won't be the motivation for most of them. They will finally get to fight their Jihad—the holy war against the hated Jews."

"Jihad includes the Christians too, as I recall. If they succeed in wiping out Israel, they won't stop. Christian countries will be next." Joanna shook her head, feeling a wave of dark premonition. "This is bad news, Dovid."

"Make sure President Baldwin understands that."

"What does the Knesset want the United States to do?"

"We need to talk about that. Our requests must be presented in just the right way. You'll always be an Israeli in your heart, Joanna, but you now understand how the Americans think. I need your advice—"

A light suddenly clicked on in Joanna's mind.

"You want the exodus put back on the burner—"

Her brother nodded. "That's our first request. Let all the Americans of Jewish heritage come back to their motherland—as soon as possible. We're asking the same terms President Baldwin agreed to before—a voluntary repatriation."

"Do you want only those who can fight—?"

"No—everyone. We want all of our people to come home."

"America is their home—"

"Israel is in the heart of every Jew. If it's not, they don't belong here. It must be stressed, Joanna, that we are not asking to abridge anyone's constitutional freedoms. But if a person decides by their own free will to come to Israel, we ask that the government provides visas and a clear channel for emigration. We can use assistance in transporting them here, but if that's a problem, we'll find a way."

"You want me to present this request to President Baldwin—?"

"I'll come over to do that in person. Of course, having you and Quinn with me would be nice."

She was studying him. "You said this was your first request. What else do you have in mind?"

"Two more items."

"And they are—?"

"Have the United States send us all the military equipment they can. Missiles. Weapons. Tanks. Trucks. Planes. Field hospitals. Medical supplies. Shells. Ammunitions. Everything to fight this war."

"You know all that is in short supply—"

"We'll take all that can be spared."

"And the third request—?" she queried.

"The Siberian leader Abraham who came with you—"

Her eyes widened again. "Are you thinking what I think you're thinking—?"

"The Ten Tribes, Joanna—they belong here. This is their homeland, not the United States."

"You don't have room for them—"

"We'll make room. We'll take room—a little more provocation, but what does it matter? The Arabs are going to fight us anyway."

"I have no idea how Abraham will react—"

"I do," Dovid told her. "That's why I was late. I met with him and Austin Wells right after the three of you arrived. We set up the meeting through the Mormons in Jerusalem as soon as we heard Abraham was coming."

Joanna gave him a quizzical glance. "Weren't you just sworn in yesterday—?"

"It's been a busy couple of days," her brother grinned.

"What was Abraham's reaction?"

"He said he couldn't speak for the entire council, but he felt sure the tribes would agree to it."

Joanna was shaking her head in disbelief.

"That's a million new Israelis—not counting the American Jews. You'll need more than a little extra real estate, brother—you'll need a whole new country."

"The Knesset will decide on where that expansion will occur," Dovid said, "probably by the end of the week."

\* \* \*

The senior NECCO officials were sitting in the presidential office. It had been decided that the image of the old Oval Office in the destroyed White House in Washington, D.C., was in need of repair and a larger, grander office was built in the New Washington residence. Next to the Grand Ballroom, it was the most elegant place in the building. Sam Baldwin felt uncomfortable in it, but he had seen the impression it made on foreign dignitaries and accepted the wisdom of the change.

There was a conference table at one end of the office, the highly polished mahogany top, with its circle of authentic eighteenth century upholstered chairs, blending well with the luxury and atmosphere of the other colonial furnishings. The table was large enough to accommodate ten people, although there were only six seated around it for this meeting. President Sam Baldwin. Vice President Anne Ashford. Quinn and Joanna Adams. Race Courtney. Aaron Stark.

Joanna finished her report on the situation in Israel, and had just presented the essence of the three requests the Israelis planned to make.

Baldwin sat back and clasped his hands behind his head, staring thoughtfully up at the crystal chandelier above the table. He wasn't counting crystals. He was trying to sort it all out in his mind. Finally he brought his arms down and leaned them on the table, looking questioningly at Aaron Stark.

"What about it, Aaron—can we send them all that military hardware? I suppose the real question is, do we have it to spare—?"

"The answer is yes, and no," Aaron replied. "Yes, we have to send them everything we can. The Israelis are fighters, but they'll need all the support in the way of materiel that we can supply. And no, we don't have much to spare. There's been little arms production this last couple of years, but we can change priorities and gear up quickly. Looks like we have no choice in that. Joanna is right—if those Muslims destroy Israel, they'll have an appetite for the rest of the world."

Baldwin switched his attention to Joanna.

"You presented the case for voluntary repatriation impressively, Joanna."

Joanna felt a little uncomfortable with that.

"I really wasn't attempting to make a case for or against it, Mr. President," she responded. "I was simply trying to explain why the Israelis plan to make that request."

Baldwin waved a hand in dismissal. "I know that, Joanna. I went through all this before with your brother. I felt it was the right thing to do then, and I feel the same way now. Quinn, I suppose it's still going to hurt to lose all that brains and brilliance—"

"It will, Mr. President," Quinn said, "but there's a lot less pressure now than when we were trapped in the Federal Zone. I don't think it will cause any problems we can't deal with."

"That brings us to the final request—and that blows my mind," Baldwin said, shaking his head in wonderment. "Your brother has brass—well, you know what I mean, ladies. Bring back the Ten Tribes to Israel—

all one million of them. It's about the most audacious thing I've heard—and I have to admit, the most logical. Dovid Shazebak is right—those people belong in Israel, not Iowa."

"I talked to Abraham about it on the flight back," Joanna said. "He feels all the tribal leaders will be as anxious to go as he is. Abrahim looks on this whole thing as being in the hands of God."

"Problem is," Baldwin muttered, "I'm not sure how many planes God has at his disposal. Getting these people to Israel appears to be a military operation, Aaron—not discounting divine power, of course."

"Combine the Siberians with the millions of our own people repatriating," Stark said quietly, "and we'll need all the divine help we can get."

Baldwin drew in a deep breath and looked around the table.

"Seems like we all agree that granting the Israeli requests is the thing to do."

"We don't have another option, Mr. President," Anne Ashford murmured. She had said little during the meeting, bowing to the experience of the others.

"I'd like you to take administrative point on this, Anne. NECCO will be doing most of the hard work, but there undoubtedly will be those who want to storm the White House. Just haven't got time to play their silly games."

"Happy to do that, Mr. President."

The President started shaking his head.

"Looks like it's chopping block time. The politicians will want Congressional approval. The lawyers will want to clear it through the courts. The committee chairmen in both houses will be drooling to hold hearings. There should be no more than three or four thousand lawsuits filed. The Immigration Service will cry rape. And somebody is going to want to know how it will affect the environment. If we're really lucky, this just might make the Supreme Court calendar two years from now."

"There's no time for any of that," Joanna gasped. She raised her hands in apology. "Sorry, Mr. President—everything you say is painfully true."

"So I'll push it through today by Executive Order." Baldwin grunted. "Anne, draw up the papers, will you. Race, set up a national broadcast as soon as you can. Quinn, your workload just exploded. Aaron, you have a logistical nightmare to solve. Joanna, tell your brother he doesn't need to come to New Washington. You did his work for him."

Joanna gave a wry smile. "I think he was planning on that—"

The President spoke to the nation the next morning. By noon, hundreds of thousands of people of Jewish heritage were already standing in line in front of registration centers. The next day, the volunteers numbered over a million.

In three days, the system was hopelessly clogged. From that point, no one was required to register, or even get a visa. They just signed their name and got in line at one of the designated airports.

Both the United States and the Israelis shuttled huge transports back and forth to Tel Aviv twenty-four hours a day. That went on for two weeks, until the last line of emigrants was boarded and delivered to Israel. An accurate count was never tallied, but it was estimated that between four and five million American Jews, along with the Siberians, went to defend their Zion.

It was a magnificent gesture of faith and sacrifice. It created a bond between the two countries that far exceeded the ties and sympathies existing since the birth of modern Israel.

# 42

## COUNTER ATTACKS

Israel launched lightning attacks on surprised neighbors even while its new citizens were pouring into the country. The Sinai was quickly overrun. It changed hands in a matter of hours.

The Palestinians paid for decades of defiance as they were crushed by tanks and a ruthless wave of Israeli soldiers. There were no longer any political niceties to be observed, and no hesitation in delivering deadly retribution.

Lebanon and Syria were not prepared for the suddenness, nor the ferocity, of the assaults launched against them. There was stiffer resistance in Jordan but it too was drowned in a staggering blood bath. Uneasy alliances and tenuous friendships of the past were erased when countries signed on to be a part of Operation Desert Sword.

There was no thought of mercy on either side. Victory would go to those who killed the most of their enemy, and everyone knew it.

In three days, Israel extended its borders tenfold.

Of the more than four million American Jews who migrated to Israel in those frantic, war-torn days, over three quarters of a million were mustered directly into the Israeli armed forces. Men, women and youth underwent intense physical fitness programs, along with crash courses in hand-to-hand killing. Those who had previous combat experience in the American military establishment became instructors for others who must soon go through the fire.

As these new citizens were training, the crack Israeli forces were cutting a bloody swathe through their Arab enemies. Almost as soon as an Arab community was overrun, it was leveled by explosives and bulldozers.

In a matter of hours, construction crews moved in to build a new Jewish community, or established a new Kibbutz.

It was a bitter victory, won at high cost, but still a victory. Unfortunately, everyone knew it was only a prelude to dark days ahead. The surprise thrusts into enemy territory had been successful, but no one doubted the real war was yet to be engaged.

With all the new arrivals, there were serious shortages. Tens of thousands lived in tent cities. There were shortages of food and just about everything else. Military hardware was the one exception as it flowed in an endless stream from the United States. With every ship and plane that brought the tanks and armaments and supplies, Israel's hopes grew that it might somehow survive.

Discovery that the Israeli's were fully aware of their impending attack came as a bitter jolt to the Arab states and their coalition partners. It should have been expected, of course, but national pride would not allow such thoughts. The massive action taken by the United States was another blow. With the element of surprise gone, and vast sections of Arab territory already seized by the Israelis, there was much to reconsider. The timetable was moved back so an assessment of the new situation could be made.

How deeply did the Americans intend to become involved?

Would they follow up the flood of armaments with troops and other military forces? The bombardments of missiles launched from American ships and planes in the Persian Gulf and later in Yugoslavia were burned into the consciousness of every Arab commander.

Was it possible the coalition would now face the full might and fury of the Great Satan?

The Arabs and their partners needed time to ponder these possibilities very carefully. A ring of cats surrounding a mouse was one thing; having an angry tiger biting into your flanks was another.

The Israelis took full advantage of their new strength and the disorganized retreat of their enemies. Air and ground attacks were stepped up against known concentrations of enemy troops and supplies, especially those identified close to Israel's borders. Fuel and ammunition dumps that could not be safely confiscated and transferred, were destroyed.

Skirmishes between Arabs and Israelis had been going on for years, stepped up during the period it was thought China was intending to throw its support behind the Islamic countries. Clashes and killing were nothing new to either side but now it was the Israelis turn to be the aggressor. The Israeli military machine thrust deep into Arab domain, leaving few survivors.

The unexpected ferocity of the Israeli raids dealt severe blows to the enemy. Every time Amman intelligence pinpointed a hidden supply depot, destruction followed. The losses in men and equipment could be ill afforded by the coalition, already plagued with shattered production facilities and broken supply lines. The Arabs were not prepared for such full-scale aggression.

Dovid Shazebak found himself in meetings with Israeli leaders discussing the possibility of keeping the country's war machine rolling through its enemies, crushing everything in its path until there were no more unfriendly neighbors. There was strong support for such a course, but those with clear heads knew that was not what the Star of David was all about.

\* \* \*

Race Courtney dozed fitfully on the plane, a parade of jumbled impressions disturbing the sleep he desperately needed. Across the aisle from him, General Frank Kantros' head was back against the seat, his mouth slightly open. Frank was so exhausted he could have slept anywhere. They were the only two passengers.

The NECCO twin-engine jet was en route from New Washington to Hill Air Force Base in the old Federal Zone. Those first months of the invasion by the combined forces of the South American countries, when the Zone was established, left vivid memories for Race and everyone else involved in the fierce struggle to keep the flag of the United States flying.

A wispy vision of his wife Stacy reaching up to kiss him goodbye drifted through Race's thoughts. She always looked so alive, so bubbly, so genuinely caring about him. They had lived through troubled times but she had always given him strength.

Then he felt his daughter's arms around his neck. A picture of her floated into focus. Leah was almost ten now, a lovable girl who had inherited her mother's outgoing personality. A separate little thought flashed through his mind: he must remember to get Leah a really special present for her tenth birthday.

Suddenly the three of them were strolling through the grounds of the new temple square in New Jerusalem. Stacy was clinging to his arm, Leah was skipping ahead, staring at statues of pioneers and admiring the huge stretches of flowers. It brought a sense of peace. Even in his restless sleep Race felt a tingling inside him, a stretching out into a sky that had no end.

But then dark memories crowded in.

Shootings. Violence. Death. They all collided together, nothing separating into coherency. That was good. He didn't want to see any of that again, his mind told him.

He was back in the meeting he had just left at NECCO headquarters. The President was there, and Anne Ashford. Aaron. Frank. Quinn and Joanna. The screen that took up most of the far wall was flashing with death again. It showed Israeli tanks blasting an Arab village into extinction. In the floating imagery of his mind, he could clearly again hear the voices of the people in the room.

"The Israelis are showing no mercy," Baldwin was muttering, awed by the savagery of what he had just watched. "Can't blame them, of course. If they leave anyone alive, they'll only have to kill them the next time. The genie is sure out of the bottle."

Anne Ashford was glancing at Joanna, who looked pale and grim.

"It must be awful for you to see this," Anne murmured. "This war is so terribly brutal."

"I have to confess," Joanna answered quietly, "it's better to see my people kill than be killed."

"All wars are brutal," he could hear Aaron Stark say, "especially when you're watching through telephoto lenses. No way to escape the ugliness."

No way to escape the ugliness.

Those words reverberated in Race's mind.

There must be some way. How much ugliness could a person see in a lifetime.

Now frightening pictures paraded through in his mind. The litter and bodies left by terrorist explosions. Senseless targets. Hospitals. Schools. Shopping malls. Not one of them a military target. Not one government building. Just innocent civilians. Men, women and children who had no reason to die. His mind became clouded with anger.

Out of the haze came the message from Nia Yao Gui, requesting he come immediately to the Federal Zone. Arab terrorists. A major nest located in California. He could still hear the alarm in his own voice.

"Don't bomb...must take alive...interrogate—"

And the urgency in Yao Gui's voice.

"You must get here quickly...must get here quickly...get here quickly—"

A hand shook him gently awake.

"We're here, sir."

Across the aisle, Frank Kantros was peering out of the small window. It was dark outside, showing only glimpses of runway lights as the plane taxied.

"That was quick," Kantros yawned. "Must have fallen asleep."

Yao Gui was waiting anxiously as they entered the terminal. The three of them went directly to small office in the rear. Yao Gui picked up some photographs from the desk.

"Heat sensor. We count about seventy-five in the camp."

Race and Frank Kantros studied the blurred images.

"You're sure these people are terrorists, Yao Gui?" Race asked. "It's not some camp of survivors from the quakes?"

"I was there two days ago," Yao Gui told them. "They're Arabs. And there's no doubt it's a killing nest. It seems to be a major staging area. Probably bringing terrorists in by ship somewhere between San Diego and Los Angeles. I guess they figure no one is paying much attention to California these days."

"What about our people?" Kantros asked. "Are you in contact with them?"

"Yes, sir," Yao Gui said. He pointed to a radio mike on the desk. "Colonel Charning, the commanding officer, is standing by for your instructions, General. Three hundred commandos are in place, as you ordered." He gave an apologetic shrug. "Sorry to have sounded so urgent about all this, but three teams of terrorists already left the camp in the last two days. We managed to take out all three, once they got far enough away from the main camp. However, I'm sure their superiors will be expecting them to check in. When they don't—well, none of us want those happy little campers to get alarmed and fold up their tents, do we."

Kantros looked at Race Courtney, got a brief nod of approval. He picked up the mike, clicked it several times.

"This is Colonel Charning," a voice said over a speaker.

"This is General Kantros. Attack, Colonel."

"A pleasure, sir."

"But remember," Race added quickly, "we want survivors—as many as possible. Maybe we can find out how many of these animals have slipped into the country."

"Did you hear that, Colonel?" Kantros asked.

"I did, sir. We'll do what we can, but these guys usually prefer meeting Allah to being interrogated."

"Keep as many alive as you can, but don't put one of your men at risk doing it. Happy hunting, Colonel."

"Can you get us to Bakersfield?" Race asked Yao Gui.

"The jet that brought you is being fueled. Should be ready for takeoff any minute now," the agent answered. "There's a small field on the outskirts of Bakersfield. The commandos will have it secured before we get there."

"How long to secure the camp?"

"Colonel Charning expects no longer than thirty minutes."

Race nodded in satisfaction. "Let's get airborne—"

Three hours later, Race, Yao Gui, Frank Kantros and Colonel Charning sat in a large tent behind a rickety fold-up table. The raid had been one hundred percent effective, with not one terrorist escaping the trap. Only five Arabs had been taken alive. Even under unusually brutal interrogation, not one uttered a word.

The four men behind the table were staring at each other, trying to decide what more could be done, when four commandos entered, carrying an Arab on a stretcher. The man was huddled on his side, wearing a blood-soaked tunic. His eyes were closed, his breathing raspy.

"Found this one hiding, sir," a sergeant reported to the military officers. "Think he did himself in." He tossed a long-bladed knife onto the table. "Took this out of his belly."

Alarm sounded in Race's head. He looked from the man on the stretcher to the Ranger sergeant.

"Did you search him, Sergeant?"

Before the commando could answer, the Arab raised up on one elbow, and gave a screeching yell of defiance. His eyes, now wide open, were almost bulging out of his head.

"Allaaah—"

Then the terrorist triggered the explosives wrapped around him under the bloody tunic.

Everyone within earshot of the man's cry died instantly.

It happened so fast, Race didn't have time to think of Stacy, or his daughter, before the darkness engulfed him.

# 43

## JIHAD

The Israeli army was told to halt its advance. Enough territory was gained, it was reasoned, and it was now prudent to turn to defensive measures.

The order proved to be a deadly mistake.

The abrupt end to the Israeli attacks provided an opportunity for the coalition states to regroup. Damage was assessed, battle plans were redrawn, attack forces repositioned.

Weeks passed with no fighting, but everyone knew it was coming.

Finally, war came in all its fury. The Islamic aggressors stole a secret from the Israelis and attacked the Jewish nation with unexpected fanaticism. The ferocity of the attacks, launched from all sides, spoke of grim determination that Jihad must prevail. The armies of the invading Islamic countries fought with a zeal matching the national pride and spirit the Israelis had shown. That was unexpected, something the Israelis had not seen in any previous encounter with the Arabs. The unified cohesion among Islamic states that for centuries had distrusted each other, gave them an advantage in this new, savage struggle. The Israelis were driven back before their onslaught.

The ground shook night and day from the heavy 'cruump' of shells. The artillery exchanges were so fierce it seemed shells must collide with each other in mid-air. Night skies were constantly lit by flame and explosions. The smell of cordite drifted through one valley into another, then another. The shouts and screams of men and women fighting and dying beat at the senses. The fury grew with each day, each flashing night.

Spaces between foes became close, often only a few scant yards apart along mountain ridges. There was no let-up, no rest. Every inch of ground was contested, the victor inevitably determined by which side had more blood to shed. This was the final test; it would not end until all was won, or all lost.

The Israeli forces were pressed relentlessly back. Exhausted soldiers glanced over their shoulders and saw the hills of Jerusalem coming ever closer.

That sight spurred them to fight with renewed fury. The old and feeble joined alongside the young, killing every enemy they could. It seemed to give most of them a renewed vigor that pushed aside infirmities. The wounded who no longer could move, found a place to keep killing until life ebbed away. The Israelis drew strength from each other. They became one person, feeling the same pain, the same desperation, the same resolve.

Amid the smoke and flames, lines of contact became almost indistinguishable, eddying through valleys veiled in the smoke of battle. It was difficult for those in command on either side to tell one army from the other. Those running and stumbling semi-concealed in the haze frequently faced a split second decision if an approaching shape was friend or foe, a decision on whether a shot was fired or a bayonet plunged into the shadowy body. Numbed senses had difficulty with such urgent reactions. As enemy hordes moved closer to the hills of Jerusalem, valor and death was decided the old-fashioned way. There was no space, no time, for modern battle strategies. It was warrior against warrior. One always died, one went on to challenge again.

\* \* \*

In the United States there was an agony of indecision. More satellites were launched to provide detailed reconnaissance of the battlefields, but the additional data received only caused the debates to rage hotter. Television screens showed heart-rending pictures of the fighting, coverage continuing twenty-four hours a day.

Many thought intervention must be avoided, even at the cost of losing Israel.

Many violently opposed that position, demanding immediate intervention.

Lights burned in Congressional committee rooms day and night, week after week. There were public displays of sympathy and public displays of angry opposition.

The nation had given enough, some said. There was no more to give.

The nation could never give enough, others said, not while the Israeli people fought to survive.

The only thing that really came of the debates and confrontations was the pushing of everyone into one camp or the other. There was no one left in the United States who did not have an opinion on what should be done about the war in Israel. And there was no one who did not watch the dreadful sights of death on their television screens.

The situation posed a dilemma for Sam Baldwin. He knew it must ultimately come down to a presidential decision. The tide of battle had definitely turned against the Israelis. The moment would come when the United States could no longer debate the issue, but must either intervene, or not intervene. Baldwin seriously doubted that any committee now holding hearings would come out with a recommendation. No one would want to stick out their neck, not until after the President had made the final decision.

Baldwin was in his office now, looking across his desk at the people seated gravely around him. Anne Ashford, sitting with arms folded, staring intently down at her shoes. Aaron Stark, appearing almost belligerent in his frowning concentration. Quinn, legs outstretched in front of him, looking too tired to draw them in. Joanna, looking worn and worried. Baldwin silently applauded his decision to exclude all Congressional and administration officials from this meeting.

The reactions he was seeing were bad enough without the bickering and squabbling the others would certainly have brought to the meeting.

"All right," Baldwin grunted, "someone say something. Aaron, you look like you're thinking pretty hard—you have any suggestions?"

"I don't understand what there is to debate," Aaron said. "We have a clear commitment to intervene, morally and legally. We have the military capability to intervene. The only thing we don't have is time."

Stark looked around the room, then back to the president.

"We must intervene, sir, and do it immediately."

Anne Ashford frowned. "We all feel the same way, Aaron, but we don't have a clear-cut legal mandate. A lot of people believe we have more than fulfilled our obligations already."

Baldwin interrupted impatiently. "We've all heard the arguments a thousand times. What I want now from each of you is a firm recommendation. No rationales—just give me your opinion."

"I favor immediate intervention, sir," Aaron repeated.

"Anne, how about you?"

The Vice President sighed. "I'm not usually hung up like this, Mr. President. but I can see both sides. This country has bled a lot these past two years. We gave up a lot letting our people go back to Israel." She shook her head. "It's difficult, but I have to go along with Aaron. We must intervene."

Baldwin looked at Joanna. "No doubt where you stand on this, Joanna—"

"No, sir," Joanna said. "Not just because of the Israelis. This Jihad—this holy war—has to be stopped before it sweeps worldwide."

"And you, Quinn?"

"Intervene."

"Nothing to add?"

"No, sir."

Baldwin looked around the room again. "It seems to be unanimous. This isn't a voting situation, of course, but I appreciate knowing your positions. No doubt how both Houses would vote. The House will certainly oppose intervention because it isn't politically correct with the polls. The Senate will want more time to lay a groundwork. We don't have time to get laid."

"We can't completely ignore those polls, however, Mr. President," Anne murmured. "It shouldn't determine the decision, of course, but the people do not want to run the risk of war, not even to save the Israelis. A popular referendum would show overwhelming support for non-intervention."

The president leaned back in his chair, drumming fingers on the top of his desk. His attention finally lifted to Quinn.

"You and Joanna are the experts on that part of the world. What do you think will happen if the United States doesn't intervene?"

There was no hesitancy by Quinn.

"The Israelis will go down the tube, sir. They won't surrender—the Muslims wouldn't let them, in any case. Surrender is not an option. The Muslims will only be satisfied when the Jewish nation ceases to exist—every man, woman and child. That's what this is about—annihilating the Jewish race. Without our help, Mr. President, that is exactly what will happen."

\* \* \*

The tide turned inexorably against the Israelis. They fought like lions, but it was not enough. Each week saw battered remnants of fighting units pushed back closer and closer toward the nation's last remaining bastion, the mighty mountainous throne of Jerusalem.

The city already lay in smoking ruin. With so many Israelis now jammed inside its ramparts, every shell took a toll as jagged shrapnel ripped swathes of death.

Jerusalem was a proud symbol of the Israeli nation. In recent years, growth pushed the city limits steadily outward, encompassing hills and villages in its sprawl. Now it was being pounded into rubble. Hardly a building did not show the scars of war. Millions of desperate, frightened people crouched in the corners of ruins, seeking shelter, seeking to survive. Missiles and shells whistled into the city with increasing fury.

When the fighting neared the suburbs of the city, Dovid Shazebak knew the hours were numbered. The Israeli lines still held in a rough triangle, with Jerusalem its eastern point, facing the main onslaughts. The southern line stretched irregularly west to the city of Ashod, on the Mediterranean, holding off largely disorganized assaults from Arab and black African nations. The northern line, under heavier attack from European and Asian armies, reached from Jerusalem northwest to the coastal suburbs of Jafo, on the northern edge of Tel Aviv.

Inside this triangle, the airports at Lod and nearby Tel Nof remained intermittently in service, construction crews working round the clock to keep runways repaired, filling shell holes almost as quickly as they appeared. Reluctantly, Dovid left Israel in the dark of night aboard a secret, ultra-fast jet loaned by the Americans for just such emergency flights. The plane raced through the skies toward the United States.

Twenty minutes after landing at Stark Field in New Washington, Dovid was sitting alone with Sam Baldwin in the presidential office. After giving Baldwin a hurried briefing on the desperate plight in Israel, Dovid came to the point of this most urgent meeting.

"The United States must intervene, Mr. President," Dovid said grimly. "We can survive only a few more days without your help. I'm not exaggerating the seriousness of the situation, Mr. President."

"I know you're not, Dovid—Mr. Prime Minister."

"Dovid, please." His eyes bored into the president. "In the next few minutes, you and I must decide the course of history."

"First, let me tell you how deeply sorry I am that my country has stayed on the sidelines. Our people are very divided. They're concerned about bringing the horror of this war to our own shores."

"I totally understand, Mr. President."

"Do you have a plan, Dovid?"

"Yes, sir," Dovid nodded. "However, it may mean the end of your political career if you accept it."

Baldwin shrugged. "Only got a year left anyway. When this term is over, if I'm still alive, I'm going to find a deep cave and crawl into it."

"I know the feeling," Dovid grimaced. "My plan carries a greater burden than political repercussions, I'm afraid."

Baldwin was staring at him. "What do you have in mind, Dovid?"

"I call it Operation Armageddon," Dovid answered quietly. "It is appropriately named."

"Operation Armageddon—"

"Sounds historical, doesn't it."

"Sounds scary."

Dovid leaned forward. "Unless this plan is carried out immediately," he said, his face grave, "not one Israeli will be left alive by the end of this week. Do you believe that, Mr. President?"

"Yes. It's our own assessment, unfortunately."

Dovid clasped both hands on the desk. "You are the only man on earth who can stop that tragedy, Mr. President."

"I do that by accepting your Operation Armageddon—"

"Accepting it, and executing it."

"What exactly does Armageddon call for?"

"Nuclear holocaust. The most massive, destructive military attack in the history of mankind."

Baldwin was staring at him. "I thought you had something big in mind—"

"I'm serious, Mr. President. Nuclear holocaust."

"You're crazy, Dovid."

"It's the only way, Mr. President."

"It should work," Baldwin nodded. "If I'm getting the picture, you Israelis will win because there won't be anyone else left alive—"

"Not quite true, but close."

"Dovid, when did you last get any sleep?"

"Hear me out, sir, please."

Baldwin leaned back in his chair. He studied the Israeli across from him with piercing intensity. Dovid's voice and manner matched the gravity of what he was proposing.

"Israel must not be exterminated. We are one of the oldest races in all of history. We are a people that God himself declares to be His chosen. Your own Bible tells you that."

"What is entailed in this Operation Armageddon?"

"Simultaneous nuclear strikes on all coalition countries. Hand-to-hand fighting is going on in the streets of Jerusalem as we speak, Mr. President. Every moment these strikes are delayed, the less chance there is that Israel will survive."

"But nuclear weapons, Dovid—we would destroy your own people as well as the enemy."

"I have prepared a list of fifty-seven cities. Destroy them, and the lifeline of the coalition is gone. Their entire war machine will collapse. I am also calling for the use of tactical nuclear strikes against the Islamic perimeters around Jerusalem. Their forces are being massed for the final push into the city. Tactical nuclear can pinpoint them and take them out."

"So only Islamic troops in direct contact with your people, inside the tactical destruct zone, are left—"

"Yes, Mr. President. We will kill those with our bare hands if needs be." Unconsciously, Dovid's fists clenched. "They have made a pact against God. Being struck down by fire from heaven is only just."

"Fire from heaven. That's a pretty fancy description of a nuclear holocaust."

"I'm not trying to portray Operation Armageddon as anything other than what it is, Mr. President—a plan to destroy every key city within the Islamic coalition, and every troop concentration in the field. Those men are waiting to rob our dead, rape our women, murder our children. They will let no one live. Either we kill them, or they will kill us."

Baldwin stood up slowly, turned to stare out of the window.

"Do you realize the enormity of what you are asking?"

"I do, sir, but there is no other way. If you were to send every soldier in this country to our aid, they could not arrive in time."

"Millions will die—"

"Millions will live, Mr. President, many of them citizens of your country."

"This will wipe out the last traces of civilization in some of those countries—"

"The dark ages have already settled on them, Mr. President. This action will give a chance for rebirth, for a new future, just as you have done in this country."

Baldwin sat down again, rocking slowly back and forth.

"You realize there is great danger for your own people in such close tactical action. We can take out the rear troop concentrations, but no one can be sure where the radiation clouds will drift."

"All that matters is that some of my countrymen will survive. However many that is, Israel will be rebuilt."

"There must be some other way—"

"There is no time, Mr. President. Even now it may be too late."

"Is this Operation Armageddon cleared with your Knesset?"

Dovid quickly shook his head. "This must be solely upon my head."

"It's on my head too, dammit."

"Our moment of vision—"

"Our visions are different, Dovid. You see a nation surviving. I see the bloodiest death toll ever ordered by one man. If there is right or wrong here, I can't separate it."

"But you will order the strikes?"

"It seems history has left me no choice."

"God has left you no choice, Mr. President," Dovid said softly.

"I hope so, Dovid. I hope He accepts responsibility for what I am about to do. God knows I may never have a peaceful moment for the rest of my life."

With U. S. forces already on full alert, the nuclear strikes were launched within hours. Aaron Stark, anticipating that intervention must inevitably take place in some form, had taken it upon himself to prepare for almost any eventuality. The oceans were still dangerous, even this long after the great crustal disturbances, but he ordered submarine fleets to sea weeks ago. Although there was no thought of any action like that called for in Operation Armageddon, Stark's planning put most of the systems ready for rapid execution of the Israeli plan. All that was needed was the feeding of specific target data into warheads, and the order from President Baldwin.

U.S. high-altitude bombers took off in waves. In both the Atlantic and the Pacific, nuclear submarines moved into position to attack designated targets stretched across Europe and Asia. Ground troops stood on alert at U.S. bases, minutes from loading and taking off if they were needed.

At zero hour, dawn on Sunday, Sam Baldwin sent the final coded message. Minutes later, the holocaust struck.

The enemies of Israel were consumed in blinding, searing heat. The whole attack on the target cities was over in fifteen minutes. In fifteen minutes more, tactical nuclear weapons left seared corpses all around Israel's perimeters.

One minute, Israel was locked in desperate combat, with but a few hours left as a nation.

The next, the war was won.

As the nuclear explosions erupted in the mountains and plains beyond Jerusalem in an awesome spectacle of destruction, the enemy stopped fighting in the streets and turned to stare in numbed disbelief. Without knowing how or why, they knew victory had been unexpectedly snatched away from them. No one was alive behind them. The circle of billowing, mushrooming clouds told it all.

Even as the enemy stood in paralyzed shock, weary and tattered Israelis, most as surprised as the sons of Islam, threw themselves upon the enemy with renewed fury. The edge of the sword turned, and the blood that was spilled was no longer Jewish.

Back in New Washington, grim-faced leaders learned the truth of what had just happened. There was too much shock for the moment to even express anger at Baldwin or anyone else. Satellite photographs showed the devastation clearly. Operation Armageddon had accomplished its deadly purpose.

There was no immediate estimate of the dead across Europe. No one really wanted to know. The photographs showed cities flattened, battlefields littered with bodies, many of them already skeletons from the heat that had consumed flesh.

Satellite television relays showed people dancing in the streets of Jerusalem. It was a gruesome reaction, with so many bodies strewn in the gutters. But everyone understood.

That evening, church bells peeled for the Israeli victory. They tolled in every city across the land, and in most of the cities in the Southern Hemisphere too.

Baldwin heard the bells, but for him they tolled a different tune. He shut himself in his office and ordered no more reports and no visitors. For hours he sat in his chair, staring out of the window. He wondered if the images in his brain would ever go away.

# 44

## Aftermath

Israel gathered its dead into funeral pyres and black smoke soon rose again over the land. Memories of the plague of maggot flies spawned among the bodies of those killed in the recent earthquakes lent an urgency to the task. The terrible stench and the sickening clouds of ash could not be escaped.

There was too strong a feeling of national sorrow to mingle the bodies of Arabs and Jews. The dead Islamic foes were transported away to several valleys designated as sites for mass burials. For weeks, bodies piled up. When there was room for no more in a ravine, bulldozers and dynamite went to work, sealing the grave under tons of earth and rock, creating unmarked tombs for millions. The task of burying the dead went on for seven months.

As in the aftermath of all wars, stories of heroism and sacrifice and miraculous survival surfaced. Some spoke of incredible human endurance, of self-less love and compassion, of bravery against all odds. Other stories, however, could not be explained in such human terms.

Many of them centered around a mysterious bearded man in a girdled tunic, wearing no uniform or armor, who had appeared out of the smoke and flames in several scattered locations, reaching out to save a soul staring death in the face.

There were the two high priests of the temple who had died in the streets of Jerusalem, killed by Islamic gunfire. For three days their bodies had lain there, undeniably witnessed by television cameras. Then while people around them backed away, it was told that the two priests stood up and walked away. That too was caught on camera. It was easily explained to millions who watched from far lands; the priests had not been killed after all, but had lain wounded, or in shock and coma, for those three days, with no one to care for them in the heat of battle. Little credence was given to the few who claimed to have witnessed a miracle, seeing dead men resurrected to new life.

One surprising fact came to light in the days following the destruction. The missionaries of the Mormon church that were sent among the Siberians in Iowa and Illinois had apparently met with greater success than anyone thought. Many thousands had embraced the Mormon faith, In fact, before the tribes joined the exodus to Israel, a large number of them received special priesthood blessings that they would be protected in the conflict ahead. Twelve thousand from each of the tribes, along with twelve thousand from each of the two tribes represented in the general population of American Jews, received this special blessing. It came to light weeks after the war had ended, when an accounting revealed that not one of those hundred and forty-four thousand had been killed, or even wounded. It defied all statistical logic, yet apparently was true.

There were many such stories, different yet strangely similar. Later, when historians and theologians and agnostics pondered these recorded events, most were explained according to the logic of each group. Some simply couldn't be explained.

Scientists discovered that during the height of the nuclear bombings, an earthquake had struck central Israel. It was not particularly large, and apparently was centered directly under the Mount of Olives, just east of the main city of Jerusalem. In fact, the Mount was fractured right through the middle. In the midst of all that nuclear horror, the quake had not even been noticed.

The rebirth of Jerusalem was startlingly swift. The center of Jewish faith for thousands of years, Dovid Shazebak and the other Israeli leaders knew that rebuilding the city out of the rubble of war was not only needed, it was psychologically and emotionally important to the whole fabric of Jewish renewal.

American aid was sought and quickly delivered. A plant to produce the remarkable solar panels rose almost overnight in the Sinai, and in weeks, it was producing construction materials.

The first project was building a new temple, this time on the site of the former Dome of the Rock. The Arab shrine had been destroyed in the battle for Jerusalem, along with every other historical landmark in the city.

The Dome, or Qubbat Assakhrah as it was called by the Arabs, was built some fourteen hundred years ago, the oldest Islamic shrine. It was a sacred spot to every son of Islam for they believed it was from here that their Prophet Muhammad, founder of Islam, ascended to heaven.

The spot was also revered by Jews, for they believed it was the spot where Abraham prepared to sacrifice his son Isaac.

This time there was no Arab population to protest the new temple, and it rose in an amazingly short time.

One startling event occurred during the construction. While blasting foundations for the new structure, water began to seep up through the rock. It had been known for some time that underground springs were in the area. They had been discovered and capped years earlier, but the newly disturbed source quickly became a river of swiftly flowing fresh water. Geologists surmised the blasting had tapped a huge underground flow from the Sea of Galilee, much larger than the springs indicated, fed by rivers and melting snows from mountains to the north.

The river was quickly diverted down into the Dead Sea. If the river gushing forth from the temple construction was startling, it was even more startling to see the change it brought to the salty waters. The level of the lake doubled and now fresh water was fed directly into irrigation systems, no longer needing desalinization. The new river needed no miraculous explanation but many were convinced it was a divine act.

The temple was finished and with the glowing solar panels towering into the air, it became a breathtaking symbol of national pride.

Soon other developments were springing up and the joy of being in a homeland even larger than in ancient times swelled in the breast of Sabra and immigrant alike.

Too soon, however, the devastation in the Islamic countries surrounding Israel became a grave concern. In those lands, there was no organized effort—no effort at all—to cover the scars of war, to bury the millions of dead, or give rebirth to government and society.

Dovid Shazebak once again contacted Quinn Adams. He was talking now on a new Comint satellite link to the United States. When it was identified who was on the link, Joanna had quickly taken the phone from her husband.

"Dovid. I'm so happy to hear your voice. How are you and Sophie doing? The satellites show marvelous progress—"

"We'd have you over for dinner, only there isn't time these days to fix it," Dovid told her. "We're surviving, like everyone else. But those pictures are right—it's beginning to look like a country again."

"Take care, brother," Joanna whispered. "We love you. Here's Quinn—"

"How can we help you, Dovid?" Quinn asked.

"Well, you know things are going well here in Israel," Dovid said, "but reports out of the Islamic countries are pretty grim."

"We've been getting the same reports."

"Quinn, probably no man on earth has more experience in coping with disasters than you do. I'm asking another favor, officially, with the approval of the Knesset—although that's a quarter of its normal size."

"Sounds pretty ominous—"

"Not at all. We'd like you to come over here and assess what can be done to stabilize the region. We're well on the road to recovery in Israel, but there's a real threat from our neighbors—not military, thank goodness, but potentially just as disastrous if we don't do something to help them."

"Are you asking official assistance from the United States?"

"Not yet," Dovid said quickly. "Just you and Joanna to survey the situation."

"We've already been talking about sending a mission out there," Quinn told him. "Joanna and I can be on a plane tomorrow. We'll decide how big a team we need once we get there."

"It'll be good to see you both. Sophie will fix dinner. There sure aren't any restaurants up and running yet—"

In the months that followed, Quinn and Joanna made several trips between Jerusalem and New Washington. Progress was slow, for dealing with the devastated peoples in the shattered Islamic countries was extremely difficult. Yet no matter how bitter and hateful the survivors felt, they knew they could not cope with the enormous problems facing them. Even so, allowing the hated Great Satan into their lands, though it was only to render aid and assistance, was almost as difficult as accepting the complete and humiliating defeat of Jihad.

Still, a glimmer of hope for the future began to dawn.

*  *  *

Jules Henshaw had not left his office for three days. He hadn't stopped frowning for three days, either. He didn't like what he was seeing. He didn't want to believe what he was seeing.

He was poring over his charts once again, comparing each notation with data received in the last few hours. Try as he might, he could find no error.

Yet something must be wrong. The data being received from around the world pointed to an event that simply couldn't occur. It was too numbing to accept.

Once again he sat down at his computer, running the models over again, checking every detail. Nothing changed. He fed in new projections taken from the last batch of information relayed by satellite. All it did was confirm the horrifying conclusion he had come to three days ago.

It was the nuclear bombings, he was sure. So massive, so concentrated.

There was no doubt in Henshaw's mind that had been the initial trigger. Nature had taken it from there, building to the enormity he was seeing on his screen.

Perhaps if he could decipher exactly how this momentum factor would impact the data—but it was impossible to anticipate how the momentum would build, and at what rate. All he could go by was the data received, and that was all too plain. All the momentum factor would do is speed up inevitable cataclysms.

He sucked in a deep breath, took off his spectacles, putting them beside the keyboard.

What could he do? There had to be some way to negate the arithmetic.

As he let the thought agonize through his mind, he knew there wasn't. Jules Henshaw never felt more helpless, or hopeless.

He put his glasses back on and reached for the telephone. He got the NECCO staff information room. His voice was recognized by the person on the other end.

"Yes, Dr. Henshaw, what can we do for you?"

"I need to get in touch with Pharaoh One. It's very urgent."

"He's in Israel—"

"Yes, I know that," Henshaw interrupted. "He was due back today, wasn't he?"

There was a momentary pause, as a log was checked.

"That's right, Dr. Henshaw." Another pause. "You say this is urgent?"

"Extremely urgent."

"Very well. He and Mrs. Adams are scheduled to arrive at Stark at ten-thirty tonight."

Henshaw glanced down at his watch. It was already ten-twenty. No way to make it to the airport in time.

"Do you know where they're going after they arrive?"

"No indication on the log. But I see there's a wake-up call at six-thirty at their residence. That probably means they'll be going home from Stark."

"Thank you," Henshaw said.

He hung up the telephone and stared at the computer screen again. He shrugged, and ran it all again.

Same result. Same frightening, unbelievable result.

He put on his coat, ran his hands through his hair. It was an unconscious gesture. There really wasn't anything but a few straggly strands across the top of his head to run fingers through. Somehow it reassured him, however. He began stuffing papers into his briefcase.

As he went to his car, Henshaw's attention was drawn into the sky. Strange streaks of light were wreathing high above. It was especially strange because he could see them clearly even against the bright glow of the city. Usually, it was almost impossible to see stars or anything else in those bright night skies. These wreaths of light, however, were brilliant, more powerful even than the reflected canopy of the twin cities.

Henshaw stopped, staring up at the long trails. Must be hundreds of miles in length, he thought. Perhaps thousands. They reached way up into the stratosphere and beyond. Impossible to tell without scientific measurement. But the wreathing plumes were very strange. He'd never seen anything like this before. It certainly wasn't a display of the aurora borealis—not the right variance in color, streaks much too pronounced. They were in the right position in the sky to be northern lights, but those were only rarely seen this far from the arctic circle, and then just a hint of a distant cloud.

What was causing them, he wondered. Perhaps an aberration in the magnetic field. The earth's crust was in such a state of disturbance that it was scientifically possible to extend shock waves into the atmosphere. As soon as he thought it, Henshaw realized he had absolutely no fact to support that theory.

The scientist in Henshaw was fascinated by the sights and the possibilities, but there were more important things to deal with. He took one last look into the heavens and got into his car.

He drove through town into New Jerusalem and finally parked in front of the Ashford Tower. As he got out, a uniformed Ranger came toward him.

"Sorry, sir, you can't park there."

Henshaw reached inside his coat and pulled out his NECCO identification. He flashed it at the Ranger.

"I know the rules, Lieutenant, but this is an emergency. I must see Mr. Adams immediately. It's very urgent. The keys are in it. Please have someone take it around to the parking lot, will you?"

There was urgency and authority in Henshaw's request—it was an order, really. The Ranger nodded. He knew Jules Henshaw by sight, and if he said something was urgent, he wasn't about to question it.

Henshaw took the elevator to the fifty-ninth floor and pressed the doorbell across the foyer. In a moment, Quinn Adams opened it, a surprised expression on his face.

"Sorry, One," Henshaw said apologetically. "Please forgive the intrusion. I know you and your wife just got back from Israel, but this simply can't wait—"

# BLUE PLANET EARTH

## PART FOUR

# 45

## A PLACE NEAR KOLOB

Race reached over and turned off the life screen. All six people in the room sat silently staring at the blank screen, visibly shaken by what they had just experienced. Seeing those last agonizing years on earth as they had lived it brought back memories and emotions very difficult to cope with.

Stacy pressed herself against her husband.

"It was so horrible," she whispered, "seeing you die like that. I never knew what happened—"

"The good news is," Race grinned, "I didn't get blown to hell. One streak of light, and here I was, in the good place."

Stacy shuddered. "Don't joke about it, Race—"

"What's really amazing," Dovid muttered, clasping Sophia's hand tightly, "is we're all up here together in—"

Dovid hesitated, and Quinn finished the sentence for him.

"— in a place near Kolob. I've got to be honest, folks, this all has to be a dream. It seems real, I know—but think about what we just saw. Either the Lifetime channel has achieved new heights, or we're having one fantastic dream."

"It's no dream, Quinn," Race said softly. "Don't know how I'm going to convince you of that, but it isn't."

"I'm convinced," Joanna murmured. "I don't understand one moment of it, but I know inside me that it's all happening." She glanced at her husband. "You do too, Quinn—you just can't bring yourself to admit it."

Stacy gave her brother an exasperated stare. "What's so difficult to accept, Quinn?" she said. "Everything that's happened is exactly what we've been told since we were children in Sunday School. We were told there's a life after death—well, here's the proof. We were told the earth is going to be consumed by fire one day—you saw that happen on the space screen in Oliblish. You've always said seeing is believing, Quinn."

Quinn was shaking his head. "If it's true, we just lived through the end of the world—"

"Not the end," Race said quickly, "just a change to a new sphere of existence. It's a new beginning for the earth, just like it is for us."

"What about all those people?" Joanna breathed. "I know less than half of the world's population survived all those terrible things, but that's still millions—"

Race shrugged. "All those worthy of being Quickened were brought up here, just like you. Those who didn't—well, they died a mortal death when the earth was consumed."

"What happened to them—?" Sophia asked.

"Everyone's here on this planet, either Unified or in the Place of Contemplation. On earth, that was called Hell, but it's actually very pleasant. People have an opportunity to review their lives, think of their choices, regret their mistakes—or be satisfied with what they did on earth. A lot of people are comfortable with who they are and want to be with people who feel the same way they do. They still have complete free agency in deciding their course. One of these days they'll get another review date. It will be decided in what degree they will be happiest throughout eternity, then they'll experience Unification. The choice is up to them, largely."

"Makes you look at death in a whole different way," Dovid muttered.

Race nodded agreement. "Down on earth, death is a big dark mystery. An ending of life into nothingness. Even the people who believe in life after death can't get a clear picture of anything beyond. On this side, however, it's like coming home from school. Most of us are gone for just a couple of hours or so."

"I don't understand why it's even necessary to go to earth," Sophia said. "Why don't we just stay here?"

"First, we need a mortal body," Race answered. "Explaining that is complicated, but everyone has to have one before they can become Unified and immortal. The other reason is to learn about ourselves, our weaknesses, our strengths, what we're really like inside."

"Surely we could learn that up here," Stacy said.

"We could," Race agreed, "but here we know what's to be gained, and what can be lost. We'd be pretty stupid to make wrong choices when we're fully aware of the consequences. We need an environment where we can really find out about ourselves, make choices without knowing what the consequences are—believing there won't be any, in most cases."

"So what we do on earth really does matter," Joanna murmured.

"A lot of people find out quickly what choices they'll make, no matter what the circumstances. They don't need to hang around too long and often are brought back early. Most people, however, need all the time they can get. Some are given special problems to deal with, others just do stupid things and end their probation before it should. All part of the learning experience."

Joanna voiced a thought she knew was in her husband's mind.

"You said Jill is in this Place of Contemplation. Is there anything we can do for her while we're here?"

"Not while you're in a Quickened state, I visit her regularly, though."

"How is she feeling about—well, all that happened?" Quinn asked.

"Suffering. She made bad choices and she knows it, but that's good. She's getting a lot of help, and already has gone through a lot of remorse. When her time comes, she'll be just fine."

Quinn leaned back again, putting his hands to his head. "This is all so incredible. It's all so—so real."

"This is reality, buddy," Race grinned. "This is immortality. The road ahead never ends."

Sophia was frowning. "But we have to go back to earth—"

"Everyone has to die a mortal death," Race told her. "Being Quickened doesn't count—it's a temporary state. But life on earth will be totally different when you go back. A terrestrial world is beautiful beyond anything I could describe. I've seen other terrestrial planets and they're unbelievably magnificent. The earth will be just like it was in the days of the Garden of Eden."

Dovid gave a little smile. "I remember what Adam said about having to start over—"

"It must have been tough for him when the Garden of Eden was put off limits—or more accurately, when it ceased to exist," Race said. "That whole thing was a lot more cataclysmic than those few verses in the Bible indicate. The earth fell to the lower telestial order, in a telestial heaven. Not to mention the continents splitting apart. Weeds sprouting must have been about the least significant thing that happened."

Sophia was still struggling to form a mental picture. "Only those of us who were Quickened—judged to be basically good people, as I understand that to mean—will return to earth?"

"Everybody else died. They'll have to wait for their Unification—resurrection—before they can move forward with their life. In the meantime, they wait in the Place of Contemplation."

"Am I right in thinking there won't be too many people going back to earth?"

"Not at first. A whole lot of people have been waiting for this to happen, though. They are assigned to go down to earth during the last millennium, so it won't take long to start getting crowded."

Stacy cast a worried glance at her husband. "Will I be separated from you again?"

"Only for fifty or sixty years."

She gasped. "Sixty years—"

"Look at it in Kolob time. Another hour and a half, and you'll be Unified. Then we'll never be separated from each other again."

"But I won't be living in Kolob time," Stacy protested. "Sixty years will be sixty years for me, not ninety minutes."

"I forgot to tell you," Race said. "I'll be visiting earth regularly on special assignments—mostly working with Quinn and Joanna, of course. There's open communication between terrestrial orders."

"I'll get to see you?" Stacy asked excitedly.

"Of course you will."

Her hands suddenly flew to her face. "But I'll look like an old woman—"

"You'll always look beautiful to me—even when you're an old hag."

Her voice fell to a mock whisper. "Will you be staying all night?"

Race grinned. "Afraid not. We can't be together that way until after you're dead too."

"That is too weird, Race—"

"Remember, Unification between mortal and spirit bodies takes place instantly in the next phase. No funerals. We'll be together before you know it."

"Together all night?"

"Stacy," Race murmured, casting an amused glance at the others, "people will think you're horny—"

"You're alive. I'm alive. I want to be with you—"

"So, yes—we'll be together all night. That's Kolob time, too."

"How long is that?"

"About three hundred and fifty years earth time, if we don't sleep in."

Stacy gave a contented sigh. "Keep reminding me, will you. Sounds like it's going to be worth the wait—and I promise you, we will sleep in."

Race had a surprise announcement.

"All right, it's party time."

They stared at him.

"They have parties up here?" Stacy frowned. "That's got to be fun—happy hour with a bunch of dead people."

"I know it's hard to understand," Race grinned, "but life 'up here' is pretty much the same as it was down on earth. People live normal lives, in a normal society."

"In a very abnormal environment," Quinn added. "I haven't seen anything so far I'd call normal."

"Life on earth was abnormal, buddy. It was patterned after the way things have always been, without all the corruption, of course. Imagine a perfect society on earth and that's what you have here. Not too many changes."

"Not counting thought transport, or thousand-year days, or very strange television programming, of course," Quinn added dryly. "Not to mention space screens—"

"You're right," Race smiled, "there are a few significant differences. Now it's time to go. Since none of you know where you're going, I'll do the old thumb trick again—"

The six of them found themselves in a large hall crowded with hundreds of people. Once again, there was no sense of travel. They were just here.

"In case you're wondering," Race explained, "this is a Unification party. There are thousands of them going on. Yesterday, millions of people were Unified and some have been waiting for that for two thousand years. It's also a welcoming party for the newly arrived Quickened—sort of a grand family reunion."

Dovid looked around. "I don't recognize anyone—"

"You will," Race assured him. "They know we've arrived."

"They—?" Sophia asked.

There was no need to answer her question.

Suddenly the six of them were surrounded by people who approached with outstretched arms, happy smiles, and tearful sobs. Utter, numbing shock seized all of the new arrivals.

"Dear God," Joanna whispered, "it's Mother—"

In moments, everyone was clinging to each other. Most in the group were parents or grandparents or great-grandparents to one of the new arrivals, some were close relatives, even old friends. It was completely unexpected, emotionally devastating—and so utterly real. They were all together again, parents and children, family and friends, and no one could speak a word through the tears.

# 46

## Oliblish Revisited

The next morning, Quinn and Joanna, and Dovid and Sophia, returned with Race to Oliblish. Stacy felt a little left out, but understood when Race explained that only persons with specific assignments on the new terrestrial earth were to attend this final meeting before all returned to the planet. Besides, she needed to spend some time with Leah and try to explain to their daughter what was happening. That would be interesting, Stacy thought. She didn't understand it herself.

As the five people entered the lobby of the Oliblish administration building, Race stopped and pointed down at the twinkling expanse of stars and galaxies that could be seen through the glass floor.

"What makes this so unusual, Quinn," Race said, "is this is not a reproduction. This is actually a view of the telestial sky the earth was in. Take a good look, because when you leave Oliblish and go back to earth, you'll see a new heaven—a terrestrial sky—overhead, and you won't even remember this one."

They continued down C Hall and entered Monitoring Room 10 again. The other members of their team were already there. Warren Hughes and Sam Baldwin were in deep discussions with Anne Ashford and her husband, Fernando Francisco de Branca. The political scene would be dramatically changed for them. Jules Henshaw was chatting with Austin and Vanessa Wells, his face frowning in concentration as he listened to Austin Wells explaining something. Everyone was glad to see the new arrivals.

The space monitoring screen in the floor was active, showing a close-up of the blue planet they now knew was the terrestrialized earth. There were no more obscuring clouds of steam and the planet could be seen clearly. The large northern land mass was green, completely covered by vast areas of vegetation. The circling mass of ocean showed many hues of blue.

"Looks pretty good," Dovid said. "Lots of grassland, rivers, forests—"

"—and a whole lot less beach front property," Quinn muttered. He glanced at his wife. "In case you haven't noticed, Oregon is gone—along with the rest of the North American continent. I guess our house is gone too."

"I loved that place," Joanna said softly. "Oh well, this new earth will be even more beautiful, I guess."

"Still going to miss that Oregon coast," Quinn muttered.

"Not when you get back to earth, buddy," Race told him. "You not only won't miss it, you won't even remember it."

The group chatted for several minutes, everyone anxious to know if the others had a better grip on this strange situation than they did. It was evident that no one doubted they were on a planet somewhere near Kolob, Even Quinn stopped fighting it. As unreal as it was, he finally admitted to himself that this was really happening.

A short while later, Adam entered the room. Everyone went to their seats at the circular conference table as Adam sat down and looked around the room.

"We are very pleased with the progress you have made," he began. "I know there is a lot to absorb, and a lot of responsibility has been placed on you, as individuals and as a team. You've shown a remarkable ability to deal with events that must seem shocking and unreal. That of course, is why you were all chosen to work together on this particular reconstruction team."

Sam Baldwin raised a hand. "If I may ask, are there many teams like us and will we be working with any of them?"

"There are hundreds of teams, Sam, representing all nationalities. You all have a common goal, to get people on the new earth organized into functioning societies, but you won't be working directly with each other. Each team has their specific assignments, but this team is integral to getting the main governmental centers in operation in both Jerusalems and New Washington. It is vital to have these centers functioning as quickly as possible. Those cities will be returned to earth intact, so that should make it a little easier. Teams have been assigned to design and implement communication systems for you, others to supervise actual construction of new cities and install public facilities.

"A lot of people of many nations will be released today from their Quickened state to return to earth and live out their mortal probation.

Providing shelter for them is not particularly important, for the elements will be friendly. The same goes for food—you will find the new earth a bounteous provider. But it is urgent to plan new cities and implement new societal structures in each nation. They will need a lot of help, and you probably will encounter a lot of opposition. It must be done, however."

Sam Baldwin started to raise a hand again but Adam waved it down.

"None of you need raise your hand. If you have a question, just think it. I'll know who you are and what you want to know." He smiled and gave a little shrug. "No magic involved. Communication by thought is something each of you will become skilled in—elemental telepathy is already very familiar to you.

"Sam is wondering about political ramifications in establishing new governments," Adam told the others. "There will be no political parties, Sam, in the new world. There is one source of civil law for every nation, and that is New Jerusalem. The same laws will be in effect for all nations, and they will come directly from our Master. He is the only one to whom allegiance must be shown. It should simplify your task."

He smiled at Joanna.

"Yes, Joanna, mortals and immortals will mingle freely together when you return to earth. In the case of this team, Warren and Race have been assigned as your official liaisons. You have all worked with them before and they understand how to get special help from Oliblish. You also should know that the Master himself will be a frequent visitor on earth. He will take an active role in directing the affairs of the kingdom, and you will have direct access whenever it's needed."

He started nodding, looking at Jules Henshaw.

"An excellent question, Jules. Perhaps a quick review of life in general on the terrestrialized earth will be helpful in determining medical and scientific needs. As you have already been told, every mortal in this last thousand years will live to be one hundred years old. At that time, Unification will be instantaneous. During your lifetime, you will experience no pain, no illness. There will be peace throughout the world, and righteousness will prevail in every nation. There will be no enmity between humans or animals, even the lowest forms of creatures and insects will not be harmful. Medical assistance will no longer be needed. As for scientific knowledge, you will soon learn things about the earth and the heavens that will astound you, Jules."

"That is exciting beyond words, sir," Henshaw said, his eyes shining.

This time Adam's attention shifted to Vanessa Wells.

"Let me calm your fears, Vanessa. There will be evil upon the earth in this next thousand years, but it will be the evil of personal choice. Lucifer, the Son of the Morning and the great Adversary to all righteousness, will not be allowed to tempt mankind. His power already has been taken away, and will not be returned until it meets the purpose of the Eternal Plan. Your concerns show the love you have in your heart, and you may be assured Lucifer will not be able to influence any person or thing for almost the whole thousand years."

He shook his head.

"No, Austin, unfortunately it does not follow that all mankind will therefor be righteous and pleasing in their actions."

He looked around the room. "The question Austin has raised is important, for all of you will undoubtedly run into it. Some people will not do what they're supposed to do—and they have the right to make that choice. The free agency of every man, woman and child cannot be abrogated, even when they make bad decisions. If they choose not to do something that is right, or choose to do something wrong, it is their right. They will do it of their own free will—Lucifer can't be held responsible. The consequences of unrighteousness, active or passive, will therefor fall squarely upon the individual."

Adam was nodding again. "Another good question, Austin. New Jerusalem and Old Jerusalem will both serve as religious centers for the entire world, but they will have different responsibilities. New Jerusalem will direct the performance of ordinances and sealings in the temples, binding the human race into one great family chain. These ordinances will be entered into the Book of Remembrance, and that great sealing work must be completed by the end of time. I might add, Austin, you will be receiving considerable assistance from right here in Oliblish. You can expect lists of names to be delivered every day showing what temple work needs to be done."

"That will be a tremendous help," Austin said, relief showing on his face. "From what you've said, I take it the veil between earth and Oliblish will be very thin."

"There will be no veil at all for those worthy to see through it," Adam said quietly. He pointed toward Dovid.

"I hear your question, Dovid. You have been called to be the leader of your people for the remainder of your life. Your Jerusalem, with its wonderful new temple, will be the religious center for all mankind."

He swiveled his head toward Sam Baldwin.

"No, Sam. That doesn't mean everyone will have to embrace the Jewish faith—or any other faith, for that matter. Those of you who were

Methodists before—and you are one of them, Sam—or Presbyterians or any other denomination, are free to continue to worship as you choose. All that is required, from every member of every church organization, is that they bow their knee and confess that Jesus, the Christ, is Savior of all mankind. Anyone who refuses to acknowledge that will be sent to the Place of Contemplation. This new world has only one king, one ruler, one lawgiver. You may deny the Christ if you wish, but you cannot live in his kingdom if you do."

It was surprising news for a lot of people in the room. Secretly, some feared they would have to abandon their former beliefs and religious practices and be forced to join a designated church. Adam had just made it plain that would not be the case, at least not for any Christian denomination. That was heartening. And like Dovid and Sophia, there was not a Jew who, after the experience of Jihad, did not already recognize their Messiah.

"Now I would like a final rundown on your individual assignments, though they are all connected to the team assignment. Sam—Warren—are you clear about what is expected from you?"

The two presidents exchanged glances, and Warren deferred to Sam Baldwin.

"I believe we are, Adam. We're to concentrate on preparing democratic forms of representation for people in all lands. Hopefully, they'll all sign on to a similar type of government. From what you've said, I don't foresee many problems in accomplishing that. Certainly not with Warren helping out," he added.

"Good," Adam responded. "Remember no one must feel that a strictly religious form of government is being imposed on them. They have the responsibility to govern themselves."

He next fastened his gaze on Dovid and Sophia.

"Do you have questions, either of you?"

"I am fearful of the responsibility for leadership of my people, Adam," Dovid said quietly. "I'm not much of a politician, and even less of a spiritual leader—"

"You are loved and respected, both you and your wife," Adam replied. "Your primary responsibilities will be to keep all the tribes working together as a nation, and to maintain close cooperation between the two Jerusalems. As for spiritual leadership, you will be given priests and prophets to support you in that area."

"Do you think nations will accept us as the standard bearer for Jesus Christ?" Sophia asked. "After all, we denied him for over two thousand years."

"You are His chosen people, Sophia—chosen before the earth was created," Adam reassured her. "He would have no other people, no other place than the Jerusalem he loved, to be the center of worship in his new kingdom."

In his mind, Adam could hear the questions and uncertainties that Austin and Vanessa Wells were feeling.

"Don't worry, you two," he smiled. "I know the responsibility for directing this great work in the temple in New Jerusalem must be frightening—having ordinances performed for the whole human race. But you are both very familiar with the work. Don't forget you will have the assistance of a host of messengers from here every day. The task is enormous, but you will have legions of temple workers assisting you. Don't even worry about getting it all done in your lifetime—there is so much to do it may well take the whole thousand years. Once you are both Unified, you will still be engaged in the work."

Anne and Fernando were staring at him, knowing it was their turn. Adam stared at them for a moment without saying anything. Then a smile of pleasure touched his lips.

"Such a great work for the both of you," he said softly. "So many of your people, Fernando, were spared much of the agony of those last years. Now you and Anne must mold them into a great nation. I don't know if you realize that the blood of Israel runs deep within them—runs in your own veins. Soon you will blend into one nation with Anne's people, and become a great force for the next thousand years. Guide them well, both of you."

Adam looked at Jules Henshaw.

"Jules, you have shown a remarkable intellect in all the sciences. I have not the slightest doubt you will find many mortal adaptations for the principles of celestial physics that will be taught when you get back. Use that knowledge to bring our new civilization to greater heights than ever before."

Jules just nodded. He didn't seem able to speak and those next to him saw tears clouding his eyes. Just the thought of being given such knowledge started a trembling inside him that would not go away.

Now Adam fastened his full attention on Quinn and Joanna.

"Your minds have been trained to find solutions to the problems that will face these new lands," he said. "The task will not be easy. People will be confused—practically everything familiar will be gone. Warren and Sam will set up a system of government for them, but you and Joanna must spearhead the effort to re-establish law-abiding societies. You'll both spend the rest of your lives trying to accomplish that, but you will leave a legacy for this new world that you can be proud of through all eternity."

Joanna put her head in her hands and began to sob. Quinn reached over and put an arm around her shoulders.

"We are both honored to do whatever we can, Adam," he told the man across from him. "It's been difficult for me to grasp the depth of what is happening, but I believe it's finally sunk home. We'll do our best, sir."

"I know you will," Adam smiled. He looked around the room. "There is no doubt you all will do your best. I am not the only one who believes that. I have been asked to extend to all of you the personal gratitude of the Master—"

# 47

## BLUE PLANET EARTH

Later that evening, Quinn and Joanna were alone in their living room. Dovid and Sophia left soon after they all returned from Oliblish, and Race went to spend some time with his wife and daughter.

There was no message or directive telling them what to do to prepare for the scheduled return to earth, so they just sat and talked, waiting until some kind of instructions arrived.

"I think Dovid is a little overwhelmed," Joanna said. "It was bad enough being made Prime Minister of Israel, but now he has to lead a nation that is ten times larger than it was. I know he doesn't feel up to it."

"He'll do fine," Quinn assured her. "It's our assignment that's freaking me out. All we have to do is organize every society in the entire world, in countries that don't even exist yet." He shook his head. "I don't even want to—"

Quinn stopped in mid-sentence. He looked so peculiar that Joanna was worried. Quinn said nothing for a moment, then a grin slid across his face. But he still sat silently on the sofa beside her. She had no idea what was going on.

"That you, Quinn?"

"Dovid—where are you?"

"Home, sitting here with Sophie."

"This is crazy—"

"It works. It actually works."

"You're referring to this conversation—"

"I just thought I'd try it. It really works."

"We're talking to each other in our thoughts—"

"Weird, isn't it."

"We're actually holding a conversation in thought. This is thought transfer."

"Hope it works long distance."

"This is a long distance."

"I mean when we get back on earth. Well, I'm going to hang up—"

"How do we do that?"

"I don't know. Stop thinking about me."

"I wasn't thinking about you. You started this—"

"Is your wife staring at you like you've gone crazy?"

Quinn looked over at Joanna. He didn't know if she could hear the conversation going on with her brother, but she certainly was staring at him funny.

"Yes."

"So is Sophie. There must be some way to hang up—"

Quinn's mind suddenly went blank. No more voices. He looked at Joanna again.

"You are not going to believe what just happened—"

"You were certainly acting very strange."

"I was talking to your brother."

"To Dovid?"

"Thought transfer. He called me on thought transfer." A wide grin broke over his face. "It works, Joanna. Just like Adam was doing at the meeting. We were holding a conversation—"

"You were talking to Dovid?"

He nodded.

"Your lips weren't moving."

"We weren't talking—"

Joanna sighed. "We'd better get some rest. It's finally got to you."

The telephone rang. It startled both of them. The phone hadn't rung since this whole transference thing started.

"The phone's ringing, Joanna—"

"Maybe you should answer it."

Quinn picked up the receiver. It was Race, sounding cheery and enthusiastic.

"You looked outside lately?"

Quinn wasn't really concentrating. His mind was still going over his conversation with Dovid.

"We were out on the balcony awhile ago. Everything looks the same."

"That's where you're wrong, buddy. What time is it?"

Without looking, Quinn shrugged. "It's been three-fifteen ever since we got here. I suppose it still is."

"Look again."

Quinn looked at the clock on the mantle over the fireplace.

Ten-twenty-seven.

Quinn looked at Joanna and she followed his stare. Someone had changed the time on the clock.

"This some kind of a joke?"

"In one minute, it will be ten-twenty-eight."

Quinn stared at the clock. Both he and Joanna saw the minute hand creep to the next minute. Time was once again running.

"What's going on?"

"Outside—that's Missouri. Well, it used to be Missouri. Now it's Eden, I suppose. That's what earth was called in its previous terrestrial state, so that's probably what it is again."

"We're back on earth?" Quinn gasped. "How can that be—?"

"Little quieter coming down, wasn't it. Don't ask me why. Must be something to do with celestial physics."

Joanna leaned close to the phone. "Is it true, Race? Are we back on earth?"

"We sure are. Get some sleep. I'll meet you both in your office at nine tomorrow morning. And remember, we're not on Kolob time—"

## ABOUT THE AUTHOR

John McRae was educated in English schools and has traveled extensively throughout the world.

As a writer and producer of trade and educational films and television commercials, Mr. McRae has frequently been honored with top national awards, including such prestigious awards as an Emmy, a New York Art Directors award, top national Telly awards, and several Best In The West awards.

Prior to moving into advertising and filmmaking he worked as a newspaper feature writer. He retired as president of a Northwest advertising agency, headed his own marketing consulting firm, and now has turned to a full-time career as a novelist.

He has written seven novels, including two sequels to the best-selling novel FIRE in the SNOW. These follow Carn Tregale and his friends through historical events occurring in 1856, 1857, and 1858.

John McRae lived for many years in the Pacific Northwest and now lives in Utah